First published in the United Kingdom in 2016 by
Mosaic (Teesdale) Ltd, Snaisgill, Middleton-in-Teesdale,
County Durham DL12 0RP

ISBN 9780993597039

Design, layout and typesetting by
Mosaic Design and Print, Middleton-in-Teesdale.

Front cover image © stokkete
Back cover image of 1959 Bristol Lodekka courtesy of Cumbria Classic Coaches

Acknowledgements

Mrs Anna Burgess whose first reading identified changes and revised focus for some characters in the story.

Dr Bryn Massey who gave guidance on medical issues in the story.

Judith Mashiter, of Mosaic Design and Print, who applied her editorial and design skills to turn the manuscript into a finished product ready for publication.

List of characters

Lucy Platt

Fred Platt, Lucy's husband

Richard Platt, son of Fred and Lucy

Dr Poxon, Deputy Head, Leeds Grammar School, and Maxwells Motors board director

Dr Adams, Headmaster, Leeds Grammar School

Sam Maxwell

Bob Maxwell

Edith Maxwell, Bob's wife

Eva and Paul Benfield, owners of Benfield Motors

Joe Lidgett, of Lidgett Bus Company

James Low, solicitor for Maxwells

Ken Straw, Luke Construction site manager

Martin Luke, joint owner of Luke Construction

James Green, project manager for garage extension

Mrs Senior, neighbour and help to the Platts

Matthew Senior, her son, friend of Richard Platt

Captain George Grey and his wife, Susan, coach tour clients

Mr Higson, a Maxwells taxi regular customer

Leslie Fortune, Manager of Priestley Travel Agency, Harrogate

Diane Rhodes, manager of employment agency, Lucy's friend

Maxwell Motors staff

Mavis Freeman, office manager

Elsie Brown, taxi and wedding car driver

John Wall, maintenance department

Mike Best, accountant

George Clay (management committee member), driver

Joe North, bus cleaner

Marion Stead, south coast tours courier

Lilly Young, housekeeper to the Platts

David Young (Lilly's brother), part-time fuel pump attendant

Margaret Mason, office clerk

Pearl Featherstone, wedding taxi driver and office clerk

Brian Hunt, general worker

Audrey Worth, luxury coach tours courier

John Bright, driver

One

Lucy Platt decided that tonight was the time to reveal her secret plan to the family. She would do it over the Friday evening meal.

It was eight years since Lucy had married Fred Platt, in 1951. Some folk said he had married above his status when he wed Lucy, but she had other ideas. As the daughter of a schoolmaster, she considered it was her responsibility to keep organising and uplifting Fred. At the time they got married, Lucy had had a job in a ladies' fashion shop, but after twelve months Richard was born and she became a devoted mother and a full-time housewife. Fred managed to keep her going with money from his job at Wilkins Engineering, enhanced by regular overtime. Lucy had the best handyman in the community and their house showed it. She was forever producing plans and projects.

Lucy and Richard had been patient waiting for Fred to arrive back from work. He was late because he had done two hours' overtime at Wilkins to complete a job for one of the local coal mines. Tomorrow he was booked to work a full day on another job for a different coal mine. The original foundry had been extended to include a large fabrication workshop which had been in operation for over a year. Fred's time was now split between foundry work and fabrication work. He had been given additional training for welding and marking out the fabrication jobs. His boss realised that Fred was bright and reliable. The works manager had even hinted to him that in the future he might be used as a foreman to supervise the assembly of the fabrications on the various sites. Fred had never discussed this with Lucy, but he was sure she had noticed that his hourly rate had increased. His firm was doing very well and their one salesman had good contacts with several Yorkshire coal mines. The trouble was that the mines always wanted the jobs completed at short notice.

Fred was tired but he put his wage packet on the table with the satisfaction that it reflected a very good wage for a working man in the engineering trade.

'There you are, Lucy; another good week's pay. You'll be able to save a bit out of that.' She took the pay packet and examined the figures on the payslip.

'You're doing very well, Fred, but I see that the tax man is getting more than he used to! Don't worry, though, I keep calling in the Building Society and putting the spare money away. The assistants give me a smile now; they probably think we might decide to buy our own house in the future to move out of this council estate.'

'I think that will be a good few years away,' Fred replied.

'Oh I am not so sure, Fred. I've been thinking. There might be some possibility for changes in this family.' Lucy was wearing one of her 'I-know-best' looks. Fred knew that she would spill the beans when it suited her. He was a touch worried, though, because her plans often involved spending money to undertake more modifications to the house.

When Fred was ready to eat, Lucy went to the back door and called out for Richard to come in from the garden where he was playing with a friend. Richard had just had his seventh birthday. He was settled at school and was doing well, with good reports from his teacher. Lucy was proud of him. He would be an only son, as she had decided that she did not want to tackle any more pregnancies.

Richard washed his hands and then took his place at the table. The meal was a Friday favourite of meat and potato pie with peas and carrots. Richard didn't like the vegetables but ate a few to avoid his Dad's critical looks.

'What are these changes that you're thinking about, Lucy?' asked Fred. 'Are you going to share them with the men of your family?'

Lucy paused for effect; she was not going to be harassed.

'It began two weeks ago. I met a woman called Pauline when I was in town shopping. We were in the same class at school. We had a talk. She is now a private secretary to a consultant at the hospital. She isn't married, but she is doing well for herself. She told me how she got to where she is now and I was most impressed. She suggested that I should consider the opportunities that are around. She went to nightschool and did shorthand and typing; then she did a correspondence course on office management.'

'Surely you are not considering going back to work, Lucy? I thought your job was to run the house while I earned the money.'

'I've given this some thought over the past two weeks. Why can't I consider going back to work, Fred? Richard is settled at school now and he can go with his mates to the school which is only two streets away. But I'm not thinking of going back as a shop assistant, Fred, I am aiming higher than that. I've already signed-on for a shorthand and typing course which starts in three weeks' time at the technical college. I've also written off for details of the office management correspondence course. I plan to complete my training in the next nine months and then look for a real appointment.'

Fred looked at Lucy with new eyes. He thought she looked smarter, and he imagined what she would look like as a secretary to some senior manager. She would rule the office like she ruled her house. She would not stand any office backchat, and she would guard her boss in his office like a lion guarding its cubs. When her boss had distinguished visitors, Fred could see Lucy, in her smart clothes, turning on the charm and providing a first-class welcome. Yes, he thought to himself, Lucy's plan was a surprise, but it might be a good one.

'But this will be a major change in our household arrangements, Lucy. It will add to your responsibilities.'

'I've considered that, Fred and I'm sure I can take it on.'

'I accept that, Lucy; but what about Richard and me in these plans? Who is going to look after the house and do the cooking and cleaning?'

'You have no need to worry about that, Fred. If I get a responsible job that requires me to do long hours I shall arrange for some household help. I want my husband and my son to be proud of me and thank me for changing all our lives. I hope to succeed as you have done, Fred.'

There was no answer to that, so Fred decided to just wait and see what developed.

It was an interesting period for the Platt family. Fred got a promotion and became a foreman at Wilkins. He was in charge of the fabrication shop, with responsibility for preparing the orders on time and arranging the assembly on site. He still enjoyed getting involved, hands-on, with the work, but he also developed contacts with the colliery engineers, agreeing with them simplified designs or increased reliability by using better quality materials. He'd never enjoyed his work so much, and the variety of his job was a bonus to him. When the works manager brought visitors or customers around the workshop, he always introduced them to Fred and explained to them that Fred was 'Mr Reliability,' who always delivered jobs on time and to specification. The manager had also arranged for Fred to receive a monthly technical journal on the latest fabrication and manufacturing systems.

Lucy completed her 'education upgrade' in nine months, as planned. She worked hard and studied intensively in the evenings and at weekends.

Fred was impressed but slightly concerned. 'Are you sure you're up to these courses, Lucy?,' he'd asked, on more than one occasion.

'Don't worry, Fred. I can master these courses, I'm sure.'

Her efforts paid off and her Technical College results for both shorthand and typing were near the top of the course. And she achieved 'distinction' for the correspondence course. Throughout the study period she was careful to demonstrate to her husband and son that she could still run the house efficiently and feed the family excellent food.

Fred held her in high regard. He respected what she was doing, and was proud of his wife. He was sure that she'd dropped a few pounds in weight, too, and that had given her a more distinguished figure, which in turn she'd exploited by buying clothes and underwear that emphasised her curves. Lucy had also sought advice on the best use of cosmetics to suit her colours; she went to a better hairdresser and this resulted in styles that built up her hair and made her stature more imposing. When they went out together Fred had noticed that she certainly caught the attention of any men, young or old, who had wanderings eyes.

'What is your next move, Lucy?,' asked Fred when Lucy received her college results. 'You now have the qualifications, so how are you going to use them?'

'I've thought about that Fred. I don't want to jump into a dead-end job and I realise that I need to get some experience, but I want it to be varied. I've decided to try an agency which provides temporary staff appointments for companies who need cover for sickness or to meet a short-term, rush job. I've spoken to one agency that might be alright, but I want to meet another one before I make my mind up. The one I went to seemed happy with my qualifications now.'

After visiting the other agency, Lucy went back to the original one and signed-on with them. She reported back to Fred with a caveat. 'The agency has offered me an appointment and the rate per hour is quite good. But they need to be able to get hold of me at short notice, so I have set the wheels in motion for us to have a telephone installed. There are spare lines down this street, so the engineer said he would give it priority.'

'I suppose it would be an advantage to be on the phone,' replied Fred, hesitantly, but silently he wondered how much this would cost over a year.

In bed that night, Lucy laid in Fred's arms for a kiss and cuddle. Fred was aroused by the feel of her wonderful body, but Lucy's mind was on things other than sex. 'The neighbours will really see that the Platt family are going up in the world, when we get the telephone installed.'

For the next year, life in the Platt family was very busy. The neighbours noted that both Fred and Lucy left for work each morning and that Richard went later to school with his friend from down the street. After school, Richard stayed at his friend's house until either Fred or Lucy got home. Pound notes were passed to Mrs Senior, Richard's friend's mother, at the end of those weeks when Richard had had to spend several hours there before he was collected. The neighbours understood that Mrs Platt was a kind and generous woman.

Lucy was paid by the agency on a monthly basis, meaning that the Platt family had five paydays each month — four for Fred and one for Lucy. Richard watched with interest the review that took place on each payday of the amount earned and how it should be spent or saved. One outcome he was delighted about was that he started to receive pocket money. Fred was impressed with Lucy's earnings and he realised that the family was around the top of the earnings league for their neighbourhood.

The employment agency had a high regard for Lucy, and had used her on a range of positions. Always, when the appointment finished, the company using her reported how satisfied they had been with her and their willingness to use the agency again. On one occasion she spent six weeks as private secretary to the managing director of a small company while his secretary had a serious operation in hospital. Lucy was so successful that the managing director himself rang the agency to record his praise and appreciation for the way Lucy had carried out her responsibilities. Fred wondered how long she would continue with this itinerant lifestyle, though, and one night, in bed, he put the question. 'Aren't you getting fed up, Lucy, with this carry-on of changing jobs every few weeks? Wouldn't you be happier with a permanent appointment, in one place?'

‘That’s a good question, Fred. I’ve enjoyed the variety, and the fact that the agency is using me now with more senior positions. It’s all good experience, but yes, I think I might soon start looking for a permanent post.’ She turned over, indicating that she did not want to continue the discussion. She needed to get some sleep as she had a long journey across Leeds the next morning to her current posting.

Lucy’s move to a permanent job came about through the manageress of the agency, Diane Rhodes. She asked Lucy to come into the office for a discussion. She explained that she lived in Horsforth, four miles from the centre of Leeds. Within Horsforth there was a private bus company, Maxwell Motors. The firm had started with one bus, in the 1920s, which replaced their horse-drawn vehicles. Mr Maxwell, the founder, had passed the firm on to his two sons, who were both now in their fifties. They’d expanded the business and now had four vehicles — two service buses and two luxury coaches — and they’d recently built a large garage. The rumour was that they intended to purchase more luxury coaches to expand their business. They had the license to operate a service from Horsforth into the centre of Leeds, running an hourly service throughout the week, and at busy times they had two buses on the route.

Diane Rhodes explained to Lucy that the Maxwell brothers needed someone to manage the office, because they had relied on Bob Maxwell’s daughter to do the job and she was now getting married and moving away. Bob Maxwell, the senior of the two brothers, had spoken to Diane to get her advice. She’d taken a look at the current arrangement and admitted to Lucy that the daughter had muddled through without any proper systems in place. Would Lucy be interested? Lucy was indeed interested and it had been agreed that Diane would take Lucy and introduce her to Bob Maxwell.

They went the next evening and Lucy had decided not to tell Fred. They spent over two hours touring the garage, inspecting the buses and coaches, viewing the one taxi that they had, looking at the two pumps that sold petrol to the public as well as filling up the fleet. In the office, which was a single-room building adjacent to the garage, Lucy asked lots of questions about the systems used to operate the business. Reflecting on the responses she received she indicated that she was familiar with better systems which could be applied to make the operation more efficient and more profitable. Bob Maxwell and Diane Rhodes were both impressed by Lucy's questions and her observations and they realised that she might be an asset for the company.

Bob Maxwell was so pleased that he asked Lucy there and then if she would be interested in the post. Lucy thought for just a minute before replying that she would be. The post would be a challenge for her, particularly if there were to be more coaches in the fleet, and of course, it would depend on the salary and terms of the appointment. Bob said that there would definitely be more coaches in the fleet as two more were on order for delivery later in the year. He would like five minutes to discuss the salary and terms with Diane in private and then Lucy could have a firm offer on the table. When he stated his figure for the salary Lucy was somewhat shocked but, when he stated her title — 'Operation Controller and Office Manager' — she realised the scope of her responsibilities were far-reaching.

'Me and my brother are getting a bit old and past our prime,' explained Bob Maxwell. 'This firm wants some young blood and we have no sons to follow us. From what I have seen of you, young lady, you are just what we want. So it will be up to you to make Maxwell Motors really grow.'

Diane Rhodes agreed to prepare the necessary appointment documents and Lucy agreed to start work in two weeks' time.

Lucy arrived home after nine o'clock and Fred was waiting for her with a look of concern on his face.

'You're late, Lucy. I've been a bit worried about you. Where have you been?'

'I've been out with the manageress of the agency, Diane Rhodes, looking at a job prospect. We had a good visit and saw the company and its set up. I asked a lot of questions and got a lot of answers. The detailed discussion then led to a job offer and I decided to accept it.'

'That's a big decision, Lucy. Were you happy to accept it without my advice? What's the job?'

'I have agreed to become Operation Controller and Office Manager of a bus company,' announced Lucy.

'That's a strange line of business for you, Lucy. Are you sure that you're right to take on that sort of job?'

'Well it will pay me well, Fred. I start at £110 per month, with a review after six months. It's with Maxwell Motors, in Horsforth, and they're an expanding company in the luxury coach business. They also have a licence for one route from Horsforth into the centre of Leeds. And they have petrol pumps selling to the public as well as for filling up their vehicles. They also have a taxi for hire. So my first job will be to have driving lessons so that I can get a driving licence. I want to be able to drive the taxi as well as my other jobs.'

'Bloody hell, Lucy; what next?'

They went to bed and Lucy was very excited about the evening's events. She wasn't ready for sleep, so Fred was treated to her ravishing body and half an hour of passion.

The day before she started her newjob, Lucy telephoned Bob Maxwell to say that she had decided to get to the town centre to catch the first Maxwell bus out to Horsforth. It left the bus station at six-forty-five. She explained that she wanted to get settled in as quickly as possible. He'd suggested it was a bit early, but he would see her as he was driving the service bus on the early rota. Fred had asked her if she would be leaving this early each morning, as he left for work at seven o'clock. His concern was what would happen to Richard. Lucy reassured him that she had already made arrangements for him to go to Mrs Senior's and have breakfast with his school friend.

At the terminus Bob Maxwell shook hands with Lucy and introduced her to the bus conductor, who was a young woman. Bob noticed that Lucy was dressed in her smart office attire. She'd brought a bag that contained two smocks and a waterproof coat, with a pair of gloves and a waterproof hat. Lucy was prepared for spending time on the forecourt and in the garage, as well as the office. When Bob saw her later working the petrol pumps, then in discussions with the man who washed the buses and the woman who cleaned them inside, he realised that she was going to get involved in the whole of the operations. That was more than his daughter had done, he thought, as he heaved a sigh of relief.

Lucy had a busy first day meeting the other drivers, taking an order for the taxi and checking all the money handed in from the service buses. She also answered a request, from a society in Leeds, for two coaches to take a trip to Blackpool. This involved agreeing the price and the times for pickup and the time for arrival back in Leeds. The bookings for the coaches had normally been entered in a book, often in pencil, but Lucy decided to prepare a typed sheet for each booking, which would be kept in a loose-leafed file. She discussed it with Bob and, with his agreement, converted all the existing bookings into the new format. It was five o'clock by the time she had put all the money in the safe. Bob suggested that she came an hour later on the Tuesday morning and Lucy agreed to the later start. She was satisfied that she had made some progress for her first day.

Bob Maxwell drove her in the taxi to the bank the following morning. They paid the money in and got a receipt for it before being led into the manager's office where they were treated to a cup of coffee. Lucy realised that Maxwell Motors was an important customer for the bank. She discussed with the bank manager the arrangements to pick up the money each Thursday for paying the staff wages. Bob explained that making up the wages and paying them out would be a part of Lucy's responsibility. He also wanted her to be able to sign cheques for the company, so signed the necessary bank documents authorising this.

As they were driving back Bob said that, as a security procedure, he would arrange for Lucy to be driven to the bank in the taxi by one of the drivers. Lucy accepted that this would be necessary for the Thursday run due to the amount of money involved. She explained that she was hoping to take her driving test in the next few weeks. He didn't say as much but at that moment Bob Maxwell had an idea to increase the efficiency of the business.

During the rest of the week Lucy took over all the office systems from Bob's daughter as she was spending less and less time in the office under the excuse of finalising the arrangements for her wedding and the move into a new house in Liverpool. Lucy changed the systems as she went along. The drivers' rota, which had been a single sheet, often written in pencil, became a typed sheet posted up on a board in the garage. Bob and his brother often took spells on the service buses but they were reluctant to do the long day trips with the touring coaches. Both the coaches were due to be out first thing on Saturday morning, so Lucy checked them on Friday afternoon to see that they were all prepared for the day. She spoke to both the drivers to confirm that they knew the time of departure and the pick up points. Before she left she had a word with Bob. 'I think I've got the hang of things now and all the plans for the weekend and next week are in place. I have one or two other ideas that I will discuss with you next week. I've really enjoyed the challenge.'

'We've been glad to welcome you, Lucy. I think the drivers and staff will be happy to work with you. You go off and enjoy your weekend.'

Lucy picked up her bag and went to the door of the office ready to catch a bus into town.

'Don't rush off, Lucy," said Bob, as he followed her to the door. 'I'm going out in the taxi now, so I'll go round by your house and drop you off.'

'That's very kind of you,' she replied, concluding that it had been a really good week.

It caused quite a stir when the taxi drew up at the Platt house and she got out and smiled to Bob Maxwell as she closed the door. Fred happened to be looking out of the front room window and so were one or two of the neighbours. Another story about Lucy Platt circulated around the houses.

During the next four weeks Lucy took over her role fully. Bob Maxwell gave away his daughter at a lavish wedding and she departed on her honeymoon and then to her new life in Liverpool.

Lucy had several lengthy chats with Bob Maxwell. She was told the provisional delivery dates for the two new coaches but that there might be a delay as Bob was having them upgraded to the latest specification. She suggested that the firm should do some advertising, to let people know that they would soon have additional capacity for trips. Bob interviewed for extra drivers who could be called on for the tour coaches when they were booked. Lucy persuaded Bob to split the accounts into the separate operations. He brought in a young man. Mike Best, from the firm who did the annual accounts, to show how to apportion the income and the costs to each section — the service buses, the tour coaches, the taxi service and the fuel sales. It was relatively easy, Lucy found, until she had to share out the costs of the two brothers, who took only a small salary each month, but shared out the profits of the company.

Lucy agreed an enlargement to the office, with a completely new layout. As well as a desk for herself and a spare one, there was an area with seats to accommodate anyone visiting the office to place an order. There was also a small kitchen so that visitors could be given a cup of tea. She'd explained to Bob that people visiting the office should be made to feel important, and reassured that they were dealing with a professional firm. Two new, linked telephones were installed, as Lucy emphasised that no enquiries should be lost because the telephone was engaged. Bob also agreed that they should appoint a suitable young girl who could be trained by Lucy to help with the additional work as the company expanded. She spoke to several schools to tell them the type of girl she was looking for.

When Lucy passed her driving test she told Bob that she would be able to drive the taxi when she got the girl started in the office, as she thought there was scope for more taxi bookings.

Four months after Lucy started, a sixteen-year-old girl, Elsie Brown, started in the office. She was keen and Lucy arranged a training programme to show her how the operation worked. Elsie helped with cleaning the buses and coaches and skillfully served petrol at the pumps. She had an attractive appearance, so Lucy bought her some smart clothes that emphasised her figure and encouraged her to smile and be friendly to the customers. The petrol sales started to increase.

Elsie became proficient in all the office systems, but Lucy was particularly keen to ensure that she operated the telephones as though it was a major company. 'This is Maxwell Motors and I am Elsie, how can I help you?' was the standard answer Lucy wanted her to use with an incoming telephone call. She also insisted that Elsie should sign-on for courses in shorthand and typing at nightschool. Lucy aimed to develop Elsie so that she could take on a bigger role in the future, as Maxwell Motors expanded.

It was the Friday marking the completion of Lucy's first six months with Maxwell Motors. In the afternoon a new vehicle was delivered to the garage forecourt. It was a small pick-up van bearing the company colours. On its sides was an illustration of one of the coaches and the telephone number of the garage. Lucy sought out Bob Maxwell, as she was not aware that the van was on order or what it was for.

'There's a van been delivered to the forecourt,' she said. 'It must be for us because it's all set up with the company colours and it's advertising the garage telephone number on each side of the van. What is it for?'

'Actually, it's mainly for you to use,' Bob replied. 'You said we needed to do more advertising, so, wherever the van is, it will be advertising the company. You can use it to travel between your home and the garage; you can use it to go to the bank and also for picking up drivers, or any other odd jobs.'

'You really mean that I can use it to travel from home to the garage?'

'Yes, it will save you a lot of travelling time. And before you go, there is a letter in the house for you.'

Bob came into the office and handed Lucy the letter. She saw that it was from the employment agency and didn't know what to do with it.

'Go on, open it. It'll not bite you,' urged Bob.

Lucy opened the letter and read that her salary would be increased by twenty pounds each month, with a further review when she had completed a full year with the company. Lucy was genuinely shocked.

'Oh, Mr Maxwell, thank you very much. I don't know what to say.' She moved towards him and shook his hand and then she placed a kiss on his cheek. He blushed and went out into the forecourt.

Lucy drove home in the van and parked it on the short driveway to the house. It had only taken her fifteen minutes to drive across town, so she immediately realised what a benefit the van would be to her working day. She went into the house and met Fred in the kitchen. He was starting to make the evening meal.

'Just leave that a minute, Fred. I'll help get the meal ready, but first I have something outside to show you.' She took Fred's arm and led him out of the front door.

He looked in disbelief at the van. 'What's this, Lucy?'

'It's the new arrival at Maxwell Motors. It's mainly for my use and it's designed to be a mobile advert for the company. We need to build up the business when the two new coaches are delivered next month. I didn't know it was coming. But that's not all, Fred. I have something else to show you.'

They went into the house and she showed him the letter about her salary increase. Fred stared at the figures and he was amazed at the increase of twenty pounds each month.

'Lucy Platt, you are full of surprises.' He pulled her into his arms. 'And they are all bloody good ones!'

Two

It was an important day for Maxwell Motors in April 1962. Lucy Platt was alone on the garage site as the Maxwell brothers had gone to Scarborough to collect their two new coaches from the Paxton body building company. She had taken them in the taxi to Leeds station to catch the train to Scarborough. Bob had hoped to have the new coaches in the fleet earlier in the year, to catch the main holiday traffic, but there had been a delay. The regulations governing the design of coaches had changed, allowing single-deck coaches to be six feet longer. This made room for two extra rows of seats and increased the capacity to 52 seats, compared with the earlier designs with 44 seats. Bob Maxwell wanted his new Leyland Royal Tiger coaches to be to the new design, and he had ordered them with the Paxton Panorama body. There had been a rush of orders for the new designs and this had caused the delay.

Just before four o'clock the two new coaches pulled on to the forecourt of the garage. They looked very impressive and Lucy and Elsie excitedly rushed to take a close look.

'Well, here they are, at last,' said Bob. 'We now want some jobs for them, Lucy.'

'I'm working on it,' she replied. 'I've arranged for the local paper to do a piece on Maxwell Motors this weekend, with a photograph of the two new coaches. The photographer will be taking his picture this evening. He might want them moving to a different line-up.I've started asking our current bookings if they would like to change to the bigger coaches which would allow them to have extra passengers. I'm also going to meet the local churches, and any other societies who run trips, to let them know what we can now offer. I am sure it will let us deal with bigger contracts. The four coaches have 192 seats in total, but if there are small children on the trips, they will be able to fit three children on each double seat, so we could be talking about a total of well over two hundred passengers.'

'That's great, Lucy. You have something to get your teeth into now.'

'And I've got a new regular order today for the taxi. A Mr Higson wants to use us on a regular basis. He's managing director of an engineering company in Leeds and he lives just outside Horsforth, in a very large house. He travels regularly by train to London and is to use us exclusively. I've assured him of my personal attention; if he's arriving on a late train I will take the taxi home instead of the van so that I can meet him.'

'That seems positive, Lucy,' replied Bob, giving a tired stretch as they stood on the forecourt. 'It's been a long day and both of us are ready for a rest,' he added, looking across to his brother, Sam, who liked driving but nothing else. 'The coaches certainly look smart and the engines are very powerful. I think we have made a good buy.'

'I am sure you have, Bob,' she replied.

The new coaches immediately proved attractive to the wider Leeds market, as well as the local Horsforth community. In September, with the start of Blackpool Illuminations, there were often four coaches booked for Saturday and Sunday. It was a very long day for the drivers as the trips usually left around nine o'clock in the morning to get to Blackpool for a late lunch. The passengers had the afternoon in the town and re-joined the coach in the early evening when it got dark. The journey home started with a drive along the Blackpool front from south to north to see all the lighting displays. The coach then looped round and drove back along to the south end of town for a second look at the lights before taking the road home. Some coach trips only passed along the front one way, which was good for getting on the road home but not very good for seeing all the displays. Lucy had spotted this and, in agreement with Bob and the drivers, had established the double-pass option which was a good selling point for Maxwell Motors. It was usually midnight when the coaches returned back to the garage, so the cycle of cleaning and washing had to be completed during the night. Lucy was often on site early on Saturday and Sunday mornings to see that the coaches got away on time.

On her request, Lucy had been instructed by Bob how to drive the coaches, so that she could manoeuvre them to the petrol pumps to fill them up with fuel for the next day. Bob had watched her very carefully when she first tried this, but he was impressed with her driving skills.

Fred often joined Lucy on the early Sunday mornings and he admired the sight of the four coaches leaving the garage in convoy. There was no doubt that Maxwell Motors were making significant profits from the coaches, but that was not the full story of the business.

Lucy had been keeping separate accounts for the different aspects of the operations. Mike Best, who had set up the separate accounting system, came to go through the figures with her. While the coaches were doing well, the cash cow for the business was the service buses. They were operating seven days a week and it was a reliable service starting early in the morning until late at night. The buses provided transport for a lot of workers in and around Leeds, but they also carried shoppers and people going into the city for entertainment. Maxwell Motors ran a late night service, leaving the centre of Leeds after eleven o'clock at night, out to Horsforth. There was usually someone on board to support the bus conductor in case there were some passengers who had exceeded reasonable alcohol limits. It had been known for the bus to be stopped and any passenger put off to walk home to sober him up, if he was thought to be a problem.

The route was so busy that a second bus was used at peak travelling times. The accountant asked Lucy if she had considered using a double-decker bus. She explained that it hadn't been raised because the financial picture was only now becoming clear. Later that day she arranged for him to see Bob.

'Bob, this is Mike Best from the accountants. He helped me set up the accounting system so that we could see how the different parts of the business are performing. We have had a session today evaluating the results and it has shown a different picture to what I expected. I suppose I should have seen this with the way the money is coming in, and what I am taking to the bank on a day-to-day basis, but I didn't see it. The fact is that the cash cow for Maxwell

Motors is the service buses. You can see the figures.' She asked Mike to go through them.

When Mike had finished explaining the analysis to Bob, he posed the question. 'Have you considered how you could increase this part of the business? You have to put two buses on at peak times. Why don't you consider using a double-decker? It would carry more passengers and it might avoid running two buses on the route at certain times.'

Lucy supported the argument from her own observations 'I think we could see an increase in passengers, Bob, as there are some times when there are queues of people at the bus stops and, if the bus is full, they move to a different bus stop and wait for an alternative service.'

Bob agreed to consider the option and promised to look at availability. Lucy had one last card to play. 'I think it would be helpful if we had Mike in every three months to review the finances with me. He knows what to look for and it would help him with the annual accounts.'

'If you want him on that basis, Lucy, you set it up.'

Bob knew a winner when he saw one.

Bob researched the latest designs of double-decker buses before settling on the Leyland Atlantean design. He took Lucy to see the bus at the Leyland factory before the final decision was made. The bus was thirty feet long, with a sixteen-foot-three-inches wheelbase. The engine was in a rear-mounted compartment outside the main body of the bus. As a result of this feature the noise levels inside the bus were very low compared with a bus with a front engine mounting. It had a seating capacity of seventy-eight and was a front-entrance bus, so allowed the driver to supervise the loading and unloading of passengers while the conductor collected the fares.

Bob went with Lucy to see the bank manager to agree a loan. In fact, the loan was quite small compared with the total cost of a double-decker bus, as the reserves of Maxwell Motors were consistently building up. There was a waiting time of four months to delivery from the time of order.

Life continued at a fast pace for Lucy. She was picking up more taxi fares as word spread about her service. She often left home to meet a late train from London and pick up Mr Higson or his wife when they were returning from a spell in London. Lucy suspected that Mr Higson, had passed on news of the service to some of their friends, as she started to get other taxi requests from senior executives travelling by train to London. This resulted in her having some very early morning fares, as well as the late night ones. Fred raised the question one night as they were preparing to go to bed. 'Lucy, don't you think you should go a bit easier, particular with the taxi fares? You're putting a lot of extra hours in, and a lot of weekend work as well."'

'Fred I'm not the only one putting extra effort in; you are doing a lot of overtime for your firm. How do you account for that?'

'The firm is doing well and I have a responsibility to see that we keep doing well.'

'There you are, Fred. Maxwell Motors is also doing well and I have the responsibility to see that the company gets bigger and bigger. I am enjoying success just as much as you are. We are a successful couple; we have a lot to be thankful for'.

'I do get paid for my overtime,' put in Fred, warily.

'You can be sure that I will see my salary increase as the company grows,' she replied, aiming to end the conversation. She had to pick up Mr Higson at six-thirty the next morning to catch the London train.

That day, Lucy received a bunch of flowers sent to the garage from Mr Higson's secretary, as a special thank-you from him for the service he was receiving. Lucy took them home and put them in a vase in the front room. When Fred looked quizzically at them she gave the answer before he could ask the question.

'A thank-you from one of my male taxi fares,' she said. 'Don't worry Fred, it was for my good driving, nothing else.'

The delivery of the double-decker was delayed, just as the new coaches had been, but it arrived at the garage on a Saturday morning when the four coaches were out on a day trip to Scarborough. Fred was working during the morning but he was free for the rest of the day. Lucy went home and made lunch and then announced that they were going out in the afternoon. She had taken the taxi home to ensure that they had a comfortable ride. She suggested that Richard could take his school friend, Matthew Senior, along.

'You must bring your camera, Fred. There might be some very special pictures.' Fred had bought a good camera, which he used at work for taking photographs of fabrications before they left the workshop. The works manager approved of this, as it gave the company some good publicity material when they were talking to potential clients.

Lucy drove the taxi onto the forecourt where the new double-decker bus stood proudly on view. Bob was at the fuel pumps filling up a customer's car.

'I've brought you some extra admirers who want to view your new purchase, Bob,' said Lucy.

'We've had a few people having a look during the last couple of hours,' he replied. He went over to the bus and unlocked the front doors so that Lucy, Fred and the boys could get onto the bus. It had the smell and feel of a brand new vehicle. The two boys looked at the driver's seat and all the dials on the dashboard.

'Sit in the seat, boys, and see what it feels like to be the driver,' said Lucy. 'Come on, Fred, get that camera out and let's have some pictures.'

Fred got some excellent shots of both the boys with thrilled smiles holding the steering wheel as though they were driving. Fred also sat in the seat and Lucy took his picture.

'What does it feel like to be in charge of this monster, Fred? It will carry nearly ninety passengers with seventy-eight seats and a few standing downstairs. It'll make a big difference to the Maxwell Motors business.' They sat in the seats and then went upstairs and checked the views out of the top deck windows.

'When are you planning to put it into service, Bob?' asked Lucy. 'I wondered if we should let the drivers have a dry run first, just to get the feel of the bus in traffic. It is a big vehicle.'

'I think that is a good idea, Lucy. Let the rota stand with the single buses on Monday and arrange for the drivers to have a run with the new double-decker. Then we can feed it into the service on Tuesday.'

'I'll arrange that, Bob, she said. 'From the look of these lads,' she added, indicating her son and his friend, 'we could have a couple of new drivers in ten to twelve years time.'

They were fortunate in that the usual route did not pass under any bridges that presented a height restriction problem for the double-decker. The bus was attractive with the local Horsforth population and there was an increase in the number of passengers being carried. Indeed, such was the increase that Lucy decided, at the peak times, to still run an additional single-deck bus on the route. This left one spare single-deck bus in the garage and raised the option of selling the bus or trying to find extra work. Lucy had a suggestion for Bob.

'Why don't we hang on to the bus for the time being and let me see if I can get some extra work for it. It is the oldest bus and not very smart but it would be alright for a works bus or a school bus. Bob agreed that Lucy should explore the options.

When the double-decker had been in use for a full month, Lucy showed Bob what the income had been from the service buses. 'You can see, Bob, that the service income has increased by over fifteen percent since the double-decker went into use. I know it cost a lot of money but it will have paid for itself within the next year. We shall have paid-off the loan from the bank in the next three months.' Lucy had signed the two cheques for the bus, one to Leyland and one to Paxton. She had told Fred, the night after she'd posted them, that signing the cheques was the most thrilling thing she had ever done in her life.

Bob was very impressed by the figures, but Lucy had another piece of good news. 'I think I've got a couple of jobs for the oldest bus. I just need to tie up the contract details. Rothwell coal mine is looking for a new contract for a service from two districts in Leeds to the pit. They've been let down by the existing contractor, who has used a very old bus that has broken down on a few occasions and left the men stranded. It will involve three runs each day, one at five o'clock in the morning to take the day shift men to work and bring the night shift men home; a run at midday to take the afternoon shift men to work and bring the day shift men home; and the final run will be a- eight thirty in the evening to take the afternoon shift men home and bring the night shift men to work. And there's a chance that I might be able to fit in a school run in the morning and afternoon with a city-centre school, if I can finalise that contract.' Bob was very impressed with Lucy's news. It had been well worth keeping the oldest bus as a stand-by.

Lucy had two additional matters to discuss. 'I think we should get a new driver to carry out the pit and school contracts. If I can persuade him to be responsible for the contracts on his own, it will mean that he does not become a part of the service rotas. We can pay him a full wage, although his day will be made up of short bits through the twenty-four hours.'

'That sounds like a good idea, Lucy,' replied Bob. 'But you'll need a fellow who is very reliable.'

'I agree, Bob. Do you know anyone who fits the bill?'

'I'll have a think about that, Lucy.'

'There is one other thing, Bob. I think I should get a Public Service Vehicle licence. There might be times when something goes wrong out on the road and we need a relief coach or bus to go to the rescue. There are often times when there's no driver available on site or a spare one that I can send for. If I could take a bus out on the road it would be the quickest way to solve the problem. It would certainly impress the stranded passengers,' she added with a laugh.

'Well that is a surprise request,' said Bob. 'You could be right to suggest it. I suppose in the future there will be more female drivers. Maxwell Motors might as well take a lead in this. I'll make enquiries. I will want you to be trained at some driving school away from Maxwell Motors. We have some good drivers here, but all of us may have developed a few bad habits.'

Lucy went home that night with her mind full of things to discuss with Fred. He was late home as the fabrication shop had been completing a job for one of the big Yorkshire coal mines. Actually, Fred was aware that the pit was desperate for the delivery and by staying one hour as overtime the fabrication would be delivered the next day. This was in fact two days earlier than the promised delivery date and Fred knew that the early delivery would guarantee more orders from that mine in the future.

'We have had a very interesting day at the garage today,' said Lucy, nearing the end of their meal. 'If you like, I can to tell you about it.'

'That's okay, Lucy. We have had an interesting day in the fabrication shop, as well.'

'Well you tell me your news first.'

Fred explained to her the job that they had finished early. The managing director was so thrilled at the news that he had come into the fabrication shop to tell them how pleased he was.

'Well done' said Lucy. She was proud of Fred's success. She was aware that Richard was listening to the conversation as she explained all about the success of the double-decker bus and the way the finances were improving at Maxwell Motors. She described the two contracts that she was finalising for the oldest bus in the fleet and the need for an additional driver and she finished with the pronouncement about her latest initiative.

'I've decided to go for a PSV licence, so that I can drive a bus on the roads. Bob is going to arrange for me to go to a training school to get the best possible qualifications.'

'Why on earth do you want to do that, Lucy?,' said Fred. Haven't you got enough on at Maxwell Motors?'

Lucy explained her thinking behind the plan – that it was

for her to be able to drive a bus on the road if there was an emergency with a breakdown with one of the buses or coaches.

'I can understand what you mean, Lucy, but I just think that you are taking on too much,' said Fred emphatically.

'Fred, I've sorted that out today. I've arranged for Mrs Senior to do extra hours here, not only cleaning, but she will do more cooking if I'm delayed at the garage or doing extra taxi runs. So you will have a woman here when you get home, Fred. I have told her that she can have Matthew here on an evening and feed him and Richard and herself if she likes. Her husband is working away now, on civil engineering contracts in London, so she is a bit lonely and short of something to do. She's very glad to be involved.'

'That's alright then,' agreed Fred. 'She's a nice woman as far as I can see. There are some women in this neighbourhood that I would not welcome one minute into this house.'

'There is one other thing, Fred, that affects you.'

'What on earth now?'

'I am arranging for you to go on a course at the Technical College. I want you to get a qualification as a motor mechanic. I'm not happy with the service we are getting from the company who are maintaining our fleet.'

'You can't be serious, Lucy! How can I fit that in?'

'Yes, I am, Fred. I am very serious. It's a night school class. You are a good engineer. Another string to your bow could be very useful.'

'Bloody hell, Lucy, what next?'

'Don't swear, Fred, you know that Richard is listening.'

Three

Maxwell Motors appeared to be a successful operation for both the community of Horsforth and to the wider districts of Leeds. More people were travelling on the service buses, where the conductors and drivers were noted for their courtesy and smiling faces. Lucy had been having short sessions with the staff to make sure that they realised how much their demeanour affected the passengers. She qualified for her Public Service Vehicle licence and the drivers and the rest of the staff were impressed when they saw her driving. She didn't drive on the roads much, but she used her new skills to move coaches on the garage site to fill them with fuel or to re-arrange the parking in the garage.

Good recommendations from societies that had used the coaches for trips led to additional bookings and Lucy was pleased to see that they were winning more mid-week trips. The growth was continuous and positive and was not generated by an advertising programme; it relied on word of mouth.

Lucy had a policy, which was followed by Elsie, to try to persuade any telephone enquirer to visit the garage so that that the matter could be discussed in detail. She was confident that once she got anyone into the office, and they were primed with coffee and biscuits, she could almost guarantee a firm order. She had a feel for the success financially from the money she was paying into the bank each week. After their quarterly meeting, Lucy and Mike Best met Bob Maxwell to discuss the latest figures.

'Mr Maxwell, you are running a business that is making more profit than any I have ever been involved in. Your profit has gone up by twenty-five percent over the same period as last year and your costs have stayed about the same. It is quite a remarkable performance,' said Mike.

'We are all working hard,' replied Bob. 'But this young lady here has the magic touch in dealing with the drivers and with our customers. She also sets an example in the way she does her job; so nobody can refuse when she gives an instruction.'

'I have to say that she is also a very good administrator,' continued Mike. 'Her bookkeeping is excellent and everything is carefully recorded.'

Lucy blushed slightly at these remarks. 'I'm only doing my job,' she said, with a dismissive wave of her hand. 'It's in my job specification that I have to grow the company. That is what we are doing and we have still a long way to go.'

'I suspect that you have an excellent team here who are all working hard to be successful. Have you considered some financial recognition for the staff, Mr Maxwell? Say a Christmas bonus in their pay packets? You have plenty of cash in the bank and can afford it.'

'We have never done that in the past. We pay a fair rate

but not any more than is normal in this business,' replied Bob, rather defensively 'We're lucky that the drivers stay with us. There have been occasions when one or two drivers were approached by other companies but they didn't move. What do you suggest?'

Mike looked across at Lucy. 'Have you any thoughts?'

She replied immediately, 'I think it's a good idea. But we can't pay everyone the same. Some are part-time and some are full-time. I think we should pay all the drivers one rate of bonus and the rest of the staff a lower rate. Whatever we decide, it must be a pleasant surprise for everyone.'

'I think you're right,' replied Mike. 'I would suggest £100 for the drivers and £50 for everyone else. That will have little impact on the bank balance, Mr Maxwell.'

'I'll discuss it with Bob outside this meeting,' said Lucy.

'We'll sort something out,' said Bob, non-commitally.

Two days later Lucy got an opportunity to talk with Bob again.

'I've been thinking about having a function around Christmas, as a treat for the staff. The trouble is that there's virtually no chance of getting them all together as we are so busy. And I don't think you or Sam, are keen on Christmas functions. So I think we should just put the extra bonus in their Christmas pay packets with a little note thanking them for their hard work through the year.'

'Now you're talking,' said Bob. 'My view is to let everyone enjoy Christmas with their families as they want; I have no time for these special events. What often happens at these parties is that some folks have too much to drink and show themselves up. I think you have the right answer, Lucy. Let's stick to what we do best — running a bus company, — and not try to be party organisers.'

Bob was clearly happy to get rid of any ideas for Christmas parties. Lucy wanted to raise another matter, but she approached it cautiously. 'I've been thinking, Bob, about another initiative that we might consider.'

'Come on then, spill the beans.'

'Well, some of the big coach companies lay on tours for several days, or even a week, to visit towns on the south coast, staying in hotels. They then use the coaches to tour around and visit places of interest in that part of the country. As you know, the very big companies also arrange tours on the continent. I don't think we should consider foreign trips, but I suspect that we could do good business with tours to the south coast seaside towns.'

'How do we go about investigating this?'

'We need some help, Bob. What I suggest is that we find someone who has experience of these trips and pay them to do an investigation for us. If you agree, I will hunt around and find someone who I think would be suitable.'

'You do that and then we'll evaluate the options.'

'We will have to modify one of the coaches so that it is equipped with a microphone and speakers throughout the coach, so that the driver or tour manager can talk to the passengers. I know that the driver has to be a person who is good at talking to the passengers and satisfying all their needs. I've spotted one or two of our drivers who I think might be suitable for this job. What we are after is repeat bookings from one year to the next. So we will want to develop several tours using a range of hotels in different seaside towns.'

'Let me know how you get on.'

Lucy had not shown all her cards. She had already met a young woman who had experience of arranging these tours. It was early December 1964 and to get these tours on the road in March or April of 1965, Lucy realised that she had a lot of work to do.

Mavis Freeman was sitting in the Maxwell taxi being driven to the garage to have a meeting in the office. Lucy wanted to show her the garage and the coaches. When they were drinking their tea, searching questions quickly revealed a portrait of Mavis. She was twenty-four years old and had left school when she was seventeen, after successfully taking her A-level exams. She had decided not to go to college or university, but had worked for two years, firstly in a solicitor's office and then in an accountant's office, but in both cases she found the work boring. Mavis then had a spell of nearly two years selling ladies' clothes. She was a good sales assistant, dealing with the upmarket ladies of Leeds. That came to an end when she was away on holiday and met a young man who charmed her and implied that they were made for each other, possibly for life. Mavis left Leeds and went to Birmingham where her boyfriend lived. It was there that she had worked for a bus company who operated tours to the south coast towns. She became involved in the contracts with hotels and acted as a guide on some of the coach tours. She was away quite a lot and after of eighteen months her boyfriend deserted her and went off with another girl. Mavis came back to Leeds and was working part-time in a ladies' fashion shop.

It quickly became clear that Mavis didn't fancy being a shop assistant full-time, but she did have 'hands-on' experience in the travel business. She was just the person that they were looking for to set up coach tours to the south coast. Lucy decided to take a risk. She painted a picture of Maxwell Motors moving into tours in a significant way and stated that there was a vacancy for a full-time job if she was interested. Mavis was keen and so Lucy agreed to have discussions with Bob Maxwell, and she promised to contact Mavis when the plans were finalised.

When Lucy got home that night, she parked the taxi in the drive because she had an early taxi fare the next day. She entered the house with a worried look on her face and didn't speak to Fred, but put the kettle on to make a cup of tea.

'I reckon that you've got something on your mind tonight, Lucy,' said Fred. 'You don't usually look worried when you've been at work. Has something gone wrong?'

'Sorry, Fred. I'm afraid I am a bit preoccupied tonight. Nothing has gone wrong, just the opposite, really; something has gone very right. But I have stuck my neck out a bit more than usual, and I've now to put the idea to Bob. That might be tricky. I'll have to sell it to him in the next couple of days.'

'You'll be alright. You are on top of your job at Maxwells'. You have nothing to worry about. Come here and let me give you a cuddle.' She went and let Fred take her in his arms and she felt relief from the stress of what she had done. Fred felt her body pressed against him and he realised again what a lovely figure Lucy had.

'Thanks, Fred. I appreciate your support. But these business decisions get bigger and bigger.'

At that moment Richard came into the room. He had been studying in his bedroom. He was now a big lad, nearly up to his mother's shoulder. 'Oh dear,' he said. 'More cuddling; I don't know what this family is coming to.'

'Don't you be cheeky, young man,' laughed Lucy 'Come here, let me have a cuddle with you. I need a lot of support from my family tonight.' She took Richard into her arms and he shyly put his arms round his mother's waist. Fred Platt looked on with pride at his son comforting his mother just when she needed it.

Lucy had prepared in her mind what she would say to Bob, but the next day was very busy. All the buses were out and both Bob and Sam were out driving. The final coach was scheduled to take two rugby teams from Leeds Grammar School to Pocklington, but the driver rang in to report that his wife had been taken to hospital after collapsing on her way to her teaching job at a local school. Lucy realised that this was an occasion when she could use her PSV licence and drive the coach. She gave strict instructions to Elsie to hold the fort until she got back at around six o'clock. The pick-up was scheduled for twelve-thirty so she drove out of the yard at twelve o'clock to be at the school in good time.

Lucy parked the coach in the school grounds in Pocklington but took the opportunity to walk up to the playing fields to observe the games and chat with the children and staff who were spectating. Richard would soon be taking Grammar School entrance exams at the end of his last year at the junior school and her afternoon on the sports field strengthened her ambition that Richard should go to the Grammar school. She got into conversation with one of the masters on the touchline and he was somewhat surprised to meet this woman who had a key role in running Maxwell Motors. Lucy wondered if she might meet him in the future at some parents' evening.

Back at the garage, Elsie reported that there was a taxi fare from Leeds station at nine o'clock, which she had accepted as it was a key client of Lucy's. She had also arranged a meeting in the office with a potential customer who wanted to hire four coaches for a church trip to Scarborough. Lucy went home with the taxi, but she put off talking to her husband about what she had seen on the school trip. However she was aware that they had to decide how they could encourage Richard to prepare himself for the school exams.

Lucy's meeting with Bob took place two days later. They first discussed the two new coaches that were on order for delivery in early March the following year. Lucy considered that both the coaches should be wired up with speakers and a microphone system. If the tours were successful, it might be necessary to retro-fit the same system into some of the existing coaches. Bob agreed to amend the orders to include the sound system in the specification of the new coaches. She then went on to discuss Mavis Freeman. She decided to go in at the deep-end and explained what a competent woman Mavis was, with the right experience to set up holiday tours to the south coast. But she stressed how she saw Mavis having a more general role in the business and finally made her suggestion that Mavis was appointed to a full-time role at the beginning of January. Lucy described how Mavis could take on some of the taxi fares and become familiar with all the office procedures so that she could stand in for her when she was away. As Lucy explained, when they had six coaches for hire, the logistics would be significantly increased and she was not sure that Elsie and herself could manage without some help. Lucy emphasised that Mavis would bring managerial experience with her, which would be a better option than appointing another junior person like Elsie.

'Won't Elsie be upset by this?' asked Bob.

'I will handle Elsie,' replied Lucy. 'She is developing very well and I think we should pay her a bit extra. I think we should initially use Mavis as a tour manager on the coach to make sure that the service throughout the holiday is very good and the passengers come back year after year because the holidays are interesting and very good value.'

'Right, I think you should arrange for Mavis to come and meet me,' said Bob. 'If she is as good as you suggest, we want to get her before any other bus company gives her an offer.'

'I agree with you. I will see her and set up a meeting as soon as possible.'

Lucy saw Mavis and had a long discussion with her and explained what the appointment would involve. She was glad to learn that Mavis had a clean driving licence so she could take on some taxi fares straightaway. She emphasised to Mavis that it would be a full-time appointment, covering many parts of the Maxwell business, and it was essential that she impressed Bob Maxwell at the first meeting with him.

When the meeting took place, Lucy was pleased to see that Mavis had taken her advice. She was dressed smartly in a skirt and blouse that emphasised her figure and indicated that she knew the latest fashions in ladies' clothes. She gave a very good account of herself and her experience and she indicated her willingness to become fully involved in the operations of the company. Lucy watched Bob and realised that Mavis was everything that his daughter had not been when she had worked in the business.

When they discussed the meeting after Mavis had left, Bob concluded, 'I'm pretty sure you have picked another winner, Lucy. You have a word with your friend, Diane, at the employment agency and get her to draw up a contract for Mavis to start at the beginning of January.'

Lucy went home that night and reported of her success. Fred had a question.'Maxwell Motors is going to be a big outfit when you have six coaches and the service buses. How are you going to pay for the two new coaches?'

Lucy replied very carefully to his question.'You might be surprised to learn this, Fred, but I think there will be enough money in the bank account to pay for the new coaches by the time they are delivered.'

'Goodness me, Lucy, you must be doing very well.'

The reaction of the drivers and staff when they got their Christmas pay packet was surprising and very pleasing to Bob and Lucy. Everyone made a special effort to have a word with them. It was usually just a brief word such as 'Thank you, Boss, we appreciate the bonus. The wife is most impressed.' Or 'That is the best thing that has ever happened here. Have you had a hand in it, Lucy?' They just smiled in reply and wished them all a happy Christmas.

Mavis spent the first three weeks of January getting involved in all aspects of the business. She did quite a number of the taxi journeys and Lucy was pleased to see that she impressed her clients so much that a number started to use the taxi service on a regular basis. She also worked the fuel pumps when Elsie was busy and, much to Lucy's surprise, when there had to be a quick overnight clean of the four coaches, Mavis changed into some old clothes and helped to clean the inside of the coaches.

Lucy spent two days of the last week of January with Mavis working through all the financial aspects of operating tours on the south coast towns. They agreed the maximum levels that Maxwell Motors could afford to pay for the hotel facilities and Mavis departed for a ten-day tour to four south coast holiday towns with appointments arranged at twelve hotels.

Every other day Mavis rang Lucy to report on her progress. She had clear preferences for which hotels to use and she rated their facilities on a scale of one to five, with five being the top grade. The level of charges suggested by the hotels was generally a little lower than the maximum levels that they had agreed. No decisions were made over the telephone but the day after Mavis returned to Yorkshire, there was a meeting with Bob Maxwell, to agree a plan for operating holiday tours to the south coast.

It was a long meeting as Mavis listed requirements by the hotels that would reduce the rate of charges. For instance, it would be better to have seven-day holidays on a continuous basis at one hotel rather than six-day holidays which would mean that the hotel had lots of rooms available for one night. However, six-day holidays would have the advantage that only one coach would be exclusively doing the tours. They finally agreed to offer seven-day tours, meaning that one coach was taking a new tour south while the other coach was bringing the previous tour back to Yorkshire.

They agreed to book four weeks continuously in one town and then book four weeks continuously in another town. After four weeks in a third town, the sequence would then be repeated to cover the six months from April to September. They also agreed that for this year, Mavis should operate as the tour manager, staying at the hotel when the tour party left to return back to Yorkshire. She would be able to welcome each tour as they arrived and travel with them on the excursions. Lucy agreed that she would do three weeks as tour manager during the cycle, to give Mavis a break, but on those weeks Mavis would have to cover Lucy's responsibilities back at the garage.

It was agreed that Bob would investigate the delivery of the two new coaches to ensure that they would be available to start the tours at the beginning of April. Mavis would have discussions with the hotels and resolve the contracts, if possible getting prices that lifted the margins for Maxwell Motors. Lucy would prepare an advertising campaign to be started immediately to get bookings for the tours. They all knew that it was critical to fill the seats on the coaches or the venture could lose significant amounts of money.

The prices proposed by Maxwell Motors were slightly lower than other bus tours to the same towns. Lucy also knew that it would be necessary to have support from travel agents in Leeds to sell the trips, as well as direct sales from the garage. Within a week there were posters on the service buses advertising the tours. Lucy did a circuit of travel agents in and around Leeds, distributing information packs and agreeing an attractive commission for tours booked by the travel agents for that year, 1964. She also displayed information about the tours in churches and clubs that used Maxwell Motors for trips and special outings.

There was a sense of relief when bookings started to drift in. Advertising in March in local papers was effective and Mavis did an interview with a reporter from the local paper and explained what Maxwell Motors was including in the tours. After the article was published there was a rush of bookings such that the tours would at least cover their costs during April. If the feedback from these tours was positive, Lucy was hopeful that word of mouth would fill the coaches during the main holiday season. There was relief when the two new coaches were collected from Paxtons in Scarborough during the third week of March. Mavis tried the sound system in both the coaches and insisted that the two drivers who would be involved also tried speaking with the microphone. Mavis adapted her accent and sounded very professional. One of the drivers stumbled with his broad Yorkshire accent, but Mavis insisted that he practised until he became comfortable with passing on information to the passengers.

Saturday 4 April 1964 was an important date for Maxwell

Motors. It was the day of the first coach tour holiday to the south coast. The coach was parked in the garage forecourt and the driver and Mavis Freeman were there to welcome the passengers and show them to their seats once their luggage had been stowed away. All the passengers had been allocated a seat for the initial journey on a first-come -first-served basis, but it was clearly explained that during the holiday the seating would be rotated. Mavis and the driver looked very smart as they were dressed in the green and cream outfits matching the Maxwell Motors livery. The driver had green trousers and a green blazer with cream piping around the lapels and a cream shirt with a cream and green tie. Mavis also had a green blazer with cream piping and a cream blouse, but she wore a knee-length green skirt which showed off her legs and drew attention to her cream shoes.

Some passengers, who lived outside Horsforth, were picked up by a special bus which toured around Leeds. When that bus arrived ten minutes before the departure time of nine o'clock, Mavis checked the list and reported that everyone who had booked had turned up on time. This meant that there were forty-eight passengers on the tour and there were just three empty seats. There were smiles from the passengers as Lucy waved the bus away. She was also smiling as she knew that Maxwell Motors would make a profit from the tour.

Mavis rang Lucy on two evenings during the week to report on the progress with the holiday. It was clear that the hotel was making special efforts, with food and evening entertainment, to satisfy all the needs of the passengers. Mavis ascertained from the barman that the bar takings were exceptionally high compared with previous weeks, so the hotel manager was delighted to host the thirsty

Yorkshire visitors. The local tours had been successful but Mavis had plans to revise the timings for the following weeks to improve the experience of the passengers.

Lucy was on the garage forecourt on the following Saturday morning to see the second trip away. There were forty-five passengers this time and she helped the driver loading the luggage and guiding the passengers to their seats. When they were all assembled Lucy took the microphone and welcomed them aboard and introduced the driver. She also explained that they would be welcomed at the hotel by Mavis who would be with them throughout the holiday as tour manager. Using her information from Mavis she concluded her remarks with a very positive promise about the holiday. 'I can assure you that you are going to have a wonderful holiday. The reports from the first tour, which will be starting back to Yorkshire about this time, have been full of praise for the hotel — its food, its service and the entertainment. Also the daily trips around the countryside have been well received. Just relax now and enjoy the journey. If you are at the half-way stopping point at the same time as the other coach just make sure they don't sneak into your seats to get another week's holiday.'

These remarks caused some laughs and she jumped off the coach and waved it away with many happy, smiling passengers waving down to her.

Lucy was back there in the afternoon to welcome the other coach returning at the garage. She managed to speak to several of the passengers and she was reassured that it had been a very successful tour. She guessed that some of them might be booking for another tour later in the year.

Later on that Saturday night, in bed, Lucy reached over to Fred. 'I think we have another winner at Maxwell Motors. Come over here and let's celebrate.'

And celebrate they did!

Four

It was the third Saturday in May, and Lucy was having an early breakfast at home before going to the garage. She was dressed in the Maxwell uniform ready to do a week as tour manager for the holiday to the south coast, while Mavis had a week back in Yorkshire at the garage. The tours were proving very successful, with the bookings filling almost all the available seats. But Lucy had regretted the timing of the exchange arrangement when she'd found out that she had chosen the week when Richard was taking his eleven-plus exam and the entrance exam for the grammar school.

'You look very smart this morning,' said Fred, in an effort to calm Lucy down as he realised that she was very tense.

'I know I look okay for the job, Fred, but I should not have picked it for this week. I should have made sure that I was here to support Richard in his exams.'

'Don't worry about that, Lucy. Our Richard has his head screwed on the right way and I'm sure he's well prepared.

I'll keep my eye on him.'

'I know you will, Fred. But I am letting him down. It's a very important time for him.'

'You have no need to worry. You enjoy your trip to the south coast. Make it a sort of holiday. I know you're in charge, but from what you've been saying, these tours are so well organised now that they run like clockwork.'

'True, Mavis has done a first-class job in setting them up and running them and she deserves a week's change. And I've done my best to set up the house here so that you and Richard are well looked after. Mrs Senior will be virtually living here this week. She'll be doing all the housework; the cleaning, the washing, the shopping and the cooking, so neither you nor Richard will have any household responsibilities.'

It was at that moment that Richard came into the kitchen.

'Morning,' he said. 'You look very smart, Mum. Have you got a new job?'

'You know what I'm doing this week, Richard. But why are you up at this time?'

'I'm going out with Dad. We're coming to the garage to see you off on your trip.'

'You are not going to see me off, are you, Fred?' Lucy was quite shocked by this suggestion.

'Of course we are, Lucy. You deserve a send-off. I told the boss I would't be in until ten o'clock and he was quite happy. We have another rush job to work on over the weekend.'

'Well, don't you be working any overtime on an evening during this next week. I shall want to ring you some nights to see how you two are getting on, and to give you any news from my job.'

Lucy drove to the garage in the Maxwell van and took Richard with her. Fred followed them in the family car. Richard chatted as she drove and tried to stop her worrying about his exams. 'Don't worry about me, Mum. These exams will just be a normal day's work for our class. We've been doing past papers for weeks now and our teacher has taught us to tackle the papers the right way.'

'How's she done that Richard?'

'We've got to read each question twice, so that we really understand it. We've not to rush our workings, and if we finish early we have to go back and check our answers. She argues that many people fail exams because they don't tackle them the right way.'

'I was impressed with her when we went to the parents' evening. You just do your best, Richard.'

'I will, Mum. Don't you worry, I'll not let you down.'

Lucy had a lump in her throat after Richard's last remark. She was very proud of him.

They got to the garage at a quarter past eight and Fred and Richard looked on as Lucy got to work. She checked with the driver that everything was arranged, then she collected all her papers from the office. Bob came out into the yard, and spoke to Lucy about the organisation for the coming week. Lucy told Bob that she'd arranged to spend a ten-minute briefing sessions with Mavis when the buses met at the half-way stop.

The holiday-makers started to arrive and Lucy busied herself with the driver stowing their luggage and showing them to their seats. Both Fred and Richard had to admire the efficient way that Lucy welcomed everyone with a smile and put them at their ease. She also willingly answered any questions they asked. Bob came over and stood with Fred and Richard watching what was going on. There were fifty bookings for the tour and they all arrived before the scheduled start time. When the last one was on board, Lucy took the microphone and welcomed everyone onto the coach and introduced the driver.

'Now, before we start, I have one last job to do,' she announced. She jumped down off the bus and ran across to the group of on-lookers. She nodded to Bob, gave Richard a big hug and finally she gave Fred a hug and a kiss. She then ran back to the bus and took her seat at the front and waved to them as the bus pulled out of the yard.

'There you are, young man,' said Bob, looking at Richard. 'You have just seen an example of what a remarkable woman your mother is.' That evaluation of his mother was to stay with Richard for the rest of his life.

Lucy used the early miles of the journey to brief her passengers with more details about the hotel and the coach tours scheduled for the week. She announced that, due to popular demand by Maxwell clients, the hotel was laying on two extra nights of dancing as part of the evening entertainment programme. 'I hope you've all brought your dancing shoes,' she joked She also explained the plan was that they would meet the coach returning from the previous week's tour at the half-way stopping point, and she explained that she was exchanging roles with the regular tour manager for a week. She concluded her remarks with a note of confidence. 'While you're having a cup of tea you'll be able to speak to the passengers from last week's tour and get their reactions to their holiday. We're happy to let you do that because we're confident that these tours are providing what our customers want and at a good price.'

Amazingly, the coaches arrived within five minutes of each other. The meeting with Mavis was intensive for fifteen minutes. Mavis suggested that Lucy meet with the hotel manager to discuss the room rates for the bookings later in the year. She'd managed to obtain figures for the bar takings that indicated the hotel was making significantly higher bar income from the Maxwell guests than normal. In Mavis' view the rates charged for future room bookings could be reduced while still leaving the hotel with increased profits. Lucy was attracted to this idea, knowing that any saving in costs would flow straight through into profits.

Mavis had provided a brief for the arrangements when the coach reached the hotel, which proved very effective. There was a welcome drink for the passengers while they were registering. The hotel manager met Lucy and gave her the list of room numbers so that the luggage could be marked-up. Within twenty minutes of arriving, the coach was parked in the car park, all the luggage had left the hotel entrance and all the guests were booked in.

Lucy went to the reception desk and collected her own key and took the lift up to her room. It was an exceptionally large room, with a sea view, and again Lucy guessed that Mavis had influenced this allocation. She rang home to report that the coach journey had been very good and that she was impressed with the hotel. Fred, prompted by Richard, reported that Mrs Senior had made their favourite pudding — jam sponge and custard — at lunchtime and that they were having ham and pork pie for tea.

'I think that you're telling me, Fred Platt, that you are going to have a week of feasts while I'm away!'

'No, Lucy. I just want you to know that we are in good hands here,' he replied.

'I will ring you again on Monday night, Love.'

She rang off and had a quick bath before getting changed to join the passengers for dinner. She put on a new dress which she had bought for the trip. It was knee-length, in light-blue satin with a flared skirt and a v-neck. She'd also bought a new bra and underskirt to go with the dress. She went to the mirror and checked her appearance, noting that there was a clear view of her cleavage emphasised by the new bra. Her outfit was completed by fine denier light-grey stockings and high-heeled blue shoes. She decided that she would apply only pale-coloured lipstick and a light-coloured face powder, as she did'n't want to appear over-the-top. She did, though, want the passengers to realise that she was a senior person at Maxwell Motors.

Before dinner time, she looked at the passenger list and tried to memorise some of the names so that she knew who she was talking to. She went down early to inspect the dining room layout and was met at the door by the head waiter, who clearly knew who she was.

'Good evening, Mrs Platt. Welcome to our dining room. Can I show you how we have laid out the area for our Maxwell guests? This layout was agreed by your colleague, Mavis.'

Lucy followed him into the dining room. A section of the dining room was identified with a notice, 'Welcome to our Maxwell Clients.' She noted that her party had been allocated a range of table sizes and that the menus looked interesting, with plenty of choice. She chose a table for eight, thinking that this would give her a chance to get to know seven of her clients on this first evening. Lucy welcomed all her party at the entrance to the dining room and directed them to the Maxwell area. The meal was served efficiently and the food was better than she had expected and, she noted, was approved by her guests. After dinner, almost all the Maxwell guests went through to the concert hall, which was set up with tables but had an area by the stage for dancing. The entertainment was a lively sextet, whose female saxophonist also performed as the singer and she was a hit with the holiday-makers. They had a very good rhythm and soon many of Lucy's party were up and dancing.

Lucy, as an unaccompanied woman, expected to watch the dancing, but she was approached by one of her group — a tall man with grey hair and a moustache. He introduced himself as Captain George Grey, and requested the dance. He motioned to his wife, who was sitting at a table in her wheelchair, and explained that she was disabled with chronic arthritis, and could only walk slowly with two sticks. Lucy recognised the name, and the information about his wife, which was recorded on the passenger list, as she would need assistance at some of the visits on the tours during the week. Lucy had met Fred at a dance-hall in Leeds and, in the early days of their marriage, they'd regularly gone dancing. But that was years ago and she was out of practice, but she accepted Captain Grey's invitation, hoping for the best. George Grey was a very good dancer and skillfully guided Lucy around the floor so that her confidence grew and she started to enjoy herself. At the end of the dance, Lucy said she would like to meet his wife and she sat with them for the next two dances. She learned about their army life, which had started before the Second World War, and had been spent in various countries of the empire after the war. In the war, George had been evacuated from the Dunkirk beaches, had been with Montgomery in the Desert and had then fought in Sicily and Italy. He'd recently retired from the army, mainly to support his wife, but he had been fortunate to obtain a bursar's post at a private school near Leeds. Mrs Grey was a charming woman who was facing a future of limited mobility, in sharp contrast to her husband who appeared to be very fit and active.

'Please, have another dance or two with George, Mrs

Platt. I'm afraid my dancing days are over now. He's a good dancer you know,' she added with a smile.

'I'll do that,' replied Lucy. 'I expected to be a wallflower this week. I can't be seen to be stealing husbands from their wives.' This caused another smile from the Greys.

Lucy had several more dances with George Grey that night. She also circulated and established name contacts with at least a dozen more of her group. Her only moment of concern was in a rock and roll number which George insisted that they try. His speed and skill at spinning her round caused her dress to ride up such that she was displaying her stocking tops and even, at times, her knickers. She blushed as they walked back to George's wife. 'If there's any danger of us doing another of those dances, George, I shall have to make sure that I am wearing a longer dress, with weights around the bottom!'

'Yes, I think some of the audience got some exciting views,' he said, with a grin on his face. 'But they seemed to be enjoying it.'

Lucy was stiff in her leg joints when she woke up on Sunday morning. But she was happy that the trip had got off to such a good start. The tour on Sunday was a success but they came back to the hotel in the late afternoon through heavy rain. It also rained during the Monday tour but they spent extra time at a stately house rather than going to a beach resort as planned. She was satisfied that she had spent time now with all her passengers and knew most of their names.

She rang home early on Monday evening as she wanted to be available to meet everyone as they entered the dining room at seven o'clock. 'How are things, Fred?' she asked for starters.

'Fine, Lucy,' he replied. 'Richard has a day of exams

tomorrow, but he seems quite calm and I'll make sure he goes to bed early so that he's well rested. Everything is fine with the house. Mrs Senior has gone home early tonight to get her son to bed ready for the exams.'

'Can I have a quick word with Richard?'

Fred gave a yell up the stairs to get him down from his bedroom.

'It's your Mum on the phone and she wants a word with you.'

'Hi, Mum. How's the trip in the deep south going?'

'The tour is going fine. We've a good crowd of people on the trip. They're drinking plenty of alcohol but no one has caused any trouble up to now. There is one lovely lady who is seriously disabled. We've been able to get her around at all the events so far. The weather has not been ideal but it's a better forecast for tomorrow. I just wanted to wish you well in your exams.'

'Thanks, Mum. Tomorrow should be straightforward. The special papers for the Grammar School exam, on Friday, might be more challenging.'

'I'm sure you will cope. I'll certainly ring on Thursday night to have a word with you. Put your Dad back on.'

Lucy gave Fred more details about the tour. She explained that she had a dancing partner and emphasised that he was an army Captain with several medals. She suggested that she and Fred should go dancing again.

'Bloody hell, Lucy! How will we ever find time to fit dancing into our lives now?'

It was dancing again after the dinner, with the same band, so everyone knew what to expect. Lucy was somewhat surprised to be approached by several other men, as well as Captain Grey, to dance with her. She suspected that some of the wives might have been making mischief by daring their husbands to take her onto the dance floor. As a result she had a busy night, but she thought that without doubt Captain Grey was the best dancing partner. She'd learned from him that it was his wife's birthday on the Friday, and she'd said she would arrange with the hotel to mark the event. She met the manager and asked that a birthday cake be paraded into the hall during the entertainment session on Friday night. She would say a few words from the stage and she would get everyone to sing Happy Birthday. She wanted the staff to serve pieces of cake to everyone, including the non-Maxwell guests. The costs for this should be put on her account, she'd agreed.

The weather was much improved from Tuesday onwards, which made the trips more successful. On Wednesday and Thursday afternoons Lucy left the driver to supervise the tours. She was confident that he understood the role of manager/driver and she heard him brief the passengers on the speaker system in the coach before he drove off. She used Wednesday afternoon to talk to Mavis back in the office about events in the garage. There had been one coach breakdown but luckily Bob was available to take a spare coach out to rescue the passengers.

'You need to get a PSV licence for such eventualities,' suggested Lucy, with a laugh.

Mavis updated Lucy with the coach bookings and the latest numbers of passengers booked for tours to the south coast. Another week was now fully booked and a waiting list had been established. Mavis commented on the increase in taxi bookings. 'We're getting so many requests that we can't fit them all in. We might have to get another taxi or a mini bus. You need to think about that Lucy.'

They then discussed the arguments to put forward at the

meeting that Lucy had arranged for the Thursday afternoon with the hotel manager. 'He knows he's on to a good deal,' said Mavis. 'He will want us to use the hotel next year.' Lucy looked forward to the meeting as she was realising that these coach tours could be a growth area for the firm.

On the Thursday afternoon, Guy Lucas, the hotel manager, welcomed Lucy into his office and saw this as an opportunity to learn more about Maxwell Motors. He addressed her as Mrs Platt, but Lucy suggested that they used first names to make the discussions less formal.

'Tell me about Maxwell Motors. It's not a company that we're familiar with in these parts?'

Lucy explained the history of the company and then gave details of its growth since she had taken over her role.

'You seem to have a major role in the company, and its growth is impressive,' said Guy.

'I had a clear objective to grow the company. I've been very well supported by Bob Maxwell and, so far, all the initiatives that we've tried have been winners. And we all work very hard,' she added, with a smile.

'What are your plans for the future, as regards these tours?'

'That is one thing that I want to discuss with you, but that will be near the end of our meeting. I want to start with the current programme.'

'That seems to be working very well,' responded Guy, implying that it needn't be discussed.

'You're right,' said Lucy. 'Our original projections, when we launched the tours, was for a lower uptake of passengers. We were playing safe. When Mavis did the negotiations with you she was looking at less room bookings than we have needed.'

'Yes that's true,' replied Guy. 'And we have been glad to provide the additional rooms.'

'The other thing that has happened is that our guests have preferred to stay in the hotel at night rather than tour the town.' Guy nodded at this statement. 'We got those projections way out. Our original publicity mentioned shopping and shows. We don't do that now, we emphasise the daily coach tours and the entertainment in the hotel. I think we are tiring our guests during the day so that they are happy to spend their evenings in the hotel. I know that you've reacted to demand by providing more entertainment, but your bar receipts must be much higher than you'd expected.' Lucy looked at Guy to see if he knew where she was heading, but he wasn't showing any change in his facial reactions.

'What I can tell you is that the bookings going forward for this year will continue at the high levels. Some weeks are fully booked, so between us we have a very successful programme.' Lucy waited for Guy to comment.

'I can agree with your review, Lucy,' he replied. 'And I'm pleased to learn that the future prospects look good.'

'Well what I want to propose, before we talk about possible changes for next year, is that we should review the room rates charged to Maxwell Motors for the other four week programme that we have scheduled for later this year. I suggest that the rates could be reduced by a few percentage points to reflect the higher occupancy that we shall be providing and the increased bar takings that our thirsty Yorkshire travellers are paying.' Guy had not anticipated this move and he was a little shocked. He decided to use his superiors as a possible get out.

'The concessionary rates that we use are provided by our marketing team in head office and I would need their approval for any changes,' he said, defensively.

‘Now come on, Guy, I know that you will be submitting weekly results for the hotel to your head office. You must know now that you are doing much better than normal on the weeks that you are hosting our tour.’ Lucy adopted a challenging role. ‘Ask them if they want it to continue. Dangle the future in front of them, Guy.’

‘What do you mean by that, Lucy?’

‘Well, we will be reviewing these tours as a separate part of the business. If this part of our operations proves to be as successful as I think it will be, we might decide to double-up and have a tour in two towns each week next year. We have the coaches and we will have trained the drivers by the end of this year. This would mean that, if your hotel was selected, you would have twice the business that you have had this year. You could make a real name for yourself, Guy.’ Lucy could see his mind working on the possibilities.

‘What sort of percentage are you thinking about, Lucy?’

‘Well, I would like a five percent reduction; but I am not greedy. I could settle for four per cent and still think that I had achieved a fair deal. But I want an answer to take back to Yorkshire on Saturday morning. Don’t let them put you off by playing for time.’

‘I’ll get onto it straightaway, this afternoon.’

‘You need to remember one thing, Guy. We know our needs much better now. I could let Mavis start a round of meetings at other hotels and I think that they will be willing to cut their rates to get the level of business that we are likely to need next year. We would, though, prefer to stay with a hotel like yours, that we can rely on to give us the total service that we require.’

Lucy left the manager’s office feeling that she had done a good job. Later that night she rang home. She had spoken to Richard after his Tuesday exams and her main aim was to have a word with him about his Friday exams taking place at the Grammar School.

'How are you feeling about tomorrow, Richard?' she asked, when Fred put him on the phone.

'I think I should be alright. It'll be strange, though, taking the exams in a strange place. The Grammar School looks a big dominating set of buildings. I might get lost in them.'

'Don't worry about that. Just ignore the atmosphere and concentrate on answering the questions. You'll get used to this as you get older. I'm often faced with imposing places. I just ignore them and get on with my job.'

'How do you mean, Mum?'

'Well, I had an example today. I had a meeting with the hotel manager to discuss some business issues. We met in his smart office and he had tea and biscuits delivered. He started by calling me Mrs Platt but I suggested we just used first names which got us both down to the same level. I knew what he wanted to discuss, but I made that wait until I had raised some revisions to our current contract. I think it was a bit of a shock to him, the way I played it.'

'Did you get what you wanted?'

'I don't know yet, but I'm quite hopeful. Anyway, good luck tomorrow. I hope you get what you are after.'

'Thanks, Mum; I'll be doing my best.'

'I'm sure you will. Put your Dad back on.'

Lucy gathered from Fred that Richard had been very sensible during the week and had shown great respect to Mrs Senior. Lucy knew that her son was growing up and that he was ready for the Grammar School.

Guy Lucas got a message to the tour coach on Friday morning, at one of its stops, to ask Lucy to meet him in the afternoon.

'Is there some problem back at the garage, Lucy?' asked the driver, who looked concerned as he passed the message on.

'No, I don't think so,' she replied. 'I set the hotel manager one or two questions when we met yesterday. He might have got some answers.'

They drove back to the hotel while the coach party was having lunch at a restaurant.

The meeting with Guy was short and successful. The original contract was for twenty rooms, to be paid for by Maxwell Motors whether they were taken or not. The hotel was prepared to consider a reduction in the room rate if the number of rooms underwritten by Maxwell was increased.

'Well, that is a reasonable request,' replied Lucy. 'I can agree to that on the basis of our experience so far.'

After a friendly discussion the room rate was reduced by four per cent and the number of rooms in the contract was raised to twenty-six. Lucy considered that her trip had yielded some financial benefits for Maxwell Motors.

Lucy rang home at six o'clock, primarily to speak to Richard. He filled her in with his news. 'You were right, Mum; it was a new experience for all of us. One lad who was sitting near me was shaking before he started the first paper and I don't think he ever settled down. When we went to lunch in the school refectory he was also near me and he hardly ate anything.'

'Did the school atmosphere affect you, Richard?'

'Not really, Mum; I followed your advice. I just ignored it and concentrated on the questions. I think I might have done alright.'

'I'm sure you will have. I'll see you tomorrow when I get

back.'

She had a final word with Fred. 'I'm sure he has done his best, Fred. I'll not be back until late afternoon, so you take him out for a treat tomorrow. See what he fancies.'

At the final dinner, Lucy was gathering favourable reactions from the passengers about the tour and she slipped in the possibility that there might be a wider choice of locations next year. This was well received. The hotel was rated highly for its food and service. Lucy was pleased by the friendly relationships within her group. She detected the group had the Yorkshire characteristics of friendliness and gossiping.

After the first two dances, Lucy was approached by the head waiter who informed her that the kitchen was ready. She went onto the stage and took the microphone from the band leader.

'Ladies and gentlemen, one of the members of our party from Yorkshire has a special event to celebrate today. You will all have seen her around. She is a very special lady who is handicapped by a disabling disease. She is special because she will not give in to that disease and we have all admired how she insists on trying to walk and join the group in all its activities. It has been a delight for us to have had her with us on this tour. Susan Grey, we all want to wish you a very happy birthday, and I am not going to disclose which birthday it is! Don't stand up Susan, just raise your hand.'

The lights were dimmed and the chefs marched in with a cake illuminated with sparklers. More waiters followed with trays full of pieces of cake. The soloist with the band took the microphone and led the singing of Happy Birthday. Many of the audience stood up at the end of the singing and applauded Susan, who waved to them. Lucy took the microphone for one last word.

'As you can see, there is a lot of cake and we would like everyone here, as well as the Maxwell Group, to share in this celebration.' The waiters went around to all the guests in the hall and even to the band. Lucy went across to the Grey's table and gave Susan a big hug and kiss.

'What a surprise!' said Susan. 'How on earth did you get to know about my birthday?'

'A little bird told me,' replied Lucy, with a twinkle in her eyes.

Susan looked across at her husband.

'You naughty boy; you were supposed to be dancing, not telling tales.'

Lucy again danced with Captain Grey, later in the evening, in a slow waltz. He held her very close and whispered in her ear. 'Thank you very much for organising the surprise. It has crowned a memorable holiday for us. Of course we both know that it will not be possible to have holidays in the future. This disease can sometimes progress very rapidly.'

'Don't say that, George. We would love to have you on future Maxwell tours.' But Lucy knew it might not be possible.

On the way home, at the half-way stop, Lucy had a quick word with Mavis, who had a full coach of fifty on the next tour. She was able to tell her of the revised contract details. Back at the garage her passengers were very kind in their comments on the holiday. One or two tried to give her a tip, but she said they should give it to the driver. For him, too, it had been a financial triumph.

Bob was out with one of the coaches, so Lucy went home. The house was empty but there was a note on the table.

'Gone with Dad to watch Yorkshire play cricket at Headingley — . Richard. (Dad asked me to write this. Bet he couldn't spell Headingley!)'

Well done, Richard, you cheeky boy, thought Lucy. She decided to have a bath and then sit with her feet up until her men got home. Life was very busy, but very good for the Platt family!

Five

After her week as tour manager on the south coast, Lucy had a meeting with Bob Maxwell to review the operations. He was pleased to hear of her success at revising the contract with the hotel for the month of August. She suggested that there was only a need for Mavis to be tour manager on the first of the four-week cycle at each hotel., as during the other weeks the driver could be left to also act as manager. This would release Mavis for three weeks in each month to help with running the office and to take on an expanded taxi business. Lucy was now confident that the coach tours on the south coast would be a success. Next year's programme would be reviewed after they had the results for the three months to the end of June. It was clear, too, that the taxi business was increasing. They were also getting requests to hire a vehicle with more seats than the taxi. Lucy suggested they think about whether they should change the taxi to one that would seat six, or possibly invest in a mini-coach that would have up to fourteen seats. Bob thought for a few minutes before answering this dilemma.

'I know that we're getting more requests to hire the taxi, but who's going to drive it, Lucy? Do we need another driver?'

'I have an answer for that Bob,' she replied. 'Elsie is now old enough to have a driving licence and I propose to send her off to have driving lessons and to take the driving test. She's told me a time or two that she wishes that she could drive, so she will be glad to learn straightaway.

'I don't think we should change the existing taxi,' said Bob, after thinking for a minute or two. 'I'm attached to that taxi. It's reliable and there are plenty of miles left in the engine. So I think we should go and look at these van conversions to make mini-coaches.'

'I agree with you Bob.'

A week later, Bob and Lucy went to view what was in the vehicle market to suit their needs. They found one that was impressive, and comparable with the high standards they had set for their coaches. Having found one so easily, Bob signed the contract to buy it on the spot. It was specified to be sprayed in the Maxwell colours and was listed for delivery in the second week of August.

At the end of June, Lucy received two pieces of news; one very good, the other somewhat worrying. Firstly, she received a letter to say that Richard had gained a place at Leeds Grammar School. She was overjoyed at this news. She was also pleased that Matthew Senior, his local friend, had also gained a place, so the two boys would be able to travel together to their new school. However when she told Bob Maxwell about her good news, he said he had some news which was worrying him. His brother, Sam, had been off-colour for a few weeks. He was not eating anything much and he was refusing to see the doctor.

'He's never ailed anything in his life and he thinks he can't possibly be ill. Can you have a word with him, Lucy, and see if you can get some sense into him? He might not say it, but he has a great respect for you.'

'I'll see what I can do,' she replied, somewhat apprehensive at this request.

Sam came into the office later in the day to check his schedule for the next day or two. He sat down wearily in a chair, looking very tired. Lucy gave Elsie the nod to make herself scarce so that she could speak to Sam in private.

'You look as though you could do with a day or two off, Sam. Are you feeling under the weather?'

'I've been feeling a bit rough for a while now, actually. I can't seem to be able to shake it off.'

Lucy looked at him with some concern, but she decided not to express her concern, but to jump in at the deep end.

'Well, you need two things, Sam, that I can fix up. Firstly, you can have a rest from driving. Someone else can take on your slots for the rest of this week. Secondly we need to get you examined by a doctor. I assume you use the same one as Bob? I'll ring up now and make you an appointment.'

Sam was about to object but Lucy waved him away and she continued ringing the surgery and made an appointment for that evening.

'I don't fancy bothering the doctor, Lucy.'

'His job is to find out what's wrong with you, Sam. That is what he's there for. You'll not be bothering him.'

'Oh, I don't know,' said Sam, not happy with the arrangement.

'Well I do know, Sam. You need to see the doctor. And

you are not going on your own, because I will take you in the taxi before I go home. And if you like, I will go in with you to see the doctor. You need a woman's help at a time like this.'

'Okay, Lucy, if you say so.' Sam left the office, agreeing to see Lucy at five-thirty.

Lucy and Elsie got to work ringing those drivers designated to do Sam's duties. Lucy also saw Bob and told him that she was going to accompany Sam to the doctor's surgery. She also rang Mrs Senior and told her that she would be late home and asked her to arrange a meal for Richard and Fred. During the afternoon she got a call to ask her to pick up Mr Higson at ten-thirty at Leeds Station. It was going to be a long day. But her greatest challenge would be how to support Sam at the surgery.

When they both entered the consulting room, the doctor looked at Sam and then at Lucy, as much as to say, who are you?

'I'm Lucy Platt, Doctor, and I work at Maxwell Motors, coordinating all the operations. As you know this is Sam Maxwell who is the owner of Maxwell Motors, along with his Brother Bob. I understand that Sam has always had good health so has probably not seen you for years. He came into the office to see me today and I could see that he is not well. I understand from his brother that this had been going on for a while and is getting worse. I'm afraid that I bullied him to come and see you tonight and I'm here with him to make sure he does see you.'

'Thank you, Mrs Platt. You have done the right thing to bring Mr Maxwell here and you have also told me the answers to some of my first questions. If you could wait outside, I will continue with my examination. But don't go away. I will want a word with you about my findings when

I have completed my consultation.'

'Lucy was relieved to escape into the waiting room. It was nearly twenty minutes before Sam came out and Lucy was called back in.

'Mrs Platt, it's not possible to give you a clear diagnosis of Mr Maxwell's problems. It could be a serious illness and I need to refer him to a specialist at Leeds General Infirmary. The hospital will undertake some tests to arrive at a diagnosis. He should rest in the meantime.'

'I have arranged other drivers to take on his schedule and I think he will be accept the rest because he has no strength to do otherwise. How soon can he be seen by a specialist?'

'It's an emergency case, so it will have some priority.'

'I can assure you that his brother will insist that he goes privately if it will speed up the hospital appointment. Money is not an issue to get him made well again.'

'I understand that, and I will arrange the consultant to see him within the next day or two.'

'Thanks for taking me, Lucy,' said Sam, when they were on their way back to the garage.'The Doc hasn't told me what's wrong with me, or given me any medicine. I do feel awful, though, so I can't wait to get to bed.'

'You have to rest, Sam. The doctor is arranging for you to see a Specialist in Leeds General Infirmary in the next few days.'

Lucy dropped Sam off and took him into the house. Bob and his wife, Edith, immediately began to ask Sam what had happened.

'Have a word with Lucy. I'm going to bed; I'm buggered,' he said, as he headed off up the stairs.

Lucy filled them in on the details and told Bob what she had done to speed up the consultation.

She had some warmed-up dinner when she got home and explained to Fred her concern about the health of Sam Maxwell. She then went off to Leeds Station to pick up Mr Higson from the London train. He told Lucy that he had had one of those days in London when difficult issues had been raised at all the meetings he had attended.

'I've had a similar day at Maxwell Motors, but one new problem has arisen that is very worrying.' He asked her to elaborate, but all Lucy would say was that it was a health problem with a key member of staff.

She crawled into bed at eleven-thirty; Fred was fast asleep but Lucy was haunted by the look of Sam Maxwell as she drove him back from the doctor's surgery; it was some time before she could sleep.

Two days later Sam had an appointment at the hospital. He was accompanied by Bob and Lucy drove them in the taxi. It was nearly two hours later when Bob came out.

'They've kept him in, Lucy. The consultant wants to do some urgent tests to confirm the diagnosis. He didn't say what he thinks, but I get the impression it might be something very serious.'

'Well we need to carry on and do everything we can to support Sam,' replied Lucy. She made no other comment, but it was clear that she would have to review the operations without Sam as a driver. She decided to upgrade one of the part-time drivers to a full-time role and she realised that she would have to take on more responsibility as Bob would be distracted by Sam's illness. She also recognised that Edith, who was a quiet and reserved woman, might not be able to cope with a very sick person in the house.

It was two days later that Bob was called to see the consultant at the hospital, after he'd had all the results of the tests. Lucy drove Bob to the hospital. Lucy saw Bob approaching the taxi in the car park and knew that it was the worst possible news. There were tears streaming down his face and he was sobbing. She jumped out of the taxi and opened the door to let him in. When she got back in the driving seat she didn't start the engine, but tried to comfort Bob. He leaned over and she took him in her arms and gave him a hug. Through his tears he tried to speak.

'I can't tell you, Lucy. It's too terrible to think about.'

'Just have a minute, Bob, and try to settle down. Then you can tell me.'

Lucy didn't need to know the details, she could guess the diagnosis. But she had to get Bob calmed down before they drove back to the garage. She didn't want anyone there to see him in this state. It took about ten minutes, then he pulled himself together and sat up in his seat away from Lucy.

'I'm so sorry, Lucy,' he said.

'Don't worry, Bob; I'm here to help you,' she said calmly. 'You tell me what is going to happen and then we'll have to decide what we are going to tell everyone back at the garage.'

'It's cancer of the stomach, Lucy. There is nothing they can do to cure it.'

'Will they be keeping Sam in hospital?'

'Only for a couple of days. They'll put him on drugs to reduce any pain and then he will be sent home. He'll not be able to keep much food down, so he will slowly fade away,' Bob gasped, and choked again. 'It's so cruel, Lucy. What can we do?'

'We will all have to support him. We have to give him

anything he wants or fancies. You will have to spend some time with him Bob. We can't let him suffer alone. We may have to set up some skilled nursing care to support your wife. Did the consultant say how long this period will last?'

'I asked him that. He said it could be weeks, or several months. It depends on how much the cancer spreads to other organs of his body.'

'I'll see all the staff when they are at the garage and I will tell them the position. Some of them know that they are taking over Sam's slots in the programme and I will reduce your slots so that you can spend some time with him. But you really need to carry on as normal. If you spend all your time with Sam, it will destroy you.'

'I don't want that to happen. I'll need you to help me, Lucy, over the next few weeks or months, as well as Sam.'

'You can rely on me, Bob. You know that.'

Lucy started the taxi and drove back to the garage. On the way they agreed that the message to all the employees would be that Sam was seriously ill and would need time off work. They'd explain that he would be looked after at home; so they might see him around the garage from time to time. If they did, they should have a cheery word with him and act as normal, they suggested. Lucy thought that to be around the garage might be the best therapy to keep Sam going for a while.

Sam came home two days later. The medication was helping him and it was clear that he had not been given the full diagnosis. He came out into the garage forecourt and into the office some days and he even served petrol to one or two clients. Lucy saw him on most days and did what she could to encourage him to keep his spirits up. The doctor came to see him and arranged for a specialist nurse to visit him every day. She was a cheery Yorkshirewoman with lots of experience of dealing with seriously ill patients. Sam began to enjoy her visits and he was known to smile at some of her stories. But he was getting weaker, as everyone who knew him could see, whenever he came outside to enjoy the summer sunshine.

Lucy had the quarterly meeting with Mike Best. It was their first chance to assess the south coast tours. She had been careful to put all the possible costs into that business. The outcome was that the tours were quite profitable and Mike worked out that the profit per day of those coaches was marginally higher than the daily profit per day for the coaches doing one-off hires. However the coaches on daily hire only averaged just over four days per week. Lucy explained to Mike that in the future the costs of the tours should reduce, with the lower room rates and less time spent by Mavis as the tour manager. It seemed sensible to increase the south coast tours, even if this reduced the availability of coaches for single-trip hire. They had a meeting with Bob and he was impressed by the total financial results for the quarter. Lucy explained that she intended to let Mavis start work on a programme for next year, having two tours each week to different south coast towns. It would require an increase in the number of drivers dedicated to these tours who could accept the additional responsibilities. It was agreed that Mavis would spend time in September negotiating contracts with suitable hotels and that there would thus be a bigger range of holidays to satisfy the requirements of their clients.

Sam continued to take an interest in the garage operations. When Sam could not walk with his two sticks, his specialist nurse provided a wheelchair. Lucy made a special place in the office for him to park, and when he was in the office she talked to him and explained what was happening. She was happy to have him there when she was negotiating with someone placing an order for the hire of coaches. Elsie had passed her test and was able to do some taxi journeys. Lucy stressed to Elsie she must always look smart and professional when driving the taxi. Elsie cut an impressive figure when she wore her driving outfit and her peaked cap. Sam smiled whenever he saw her leaving the office to do a taxi fare.

Sam was also interested in the mini-coach that was being introduced to cater for bigger numbers.

'Do you fancy a ride in it, Sam?' Lucy asked him one day. Sam nodded and gave her a smile.

'Let me get some strength to lift you in.'

It was not that Sam was heavy, but they had to lift him without hurting him at all. They used the blanket under him in his chair as a sling and placed him in the front seat next to Lucy and strapped him in. Elsie was left in charge of the office.

'Where do you want to go, Sam?'

'The airport,' he answered.

'We can do that, Sam. Leeds Bradford airport isn't too far away.'

Lucy knew a parking spot alongside the runway and they stayed there for two hours and watched two planes take off and two land. Sam had a smile on his face. It had been a real treat for him.

The drivers who saw Sam on a regular basis were amazed that he looked so thin and grey.

'How long will this go on, Lucy? He's only a skeleton. It's cruel to keep him going.'

'The will to live is a very strong motivating force. We have kept him involved in what is going on in the business. I think this has helped him. It is far better than him being in his bedroom watching the clock ticking away. It has also helped Bob who was dreading this period at the end of Sam's life.'

'Bully for you, Lucy. You're doing a great job.'

But Lucy too was wondering how long it would last. There were two developments that interested her. Sam and Bob were visited by the accountant, who spent an afternoon with them. And on another afternoon, the solicitor for Maxwell Motors spent two hours with Bob and Sam. She dared not ask Bob what was happening, but Bob had noticed Lucy's concern and a week later he saw her on her own in the office.

'I think we have it all organised for when Sam goes now.'

That was still no answer about the future, as far as Lucy was concerned.

Six

August was a strange month for Lucy. She'd planned to take a week's holiday but she deferred that as she wanted to be around to support Bob and help with Sam. Wilkins engineering workshop was closed for a holiday week, so Lucy persuaded Fred to go to his sister's in Scarborough, with Richard, for the week. Before they went she had spent some time with Richard getting all his clothes, sports gear and other equipment ready for him starting at Leeds Grammar School. She was immensely proud when she saw him fully dressed-up for school, although Richard was embarrassed by Lucy's efforts.

On Richard's first day at his new school, Lucy had delayed her start at the garage. She was very proud as he prepared to set off with his friend, Matthew.

'Stop making a fuss, Mum. It's only another day at school.'

'Oh no, Richard, it isn't just another day at school; this

school will give you a passage to the very best education in the country. It will be tough, but I am sure you are up for it.'

It was at the beginning of September that Lucy had an idea which she discussed with Mavis. She wondered whether they should offer a free trip for two staff from a newspaper, on the last week in September, to get possible publicity for Maxwell holiday tours. Mavis agreed and so Lucy visited the Yorkshire Post and agreed that two reporters, a husband and wife, would travel incognito on the last tour of the season. She got a commitment that she would be shown the draft of any article to check for inaccuracies. A photograph was taken of the group alongside the coach before they set off. Mavis travelled on the coach as tour manager but she planned to spend part of the week discussing the contracts with the hotels for the next year's tour programme. There would be six hotels used, in six different towns, and Mavis was aiming to agree rates that were marginally lower than those of the first year, based on the good business prospect of Maxwell tours for the hotels.

September was a busy month for the garage. The Blackpool Illuminations became the major attraction for coach trips, particularly at weekends and it was a challenge to prepare the vehicles on Saturday nights for use again on Sunday mornings. Lucy had to take on additional part-time staff to cover this work.

On most days in September, Sam was wheeled out onto the garage forecourt so that he could feel a part of what was happening. He began to look weaker and he had a ghost like appearance, with his shrunken face and protruding teeth. Lucy realised that he was failing fast and would soon be confined to his bed.

The nurse visited him every morning and evening to wash him and make him comfortable. Each afternoon Lucy sat at the side of his bed and held his hand. Sometimes he opened his eyes and she thought he recognised her; at other times he was in that hazy limbo state between life and death. He passed away on Thursday 8 October, 1964.

Everybody thought it was a blessing, but there was sadness among the drivers and staff who had known Sam for many years. It was agreed that everyone would wear a black armband on duty until the day of the funeral. Elsie was very upset and wept openly in the office. Mavis and Lucy comforted her but decided to let her take on most of the taxi bookings to take her mind off her sadness.

The funeral service was on Thursday 15 October, in St Margaret's Anglican Church in Horsforth, and he was to be buried in the cemetery alongside his father. Every member of staff was informed of the arrangements but it was a busy day for coach bookings, so only a limited number could attend. Lucy persuaded Fred to take a couple of hours off work so that he could attend the service but he could not stay for the reception in the Church Hall.

Mavis remained in the office in charge of operations. Lucy went to the church early, with Elsie. When the other Maxwell staff saw Lucy they came and sat around her so that there was a block of Sam's colleagues all together. Some of them seemed uncomfortable at being in Church anyway, so were pleased to sit among their work colleagues. When all the mourners had arrived Lucy looked around and she estimated that there was over a hundred people in the congregation.

Four Maxwell drivers carried the coffin into the church; it had just one wreath on it, in the company colours. It was followed by Bob and Edith and their daughter and her husband. Sam must have had a lonely life, with no friends to follow him to his grave.

The service followed the normal format. Lucy had wondered whether Bob would give the eulogy for Sam but it was done very effectively by the vicar who had been well briefed. He concentrated on the fact that the two brothers were only in their twenties when they took over the business. He emphasised that Sam had been the quiet one who was totally reliable and an excellent driver. In thirty-five years of driving he had maintained an accident-free record. The vicar concluded by referring to the last months of Sam's life and the interest he had retained in the company despite his failing health. The congregation was encouraged to go to the church hall for refreshments after the burial.

The burial at the grave gave rise to some tears. Bob had to be comforted by his daughter and her husband. Some of the drivers could not hold back their tears as they cast soil on to the coffin. Most of the Maxwell staff followed the invitation and drifted to the church hall for the refreshments.

Lucy circulated around the church hall and was surprised that several people from around the district wanted to meet her. Presumably they had heard about her role in the business. As people started to drift away, Lucy went to have a word with Bob.

'I think that Sam would have been proud of the support he has received from our staff and from the community today, Bob.'

'Yes, I did wonder if the congregation would be very small. Our Sam was a bit of a loner.'

After the funeral, the operations of Maxwell Motors settled down to their normal busy schedule. Lucy had a pleasant surprise when she was sent a draft of the article proposed by the Yorkshire Post staff who had been on the final south coast tour. The piece was to be a major feature in the paper. It was quite positive, without being sugary, Lucy thought. There was a well-reasoned evaluation of the cost of the holidays and a conclusion that they represented good value for money. There was a gap in the story as there was no reference to the plans for next year. Mavis drafted a paragraph listing the six holiday towns in the programme and the fact that there would be two coaches each week from April to September. They sent back the duly amended draft.

'When it's published, it will be a bit of good publicity for us,' said Mavis. 'It will hopefully attract clients from a much bigger area.'

One or two of the drivers asked Lucy what was going to happen to the business following Sam's death. She could only tell them what Bob had said — that it was all organised — but in response she received some worried looks. Sam's will was to be made public at the solicitors. Bob wanted Lucy to be there and any of the staff who were available could attend. There was a sense of relief that the issues were to be resolved. Bob and his family went in the taxi and Lucy drove the mini-coach with eight members of staff. They crowded into the conference room at the solicitor's office and there was a sprinkling of press also there.

The solicitor presented the will in two parts. Firstly, Sam had accumulated approaching fifty thousand pounds in his private banking accounts. He had disposed of one thousand pounds by making small gifts to some charities and local organisations. He made a specific gift of two thousand pounds to the specialist nurse who had looked after him through his final months. This left a figure of forty-seven thousand pounds, which he left to Bob's daughter and her husband.

The solicitor then turned to Sam's shares in Maxwell Motors. He explained that Sam wished to preserve the financial resources of the company. There was a total of three hundred thousand shares in the company, divided equally between Sam and Bob. The current value of each share was just over two pounds, which gave the company a value in excess of £600,000. The solicitor announced that Sam's shares would be allocated as follows: one hundred thousand shares would be transferred to Bob Maxwell and fifty thousand shares would be transferred to Mrs Lucy Platt. There was a ripple of surprise at this last statement, and Lucy felt a flush come to her face.

That completed the proceedings.

In the mini-coach travelling back to the garage, one staff member reflected the general feeling about the will. 'I couldn't have wished for anything better. Now that you have got shares in the company, Lucy, we know that Maxwell Motors is in good hands. I was fearful that Bob's daughter might come back into the company. If anybody came with an offer above half a million pounds she would have bitten their hand off and agreed to sell up and take the money.'

Back at the garage, Bob took Lucy into the house and explained the way the company shareholding affairs were operated. Each year a dividend was paid — usually about five percent — and any further surplus profits were added to the value of the share price.

'So you should be able to look forward to a dividend of about £2,500 each year, as well as your salary, which will be increased due to your added responsibilities.'

‘I don’t know what to say, Bob,’ said Lucy. ‘I’m deeply honoured to be a shareholder in the company. You know that I will be working flat out to keep the company growing.’

‘Lucy, you are the best thing that has happened to this company. I think back to that evening when you came with Diane Rhodes, the employment agency manageress, to see me. You kept asking questions and telling me you knew of better ways to run the business. I couldn’t believe what I was hearing. What a find you were!’

Lucy went home bursting to tell Fred what had happened with Sam’s will. But there was other, more important, information waiting for her.

‘Just you listen to Richard’s news, Lucy,’ said Fred, as soon as Lucy entered the house.

‘I’ve been promoted into the under-thirteens rugby squad,’ said Richard. ‘I’ll have to do extra training two afternoons each week. Then, if I get picked, I’ll be playing at other schools around Yorkshire. I tackled one of the big lads in the squad and flattened him. The games master was impressed. He thinks I might have a future in the rugby teams.’

‘That is wonderful news, Richard. Rugby’s a bit of a rough sport; are you happy getting knocked about a bit?’

‘You have to get fit so that you don’t feel the bumps. Do Maxwell’s provide the transport for the rugby teams?’

‘Yes, we do.So you won’t mind if your mother is driving you to an away fixture will you?’

‘I suppose it will be classy if that happens,’ concluded Richard.

It was later in the evening when Lucy revealed her own news. Richard had completed his homework and had come back into the living room from his bedroom.

‘I got a very big surprise today when I went into Leeds to

hear Sam Maxwell's will read.'

'Was it good news?' asked Fred.

'It was fantastic for me,' she replied, 'and reassuring for all the Maxwell staff. Sam left his shares to Bob and myself. So the future finances of the company are secure. I have been allocated fifty thousand shares, which are worth just over £100,000.'

She went on to explain how the company shares worked.

'So we are rich now,' concluded Richard.

'You could say so,' replied Lucy. 'Effectively I own one-sixth of Maxwell Motors.'

'That's cool,' said Richard.

Fred thought it was amazing too, and saw this as a milestone marking the fact that his wife was now a businesswoman in her own right.

Seven

'Lucy, I want you to come to a meeting tomorrow at our solicitor's office in Leeds,' said Bob.

'Is something wrong?'

'Not really, Lucy. It seems that we are doing very well and the figures are getting better so fast that some people can't understand them. Our accountants will also be there.'

At the solicitor's office, the accountant set the scene. 'The problem is that we have to submit the annual accounts to Companies House in London. We are happy with the figures but we need evidence of the decisions that you are taking to achieve these results. You do not appear to have regular meetings to agree the actions you are taking to make changes to the company.'

'There are discussions between Bob and myself on all manner of issues, and from those discussions we agree what we will do,' explained Lucy, with a touch of defensiveness in her voice.

'You are clearly making the right decisions, because the results for the company get better and better. However we need to have a record of when the decisions are made.'

It was a long meeting, and out of it came a structure for managing Maxwell Motors. It was agreed that there should be five directors of the company: Bob would be Chairman and Lucy would be a director; there would be a company secretary provided by the solicitor's office; Mike Best would be the finance director and there would be one other non-executive director appointed when a suitable person was identified. The board would meet every six months, but the main meeting would be to agree the annual accounts and the dividends to be paid.

It was also agreed that there would be a management committee meeting every other month to monitor the financial results and agree policy decisions. This committee would consist of Bob, Lucy and one member of staff to be elected by the staff. Mavis would act as secretary of these meetings and would provide the minutes. Mike Best would be a member as the finance man.

'It is a simple organisation,' said the accountant. 'You must remember that Maxwell Motors is a very successful company turning over a large amount of money each year. There are bound to be people watching your results.'

Lucy turned her attention to finding the right person to be non-executive director for the board and discussed a few suggestions with Bob. They decided that she should approach the Deputy Headmaster of Leeds Grammar School, Dr Poxon, who she knew and had dealt with on transport matters. Lucy approached him and he was delighted to accept the appointment, although he professed to know nothing about the operations of bus and coach transport.

Lucy had many discussions with members of staff regarding the staff member of the management committee. She emphasised that the person would know what was happening in the company and would be able to brief other members of staff. Two drivers showed an interest and Lucy persuaded them both to put their names forward for a ballot. It was a close-run vote but Lucy was happy that the winner was George Clay. In her opinion he would be a sensible member of the management committee and he was respected by his colleagues.

Lucy was so busy at work that she had little chance to support Richard when he was playing for the under-thirteens rugby team. Fred, however, was a regular supporter and reported to Lucy the result of each match and how Richard had played. He saw that Richard and one of his friends in the team had formed a close playing relationship. They were often together in the loose play around the scrums. They slipped the ball to each other and then passed it out to the backs. The rugby master in charge of the team noted their play and praised their initiatives. 'Well done, Platt, keep up the pressure.'

The team was winning most of its matches, but one hard-fought match with Bradford Grammar School ended in a 13-13 draw. Richard had played flat-out and was exhausted after the match. 'I need to get fitter, Dad, to manage games like that,' he panted as they met on the touchline.

'You'll get fitter as you gain more experience,' advised Fred.

There was a fixture at Hull Grammar School when the first and second teams, and the under-thirteens team were playing. Lucy realised that it would need one of the largest coaches to get every player and the staff on board. She decided to drive the coach, leaving Mavis in charge of the office. On the journey, Richard kept his eye on his mother, so much so that one of his team put the question. 'Is that your mother driving the coach, Platt?'

'As a matter of fact, it is,' replied Richard, proudly.

'She's a cool driver. Is that her job?'

'No, her job is to coordinate all the operations of Maxwell Motors. She is a director of the company. She just drives occasionally, for a change.'

'Wow, some mother!'

The matches were played on three adjacent pitches. There was a crowd of supporters from the Hull school supporting their first team, but they had little to shout about as the Leeds team were the stronger side and they converted their attacks into points. It was a similar story with the second team.

Lucy was watching the under-thirteens team. Within the Hull side there were several players who seemed oversized. Whether they were just very big for their age or whether they were really from a more senior side, no-one knew, but they put up a strong showing against the Leeds team and at half-time Hull had a lead of 9–6. The Leeds master in charge gave his team a pep talk at half-time and instructed them to concentrate on the three big members of the Hull team and give them some hard tackles. He allocated the task to Richard and his mate.

The second half began with several Leeds staff watching the match alongside Lucy. Five minutes after the start, one of the Hull big boys got the ball and started to advance into the Leeds half. He was tackled by Richard and his mate — one took his legs and the other hit him with full force in the chest and flattened him. 'Well tackled, boys,' shouted the Leeds master. That big boy turned into a passenger for the rest of the match. A similar approach sorted out a second of the big boys in the Hull side. From then on the Leeds team began to dominate the play and the scores were soon equal at 9–9. The Leeds team had to press for the winner. Lucy was jumping in the air when Richard's mate slipped him a pass about fifteen yards from the Hull line. Richard advanced and pushed off one tackle, side stepped another tackle and touched down for a try.

'Well played, Platt, an excellent try,' shouted Dr Poxon. He complimented Lucy on her son's skill and commitment.

It had been a good afternoon for Leeds Grammar School as all their teams had won, thought Lucy as she drove them all safely home. And it had been a bonus for her to see her own son playing an excellent game of rugby.

The minutes of the first meeting of the management committee at the beginning of November were brief. The financial results to the end of October, which showed a fourteen percent increase compared with the previous year, were noted. On the south coast tours for the next year, it was agreed to run two tours each Saturday to different towns. If they were well supported then an additional monthly tour starting on Sundays would be introduced. It was noted that two new coaches were to be purchased, bringing the total fleet compliment to eight coaches, one double-decker and a single-decker service bus, one colliery coach, the mini-coach and the taxi. The number of part-time drivers was increased so there would be no problems in manning the fleet. On a proposal to install new fuel pumps and tanks, Lucy was required to have meetings with two suppliers to obtain quotes for a project. It was agreed to recruit a teenager who could be trained to do odd jobs around the forecourt as well as serving petrol and diesel.

It was decided to have a meeting of the Maxwell Motors board at the end of November. The main meeting would be in March, to agree the annual accounts for the previous year. However this year it was thought important for the board to get to know each other and review the business to the end of October, which would provide a guide towards the annual results.

The board was briefed on the operational and financial performance of the company. Lucy sought the approval of the board to place the order with Shell for the new fuel facilities. She discussed the Christmas bonus payment at the new rate of £150 for drivers and £75 for other staff and both requests were approved.

When the meeting was finished, the board members were entertained to a sandwich lunch in the reception area of the office.

The next afternoon Lucy and Mavis interviewed Brian Hunt, the young lad suggested by George Clay to be brought onto the staff. He was a smart lad, but obviously very nervous. Mavis confirmed that he could read instructions and understand figures. He was obviously quite fit and when Lucy suggested to him different jobs that he might be asked to do, he responded very positively. 'Mrs, you can give me any job that you like, and I'll stick at it until I master it. Once I've got it sorted you won't have to worry about me on that job ever again.'

'That's good enough for me, Brian,' said Lucy.

Brian started work at the beginning of December. He looked very smart in his Maxwell uniform and he was indeed keen to tackle any job offered to him. Lucy noted that George Clay often had a quiet word or two with Brian when he was in the garage forecourt. After a few weeks Mavis said. 'I think we have another winner here, Lucy.' On some nights Brian was still in the yard when he really should have been at home.

The Christmas period was exceptionally busy. The service buses were both in use as there was a lot of shopping in Leeds and the late-night service was packed with passengers. There were also numerous coach bookings for trips to pantomimes, Christmas concerts and works outings.

'There seems to be more money about this year,' commented Mavis. 'And people are keen to get out and enjoy the festive season. It's good that we are getting our share of their extra spending.'

When the staff got their Christmas pay packets and saw their special bonus there was an excited reaction going through the company. There was a parade to the office to show their appreciation.

There was also excitement in the Platt household when Richard broke up for the Christmas holidays and brought home his first report from the Grammar School. While there were boys in his form who were brainier and more experienced at the studies they were undertaking, Richard was praised for his commitment and hard work. It was suggested that he could expect to do better academically if he continued to work hard. And he got a very positive comment from the sports master for his efforts on the rugby field.

Lucy, Fred and Richard sat down on Christmas Eve and looked back over the year. It had been a great year for Fred and Wilkins, where it was very busy and the contracts for the mines were getting bigger and there were more of them. 'We're going to have to take on a few extra craftsmen in the New Year,' concluded Fred.

'It's been a sad year for us, losing Sam,' said Lucy, 'but we are better organised now and the future looks good.

Everyone seems keen to see the company growing and the Christmas bonus has been very well received. But I think the star performer of the family this last year has been Richard Platt. You have worked hard and got yourself into a school that will stretch you and give you opportunities better than any of us in the family have ever dreamed about.'

'How can you say that, Mum?' replied Richard, who was slightly embarrassed. 'What about what you are doing at Maxwell Motors and what Dad is doing at Wilkins? You are both achieving great results.'

'Yes, Richard, we are both doing well. But your education will open doors for you into fields that none of us dream about now.' Richard didn't understand what Lucy was getting at, and neither Lucy nor Fred could define exactly what she meant. But Lucy was sure that education for Richard would be far more important than any of them realised.

Eight

The contractors moved on to site in the second week of January 1965 to install the new fuel tanks and delivery pumps. They marked-off quite an area of the forecourt which they would need to operate in to do the work. Lucy realised that there would be congestion and she'd had discussions with the drivers to ensure that the coaches and buses were parked in the confines of the garage as much as possible until the work was completed. The first task was to dig out a significant hole into which the three large fuel tanks would be placed. The size of the hole amazed all the staff and there were questions and comments.

'Are we planning to store enough fuel for the next world war?' asked one driver.

'The capacity of the storage tanks will mean that we will have fewer deliveries and we get fuel at a discount,' explained Lucy. 'Also, I didn't want the forecourt affected by fuel deliveries more that is absolutely necessary.'

'I can see the sense of that.'

Lucy expected that Brian Hunt would earn his keep by looking after the increased fuel sales to the public and she was also satisfied that the new system would lead to lower fuel costs for the buses and coaches, which should lead to increased profits.

The new tanks were installed and the whole system tested and calibrated so that it could go into operation on 1 March. The old pumps and tanks were removed and the forecourt tarmac was replaced by the third week of March. It was impressive and attracted local car owners. Lucy was determined to keep her fuel prices competitive. A small, secure office had been built as part of the scheme and Brian Hunt enjoyed the new responsibilities he was given and became very popular with the locals as he cheerfully served their fuels.

'You have a responsible job now, Brian,' said Mavis, when she had finished his training. He marvelled when he saw the amount of cash collected at the end of the day.

Before the March board meeting, the directors inspected the new fuel facilities and one of the newly delivered coaches. They were duly impressed. They also noted the increased fuel sales to the public and the overall estimated two percent annual reduction of fuel costs for the company. Mike Best reported that the valuation of the company had increased to £655,000 and the board approved his proposal for an annual dividend of six percent. All the different business units were performing well and forward bookings for coach trips and tours were very good. There were favourable comments by the board members about the company results, including those of Dr Poxon who was full of praise for the service his school was receiving from Maxwell Motors.

It was the day after the board meeting when the accident happened. Three coaches were taking a Club outing to Skegness. On the outskirts of Doncaster the third coach was passed at speed by a motorcyclist who then swerved in front of the coach. He lost control of his machine and was thrown off to the side of the road and severely injured. The motorcycle, despite emergency braking by the driver, passed under the coach with a grinding crunch. All the passengers were shocked but there was some relief when they realised the motorcyclist was not with his machine. The emergency services were on the scene quickly, although the medical team took some time to get the motorcyclist into the ambulance as he was suffering with head injuries. The coach driver spoke to the garage and suggested another coach should be dispatched to the incident as quickly as possible. His view was that it might take some time to extricate the motorcycle from under the coach.

Lucy took the call and fortunately there was another spare driver on site. She explained to him the problem and told him to take one of the new coaches to the site. She took the mini-coach and arrived on the scene first. She immediately spoke to the coach driver who described what had happened. Lucy then went onto the coach and tried to calm the passengers. She explained that a brand new coach would be on site within minutes so that they could all transfer and continue with their trip. One or two seemed apprehensive, so she said that she had the mini-coach available and she would take back anyone who didn't want to continue. In the end, only two women decided to go back home, despite pleadings from their children. Lucy left the original coach driver to salvage his coach and the spare driver set off for Skegness. Lucy delivered the two families back to their homes. She thought to herself that the women were making something out of the incident, but she was relieved the next day to learn that the passengers in the spare coach had enjoyed their day out and were full of praise for the way Maxwell Motors had reacted to the emergency. There was even a short piece in the local paper about the accident and the way a new coach had been provided to ensure that the day trip could be completed.

'That is the sort of incident that I dread,' confessed Lucy to Mavis and Elsie. 'But I think we handled it well. Maxwell Motors got positive reactions from the passengers and the press; you can't do better that that.'

Lucy drove another rugby trip outing, to Wakefield Grammar School, again with the three teams involved in fixtures. It was a disappointing day for the Leeds teams as the Wakefield teams were strong and well-trained. Wakefield first team won 23–8 and their second team won 17–5. The under-thirteens' team match ended in a draw at 12–12 but there was an incident near the end of the match when one of the Leeds players was kicked on the head in a loose scrum and was effectively knocked out. He had to leave the field and was given a cold sponge by the Leeds master in charge but he was not allowed to go back onto the field. Lucy was a little worried about the injured player as she waited back at the coach while the teams had tea in the refectory.

When the teams started to drift back to the coach Lucy was surprised to see the Deputy Head of Leeds School, Dr Poxon, approaching, accompanied by a Wakefield master. Lucy moved away from the coach to meet them.

'This is my opposite number at Queen Elizabeth Grammar School. This is Mrs Lucy Platt, who is Operations Coordinator and Office Manager for Maxwell Motors. I have been telling my colleague what an excellent service we get and I have also added some of my additional knowledge about the company from my new involvement with you.'

Lucy shook hands with the Wakefield master and immediately went into sales mode. She handed him her card and invited him to visit the garage site where she could discuss the services that they might be able to offer the school.

'I recommend that you accept the invitation to visit the site,' said Dr Poxon. 'I'm sure you will be impressed with the company and you might also be surprised at the commercial terms on offer.'

Lucy went back to her driving role. She had a quick glance at the boy who was injured. He looked a bit pale but the master told Lucy that he was sure that he would be alright. It had not been a good day for rugby but there might be more business available for Maxwell Motors if Wakefield Grammar School could be persuaded to become a customer. She was beginning to think that her choice of a non-executive board member for the company had been a good one.

A few days later, Lucy was on the forecourt when one of her taxi clients called in to see her.

'Good afternoon, Mr Higson,' she said, as she shook his hand. 'I don't think we have seen you here before.'

'No, I'm having a day or two off and I decided to fill the car up with fuel while I was here. This young fellow of yours says that this is a new system that you have installed recently. He also says that you are selling a lot of fuel to other clients.'

'That is true. We use a lot of fuel for the business but we decided to offer fuel services to the community. Our Brian is proud of his set up and he is a good salesman,' Lucy added with a smile. Brian touched his cap to acknowledge the compliment.

'I might be interested in doing some business with you,' said Mr Higson.

Lucy took him into the office reception area and offered him a cup of coffee. Mr Higson looked around and saw the literature for the company and brochures about the coach tours. When they'd drunk their coffee Lucy suggested that they look at one of the coaches parked on the forecourt. She explained all aspects of the business and the way it was monitored.

'It is a much bigger set up than I'd imagined,' he concluded.

They then discussed the possibility of the Higson motor vehicles obtaining fuel from Maxwell Motors. They had one large lorry, two small lorries, two vans and two company cars. Lucy explained how the monthly account worked and the cards that were issued to be used by anyone purchasing fuel chargeable to the account.

'This site is a little further from the factory than the garage we currently use, but that will be more than offset by the discount you're offering,' concluded Mr Higson.

It was agreed that he would send his Head of Finance to see Lucy to draw up an agreement for Higson's to have a monthly account for their fuel.

'Well done, Brian,' Lucy said to him next time he came into the office. 'I think you have attracted another major user for our fuels.'

It was certainly a growth area for the Maxwell business.

The management committee minutes listed the following items: A survey had identified that passengers on the south coast tours were coming from a much wider area of Yorkshire than in the previous year; due to increased demand one tour would be introduced to the south coast each month leaving on a Sunday morning; the six Sunday tours would be to a different town each month; increase in fuel sales had made it necessary to staff the operation to nine o'clock each evening as local people, and some company clients, liked to fill up during the evening; a contract had been sent to Wakefield Grammar School for their school transport; as well as transport for inter-school sports, it included transport for field trips and holiday tours.

Richard's second school report was carefully studied by Lucy and Fred. Their conclusion was that it was better than his first report, and they were lavish in their praise to him. Richard's aim for the summer term was to get selected for the under-fourteens cricket team. Fred suggested that he join a local sports club to get some coaching for his cricket ambitions.

The next day Bob Maxwell asked Lucy to come into the house for a chat with him. He was in the lounge, with papers spread across the table.

'How would you fancy flitting, Lucy?' he asked.

'Never given it a thought, Bob,' she replied, shocked at the question.

'Well you might get a chance,' he replied. 'Me and Edith have been looking at where we should live in the future. This place is too big for us and she fancies a new bungalow. There is the piece of land beyond this house which is big enough for a bungalow with a nice garden. We've had an architect do a design for us and he has had a word with the planners who don't seem to have any objections to the idea.'

He showed Lucy the plans of the bungalow and she said how impressed she was with the design.

'It will move you away from the garage, Bob, which

dominates your house. I am surprised that you haven't done it earlier. You deserve a bit of peace after all these years.'

'That's true, Lucy. But we didn't want to make any changes while Sam was around. I suppose his death opened up the opportunity. Anyway we'll be pushing ahead with the plans and it should be built in about eight months' time. Money is not a problem and I might as well invest some of my dividends in a new house. My idea is that you could move into our house, at a peppercorn rent. You are virtually living on the job now so you might as well have the benefit of the bigger house and not have to spend time travelling across Leeds.'

'That is a wonderful offer Bob and I don't know what to say. I'll discuss the plan with Fred and Richard when I get home tonight.'

'How is that lad of yours getting on at school now?'

'He's doing very well, Bob. He's working hard and playing well in the rugby team. We're very proud of him.'

'Well he has a good example from both his parents.'

Lucy rang home and spoke to Richard. He reported that Mrs senior had left the dinner in the oven on low heat. She had made the mixture for Yorkshire puddings and Richard had been instructed to turn the oven up to full heat and allow about fifteen minutes to cook the puddings. He was to take the stew out of the oven for that time. His Dad was not home from work yet.

'That all seems to be well organised, Richard. I shall be home in the next half hour, so I would like us all to have dinner together. I have some interesting news to talk about.'

'See you, Mum. Dad has just landed,' added Richard, as he was replacing the phone.

During the meal there was general chatter, but Lucy decided to wait until they had finished eating to spring her news.

'Bob called me into the house this afternoon and gave me some surprising news. He's decided to build a bungalow on the land beyond his house, which runs alongside the road.' She paused to see how Fred and Richard were reacting to this news. They seemed laid back. 'It is all organised, the plans are very impressive and the bungalow will have a separate entrance off the road. Planning permission should not be a problem and Bob seems to think that the building work will start within the next month.'

'What's going to happen to the house that they live in now?' asked Fred.

'That's also part of the plan. Bob wants us to move in and he will offer it to us at a peppercorn rent. It will save me a lot of time travelling across Leeds every day. I've thought about it since he spoke to me and I can't think of any snags. It's a very good offer,' she finished.

'How will I get to school from there?' asked Richard.

'That is easy. You will travel on the Maxwell service buses from Horsforth with other pupils from the Grammar School. The route goes within two streets of the school. You will get a pass like other students who use our buses.'

'It will be a bit further for me to travel to work, but I might be able to work out a short-cut to miss some of the heavy traffic,' mused Fred. 'At least we shall see more of you, even if you will be dashing out all the time to sort out problems.'

'I'll not be travelling to school with Matthew any more,' said Richard. 'What about Mrs Senior? Will you still be able to use her to help in the house?'

'I'm sure I shall be able to sort something out. Bob's house is much bigger than this one, so I suppose I will want more help,' answered Lucy.

The questions had been more than Lucy expected and the enthusiasm much less than she had hoped for. But the more she thought about it, the more she was sure that the house move would offer a new phase to all their lives.

Nine

It was 1 April 1965, and Lucy was driving the mini-coach with seven drivers, Mavis and herself to a workingmen's club on the outskirts of Horsforth. Lucy wanted it to be a day of intensive planning for the south coast tours, so she had hired a room for the day.

When they were all established in the Club committee room, which was like an elaborate boardroom, Lucy opened the meeting.

'It might be April Fool's Day, but this is a day for wise men and women, not for fools. You are the men who have the responsibility for delivering these tours to many hundreds of customers over the next six months, and we want them all to be satisfied folk who come back for more. As you are aware it is a much bigger programme than last year, giving our customers more choice.'

'The next thing that will be different is that you will not have a tour manager on hand all the time. Mavis is going down for the first two weeks, with the company van, and she will float around the four tours that will be taking place in those two weeks. She will be assessing the new arrangement of driver/managers. You will always be able to contact the office and talk to myself or Mavis if you have any serious issues. You have been chosen for these tours because we are confident that you have had the training and gained the experience so that you can operate as driver/managers. We're paying you an enhanced wage but we also know you will get some generous tips at the end of each tour. So you are the elite drivers of Maxwell Motors. The drivers of the service buses might think they should be the elite drivers, slogging away every day in all the traffic into and out of Leeds and I have lots of sympathy for them and they do earn a lot of cash income for the company. But you must have additional skills at handling people when problems arise.'

'Today is vital for you, and, at the end of the day, you must feel fully briefed by Mavis on any issues that might arise and how to deal with them. I hope to see you at lunchtime when I will bring some sandwiches and refreshments — if I remember to come!'

There were a few laughs at the last remark as Mavis took Lucy's place at the front of the group.

'Thank you, Lucy, for setting the scene so well.'

Lucy walked back into the office just as Elsie was completing the details of a booking for a south coast tour. As she put the phone down Elsie said, commented. 'That's a good one. It's for six people and for the Sunday tour in May. That is the second booking this morning for south coast tours.'

The phone rang and Elsie picked it up with the usual answer. 'Maxwell Motors, Elsie speaking. How can I help you?' When she had heard the reply she mouthed to Lucy, 'another one.'

It was like that all morning; people phoning to make bookings or calling into the office to pay and collect their tickets.

Brian Hunt came into the office and reported that the fuel was selling well and Lucy needed to ring Shell for a fill up.

It was nearly midday when Lucy left to call at the local bakers for sandwiches and cakes for the drivers' meeting. She'd arranged a tab at the Club bar for drinks over lunchtime. There was some relief by the drivers when Lucy entered with a tray of food as they'd been hard at it since she left, with just one five-minute comfort break.

Lucy ate her lunch with Mavis and heard that they would need another two hours to complete all there was to discuss. She showed Lucy the hand-outs she was issuing, which contained details of the names of hotel staff and the names of people who would likely be on duty at the places to be visited on the daily tours.

'They will have a lot to read up, but these lists should be a very good guide for them.'

Lucy then went and sat with the drivers to get their reaction to the morning. They were full of praise for what Mavis had prepared. One driver summed up his feeling, 'I had no idea, Lucy, the detail that Mavis has accumulated in organising these tours. No wonder they are a success. Nothing has been left to chance. I feel a lot happier now, with all this information as a back up.'

'She will explain briefly the contracts with the hotels for your information, so that you know what Maxwell has agreed to do, and what the hotels have agreed to do. If there are any contractual problems then we will deal with them from the office. Your worry is to see that the hotels provide the service they have promised.'

It was nearly four o'clock when Lucy got a call from Mavis to say that they had finished. Lucy drove into the Club car park and saw the drivers sitting together on a wall enjoying the fresh air. They all carried a folder containing the papers Mavis had issued.

'Has it been a good day?' Lucy asked in general, as they took their seats in the mini-coach.

One driver offered to speak for them all. 'I think you can take a positive answer to that question, Lucy. But it's been a slog. It would have been a bloody sight easier to drive a coach all the way to the south coast than go through what we've done today.'

'Ah,well; that shows that the briefing session was necessary,' said Lucy, with a smile.

Saturday 3 April 1966 was an exciting day on the forecourt of Maxwell Motors. The two new coaches were parked ready for boarding: Coach A was going to Brighton and coach B was going to Torquay. Maxwell Motors had offered a collection and return service, at £1 per head, to pick up passengers and their luggage from outlying districts. They picked up thirty-eight passengers and the schedule aimed that everyone was at the garage at least fifteen minutes before departure.

'This is the risky part of our morning,' said Mavis, who was in the office. 'We only need to have one couple stay in bed and both coaches could be affected.' The passengers clearly thought they needed them to be on time because, much to Mavis's relief, both the mini-coach and the other collecting coach arrived and parked in the forecourt before a quarter-to-nine.

Mavis welcomed the fifty passengers for Brighton and introduced the driver on coach A and Lucy welcomed forty-eight passengers for Torquay and introduced the coach B driver. They waved the coaches off and that was the start of the holiday tours for 1966 season.

Mavis and Lucy went into the office and decided to have a coffee before Mavis chased after the coaches in the van. While they were waiting for the kettle to boil, the phone rang and a most agitated young woman asked, 'Have the coaches left?' The answer was yes.

'Oh dear,' she gasped. 'What shall we do? I've just been into the bedroom and my Dad has left his wallet at the side of the bed. It has all his money in it.'

'You're very lucky. We can fix that,' said Mavis. 'I am going to be following the coaches to the south coast in a few minutes. Can you get the wallet to the garage here?'

'Yes, I'll get my brother to run me down on his motorbike. I'll be there in a few minutes. My Dad will have a fit when he realises what's happened.'

'We'll try to get a message to him when the coaches make their stop on the way down.'

'Sometimes it's just luck that allows you to provide a very special service to your passengers,' said Lucy to Mavis when the call had ended. 'It's fortunate on this occasion that we decided to have a cup of coffee.'

On 18 April the first Sunday coach tour left the forecourt carrying thirty-six passengers. Mavis wasn't worried by the fact that the coach wasn't full. It was the first Sunday booking, she told herself, and a bit of a trial, and there were already over forty booked for the May tour. Mavis was sure that the rest of the Sunday tours would operate at a profit. They waved the tour off and then two other coaches left on a day trip to Cleethorpes.

Back in the office Lucy took the opportunity to discuss with Mavis her two weeks covering the first four tours for the year on the south coast.

'What's your feeling about the tours operating with driver/managers? Will it work?'

'To be honest, Lucy I'm not sure. There were incidents on all the four tours that needed my attention.'

'Do we need to rethink our policy on driver/managers?'

'I've been thinking that there may be a better option. If we had a courier established in that region, covering all the south coast tours, he or she could spend a part of each tour assisting the drivers and resolving any issues. Some drivers might have no problems but they would all benefit by having support immediately available.'

'We'll have to discuss this with Bob.'

'Just give me a bit of time to think it through, Lucy. We'll get a better picture this week when there are three tours operating. I've told all the drivers that I will be ringing them most nights to check how they are getting on. There's a good atmosphere among the workforce and nothing breeds success like success. I suppose the Christmas bonus did encourage them to be positive.'

'The few extra drivers we've appointed all came with recommendations from our staff,' added Lucy. 'I also think George Clay is doing a very good job since he came onto the management committee. He often talks to his driver colleagues when he's at the garage, but I have also seen him speaking to the part-time staff who wash and clean the coaches. He's got a real feel for the whole of our business now.'

It was 27 April when Mavis sat down with Lucy and Bob to discuss the south coast tours. The previous week there had been three tours, two returning on Saturday and one on Sunday. Mavis brought with her several pages of notes she had made during the previous week from her telephone discussions with the driver/managers.

'I met all the coaches when they returned and generally the passengers seemed to have had a good holiday. However, the drivers reported many small issues that had arisen which they had to sort out. Some of the drivers seemed to delay resolving the problems immediately, probably hoping they would go away. They clearly missed having a courier to deal with the passengers while they did the driving.' She paused to get reactions to what she had said.

'Are you saying that the driver/manager role will not work?' asked Bob.

'I think we always knew that it would be a challenging role. We spent a lot of time giving the detailed briefings to help them do their job, but my conclusion, Bob, is that I think we have gone a bit too far. Think about an incident where one of the passengers is taken seriously ill; the driver/manager will definitely need help in that situation. He could not possibly cope on his own.'

'What do you suggest, Mavis?' asked Lucy.

'I think we have to go back to the system we used when I covered on the first two weeks of this year. It's possible for one courier to spend some days each week with both the tours and sort out any issues with the hotels on a daily visit. I spoke to the other driver each night so I was fully in the picture of what was happening on both tours. My proposal is that we should appoint a courier for the south of England. It needs to be someone who lives in that part of the country, who drives a car so that she, or he, can commute between the two tours. Driving the coaches from the garage to the destination and back we can leave to the driver/managers.'

'I think we should act on this straight away, Bob, if you agree,' said Lucy. 'It will still be a big saving compared with having a courier on each coach all the time.'

'I agree,' said Bob. 'What about the Sunday tours? I don't think one courier can cover three tours.'

'I think you're right, Bob,' said Mavis. 'I think we shall have to bite the bullet and have a separate courier on the Sunday tours. It's only five more trips this year.'

We'll have to get an advert out straightaway, Mavis,' said Lucy.

'I might have a quicker answer; I knew a couple of couriers who lived in that part of the world when I was in Birmingham. I'll check them out first.'

At the beginning of May the builders moved on to site to build Bob's bungalow. They started by making a site access from the road and then they had a machine digging out the foundations. Bob took Lucy round to see the work.

'They've got started quicker than I expected,' said Bob. 'The architect recommended this team of builders for the job. If they stick to their programme we might be moving in during September. What we've got to do Lucy, is have a look at the old house and decide what needs doing to smarten it up. Edith's full of ideas of what needs doing. What are Fred and Richard saying about the move?'

'It was a bit of a shock when I first raised it with them, to be honest, but they are alright now. Richard will travel to school on the Maxwell service buses and Fred has worked out a neat route to Wilkins. I'm looking forward to living on the job and not having to travel across Leeds each day.'

'You'll have to make sure you spend plenty of your time

in the house and not more time in the office. There is so much going on now.'

'Yes, I'll watch how I organise myself, Bob. You must excuse me. I have to go to the bank now. There is so much cash coming in that I really should bank it every day, but I am still sticking to the pattern of going every other day.'

Lucy emptied the safe and collected the cheques and money from the office. She also sent Mavis for the cash from the fuel pumps. Lucy placed it all in a special, lockable bag and put it on the seat beside her in the van. She drove with the van doors locked and parked at the side of the bank. She was always relieved to get through the bank doors. The other customers were not pleased to see her, however, as she dominated one service point for fifteen minutes or more while the cashier verified all the figures and gave Lucy a receipt for the deposit. When they flitted, Lucy decided that she would transfer the Platt family banking accounts to that branch.

Mavis, Bob and Lucy were sitting in the office looking across to an imposing middle-aged woman, Marion Stead. Mavis had worked quickly and established contact with an experienced courier from her Birmingham days. Marion was free from any courier work at the present time and had shown an interest in the role that Mavis had described. She had come up the day before and stayed overnight with Mavis. She was fully briefed on Maxwell Motors and in the discussions she had asked questions that showed she was experienced and familiar with the problems that might need solving on any coach tour. She lived near Godalming, so she was centrally placed to get to the south coast holiday towns. Her husband was a civil servant who commuted into London each day and they had no children. She ticked all the boxes, Lucy and Mavis thought, and she was available to start the following Saturday. Marion left later that afternoon with a contract to the end of September in her pocket, for a good salary and a car allowance. She also had a detailed specification from Mavis setting out her duties.

'I don't think we'll have any problems with the south coast tours from now on,' said Mavis, when Marion had left the office. 'She's a classy courier who will be appreciated by the passengers and the drivers. I couldn't believe our luck when she was available. We will need to brief the drivers about Marion and her role. They will still be driver/managers but they will have support and back up. I don't think they will complain.'

At the Grammar School Richard made it into the under-fourteens cricket team, though he was not a star player. There was one lad who was a fine opening batsman who dominated the crease once he'd got his eye in and there was another tall young player who was a really fast bowler who tended to terrify some opponents. Richard had his place as an all-rounder. He batted at number seven and was used as a change bowler with his medium-paced accurate swing bowls. In several matches he never had a bat as the team won with several wickets to spare. He did have a success in one match when the Leeds team fast bowler was off-form and was hit around the field by a particular opposing batsman. Richard was brought on and his accurate bowling stopped the run flow and he took three wickets, including that of the batsman who was scoring all the runs. This seemed to seal his place in the team.

On one particular Saturday, when the Leeds first eleven and the under-fourteens had fixtures at Ripon Grammar School, Lucy decided to drive the coach and she persuaded Fred to go along too. They took a picnic to have between the innings. It was a beautiful afternoon and Fred had put two folding chairs and a small table into the storage space of the coach.

'What a peaceful scene,' commented Lucy, as they watched the match. 'I do think life is being very good to us, Fred, don't you? I suppose that I'm really working this afternoon, but here we are having a great time together as a family. What more could we ask for?'

'We could hope that Richard gets some wickets,' replied Fred. 'He's coming on to bowl now.'

Richard did get a couple of wickets, but the important part of the afternoon for Lucy was when Dr Poxon walked around the boundary to where Lucy and Fred were sitting. He was accompanied by a younger man.

'Now this is how to enjoy an English cricket match in real luxury,' he said when he reached them. 'I want to introduce you to our new Headmaster who will be taking over the school in September. This is Dr Adams.'

Lucy and Fred jumped up. Dr Adams shook hands and gave them a big smile.

'So, this is the famous lady, Lucy Platt, who drives coaches but manages a company that is expanding very successfully, I am reliably informed.' There was a distraction at that point when Richard clean-bowled one of the Ripon batsmen.

'They also have a son who is developing into an all-round sportsman,' interjected Dr Poxon. 'I would like to bring Dr Adams up to inspect your facilities when he gets settled in, Lucy. I think he will be very impressed by your organisation and how you run the business.'

'We would be very pleased to welcome you and show you what we do and how we plan it,' replied Lucy.

That summer afternoon would always be remembered by

the Platts. Everything was perfect: the sun shone, Leeds Grammar School won both matches, Richard got two wickets with his bowling and he was at the crease with fifteen runs not-out when Leeds passed the Ripon score.

The return journey from Ripon to Leeds was easy, with no traffic problems. Back at the garage, Mavis reported that the two coaches had returned safely from the south coast tours before four o'clock and that the passengers were full of praise for Maxwell Motors for an excellent and memorable holiday tour.

'Everything seems to be in order, Mavis,' observed Lucy. 'I'll leave you in charge and have the rest of the evening at home with my men.'

'You do that, Lucy. I seem to think that you have only had late evenings during the last week or two.'

As they drove out past the new bungalow being built for Bob Maxwell, Fred commented on the progress as the shell of the bungalow was nearing completion. 'The builders are doing really well,' said Lucy. 'I'm sure that Bob will be moving in by the end of September. He wants to talk to us about what improvements we want to the old house. He seems determined to refurbish the house to a very high standard for us.'

'Mum, surely you deserve the house to a high standard as a pay-off for all that you are doing for Maxwell Motors,' suggested Richard, from the back seat.

'I accept that living there will make it easier for me to do my job,' replied Lucy. 'I also accept that my job is getting bigger, as the company expands, and that I am now carrying significant responsibility for the company. But what Bob is proposing for the house will cost quite a lot of money.'

'I shouldn't worry about the cost, Lucy,' said Fred. 'Bob Maxwell will be worth a good many thousands. He's only his daughter to leave his money to, and she got a good helping from her Uncle Sam.'

'Well, I'll be arranging for us to go over and look at the house with Bob in the next week or two. Then both of you will have a chance to air your views when we have seen the house.'

Their tour of the house took place two weeks later. Lucy was on edge about the visit and the modifications to be agreed, but she need not have worried, because help came from an unlikely source. Edith welcomed them and gave them a cup of tea and cake as they sat in the sitting room.

'I have been having a good think about this place, Lucy,' she said. 'This is the chance to convert it into a really nice house with the latest fittings. When we moved in Bob's father was still alive and he never wanted to change anything. And Sam was not much better — he didn't want any fuss to interfere with the normal set up.'

'I would appreciate your views,' said Lucy. 'You know the house and what its potential is.'

'My wife will be a great help to you, Lucy,' said Bob. 'She has a clear view of how to improve things.' Bob was encouraging Edith to speak her mind.

'The first thing to do is to install central heating,' she continued. 'It's not a cold house when we have the fires lit downstairs, but upstairs in the winter it can get a bit nippy. I suppose you will want one of the bedrooms as a study, Richard?' Richard was surprised to be brought into the conversation so soon.

'Well, yes, it would be good to have a bedroom as a study,' he replied.

'So you have got to put your hand up for central heating, Richard,' said Edith.

They then went on a tour. In each room Mrs Maxwell gave her views and Lucy just nodded in agreement. She had even made a list for each room.

When they'd completed the tour and agreed the changes, there was an impressive list:

a. Gas-fired central heating throughout the house. The boiler to be sited next to the utility room and an additional small boiler installed there which would provide hot water throughout the house.

b. A complete new kitchen with a gas-fired Aga cooker.

c. A new fireplace in the lounge/sitting room.

d. Two of the six bedrooms to be converted; one to a study for Richard and one to make a second bathroom with a shower.

e. The existing bathroom to be modified to have a shower as well as a bath with all new fittings.

f. The whole house to be redecorated with modern wallpaper and brighter paint colours.

g. The existing downstairs toilet to have new fittings.

h. The utility room to have a new washing machine.

Lucy looked expectantly at Fred and Richard for comments, but they just nodded in agreement.

'That's been useful, Lucy,' said Bob. 'We now know where we're going.'

'It will effectively be a new house when all that is done,' said Lucy.

'That is what we're aiming for,' said Bob.

As they were driving back home Lucy summed up her thoughts. 'That was much easier than I'd expected, and Edith was most helpful.'

'I think that she's been looking to make those changes for

years,' said Fred. 'She knew what was required to make it into a luxury house.'

'Don't worry about the cost, Mum,' said Richard. 'I was watching Bob all the time we were going round. He wants to spend that money as a gift for you. He knows what you are doing for Maxwell Motors.'

'We have an observant son, Fred, who is becoming an expert on human behaviour, ' said Lucy. 'He'll be studying his mother and father next, so we'll have to watch our Ps and Qs. Actually, I think that you're absolutely right, Richard.'

The compiled notes of the management committee meeting in May were in Mavis's style. The financial figures for the first three months of the year to the end of March showed that both the turnover and the profits were up on the previous year; the south coast tours had most coaches fully booked, and the Sunday tours for the remainder of the season would have very few spare seats; the appointment of Marion Stead and her role as courier of south coast tours was noted; a contract had been signed to provide all the transport services for Wakefield Grammar School; and Bob was authorised to arrange the purchase of another double-decker service bus and Lucy to arrange a short-term loan from the bank, if necessary.

Lucy spoke to Bob after the meeting about the matter of the purchase of another double-decker bus. In the meeting Bob had explained that if there was a major breakdown of the existing double-decker it could only be covered by a single-decker, resulting in the loss of a lot of passengers. He considered that it would be prudent to purchase a new double-decker which would take four months. When it was put into service the existing double-decker would be given a major overhaul and then used as the back-up at peak times. Using two double-deckers at peak times could be expected to increase the number of passengers.

'Bob, I want to apologise to you that I'd failed to consider the risks to our service buses if any major breakdown occurred to the double-decker,' said Lucy. 'I'm glad that you raised it at the management meeting and I'm sure that your plan will remove the risk and possibly lead to an increase in our passenger numbers. I'm afraid I've let you down.'

'Don't worry, Lucy; you can't be expected to spot every issue in the company. I am still around to lend a hand.'

Ten

The smooth operation of the management committee meeting changed in July when there was disagreement over one item on the agenda. It had suggested an additional tour programme to be arranged by Mavis.

George Clay was the first to voice his caution at the suggestion.

'This company is working flat-out now. By the time we get to the end of September and finish with the south coast tours there will be some tired drivers and staff around. I know everything has been a success so far, but don't you think that we need a pause; a time to reflect about the future?'

'That is a welcome comment, George,' said Bob. 'We've been taking on additional commitments every few weeks and a pause might be a good idea. What do you think, Lucy?'

'I accept the points raised by George, but in my opinion

we must always be looking for new initiatives. What Mavis is suggesting is that we offer some alternative mini-holiday breaks to other locations. These could just be in the Autumn and early Spring. The fifteen hundred passengers on our south coast tours this year are potential customers for a short break with us.'

Mavis took up the theme. 'We've had requests for other tours from some of our clients. There are lots of towns in locations that would be of interest to our clients. It's just a case of assessing them and then picking the best for a trial.'

The discussion continued with the pros and cons of the suggestion being stated. Having listened to the arguments, Bob moved matters forward. 'I can tell that you have thought about this, Mavis, and there appears to be no shortage of tours that could be offered. What do you feel then?' he asked, looking across at George Clay.

'I think we should let Mavis investigate her idea. I have no doubt she'll apply the same detailed planning to any of these trips that she always does.'

'I can back that approach,' said Lucy. 'We can let Mavis put her findings to the next management committee meeting.'

The committee agreed, and also approved the proposal that Lucy should seek another person to take over the office as a full-time role.

Lucy went to see her friend Diane Rhodes in the employment agency and asked her to find a mature and experienced person for a new role. She explained that she needed a person who would be an anchor and offer continuity in the office. Diane agreed to send two people for interview. Lucy and Mavis were to do the interviews one evening when the office would be quiet.

The first person interviewed was Pearl Featherstone, a smart young woman in her mid-twenties who lived at home with her mother and was not married. Pearl explained that she was very proficient at office organisation and asked lots of questions about the systems in use at Maxwell Motors. Lucy explained the Maxwell organisation and how it operated. At the end of the interview Pearl said that she would be pleased to work at such a well-organised and expanding company. Her current post was as private secretary to a senior official in the railway industry. Mavis was not sure she would adapt to the multiple roles of the Maxwell team and suggested to Lucy that there were some jobs that would take Pearl out of her comfort zone.

The second person was an older woman in her mid-forties, Margaret Mason. She explained that she had been married for ten years but her husband had been killed in a road accident. She had been a widow for three years and had gone back to work because she needed an income. There were no children involved, so she would be flexible. She also had the advantage of living in Horsforth, a five-minute walk from the garage. Lucy liked Margaret's appearance and thought she would be very good at dealing with the clients. She also had a voice that would be impressive on the telephone as her diction was clear and her accent was Queen's English with just the slightest inflexion of Yorkshire vowels.

Lucy and Mavis decided to offer Margaret the post but agreed to keep Pearl in mind for the future. Lucy cleared the appointment with Bob and made sure that the salary offered to Margaret was higher than her current salary.

Margaret started work two weeks after the interview. She appeared on her first morning before Mavis and Elsie were on site. She quickly settled into the office and was given a briefing on all the systems used by Mavis and Elsie. It was immediately clear to all the team that Margaret would be good on the telephone and excellent at handling people. With Margaret settled in, Mavis went on tour in Scotland and the northeast of England to begin her survey of possible short tours. Elsie continued to do office work and drive the mini-coach.

Later that week, Bob went to Plaxtons in Scarborough to collect the new double-decker. It was an impressive sight when it parked up in the garage forecourt. They decided to put it into service the following Monday morning and, as planned, send the old double-decker away for a complete overhaul so that it was ready to be used at busy periods.

In mid-July Lucy and Fred went to Leeds Grammar School for their first parents' evening. Richard had faced a series of exams on all the subjects he was taking. The results in the exams would determine which form he was in for his second year. Richard's comments on the exams had been generalisations such as 'not bad', 'I might be alright', 'most of the questions were straightforward', or 'I finished in good time and was able to check my answers'. None of the students in the first year had been given their exam results, nor were they told which form they would be in for their second year.

At the parents' evening Lucy was dressed in a smart, new, dark-blue woollen suit. Fred was in his best suit and he felt over-dressed and uncomfortable. They followed the list that Richard had given them and queued up to speak to each of his teachers, which were all men except for the Latin mistress. At each meeting point Lucy detected that she was being scrutinised by the teacher who was intrigued to meet Mrs Lucy Platt. All the teachers expressed their view that Richard had worked hard and had improved his position in the form as the school year had progressed. The sports master said that his commitment to the rugby and cricket teams had been very good and he forecast that Richard would have a role in the sports teams throughout his time at the school. No one indicated which form he would be in for the second year.

When they had seen all the teachers, Lucy dragged Fred along and joined the short queue for Dr Poxon, the deputy Headmaster. When they got to his desk Dr Poxon stood up and shook their hands.

'Mr and Mrs Platt, how nice to see you; how have the discussions been with the teachers?'

'They've been very good and left us proud and satisfied with Richard's performance,' replied Lucy. 'But no teacher has given us his exam results in any subject and no-one has told us which form he will be in next year. Is there a reason for this?'

'We want these discussions to cover the general performance of each student throughout the year,' replied Dr Poxon. 'We don't want the focus to be on marks in exams or about which form the student will be in during the next year.' He paused for a moment, searching for the right words. 'But I can tell you that, a bit like Maxwell Motors, Richard has had a fine year and the future looks good.'

'Thank you very much,' said Lucy, with a broad smile. She had her answer. 'I look forward to seeing you at the September board meeting.'

'Yes, I plan to be there. I've arranged to come back from my holidays a couple of days early for the meeting. I suppose that we will get some confidential information at that meeting, a bit like my confidential remarks about Richard.' Lucy nodded to indicate that she understood what this remark implied.

'We are expert at keeping confidential information confidential,' she replied.

Going home in the car Lucy and Fred agreed to give Richard due praise for his performance during the school year but not to give him any indication about the form he would be in during the next school year.

At the end of term, Richard's school report contained his exam results in each subject, which in total were better than Lucy had expected. There was also a separate short note from the Deputy Headmaster indicating that his form for the next year would be 2A, the top stream for the second year.

'Wow,' said Richard. 'That'll be a real challenge for me. There are some bright lads at school. I'll have difficulty keeping up with them.'

'Richard, if you continue to work hard in your new form I'm sure you'll be able to hold your own. We don't expect you to be top of the form but we think that you should be able to be in the top half. Think positive, Richard. You can do well. And you have your sports to give you some relief from the studying.'

'I wonder what form Matthew will be in next year?'

Two days later, when he learned that Matthew would be form 2B for the next year, Richard assured him that they would remain friends, even if they were in different forms.

Lucy was determined that the family should have a summer holiday away from Leeds. Fred's firm was closed for the third week in August, so they decided to take a holiday then. Lucy suggested that Matthew could come with them, if he would like, as a companion for Richard.

Lucy was back at the garage in the late evening to talk to the team cleaning the vehicles for the next day. With the heavy bookings in August, the nightly cleaning job was a huge task. The night foreman, Joe North, who operated the pressure sprayer and filled all the vehicles with fuel for the next day, was grateful for the two part-timers Lucy had recruited to help. Lucy gathered them round her and spoke of the challenge that they faced.

'I want you to know that I recognise what you are achieving each night. Maxwell coaches and buses leave this forecourt each morning sparkling clean and our passengers appreciate it and do comment to us about your standards. I also know that on some nights you have to undertake unpleasant cleaning jobs. The company has never been busier and so I cannot see your job getting easier. As you know, we have paid you four hours each night for your wages but I have decided to raise your wages to five hours each night as I know that on some nights you cannot possibly complete everything in the four hours. It does not mean that you have to stay the full five hours, and Joe will agree that you can leave when he is satisfied that the job is done. This new pay arrangement will stay in place until we see a big reduction in the cleaning work.'

It was well received by the team and Lucy noticed that they nodded to each other and had a smile on their faces. The company was doing very well financially, and she wanted some of the money to flow down to the people who were not on show, but who worked very hard to maintain the company standards.

It became clear to Fred and Richard that Lucy was adopting a new approach to their holiday in that they were going to have a no-expenses-spared break. She booked two superior rooms in a hotel on the sea front at Scarborough, on a full-board basis. They were to travel by train and Lucy had arranged transport to the station in the mini-coach driven by Elsie. Mavis was to be in charge in Lucy's absence, supported by Elsie and Margaret, and Bob would be around the forecourt to keep things moving. She explained her approach to Fred. 'I have given my life in total to Maxwell Motors since I joined them. My thoughts have always been about the company and how it was doing; so even when I had a few days off, I was always ringing up and checking how things were going. Well, this holiday will be different. I have told Mavis and Bob that I will not be ringing them and I do not want them to ring me unless it is a major tragedy, like the garage burning down. So you will have my full attention, Fred, and I want you to forget about your job. We're going to enjoy ourselves and have a week to remember.'

The journey by train was very relaxing and Lucy had refreshments in her bag to sustain them and she encouraged Richard and Matthew to buy some reading material in the kiosk on Leeds station. From the station in Scarborough they had a taxi take them to the hotel. When they were allocated their rooms it was clear that they had two large rooms, each with a sea view. Their room certainly impressed the boys. 'I think Mum has taken a different view of this holiday compared with our normal carry-on,' said Richard. 'We might as well relax and enjoy ourselves.'

The boys certainly did enjoy themselves. They were given a choice each day on how they wanted to spend their time. They swam in the sea and in the swimming pool and made friends with some young girls who were swimming there. They went into the amusement arcades with pockets full of money to play games and to try to win more money. They were unsuccessful with that objective, but the most memorable time in the amusement arcade was having several goes on the dodgem cars when Richard and Matthew combined to chase and crash into Fred. Lucy was watching and had a good laugh as Fred used all his driving skills to avoid the reckless attacks from two sides. They had early evening meals in the hotel so that they could go to shows on the pier and at the theatre. On two occasions the boys went to the cinema in the afternoon while Fred and Lucy walked in the park. On most nights, after dinner, the boys went to their room and watched television. Three times Lucy and Fred went to the largest hotel in Scarborough where there was dancing to a seven-piece band. Fred enjoyed these evenings but he was surprised at the aches in his leg muscles after the first night. Lucy, reinvigorated about dancing after the south coast tour, insisted that they should do most of the dances including the occasional rock and roll. The weather throughout the week was fine and warm, so they all gained a tan and a healthy appearance.

Fred remembered the nights more than anything else. Lucy had bought two new nightdresses which left little to the imagination and she offered her body to Fred on most nights in ways that were new to their love-making. Fred wondered where she'd found out about the techniques to spice up their love life, but he wasn't complaining. Near the end of the week, after one of their passionate sessions, as they lay hot and sweaty in each others arms, Fred decided he had to make a comment. 'Lucy Platt, you are an amazing woman and a darling wife. When I married you I never thought it could become as good as this.'

'Well Fred Platt, you are the reason that I have become as I am,' she, whispered, her head buried on Fred's chest. 'You've trusted me and encouraged me to do my job at Maxwell Motors so that I've grown in confidence and experience. We're very lucky, Fred. Compared with most folks we are now well-off financially, and it could get better. We must enjoy our life now, like we have done this week.'

Elsie picked them up from the station and was pleased to hear that they'd had a truly memorable holiday and were refreshed and ready for new challenges.

The management committee meeting was held in the last week of August and covered routine items at the start. The main item on the agenda was to receive the report from Mavis on her investigations into possible mini-holidays in the north of England. She tabled details of four options: one to Edinburgh, which would be four nights, one to the Lake District, centred in Ambleside, for four nights, one to Northumberland, staying at a hotel in Alnwick, for three nights, and one to County Durham, staying at a hotel in Durham City, for three nights. In each case she gave details of the hotels and their rates, which were lower than the south coast hotels. Mavis explained that there was no way that these short tours could cover all the places of interest that she had identified, so this would mean that the visits programmes could be varied. There was a long discussion until it was generally agreed that this might be a viable option to extend the tours season. It was decided to offer just one weekly tour to Edinburgh during October and November, leaving on Friday morning and staying four nights, returning on Tuesday afternoon. Lucy agreed to circulate this proposal to all the clients who had taken south coast tours. Mavis was instructed to produce attractive leaflets giving more details and Lucy insisted that the leaflets made it clear that, if these holidays had public support, Maxwells would be offering tours to other places in the Spring of next year.

'I can support this plan,' said Bob. 'We will be dipping our toe in the water, to test the temperature. If the mini-tours don't work we shall not lose much money. If they do work we'll have to think carefully about how many of our coaches we can commit to this programme next year.'

'I agree with you, Bob,' said Lucy. 'Our programme of south coast tours for next year could be a repeat of this year. That's a winning formula, so there's no need to change it.'

Mavis suggested a different approach. 'I think we should introduce at least one new town or area each year for the south coast tours, to keep the interest of our regular clients.'

There was then a discussion on coach deployment, which Bob brought that to a close by suggesting that they should review the vehicle fleet next Spring.

Lucy asked to have a chat with Bob before the board meeting in September and they met in his sitting room.

'Well, Lucy, what do you want to discuss now?'

'Firstly, I think you will have to report to the board that you will be moving into the bungalow and that I shall be moving into your house, but I have another reason for discussing this with you. I want to take a room of the house on the ground floor and turn it into an additional office. The current office and area to meet clients is doing its job well; but it's getting very crowded at times. When I want a confidential talk with anyone it's difficult to find a quiet corner. When I move into your old house I want this to change.'

'What have you in mind?'

'I want to form an office using the front room of the house by the roadside, but make an entrance to it with a door opening off the forecourt, to make it quite separate from the house. But the modification needs to done along with the other changes to the house.'

‘That’s a good solution, Lucy. We can arrange it as part of the building programme.’

‘Yes, but it needs to be financed by Maxwell Motors, not by you personally, Bob.’

‘Oh, I don’t think we need worry about that.’

‘Yes, Bob, the company is doing very well, so it must pay for the work. If my ideas are right, I will use the office to do my job better and that should earn the company even more profits.’

‘Assuming that it is another of your good ideas, Lucy, it will certainly benefit the business,’ concluded Bob, with a smile.

The September board meeting started with excellent reports on the operations and the financial results. It was a complete catalogue of improvements on the previous year converted into increased profits. Mavis described the plans for mini-tours to the north of England, starting with one location — Edinburgh — with a weekly tour in October and November, to test the market. ‘What if the tours are very well received?’ asked Dr Poxon. ‘I must say that I am attracted to them and might like to join one tour with my wife.’

Lucy looked at Bob and he gave her a look that suggested a cautious reply. ‘Well, we could have a problem if they are a great success. We have had a look at next year and we could have a shortage of coaches. There is a lot more work to do to evaluate our options.’

Bob decided to halt any further discussion on this subject. ‘When we have the board meeting in March next year, we’ll be able to explain how well the short tours were supported and what solution we have chosen to provide the coach capacity we need. I would now like to explain the changes to the accommodation here.'

Bob explained that he would be moving into the bungalow at the end of September and then the house was to be modernised and brought up to standard for Lucy and her family. He tabled a plan to show how a room in the house would be made into an office which would be accessed through a door from the forecourt. There were one or two questions and then Lucy added to the discussion. 'I hope, Mr Chairman, that the next meeting of the board will be in that office, where we can meet and eat in some appropriate level of luxury.'

Lucy's remark terminated the meeting.

Eleven

Bob moved out into his new bungalow in the last week in September, 1965. Lucy had had a look around the bungalow and was most impressed with the quality of the building works and the fitments.

'I've let the contract for the modifications of your house to the same firm and the work will be supervised by the architect who designed the bungalow,' said Bob. 'And I've agreed that they can move in and start as soon as we move out. I want to see you in that house before Christmas.'

'That will be wonderful, Bob, if it's possible.'

Two days after Bob moved out, the building firm appeared on site to start work on the modifications of his old house. Lucy made it clear to the foreman that she expected the same high standards that they'd achieved on Bob's bungalow, with minimum disruption to operations at Maxwell Motors.

Richard started the new school year in form 2A. He looked around his class and realised that he knew less than a third of the students. Some of them looked like swots and took their studies very seriously. He determined to try his best at all the subjects. He was particularly impressed by the young maths teacher, who used his skills to make mathematical problems easy to understand. He would approach each new topic from more than one angle to give his class the chance to grasp the concepts. Unlike some of his fellow students, Richard had no difficulty solving the questions in the maths homework.

Richard also gained a boost when he was appointed vice-captain of the under-fourteen's rugby team. It was significant, he thought, that only three members of form 2A were in the rugby team. The intensity of the homework was a challenge and on many nights he had to spend over two hours to complete his studies, but Fred and Lucy gave him their support and encouragement.

'It will be better for you, Richard, when we move into the new house and you have a room of your own as a study,' said Lucy.

Fred watched Richard on the rugby field whenever he could. He reported back to Lucy that Richard's weight and strength had increased since the previous year. He was marshalling the scrums and line-outs as vice-captain and the team was playing very well. They won all four of their first matches.

The last tour to the south coast returned at the end of September. Lucy spoke to the drivers and it was clear that the tours had been a financial bonanza for them personally. If the passengers were tipping well it was a sign that they had enjoyed the tours, but Lucy was glad to learn that many of them intended to take another tour next year. Over the last few weeks in September, when the publicity was out about the mini-tours, the option to take a short tour to Edinburgh in October or November attracted positive interest. Daily, the number of bookings increased, and when they exceeded thirty-five for the first tour, Mavis was confident that Maxwell Motors would not lose money on the trips.

On Friday 8 October the first mini-tour left the forecourt for Edinburgh with forty-three passengers on board. Lucy waved the coach off and she was confident that Mavis, as courier for the tour, would ensure that the passengers had an exciting and stimulating short break.

Lucy returned to the office to work with Mike Best on the financial results for the third quarter of the year. They discussed the separate accounts for the south coast tours and the service buses. The service buses came out on top but they had benefited from the two double-deckers being used. Lucy thoughts moved to the future.

'Looking forward to next year's tour programme, we'll need to buy new coaches and we could do with a larger taxi. Bob will not be happy borrowing from the bank to make those purchases, so I am investigating another option. It might be possible to have an agreement with another local coach company to loan each others' coaches whenever there are large bookings which exceed individual resources.'

Mike's immediate reaction was that such an arrangement would require very careful accounting. 'If anything comes of this idea, you'll probably get the job of sorting out the financial arrangements!' said Lucy, with a smile.

Lucy saw that Richard had a fixture at Ampleforth College, near York, and decided to drive the coach transporting the three Leeds Grammar teams. Richard told her that it would be a tough game, as Ampleforth had a very good rugby reputation. The team was very keen to maintain their unbeaten record for this term. Dr Poxon was among staff supporters on the coach.

Lucy parked the coach near the imposing old school. After a quick sandwich on the coach she walked to the playing fields and took up her position on the touchline. It was a thrilling encounter by two equally matched teams and the score reflected this by moving, by the odd point, to give a lead first to one team and then to the other. Near the end of the match Ampleforth attacked the Leeds line to try to score a winning try, but the Leeds team resisted every attack, throwing themselves in front of the Ampleforth players and pushing them back from the line. Leeds were relieved when the final whistle sounded and they had won by 13 points to 12.

'That is as good a win as I have ever seen,' said the master in charge of the team to Lucy as they walked back to the school. 'Your son was an inspiration today.'

'I don't know much about the game of rugby,' Lucy replied. 'But I did think that he played well.'

Dr Poxon spoke to Lucy before he got on the coach for the return journey.

'Lucy, I'd like to come up to your office to have a word with you about something that's being planned at the school. This is not the place to explain it to you.'

'I'll be pleased to see you,' she replied. 'Just give me a ring to firm up the date and time. It's not about Richard, I hope.'

'No, he seems to be doing well in his studies and he's clearly a key man now in the rugby team.'

Lucy concentrated on her driving on the journey home but when back at the garage she wondered what Dr Poxon could want to discuss. Were they considering giving the coach contract to another company? She thought that was unlikely, but was there some major change in school policy proposed by the new headmaster?

The first mini-tour to Edinburgh was acclaimed a success by the passengers and Mavis reported that it could be improved by some re-timing of the excursions. Awareness of the mini-tours spread in the community, presumably from comments by passengers on the first tour, and Margaret reported a steady increase in the bookings for the remaining seven tours. Mavis concentrated on planning a schedule for the mini-tours starting in March of the following year and going to all four locations she had investigated. There would be the question of coach availability to resolve.

Dr Poxon came to see Lucy in her office after school. It was a relaxed atmosphere as he began to explain the reason for his visit. 'We have a very successful music department in the school, Lucy. The music mistress, who has been with us for two years now, has been effective in bringing in peripatetic teachers to the school. Of note has been the number of students taking up brass instruments and some of them are becoming very good players. We have a brass group who play at some morning assemblies and have even performed as a part of other youth concerts in the town. At a recent staff meeting someone suggested that we should arrange a concert by a major brass band, in the school hall. It would be aimed at raising money for music initiatives in the school but it would also inspire the brass players by hearing what can be achieved in brass band music. We'd like to arrange for the Grimethorpe Colliery Band to give a concert, as they're recognised as one of the best brass bands in Yorkshire. We think the cost would be around six hundred pounds for a concert booking. The music teacher has come up with another idea and she would like to approach the band to see if they would agree to let some of the best school brass section play with the band for one item of their concert. It would be a thrill for the students and it would encourage parents to support the concert. The selected players would have to rehearse with the band and to have approval of the conductor.' He paused for breath, so Lucy took the initiative.

'It all sounds very exciting, but where do Maxwell Motors come in?' she asked. 'Apart from transporting your brass players to the rehearsal in Grimethorpe,' she added hastily.

'I wondered if Maxwells would consider sponsoring the concert and making a contribution to the cost of the event? Our hall will seat over four hundred people and we'd want to fill it to make it a memorable occasion. As well as the band cost there are other ancillary costs, like tickets, programmes and advertising. Some staff worry about the risk of the school losing money if the concert failed to attract a big audience. Let me say at this point, Lucy, that I am here on my own behalf to seek your help. I haven't suggested this to anyone at the school yet, but I think it would be very good publicity for Maxwell Motors. Your sponsorship would be noted in the advertising and in the concert programmes. We would hope that the concert would be reviewed in the local press, who will be invited. What do you think, Lucy?'

'My initial reaction is to say that I am honoured that you have raised this idea with us. It is the first time we've been approached to sponsor an event. As you know, Maxwell Motors is in good financial shape but we don't have a policy for spending money on community activities. I will talk this through with Bob tomorrow and get back to you. I assume there will be some complimentary tickets for the sponsor? I have a feeling that Bob might like brass band music.'

'Of course there will be complimentary tickets for the company. Dare I ask what sort of sponsorship figure you have in mind, Lucy?'

'My answer is simple. If we are sponsoring the concert we will at least be talking about the total cost of the band.'

'That would be magnificent, Lucy!'

She realised that it had not been easy for Dr Poxon to approach her for financial support to the project.

The next morning Lucy met Bob in his bungalow. 'Do you like brass band music?' she asked.

'As a matter of fact, I do. My father was keen on brass band music and took us to some concerts as a family. He wanted me to learn the cornet, but I was too busy getting involved with the business. We went to a brass band concert on our honeymoon, didn't we?' he said, turning to his wife.

'Yes, we did. I enjoyed it, but that's a long time ago and I don't remember any more concerts.'

'Well, I think you will have to put a date for a brass band concert in your diary,' said Lucy and she proceeded to give Bob a full explanation of her meeting with Dr Poxon. She emphasised the good publicity that would benefit Maxwell Motors and suggested that they should pledge six hundred pounds to sponsor the concert, the sum which would allow the school to finalise the booking. She also said that they could assist with publicity by advertising the concert on the service buses. Bob agreed and told her to go ahead.

She rang Dr Poxon and gave him the news.

'That is magnificent news, Lucy. I will pass that on to the music mistress and tell her to get to work.'

Dr Poxon rang Lucy three days later about the concert.

'There's been an interesting development regarding the Grimethorpe concert. The music mistress met the band secretary and their conductor. They have agreed to give a concert at the school in March next year and they will give a firm date within the next two weeks. The conductor, George Thompson, likes the idea of some brass players from the school joining the band for an item in the programme. He's going to come over to the school and hear the brass group playing, but he will also bring some of the band with him who will take part in a masterclass with them.'

'That sounds very interesting,' said Lucy.

'The music mistress is over the moon. She says a masterclass will teach the brass group techniques that they would never learn with their normal teachers. The headmaster is also excited by this concert and what it will do for the school. Don't be surprised if he rings you up.'

Lucy thought to herself that her six hundred pound might prove to be a good investment.

The work on modifications to Bob's old house continued at a fast pace. The new office was given priority as it could be accessed from the forecourt once the new door was installed. Lucy was consulted on the curtains and carpets, as well as colours for the paintwork. It was clear that it would be available for use early in November.

'You'll have to decide what office furniture you need, Lucy,' said Bob, when he inspected the progress of the conversion.

'My plan is to have an office desk with a chair, and a large table in the rest of the office that can be extended for major meetings. There will be other chairs to use round the big table. No settees or easy chairs for relaxing,' she added with a grin. The architect provided examples of prestigious office furniture. Lucy was shocked at the prices but Bob said that price didn't matter as it had to be an impressive office.

There was excitement when the Aga cooker for the house was delivered. It was a dark green colour and its weight presented the builders with a challenge to manoeuvre it through the door into its place in the kitchen.

'I might have to go to cookery lessons to learn how to use it,' laughed Lucy. 'It's so big.'

'It's only like a double-decker bus,' replied Mavis. 'My rich sister has one. She swears by it for helping her cookery exploits.'

Carpets and curtains and all the decoration colours for the house were agreed with the architect. When the carpet fitters appeared on site Lucy realised that she should make plans to move into the refurbished house before Christmas.

The November meeting of the management committee took place in Lucy's new office and there were comments that Maxwell Motors now had an office appropriate for a company of its size. The financial results to the end of September were noted, with a favourable comparison with the previous year. It was reported that the mini-tours to Edinburgh should show a small surplus by the end of November. Mini-tours could be introduced in March next year, one tour each week in sequence to the four towns that had been studied, depending on coach availability. An exercise was to be undertaken to evaluate the requirements and availability of coaches for the tour season next year and the results would be reported to the next meeting. The Christmas bonus would be paid to all staff on the same basis as last year.

Outside the meeting Lucy had a discussion with Bob about the bonus. She realised that the driver/managers had made a lot of money from tips on the south coast tours but she could think of no way of excluding them from the company bonus. They agreed to introduce some new drivers on the south coast tours during the next year's programme and they concurred that this should avoid any drivers becoming prima donnas in the company, who thought that they could command their own deployment.

Unbeknown to her colleagues, Lucy had started to do a tour of other bus and coach companies around Leeds to see if there were any possibilities of a partnership agreement. Her method was to park outside the garages and view any coaches that were on the forecourts. A bad impression quickly ruled out some companies. One or two that she looked at were obviously significantly bigger than Maxwell Motors, which meant that in any negotiations Maxwells would be the minority partner. Lucy didn't favour that option. There was one small coach company that she had observed from a distance that interested her. They appeared to have only three coaches, but they were modern coaches and they were cleaned and presented on the forecourt with some pride. The garage facilities were small and would only take a maximum of four coaches. They had no fuel pumps on the site, so the company must fill up elsewhere. To extend her research she asked Fred to visit the bus company as a potential client and ask for a quote for three buses to take a trip to the seaside. Lucy also prepared a list of questions for him to ask about the company while he was there.

Fred learned that the company had only been in business for two years. The owner, who turned out to be the person Fred was talking to, was the only full-time driver and he used part-time drivers when he got a booking for more than one coach. They didn't have any regular work, so their business was mainly seasonal in the summer months. Fred had a look at one of the coaches that was on the forecourt. He checked the mileage on the clock and realised that it was low for two years' work. He asked why they had gone into the business. The reply was that his wife had inherited a six-figure sum from her father and they had decided to invest it in the travel business, but they were not as busy as they would like to be. Fred thanked him for the information and promised to get back to him.

'He might be interested in doing a deal with you, Lucy,' he reported back to his wife. 'They must have some spare capacity on many days of the year. I would suggest that this fellow is an innocent abroad as far as the coach business is concerned. What are you going to do?'

'I'm going to have a big think about this one, then I'll have a talk with Bob.'

After a few days, Fred rang up the company and told the owner that he had placed the order elsewhere. He noted the disappointed reaction to his message.

Maxwell was experiencing a busy Christmas period, like the previous year. On one occasion Margaret reported to Lucy that she had a potential order for four coaches but she was one coach short, so she was going to have to refuse the request.

'Don't do that, Margaret,' said Lucy. 'Ring them up and say that we are doing a bit of sorting out with our coaches and you will ring them up tomorrow.'

'Right, I'll do that,' Margaret replied. 'What are you going to do?'

'We're going to try to find an answer. Come on, Mavis, we're going to look for a spare coach. Bring all the details of the booking from Margaret.'

They decided to go in the mini-coach and drove into the

forecourt of the company that Fred had visited. There were two coaches parked there, so obviously the owner was out on a job. Lucy and Mavis got out and started to walk around, looking at the two coaches. A woman came out of the small office alongside the garage.

'Can I help you?' she asked.

'You might be able to,' replied Lucy. 'We were looking for the owner of the company. Is he around?'

'He's out driving one of our coaches. But I am his wife. I'm Eva Benfield.'

'So you are Benfield Motors. I don't think I've met you,' said Lucy. 'How is business with you? Are you busy at this time of year?'

'No, we're not busy. It's our quiet time,' Eva Benfield replied. 'Who are you? I see that you have come in a Maxwell Motors mini-coach. Are you anything to do with them?'

Mavis decided to jump in, 'Yes, we are from Maxwell Motors. This is Lucy Platt, who runs the company,' she said, pointing to Lucy. 'We're here to try to do a bit of business with you.' Mavis took a sheet of paper out of her pocket. 'We are a coach short.' She read out the date and details of the booking. 'Have you a spare coach on that day?'

'I'm sure we will have,' said Mrs Benfield.

The three women went into the office and Mavis looked over Eva Benfield's shoulder when she opened the booking diary. There were no bookings at all on the day in question and Mavis noticed that many days in the diary were blank.

'Right,' said Lucy. 'Can we make a firm booking for one of your coaches on that day? We might want more than one, but I suggest that you and your husband come down to Maxwell Motors and then we can agree the terms with you. Are you interested?'

'We're certainly interested,' she said, as she wrote the booking in the diary. 'We've been looking for something to give us a boost and I'm sure my husband will be keen to meet you.'

'When he gets back, ask him to ring me and then we can finalise a meeting,' said Lucy, as she handed over her card to Eva.

As they drove off in the mini-coach, Lucy said to Mavis, 'From what Fred told me, and seeing their forward bookings, I think that they're struggling.'

'What line do you intend to take when you meet Mr Benfield, Lucy?'

'It all depends how the meeting goes. We've got to show them that they are playing in a very small pond compared with Maxwells. Our initial aim will be to use their coaches to boost our fleet, but we will have to agree strict terms to cover all our overheads. We must have additional coaches available in the New Year if we want to expand our tour business.'

Mavis knew that there were some difficult decisions to make.

Lucy asked Bob to be at the meeting she'd arranged with Benfield Motors. She wanted to concentrate on the rate for hiring a coach on a daily basis. The meeting took place in the new office two days after Lucy and Mavis had first spoken with Eva Benfield. Both Mr and Mrs Benfield arrived at the appointed time, and Eva introduced her husband, Paul.

Lucy welcomed them and introduced Bob. She explained that she would tell them about Maxwell Motors and show them the way they operated later. But her first objective was to agree a daily rate that would be paid for the hire of a coach, assuming they were willing to agree to hiring out spare coaches. They immediately indicated that they were indeed willing to consider an agreement, but they asked who would provide the drivers. Lucy said that Maxwell Motors would prefer to use their own drivers. Paul Benfield said that such an arrangement would suit him as he was the only regular driver on the company books. Lucy then asked if they had considered what daily rate they would charge. Eva Benfield gave a figure, which Lucy wrote down in her notebook. She looked across at Bob. The figure was less than the one they had been prepared to pay.

Lucy pretended to do some calculations and then she replied. 'I think we can meet your figure, but I'm assuming that the rate is independent of the distance covered. It could be a local trip of twenty or thirty miles or it could be a long trip of over two hundred miles?'

'Yes, we accept that,' replied Eva.

'Can I ask you another question?' said Lucy. 'Where do you get your fuel for the coaches?'

'We fill up at local filling stations,' replied Paul Benfield. 'I've tried to set up an account at one or two of them but they wouldn't give me any discount.'

'Well you can see that we have a big business in fuel sales and I'm sure that we could give you a better deal. We need to explore that if we are going to be working together.'

They discussed other details as a result of which Lucy agreed that Maxwell Motors would be responsible for cleaning the coach after its day's hire. The payment would be made to Benfield Motors at the end of the month during which the coach was hired.

'Might you want to hire coaches from us on a regular basis?' asked Eva, somewhat hesitantly.

'I think you will get the idea of the potential if I describe our business to you,' replied Lucy. She suggested that they look at the office organisation and the garage facilities before they asked any more questions. Margaret demonstrated the bookings system for coach hire, rotas for the drivers and the programme for the deployment of the coaches. They went out onto the forecourt and inspected the only coach on site, which was equipped with the sound system for the touring holidays. Back in the office Lucy reviewed the situation.

'I think you can see that we are very busy. But we are getting bigger bookings from organisations that require five or six coaches. These orders usually go to the very big coach companies. We need access to spare capacity to allow us to take on these bookings, so we could want to hire from you frequently if these big orders keep coming in.'

Going back in the car, Eva Benfield was buoyant and her hopes were raised. 'This is what we have been waiting for, Paul. They will do all the work of getting the bookings and all we have to do is provide the coaches.'

'And we will lower our fuel costs if we fill up on their site. It's been a good afternoon's work.'

Lucy discussed with Mavis what had gone on at the meeting. 'In reality, we have added two or three extra coaches to our fleet at a cheap daily rate and we will lift our fuel sales. On some days we might take all their three coaches. I think it has been a good afternoon's work.'

Twelve

It was the end of the second week in December 1965 and the furniture van drew up at Lucy's house. She was at home, with Fred, to supervise the move to Bob's old house. They'd packed lots of boxes and marked on the furniture which rooms in the new house it was to go in. There would be more space in the new house than was needed for the furniture. When the refurbishing was complete Lucy and Fred had done a tour of all the rooms and they'd been thrilled with the house and its fittings. They were excited that the day of the move had arrived.

The three young men, with bulging arm muscles, from the removal firm surveyed the house and decided that it was a straightforward job. Fred and Lucy stood back and watched the furniture and boxes disappear into the van with hardly a word between them. The men declined the offer of a drink until the house was empty. Just before midday the loading was complete and Lucy had the tea and coffee ready. The men sat in the empty front room and rested their arms and replenished their fluids as they ate a complete plate of chocolate biscuits.

The furniture van left for the garage at twelve-thirty, followed by Fred in the family car. Lucy walked down the street to say farewell to Mrs Senior, who had decided that she couldn't accept the post of cleaner in Lucy's new house as she needed to be at home to look after her husband who now had a job in Leeds. She then followed Fred in the Maxwell van.

When Lucy arrived at the garage there was intense activity as the removals men were emptying the van. Fred was acting like a policeman directing the men to the different rooms.

'Are you looking forward to living here?' asked Margaret, in the office.

'It will take a bit of getting used to, said Lucy, 'as we've been in the old house for over eighteen years.'

Lucy spent the afternoon emptying boxes. At four o'clock the van was empty and the men had a final look around. Lucy met them at the door and placed a sizeable tip in the hands of the foreman. When he realised how much it was he was very appreciative. Shortly afterwards, Richard came in from school after his first ride home on the bus to Horsforth. He had a walk around the house and then declared, 'There seems to be a lot of gaps in the furnishings. Is there another van load to follow?'

'No, there isn't another load!' said Fred, with feeling. 'We'll fill the place up in the future when we get used to living here.'

'Come on, both of you,' shouted Lucy from the kitchen. 'Let's have our first meal together. At least I have managed to boil the kettle on the Aga. It's really a picnic tea until I get things organised.'

‘I assume you’re going to get some help in the house, Mum,’ said Richard. You can’t run Maxwell Motors and look after a house this size. We need another Mrs Senior.’

‘You are quite right, Richard. I am going to start looking round for someone. There must be a lot of cleaners and home-helps in the houses of your school friends. Keep your ears open and let me know if there is anyone looking for a new placement.’

‘Mum, we’re at school to study and that’s what we concentrate on. We don’t discuss cleaning ladies!’

It was a settling-down evening. Fred got the television working in the sitting room and the radio in the kitchen. Richard arranged the table and the reading lamp in his study and then got down to his homework. Lucy sorted out the two bathrooms and then decided to call it a day. She popped out into the garage office and reviewed the bookings for the day. One of the coaches came in from an afternoon booking and she spoke to the driver. Everything was organised for the cleaning team and they started to arrive at nine o’clock. Joe North met them and gave them their instructions. They were all well wrapped up as it was a cold night and there was no way to avoid the wind blowing around the forecourt. Lucy spoke to them and then went into the house and the comfort of central heating.

When they went to bed she snuggled into Fred’s arms and then summarised the change in their lives.

‘I think that we’ll be okay in this house, Fred. We have more space for the three of us and it’s certainly a warm house, with the central heating. One other thing that I have now realised is that we are much further away from Richard’s bedroom than we were in the old house. So we can be a bit more noisy when we have a passion session. But passion isn’t on for tonight; we are both too tired.’

She turned her back to Fred to go off to sleep. He moved

his body close to her and put his arm over so that he was cuddling her breasts as she quickly fell asleep. Fred was awake for a while reflecting on the last few years and the difference Lucy had made to their lives.

It was a new morning routine for the Platt family and Lucy supervised it. Fred went off to work first, in the family car. Richard, after eating a big cooked breakfast, went out to catch the bus to school. Lucy tidied the kitchen and then walked out to the garage office. Margaret was there already and she was checking the chart which showed the schedule of bookings for the day. There were three coaches un-booked for the day.

Lucy looked at the schedule with Margaret. 'It's a quiet day today, Margaret.'

'Yes, but tomorrow is a fully-booked day,' replied Margaret, picking out the schedule for the next day. 'All seven coaches will be on the road and there are some long trips. Two coaches are going to London and one to Newcastle. So there will be some late arrivals back to the garage.'

'I always feel a bit vulnerable when we don't have a spare coach to call on,' said Lucy.

'But you could call on one from Benfield's; they have only one coach out tomorrow as far as I can see.'

'I'm going to have another meeting with them to arrange more details about how we will work together,' said Lucy.

'I have another problem to sort out, Margaret. I need a cleaner and home-help. I had an excellent woman in the old house — she was really one of the family — but she can't travel here. Let me know if you can think of anyone who might be suitable?'

'I'm sure I'll be able to think of someone, Lucy,' she

replied as the phone rang. Lucy went into her own office, where a pile of papers were waiting on her desk. It was going to be an office day.

In the early afternoon Lucy got a call from the driver of the coach on a Leeds Grammar School sports trip.

'Lucy, I'm parked up at the school but there is something wrong with the coach. It's very hot and smells of oil. I've had a look at the engine and I wonder if it is short of oil. The funny thing is that this coach was supposed to be serviced yesterday by a man from the service company.'

'Just stay there and I'll bring a spare coach out to you. I'll be there in ten minutes.'

'I will explain the position and tell them that another coach is on its way,' said the driver.

Lucy told Margaret where she was going and ran to one of the coaches in the garage. Her mind was working on what to say to the servicing company. She arrived just as the sports teams were beginning to gather at the coach. She directed them onto the relief coach and spoke to the master in charge and explained the situation to him. She then went into the school and asked to use their phone to ring the service company. She spoke to the service manager and suggested that he come out to see what the position was with the coach. She also recommended that he brought some engine oil with him. Dr Poxon came into the office while she was there and she explained to him what had happened.

'You look cross, Lucy,' he said.

'I will be more cross when I get the manager here and I find out what the problem is. They serviced that coach yesterday and if the driver had driven further it might have destroyed the engine. We're fortunate that he spotted the over-heating when he got here.'

Lucy went out to the coach and was waiting there when the service manager, accompanied by an engineer, arrived in a van. The engineer inspected the engine and identified that the oil drainage plug was missing. He looked at his boss who asked him 'Have you found the problem?'

The engineer nodded, and then explained. 'He must not have tightened the drainage plug properly when he refilled the engine with oil. I'll go and get some oil from the van and another drainage plug.'

'We'll have you back on the road in a few minutes, Mrs Platt,' said the service manager, relieved that it wasn't a serious problem.

'That's not the end of the matter,' said Lucy quite forcefully. 'That is a failure of your company's workmanship. It is only the diligence of one of my drivers that has saved a major tragedy.'

'I am terribly sorry, Mrs Platt. I agree with your conclusion and I accept full responsibility. It will not happen again, I can assure you.'

'It may not happen again because I will review your invoices and seek an alternative tender for our maintenance work. I think your rates have increased recently. Maxwell Motors have paid you a lot of money over the past year. You will definitely not get paid for any work done yesterday.'

'Mrs Platt, your contract is one of our biggest and I do not want to lose it. Let me come and talk to you before you make any changes.'

'You can do that if you like; but you will have to sharpen your pencil on your rates before I will consider you again. I do not like my days upset by sorting out somebody else's poor workmanship.'

Lucy climbed into the driving seat and started the coach engine. The engineer listened to the sound and gave her a 'thumbs-up' sign. She drove off leaving the service manager to ponder his problem.

'That is some woman,' he said to the enginner. 'The idiot who serviced that coach yesterday is in for the big drop. It might cost us the contract. I'll have to try to talk her round, but it won't be easy.'

Lucy had a talk with Bob and they decided to have another meeting with Benfield Motors. Paul and Eva Benfield seemed keen to meet again and agreed to the first date offered to them.

Lucy opened the meeting after Margaret had served them with tea and coffee.

'First of all I want to introduce you to Mavis, who will be joining the meeting. Mavis is the person who has developed the south coast tours and has started work designing mini-tours to Scotland and the north of England.' Lucy looked across at Eva Benfield. 'She was with me when we visited your garage to make the initial request to use your coaches.'

'Yes, I remember Mavis,' said Eva.

'Well, so far, we have hired two coaches from you and the arrangement worked satisfactorily,' continued Lucy. 'The drivers were happy with the coaches and so were our passengers. I think we have pencilled-in the hire of three more coaches in the next few weeks. Our impression is that you are short of jobs. I can't see how you are making any money.' She looked across at them and paused for an answer. Paul Benfield looked at his wife, waiting for her to respond.

'We organise the business to limit our costs. We only have to pay drivers if they do a day's work for us. My husband looks after the maintenance and I look after the office work and administration. We were able to build the garage and buy the coaches without borrowing any money, so we have no debts to cover. We will be in real trouble if any of our clients fail to pay their bills. You're right to think that we cannot go on as we are, but we are hoping that business might improve.'

'So, really, you're dependent on Maxwell Motors getting your operations up to a profitable level?' suggested Lucy.

'Yes, I think you could say that,' replied Paul Benfield.

'We are in the opposite position,' said Lucy. 'Mavis has worked out four mini-tours in the north of England which would be extra to our programme for this last year.'

Lucy looked across at Mavis. 'From the experience so far, I think the Edinburgh mini-tour should go weekly. Then we could start selecting one mini-tour each week from the other planned tours. I see that we will require two coaches on mini-tours. We are looking at a situation where we could provide work on most days for all your coaches through the summer months.'

'That would suit us,' said Eva. 'What are you proposing?'

'We want to make our working arrangement more efficient for both parties. We'll pay you on our existing agreement each day we hire a coach. But we think the first thing we should do is merge our booking systems. If you get an order you would say to the client that it will be delivered by Maxwell Motors, and you would pass the details on to Margaret. Margaret would then be planning on deploying ten coaches, not seven. You've seen the office set-up so you know how our operations are organised. It's a sizeable programme.'

'It's an amazing business,' said Eva. 'I didn't realise that you had so many different operations. How do you think we could benefit from working more closely with you?'

'Well, effectively we will at least double your turnover,'

said Lucy. 'But there are other ways of increasing your efficiency too We could arrange to clean your coaches each night along with ours, and they could be filled up with fuel. Your garage could effectively become a parking place for the coaches of either company.'

'It sounds to me like you are really taking over our company,' said Paul Benfield.

'Not really,' replied Lucy. 'We don't want to buy you out; we are just aiming to use your coaches so that you make some money. You will have nothing to do except receive the income from the use of your assets. It seems to me to be a good deal for you and we will be able to expand our business.'

'I think it's a good, practical plan,' said Eva. 'We'll certainly have less concern about chasing bookings. I think we should give it a try.'

'I'm not objecting to the plan,' said Paul. 'It's just that we will have to sort out the detailed costs so that both parties get a fair share of the additional business.'

'That is true,' replied Lucy. 'And we have an excellent finance man who will do that. But first, Bob and myself have to take this proposal to our management committee for their approval. They may object to mixing the two types of coaches with different company names on the same booking, but we will explain to them that this plan is really a trial. If we can make the shared operation work for the next year we can then review it and see if we want to continue it, or modify it, or even abandon it.'

'I agree with that proposal, Lucy,' said Bob. 'It is a trial to see if the two companies can work together with benefits for both parties. We are not changing either company to such an extent that we can't go back to where we are now.'

Lucy carefully observed Eva. Clearly she did not like the thought of going back to where they were at the present time.

They continued to sort out some operational details. It was agreed that Paul would be paid a daily rate for all the days he was coach driving and that Eva would be paid a small daily rate for monitoring the Benfield site. Maxwell Motors would organise the maintenance of the coaches, but any maintenance work on the Benfield site would be paid for by Benfield Motors. Bob insisted on this as he wanted them to realise that they might be back on their own after the trial period. He wanted Paul and Eva Benfield to be motivated to make the arrangement work, through fear that failure would result in them having a financial disaster on their hands.

Margaret had suggested a cleaner-cum-housekeeper for Lucy, who had agreed to see her, but she had been warned by Margaret that she would probably be surprised by the person who turned up for interview. A young girl, who was approaching her eighteenth birthday, sat and faced Lucy in her office. Her name was Lilly Young and she was smartly dressed in a skirt and blouse.

'I'm surprised to see such a young person applying for this job, began Lucy. 'Do you think you can do it?'

'I am sure that I can do it, Mrs Platt. I'm fully trained and have been doing a similar job for three years at home.' She paused for breath. 'My mother has been very ill for the last three years and I have had to look after her. She was bedridden for the last year and so I have had to do everything for her. Luckily she had trained me to cook and clean before she was taken ill, so I knew what to do. Of course, my schooling went by the wayside, but I managed to prevent my mother going into hospital, as she wanted to die at home.' She paused and her eyes were cast down looking at the floor. There was absolute silence in the office.

Lucy didn't know how to ask about her mother. Eventually, Lilly looked up and said very quietly. 'She died three weeks ago.' There were tears in her eyes.

Lucy went around her desk and took Lilly in her arms. 'I am so sorry for you, Lilly. Just have a minute and collect yourself. Sit down here at the big table. We'll have a cup of tea together.' Lucy went out to organise a pot of tea.

Margaret could see that Lucy was moved by Lilly's story so far. 'She is a remarkable young woman,' said Margaret. 'I wanted you to see her without giving you any information first. If I'd told you her story you would not have believed me.'

Lucy went back into her office with the tea and some biscuits. Lilly had recovered her composure and explained that her father had died two years before her mother was taken ill, so it had been a bad five years. Now there was just her and her fifteen-year-old brother at home.

'It's no use me looking for a job in a shop or a factory because I have missed my schooling and I have no qualifications. But I've got the skills to run a house and that is what I want to do. I would like you to come and look at our house and see how I keep it, Mrs Platt, before you decide that I am good enough to work for you. But I do badly need a job, to earn enough money to keep me and my brother going.'

'I will do that, Lilly. In fact, we'll go now, but I'm sure you will be working for me in the very near future.'

Lucy went out with Lilly and they took the taxi to Lilly's terrace house in Horsforth. It was a picture of tidiness and neatness and in the kitchen there was the smell of home-baking. Lilly insisted that Lucy also see the upstairs and it was the same — spotlessly clean and tidy.

'This was my mother's bedroom, but for the last few months she was downstairs in a bed in the front room. My brother, David, has moved into her bedroom now.'

'I am very impressed, Lilly, with all you have told me and shown me. I'm sure you are the sort of person I'm looking for. I want you to work for me and I will look after you. How soon can you start?'

'I will be with you tomorrow morning at nine o'clock, if you can spare a few minutes then to tell me what you want me to do.'

'I'll see you then, Lilly.'

That night, after their evening meal, Lucy decided to brief Fred and Richard on her new cleaner. 'As Richard has had no success in finding me a cleaner,' she started, looking across at Richard, who had an amazed look on his face, 'I have had to sort out the matter myself. I interviewed a young lady today and she'll be starting here tomorrow morning. She is a special young woman who has been remarkably brave over the past three years, looking after her mother who had a terminal illness. I want you to be kind to her when you meet her, but I'm sure that she will do a first-class job for us.'

Lucy gave Fred and Richard a full account of her meeting with Lilly and the visit to her house.

Lilly arrived on time the next morning, looking very different from the previous day. Her hair was tied back and she was dressed for housework. She was wearing an apron and, in a bag she was carrying, were brushes and cloths. She explained that, at the start, she would prefer to use the tools she was used to.

They walked around the house, which Lilly greatly admired, and Lucy said that it would all be for Lilly to manage and clean. There might be times when the kitchen needed tidying up and washing-up was required, explained Lucy, and at other times there could be clothes to wash and ironing to do. Lucy had decided that she wanted Lilly on duty every day so that she could pay her a substantial wage.

'You can see, Lilly, that this is a big job, so you will need to be here just about every day, although some can be short days. We can be flexible and work out the details later, but I intend to pay you a wage of twenty-two pounds each week.'

'You can't do that, Mrs Platt. I'm not worth that much.'

'Oh yes you are, Lilly. When you have been here a bit, you will realise how little time I have for housework.'

'You can leave it all to me, Mrs Platt; I'll not let you down.'

Christmas 1965 was a good time for Maxwell Motors. The company was busy and there was even one coach out on Christmas Day. All the staff received their Christmas bonus, as well as enhanced wages through overtime worked, so there was an atmosphere of prosperity in the air. This even spread to Richard who did quite a number of hours in the evenings and at weekends serving at the fuel pumps. He noticed the amount of money he was taking at the pumps and he commented to Lucy on the size of that part of the business.

'You will realise, Richard, that Maxwell Motors is now quite a big operation. You should see the way I am welcomed by the bank manager,' she added with a laugh. 'It's strength is that all the different parts of the business complement each other and allow us to have a very slim management organisation to oversee them.'

Two items dominated the January management committee

meeting. The collaboration agreement with Benfield Motors was explained in detail by Bob and Lucy, and they answered some questions for clarification. The proposal was accepted by the committee. A proposal to provide a taxi service for weddings was agreed and a new wedding taxi would be purchased. The existing taxi would be retained and also used for weddings, along with the mini-coach. It was agreed that the tour programme would run for seven months, starting in March, with two coaches each Saturday going to different towns on the south coast and that each month there would be a coach leaving on Sunday to one of the south coast towns. There would also be a weekly mini-tour to Edinburgh, starting at the beginning of March, but running through to the end of October. And there would be another coach each week doing one of the mini-tours to the north of England.

Lucy kept Mavis and Bob in her office after the management committee meeting to discuss the outcomes with them.

'It was an important meeting for the company,' Lucy began the conversation. 'I think the other members of the committee are realising that we have difficult decisions to make and they need to share in that responsibility. But we're now looking for expansion into a new field, with the wedding taxis. We didn't raise it with the committee, but I think you can start quietly working out new mini-tours elsewhere in the country, Mavis.'

'I think the challenge for us is to keep on expanding our client base,' said Bob.

'You are right, Bob," said Lucy. 'We certainly got bookings from the outskirts of Leeds last year. What had you in mind?'

'I was thinking about Harrogate, Lucy. There are folks

there with a lot of money and many of them have time on their hands because their working days are over. In fact some of them never had any working days, as their wealth came from their fathers and grandfathers who got it from the sweat of the woollen mills in West Yorkshire.'

'That's a good point, Bob. I'll investigate setting up an agreement with a travel agency to cover Harrogate and Knaresborough.'

Lucy told herself that it had been a good day and she had the feeling that Maxwell Motors was going to make another surge in its business. She decided to leave the paperwork in her office until tomorrow. When she entered the house there was the smell of cooking and Lilly was still around.

'I couldn't see anything for your meal tonight, so I've made a meat and potato pie.'

She opened the Aga and took a large dish out of the main oven. It had a golden crust and there was steam coming out of the holes in the top.

'You are so kind, Lilly,' said Lucy. 'I've been very busy today and I had made no plans for tonight's meal. You should be at home now getting a meal ready for your David.'

'He's staying on late at school tonight as they have a meeting with a special speaker. So I'm in no rush.'

'Well, why don't you stay and help us eat this pie? Look how big it is. My men can eat a lot, but there's no chance we can eat all that!'

'Oh, I don't know about that, Mrs Platt. I was just starting to make an apple crumble when you came in and I was intending to get peas and carrots ready to eat with the pie. So I was not planning to leave for another hour, but I don't know about staying to eat with you.'

'Lilly, I insist you stay. Richard will be home soon and Fred will be here in about an hour. They will welcome the opportunity to share some time with you. And I will drive you home, if you like, when we've finished. You won't have to do the washing-up. Richard and Fred are good at that.'

So Lilly stayed and agreed to help eat the meal she had prepared. Lucy persuaded her to go upstairs and have a wash and change out of her apron. When she came down she had let her hair down and there was a pink flush to her face. Richard looked at her and saw that she had a shy beauty which he compared favourably with the looks of the girls from Leeds Girls High School that he saw on his bus journeys.

Lucy and Fred talked to Lilly during the meal and concentrated on Lilly herself, with no reference to her life looking after her mother. Lucy tried to find out what she liked in clothes, whether she went to the cinema, whether she had other friends besides her brother, and what books she read. The answers were surprising. Lilly was a member of the local library and read mainly historical novels. She had retained one girl friend who she had known at school and now and again they would go out together, but it was usually to her friend's church events. She hadn't been to the cinema in the last five years and she had little interest in clothes. Her main concern in life, she emphasised, was to get her brother, David, to be successful at school so that he could go into the sixth form to get his A-Levels. Lilly was sure that he was working hard and she knew that he wanted to do well in memory of his mother.

Lucy realised that Lilly was a young woman who had matured way beyond her years, but also, Lucy realised, she still needed some guidance. Lucy was determined that she, and Maxwell Motors, would take Lilly under their wing and give her the support she required.

Thirteen

During the third week of January, 1966, Lucy received a bulky envelope from Dr Poxon containing flyers and posters about the Grimethorpe Colliery Band concert at Leeds Grammar School. She arranged to have the posters displayed on both decks of the double-decker service buses. Margaret had a bundle in the office and gave one to anyone booking a trip. There were also flyers in the drivers' cabin in the garage. The posters prominently stated that the concert was sponsored by Maxwell Motors.

The meeting with the coach maintenance company was also scheduled in the third week in January. Lucy, who was accompanied by Bob, had deliberately deferred the meeting for several weeks as she wanted the company to be worried that they might lose the contract. They met in Lucy's office. The maintenance company manager was accompanied by a colleague, who he introduced as the senior foreman for maintenance work on coaches and heavy lorries. Lucy opened the meeting.

'You have had time to reflect on the incident, and I am sure that you are relieved, as we are, that there was no major damage to the engine concerned.'

'We are very sorry for what happened,' said the manager. 'The person who carried out the work on the coach has been dismissed, and we did not invoice you for his days work.'

'I should think you didn't. Let me tell you that I was looking out for an invoice from you and if we had received one that would have been the end of all your contract work with us. Finished, no question about it.'

Bob jumped in to the discussion.'When Lucy described the incident to me, I had cold shivers running down my spine at the thought of what could have happened. You have been saved by a very good, conscientious driver who used his initiative. It's a good job that we have trained our drivers to look after the coaches they drive.'

'Well, where do we go from here?' asked Lucy. 'How are you going to ensure that it does not happen again?'

'It will not happen again. I can guarantee it,' replied the manager. 'I have brought along our senior foreman, who will have direct responsibility for the work we do on Maxwell Motors buses and coaches.'

'I have been looking at the contract that we have with you,' said Lucy, 'and I see that it is up for renewal on the 25 March this year.' The manager nodded at this statement and pulled a copy of the contract out of his briefcase.

'I wondered if you would prefer to find work elsewhere and not continue working for us?' suggested Lucy.

'That is the last thing that we want, Mrs Platt,' said the manager, forcefully. 'You know that this is one of our biggest contracts.'

‘Well, what are you offering for the future?’

The manager hesitated before replying.

Before he could reply though, Lucy said, ‘Let me help you. I’ll make you an offer of what we are prepared to accept.’ The manager continued to hesitate so Lucy continued.

‘We will renew the contract for a three-month trial period. In that time we will monitor how your people perform. We would expect their work to be to the highest standard at all times.’

‘I can assure you that it will be,’ put in the manager hastily.

‘But I have not finished,’ continued Lucy. ‘For the three-month period I will pay you at rates that are reduced by 5% from your current rates. If we then decide to continue the contract we will go back to your current rates. You weren’t thinking of increasing your rates for next year were you?’

‘We do try to increase our rates each year, for inflation,’ replied the manager.

‘You are very fortunate then, Maxwells can’t do that,’ said Lucy. ‘We have to keep our charges the same year on year, or we would lose out to other coach companies. So we try to increase our efficiency each year to cover for inflation. You have to make your mind up. Can you accept my offer as a solution to allow you to carry on working for us?’ The manager didn’t hesitate this time, as he’d achieved what he came for.

‘Yes, Mrs Platt. We will accept your offer.’

‘I will send it to you in writing in the next few days.’

The manager and his colleague left the office and went to their service van.

‘She’s a tough woman,’ the manager said. ‘I got what I wanted, but we’ll have to increase our performance if we are to run it as a profitable contract.’

In the office Lucy and Bob talked about the outcome.

'He certainly was desperate to keep the contract,' said Bob. 'But you did drive him to a hard bargain, Lucy.'

'Not really, Bob. I started on the basis that we all work hard here to provide an excellent service. Any firm that works for us has to have the same commitment to excellence. If they fail, then it will cost them.' Bob couldn't argue with Lucy's objective.

Lucy and Mavis undertook a period of detailed planning in the first weeks of February, resulting in a strategic plan for the company to be tabled at the board meeting in March. Parts of the strategic plan would be used in staff briefings before the tour season started. The amalgamation of the booking system to include bookings for the Benfield coaches was completed in February. Margaret generally used the Benfield coaches on discrete bookings so that there was little mixing of the types of coaches. With his agreement, she always deployed Paul Benfield as driver whenever a Benfield coach was used.

Mavis disappeared in the last week of February to research new mini-tours. The outcome was a four-night tour based in Blackpool, a four-night tour based in Chester and a three-night tour based in Scarborough. These proposals would be tabled at the March board meeting, when a decision would be made on their introduction.

At the end of February, Lucy had a call from Dr Poxon about the Grimethorpe Colliery Band concert planned for Friday 18 March. Tickets had gone so well that it was certain to be a sell-out. Dr Poxon asked Lucy if she had sorted out who was to use her ten complimentary tickets.

She answered carefully, 'Yes, they're all organised,' There

had been such a demand for tickets that she had sent Elsie to the Grammar School to buy five extra tickets. Bob had four tickets, including his daughter and son-in-law; Lucy had eleven, including Lilly and David Young, Mrs and Mrs Senior and Matthew, and Elsie, Margaret and Mavis from the office.

'We'll be arranging for seats to be reserved in a block in the balcony for the Maxwell guests, along with the Headmaster and the guests of the school. So you won't be involved in the crush for early seats,' explained Dr Poxon.

'There is a slight issue there, Dr Poxon. We have bought five extra tickets for people in the management team at Maxwell Motors and it would be very good if we could all be together.'

'Lucy, I wish you had spoken to me about the extra tickets. You should have had free tickets. I can certainly increase the reserved block by five seats. The school players are scheduled to go to a rehearsal in Grimethorpe, so you will be getting an order for transport on that evening.'

'It would be helpful if the total number was no more than fourteen so we can use the mini-coach and we will not charge you for that booking.'

'I am sure we can restrict the number to fourteen,' agreed Dr Poxon.

Lucy was relieved that all the Maxwell party would be treated as VIPs at the concert. Her aim was that it would be an exciting and memorable occasion for Maxwell staff and friends.

Bob decided to go for the top of the range in the taxi market. He ordered a TX Fairways Model, in platinum silver. It was delivered in the first week of March. Mavis trimmed it up with wedding decorations, both inside and outside. She then organised a photographer to take pictures to use in advertising the wedding service. Parked on the forecourt, it generated a lot of interest for anyone visiting the office. It had been agreed that Mavis would be the main driver for weddings, backed-up by Elsie. To add glamour to the scene, Mavis and Elsie were measured and provided with jacket, blouse and skirt in platinum silver, and a peaked hat in grey. They also had high-heeled platinum silver shoes that they could slip on when they were walking round during the day, although they were required to use their normal shoes when driving.

The management committee meeting in the first week of March was briefed on the Benfield agreement and the combined booking system whereby Margaret had ten coaches to deploy each day. The tour schedules for the south coast tours and for mini-tours were explained, and the forward bookings were reported as good. Photographs of the wedding taxi were distributed, including one of Mavis and Elsie their new outfits for weddings.

Saturday morning, 12 March, was the day of the first wedding booking. It was of special significance for Maxwell Motors. Lucy inspected both the taxis to make sure that they looked immaculate. A photographer from the local Leeds newspaper was present to capture the scene, with Mavis and Elsie posing shyly by their taxis. The photographer followed them in his car to try to get action photographs of the taxis in operation. He was in competition with the official wedding photographer to get pictures. However when he told the wedding guests that his photographs would be in a Leeds newspaper, he had their full co-operation, and succeeded in getting excellent pictures of the taxis and their passengers.

Later that morning Lucy went into the kiosk for the fuel pumps, where Richard was on duty. 'What did you think of the wedding taxis, Richard?'

'I think they looked fine. Elsie certainly looked grown up in her new outfit. What on earth will you think of next for the company, Mum?'

'I have no other plans at the moment, but I'm sure that something might catch my eye. Of you go, Richard, another customer for a fill-up,' she said, watching a car draw up at the pumps. 'Don't forget to wipe his windscreen. We want him to come back next week.'

On the same Saturday afternoon, Lucy and Fred were on the touchline at Leeds Grammar School playing fields to watch Richard playing against Wakefield Grammar School. On Thursday evening Richard had requested their presence as it would be a critical match.

'Wakefield Grammar School has a very good team this season,' he'd said, to emphasise his request for support. 'They've won the same number of matches as us, but our sports master thinks we can beat them if we play well. The Headmaster even mentioned our fixtures in the school assembly this morning. I know you'll be very busy at the garage, Mum, but when you support us, we usually play well. Actually there is another reason why I would like you to be there: our captain is injured so I will be captain of the team.'

'Oh, Richard, that is great news,' said Lucy. 'We will definitely be there.'

'I shall be working on Saturday morning to ensure we complete an urgent job for one of the pits,' said Fred. 'But I will go in early so that I can definitely be home for lunch. We can't miss this match, Lucy. Captain of the team; that is really great.'

Lucy decided to recruit more support at the match. 'I've told Lilly about the match and she says her brother likes to watch rugby, so they might be there. They're going shopping in Leeds, but they will come to the playing fields from town.'

Lilly and her brother, David, walked up to Fred and Lucy just as the teams were running out onto the field. There were quite a number of parents and boys along the touchline supporting both teams.

From the start, Richard was prominent, calling for extra efforts from his forwards in the scrums and line-outs. It was clear that it would be a low-scoring match and the winner would be the team whose forwards had the most stamina. Near the end of the first half, the Wakefield stand-off saw an opportunity and kicked a drop-goal to give his side a 3–0 lead at half-time.

In the team discussions in the changing rooms, the Leeds team decided that the Wakefield stand-off should be marked tightly in the second half. Richard and his fellow forward took on this task. Early in the second half, the Wakefield stand-off received a poor pass which he managed to collect, but he was immediately tackled strongly and floored by Richard and his friend. In the loose scrum after the tackle, Leeds got the ball and were able to release their backs. A good run by the right wing took the play to within ten yards of the Leeds line and Leeds got the scrum.

'This is our chance,' Richard yelled at his scrum. 'We need a mighty push.'

The ball was fed into the scrum and there was a roar from the Leeds forwards as they gave a magnificent push and the Wakefield scrum were pushed off the ball. It was fed out by the Leeds scrum half and a scissor move between two of the three quarters split the Wakefield defence and led to a try near the posts. The try was converted, giving Leeds a 6–3 lead and a massive confidence boost.

There were two further times when the Wakefield stand-off was tackled by Richard and his team-mate before he could pass the ball. The Wakefield plan was in tatters. Leeds began to keep the ball in the Wakefield half and apply pressure. From a Wakefield scrum Leeds won the ball with a well-timed drive and again the ball was passed out to the right wing. When he had gained twenty yards of advance he slipped the ball inside to Richard. He threw out a long pass to take advantage of an overlap. It was an impressive try and had the Leeds crowd cheering. Lucy was dancing up and down, joined by Fred and Lilly and David. The try was converted to make the score 12–3 for Leeds, which was the final score.

Richard was very happy with the win under his captaincy. Fred took Lilly and David back home with Lucy, where they were all to have tea together when Fred had been back to collect Richard from the playing fields. During tea Richard told them that he had been congratulated by the senior sports master on the way he had led the team.

The Grimethorpe Colliery Band concert, on Friday 18 March, was a hectic day for Lucy. She'd arranged for Fred to pick up the Seniors and bring them to her house for a buffet tea. She'd insisted that Fred left his work in good time to join them. Lilly arranged for David to come straight from school for tea and she'd brought a change of clothing for David and herself to wear at the concert. In the same way, Margaret, Mavis and Elsie had brought clothes to change into for the concert. The office and fuel pumps were to be covered over the evening by Brian Hunt, who had been given a special briefing by Mavis. Richard was also instructed to come home from school as soon as possible so that he could assist with entertaining all the guests at the buffet. He did as he was told, but his comments the following day amused his parents.

'The house was like Piccadilly Circus, with people using the bathrooms, and then the bedrooms to get changed, both before, and after the tea. I didn't know where to go in my own house!'

Lilly worked hard all day, baking and making sandwiches and cakes for the buffet. She had it all laid out on a big table in the dining room. Lucy and Lilly were the last to go upstairs to get changed, but everyone was complimenting Lilly for the spread she'd put on. When Lilly came back downstairs she was transformed. She was dressed in a short, blue jacket and blue skirt, with a white blouse. Her hair was loose on her shoulders and she wore high-heeled blue shoes which displayed her shapely legs. Richard sat with her and David in the mini-coach on the journey to the concert. When they reached the school, he pointed out to her all the different buildings and what they were used for. Elsie drove the mini-coach and Mavis drove the new taxi with Bob and his family in it.

The party were guided to two parking spots near the concert hall, where they were met by Dr Poxon. He carefully split up the party so that Lucy and Fred, with Bob and Edith Maxwell, sat on the front row of the balcony with the Headmaster. The rest of the Maxwell party sat together in the reserved seats on the rows behind. Richard had Matthew Senior next to him on one side with Lilly and David on the other side. There was excitement among all the party at their priority seating arrangements.

When the audience was all seated the house lights were dimmed and the stage was floodlit. Dr Poxon stepped onto the stage and welcomed the audience and thanked Maxwell Motors for their generous sponsorship of the concert. He then invited the audience to welcome the band, which filed onto the stage and stood in their places to loud applause. He then asked the audience to welcome the conductor, Mr George Thompson, onto the stage. The band took their seats and the conductor bowed to the applauding audience and then swung round and brought his baton down to start the band playing a triumphant march. The power of the band and the precision of their playing shocked the audience, and they immediately realised they were experiencing something special.

The conductor spoke to the audience after each item, describing the next musical piece in the programme and saying who had composed it and who had arranged the music for brass bands. He also introduced each soloist in the band before they played. He was full of praise for two of them who, he claimed, were the best players of their instruments in Great Britain. The soloists gave two types of solos: one type showed brilliant virtuoso playing, with variations played at break-neck speed; other soloists played a well-known piece of music with total concentration on tone and feeling which, along with the band accompaniment, caused gasps from the audience.

At one point in the programme the conductor made a point of stating that all the members of the band worked at Grimethorpe Colliery, in various capacities. 'A few members of the band work nine hundred yards underground on some days. When they've done a shift down there, I'm amazed that they have the puff to blow their instruments, but tonight you have heard what marvellous music they make.' This remark got a loud 'bravo' from one member of the audience, followed by a sustained round of applause.

Before the final item in the first half of the programme, the conductor spoke again to the audience. 'Our finale to this half of the programme is the Dam Busters March. This should stir you all up, but don't miss the start of the second half of the concert, because we will be joined by some special guests from the school. We've had a musical workshop here, with the school players tutored by our players; and they have rehearsed with us in Grimethorpe. You must hear this part of the concert because it is their show.'

During the interval the VIP guests were provided with refreshments in a separate room. Dr Poxon and the Headmaster circulated among them. Lucy introduced the Maxwell team to the Headmaster as he went around, and when she introduced Elsie, she commented that Elsie had driven the brass players from the school to the rehearsal at Grimethorpe. In answer to a question about the trip, Elsie gave a vivid description about the mine site. 'The rehearsal room was in the middle of the mine site. A man joined the coach at the mine entrance to show me the way. I wondered where we were going. There were three mine shafts, all working, with lots of conveyors taking the coal across to one big building. There was also a large coking plant near the road where I was parked. While I was waiting for the players I saw them push the white hot coke out of the ovens and dowse it with water, so there was lots of steam and noise. I didn't know whether it was impressive or frightening.' Elsie finished her description with a shrug of her shoulders.

'You see, Headmaster,' said Lucy, 'that we educate our staff about many aspects of life as they drive around the country.'

'Very impressive, thank you very much,' commented the Headmaster, speaking directly to Elsie.

When the second half of the concert began the band were joined by five players from the school — a cornet player, a flugel horn player, a horn player, a euphonium player and a trombone player. The band, along with the school musicians, played a march and the applause was deafening, with cheers from the students in the audience when the conductor asked the five school players to stand and take a bow. The conductor then addressed the audience.

'The brass band world owes much to Salvation Army musicians who have made brass band arrangements of many hymns. We are going to play one now — the well-known tune, Deep Harmony, but tonight we have made a special arrangement of the hymn tune. The band will play the first verse and then the school musicians will play the second verse, which is notated to be played softly and with feeling. The final section, which will be played by all the players, will conclude with a triumphant finale. The conductor called the five school players to stand at the front of the stage, on one side of the band. He adjusted his music stand so that he could turn to one side and direct the school musicians. There was a tension throughout the audience who were willing their school colleagues not to fluff any notes. They need not have worried. The players had music stands in front of them but they had rehearsed their parts together so many times that they could have performed without music.

The conductor began the music with the cornets taking the melody, but they were supported by a solid foundation from the rich tone of the bass instruments of the band. The school players played with the band, encouraged by the conductor. For the second verse the conductor stood to the side and gave the players an encouraging smile. They started exactly together and with a balanced harmony. There were no fluffed notes and the final phrase was played pianissimo and with perfect tone. The audience was transfixed, but the conductor didn't want any applause at that point, so he brought the band, with the school players, straight into the final verse. It rose in volume until the last few bars, when the timpani provided a crescendo leading to the final chord when all the instruments were playing fortissimo.

When the conductor stopped the music there was an outburst of cheering and applause and then the audience began to stand up to give their ovation. The conductor shook hands with each of the school players while members of the band joined in the applause.

The school players left the stage and the band took their normal places. The audience resumed their seats and there were murmurs of relief that the experiment had worked. The conductor faced the audience. 'That was wonderful for me, and for the band. You might be saying "Follow that." Well, we will.'

The concert continued with a mixture of solos and brass band music. The final piece was an arrangement of the 1812 overture by Tchaikovsky. The music concluded with the timpani imitating gun fire as the band played double forte to a grand finale. There was another standing ovation. The band finished with an encore by playing an excerpt from the William Tell Overture. This was a fast piece which required true virtuosity by many members of the band.

As the audience left the concert hall there were many comments of praise for the band. 'I have never been to a better musical performance.' 'I can't believe that those musicians work at a mine.' 'It's the first time I have been to a brass band concert. It won't be the last.'

There were effusive goodbyes to Lucy and the Maxwell party. It was clear to everyone that it had been a very successful evening for the audience and the school.

Back at the garage, Lucy bid goodnight to her staff and reminded them that it would be a busy day for the garage in the morning, with nine coaches booked for tours. Bob was on hand to have a word with Lucy. 'That was a truly memorable concert, Lucy. I am sure that it will have done Maxwell Motors a lot of good. It was nice to have all the staff there to enjoy the experience. I suppose we will get other requests for sponsorship now?'

'We'll only get involved if it is to Maxwell's advantage,' assured Lucy.

Lilly and her brother were the last to leave as they both thanked Lucy for inviting them. She wanted to take them home in the taxi, but Lilly insisted that they would walk.

Three days later Lucy received a letter from the school Headmaster. It thanked Maxwell Motors officially for the sponsorship of the concert and reported the financial figures for the evening. The band had raised £60 from the sale of the programmes, to add to the £600 they had charged for the concert. They had also sold some records of the band. The school had made a surplus from the sale of tickets, and the sale of refreshments, of £710, which would go into the School Music Development Fund. The Headmaster concluded his letter by stating that, far more important than the financial figures, was the impact that the concert would have on the school musicians. He hoped that the working relationship between the school and Maxwell Motors would continue in the future. Lucy marked the letter to be shown to Bob and then to be tabled at the next board meeting.

The board meeting at the end of March was a positive meeting from beginning to end. The turnover and profits were significantly higher than the previous year, so it was agreed that the dividend would be seven percent. The figures showed that Maxwell Motors was making a significant profit from using the three Benfield coaches.

Two large orders for day trips, which required all ten coaches on those days, were noted. The total tour programme for the year showed a significant increase on the previous year and an article in the local paper about the wedding taxis was circulated. It had led to an increase in forward bookings, some for a year in advance. The letter received from the Headmaster about the Grimethorpe Band concert was duly tabled.

During the lunch after the board meeting Dr Poxon described how the band concert was a continued topic of conversation among staff and students. There would be a report in the school magazine, he said, written by the music mistress, about the unique impact that the concert had provided for the school musicians.

After the lunch Dr Poxen stayed on to have a chat with Lucy. 'Lucy, every time I come to a board meeting, I am amazed at the progress of Maxwell Motors. Everything that you touch seems to turn to gold. What's the secret of your success?'

Lucy paused before answering. 'Well, we have a good set of people in the management team. All our staff work hard and try to be the best in this business. We also consider each move carefully before we give it the go-ahead. I don't know how to answer your question other than those factors.'

'I don't think you give yourself due credit for the impact that you make on the operations, Lucy. Is there a risk that you're pushing yourself too hard? You are now living on the job and you must be always popping out of the house and into the garage area and the office?'

'It is undoubtedly an advantage living on the job as I have no wasted travelling time across Leeds and I get to know of any problems as soon as they arise. But we all get great satisfaction from the success of the company.'

'Just be careful, Lucy. Don't push yourself too far.'

'I hear what you say. I'll be careful.' She gave him a big smile as he stood up to leave. He gave her a hug as he passed her and left the office.

Lucy considered life to be very good and she didn't want it to change in any way.

That same night, after their evening meal, Fred told Lucy about an event at Wilkins. 'We had some visitors to the works this afternoon, Lucy, who looked a bit suspicious.'

'How do you mean, Fred?'

'Well, we get plenty of visitors, but they are usually people we are doing work for — engineers or managers. But these were different. They were looking at the facilities. They looked like senior company staff. The boss introduced me to them and he said that I was the fellow who ensured that each job was finished on time and that I often arranged assembly on site.'

'Well, he was certainly being fair to you,' said Lucy.

'What worries me is that I've heard that one or two of the big firms manufacturing products for the mining industry would like some of the business from small firms like ours. The easiest way for them to get what they want is for them to buy the small firms. What they want is the orders that we're getting from a good number of Yorkshire pits. The pits know us now and they're confident that we will react quickly to any requests and get the job done as soon as possible.'

'Don't worry, Fred. If your firm is taken over and closed, I have a job for you at Maxwell Motors. You did the course on diesel engine maintenance and got your certificate, so you will be able to put it into practice. The company that does our maintenance knows that they are on trial. And they are expensive. So I could pay you a big salary and still make a significant cost saving.'

'It might not come to that Lucy, but I just have a feeling that the boss might be tempted to sell up, while the firm is doing well.'

'What you are worried about, Fred? Is it the thought of working for a woman, even if it is your wife?'

Fred laughed out loud. 'Particularly if it's my wife, you should have said!' Lucy also laughed.

They went up to bed and clung together in a passionate embrace.

Fourteen

Richard Platt was at the nets on the sports fields, being instructed by a cricket coach on his bowling action. He was keen to listen as he had been upgraded to the Colts team. The sports master thought that he could become an all-rounder and a regular member of the side, if he could improve his bowling skill.

The coach watched Richard bowling his medium-pace balls for fifteen minutes. After analysing his bowling action, the coach made four proposals to Richard. He suggested that he should grip the ball in a slightly different way, that he should bowl from different positions within the crease width, that he should develop a faster ball, and that he should develop a slower ball, both of which should be disguised by the speed of his run up.

Richard was then asked to bowl with one of the first team batsmen at the crease.

'You've got to tease him out,' said the coach. 'Keep

changing the pace and line of your deliveries so that he cannot assume where the next ball is coming from.'

Richard's style in the past had been to make all his deliveries consistent in speed and length so that the batsman could not easily score runs. He struggled at first and the batsman was able hit some of the balls so hard that they would have been fours or sixes in a proper match. But then he had some success. He ran up to the crease at full speed, but bowled a slower ball which deceived the batsman and bowled him. The coach was pleased and commented accordingly. 'That was a well-disguised slower ball and the batsman didn't spot it. You need to drop one of those in from time to time.'

After half an hour of continuous bowling, Richard began to feel comfortable with varying his deliveries. The coach was sure that, with more practice, Richard could become an effective change bowler. Richard also aimed to improve his batting so that he could claim a regular place in the team.

Fred was pleased with Richard's report on his training session, and promised support if he got a place in the team.

Late in April, Lucy was in her office reviewing the operations of Maxwell Motors. On the surface, things were going well for the Company. The routine service double-decker buses were busy, but there had been one or two incidents with late-night drunkards behaving badly. This had led to a few men being put off the bus to sober up by walking home and there had been a report in the local paper about one of these incidents. It was good news for those people who wanted to travel on the last bus from Leeds in peace, although it also generated some negative comments about the company from young men who wanted a wild night out, in a gang with their mates. The south coast tours were generally fully-booked and were going down well with the passengers, but there had been two occasions when the hotels were fully-booked and the Maxwell passengers had been placed in inferior rooms to those agreed in the contract. Both cases had been investigated by Marion Stead, the courier, and reported to the office. Mavis had had discussions with the hotel manager and agreed a rebate on the room rate for that week. Lucy convinced Mavis that they needed to take some action to avert a bad reaction from the passengers and they agreed to offer a refund of half the cost of their holiday. Marion Stead was told to brief the passengers and she'd said that it was well received. Both Mavis and Lucy had met the particular coaches when they returned, and talked to the passengers and offered their apologies and handed over the refund.

'I think we have avoided disappointing those passengers,' concluded Lucy. 'It was the least we could do.'

The mini-tours to Edinburgh and other towns in the north of England were operating with reasonable support and were profitable for the company. However, on a few occasions there had been last-minute cancellations which reduced the profits on the trip to little more than break-even.

Margaret had told Lucy that the forward bookings for coach hire indicated that on some days all the ten coaches would be needed. Lucy checked the total payments transferred to the Benfield Company each month and these indicated that the partnership agreement was working well. Lucy's thoughts were interrupted when George Clay asked to see her.

'You asked to see me, George. Is it some problem that I don't know about?'

'It might be, Lucy,' George replied. 'A couple of drivers have had a word with me. It seems that they have been on jobs where Paul Benfield was driving one of his coaches.

When the drivers asked him how things were working out, he said he was not happy with the deal and that he might have to re-negotiate, or pull out. With all the bookings you have in the pipeline, I thought this might be a problem for you.'

'Thanks for telling me this bit of news, George. It's a fact that we have saved his company.' Lucy opened her desk and pulled out the report on the Benfield financial transfers and passed it to George. 'Just look at those monthly figures. When they were operating on their own they were not getting much more than a quarter of that income.'

'That's what I thought, Lucy. Paul Benfield is a strange fellow. Maybe he's just trying to put a different picture across to our drivers. But we don't want him upsetting our lads.'

'I am glad that you have told me what he has said. You're right about our need for the Benfield coaches. I'll think about it and I'll let you know what we decide to do.'

Lucy sat and considered the situation. Was Paul Benfield just a mischievous fellow, jealous of the success of Maxwell Motors? Or was he a schemer who was planning to do a deal with some other company that would leave Maxwell Motors with a major problem? She decided to check where Bob was.

'He's doing a four-hour stint on the service bus this morning,' replied Margaret. 'The scheduled driver has had to take his wife to hospital for an examination.'

'Let me know when Bob is around, please.'

'I will. We have had two bits of good news this morning that you might to like to know about, Lucy.'

'What are those, Margaret? I could do with some good news.'

'I've had a booking for a ladies club to go on the Blackpool mini-tour. That's for twelve people, and it has filled the coach. The other one is for five coaches to take a Club trip to Bridlington in the October half-term. That's taken up all our ten coaches for that day.'

'Thank you, Margaret. I'm glad that the future is still looking good.'

Lucy saw Bob in her office in the afternoon and filled him in on what she'd heard from George Clay.

'That is a surprise,' Bob replied. 'I thought the Benfields would have been highly relieved to have had the cash we have been handing over to them.'

'So would I, Bob. I considered that side of our business was settled and in order.'

'What do you think we should do, Lucy?'

'Having had a few hours to think about it, Bob, my plan is to take it seriously and prepare a contingency plan before we see Paul and Eva Benfield. I will explore an agreement to borrow coaches from another company. I'll probably go further afield, around Bradford or Sheffield, to a company that doesn't know about our existing deal. When we have a document in our pocket, then we can see Paul and Eva Benfield and give them a choice. Putting it crudely, it will be working with us, or bankruptcy.'

'I like your plan, Lucy. It'll be a very interesting meeting with the Benfields.'

It took Lucy several trips over two weeks to find a suitable garage with coaches to approach for a deal. The garage she settled on was on the outskirts of Huddersfield. She travelled in the family car so that there was no indication she was from Maxwell Motors. She met the owner and spun a tale that she was representing a coach company in Leeds who were considering expansion by leasing coaches on a daily basis from another company. They wanted to test a new market before investing in new coaches. The owner conceded that he had additional capacity but said that the coaches he would be prepared to lease out would be his older coaches. Lucy inspected the coaches he was proposing and they did not come up to Maxwell standards, but she thought they would suffice as her reserves at this stage. She volunteered a daily rate for a lease without driver. The owner was impressed and interested. In the discussions that followed, Lucy showed that she knew what she was talking about on running a coach company. When she was sure that the owner was convinced that her request was genuine, she agreed to write to him with an outline proposal for a future agreement. She requested that he confirmed his interest in writing.

She sent the letter the following day, on official Maxwell Motors writing paper. The letter was typed by Margaret who understood that this was a secret initiative that had not to be discussed with anyone. Four days later Lucy received a reply from the owner of the other coach company expressing his interest in exploring the matter further. Lucy's letter and the reply were placed in a separate file locked up in her office.

On Saturday 21 May, Fred and Lucy went to a cricket match at Bradford Grammar School, where Richard was playing for the Leeds Grammar School Colts team. Richard had secured a regular place in the team and he was getting wickets and runs in the matches. He was batting at number eight, so in some matches he didn't get to the crease to have an innings, but he had bowled in every match. He regarded each batsman as a challenge to be got out by variable deliveries. His deceptive slower balls had claimed several wickets, but he had also taken two wickets with his faster balls that had surprised the batsmen.

As it was a week without a wedding, Mavis was meeting the coaches back from the south coast tours and she was manning the office, with Brian Hunt on the fuel pumps. There were nine coaches out that day so it was a busy day for the garage. One of the coaches was one taking the teams from Leeds to Bradford but it was driven by a regular driver as Lucy wanted to be independent. She took sandwiches for a picnic tea.

Bradford batted first. They scored twenty runs before the first wicket fell and then their number three batsman hit ten more runs off the first over he faced. The Leeds team was in trouble and Richard was brought on to bowl.

'Richard is on to bowl now,' said Fred to Lucy. 'The team needs him to do well.' Lucy knew that she should concentrate on the cricket, and stop thinking about Maxwell Motors.

With Richard's third ball, the number three batsman slashed at the ball and it flew to a slip fielder, but he dropped it. 'Goodness me,' said Fred. 'The fielder should not have dropped that catch. I hope it doesn't put Richard off.'

Richard wasn't put off. He teased the batsman with a slower ball, which he missed by playing too soon. But with the final bowl of the over his faster ball got through and bowled the batsman. There was applause from the Leeds supporters and Richard was then full of confidence. He got another wicket in his third over. This time the batsman had been frustrated with five balls that he had just managed to stop, so he had a swing at the last ball of the over. It was sent high in the air but was caught brilliantly on the boundary by a Leeds fielder. It was in his fifth over that he got another wicket with his slower ball that deceived the batsman who played too soon and gave a catch to the mid-on fielder. At the end of that over, the master in charge of the Leeds team gave a message to a fielder on the boundary, to pass on to the captain of the Leeds team. It later became known that the message was to 'keep Platt bowling'. As a result Richard continued to bowl though to the end of the Bradford innings. His final figures were ten overs, three maidens, twenty-one runs, five wickets. The Bradford team was all out for eighty-seven runs.

After the tea interval, when Leeds went into bat, Richard walked round the boundary to his parents. They were full of praise for his performance. Richard was also pleased by the comments of the master in charge of the team about the improvement of his bowling. Richard didn't bat and Leeds knocked off the runs for five wickets, so it was a resounding victory.

Richard travelled back home with his mother and father in their car. Later that evening, Lucy went out into the yard and saw that the cleaning team was in action, preparing all the buses and coaches for the next day. She'd really enjoyed her afternoon, watching Richard playing cricket, and sharing the picnic with Fred.

At the end of the month, Fred came home with news about Wilkins.

'It's happened, Lucy,' he said, as soon as he came into the house. 'The boss called me into his office this afternoon and told me that he has agreed to sell the company. It will all be completed within the next few weeks. I think he must have got a good price. It sounds as though he will be able to clear all his debts with the banks and have a nice balance left to spend.'

'What did he say about your prospects with the new owner?'

'He was a bit vague about that. He did say that they will be putting in one of the young fellows that came to view the operations as manager. If it's the one I remember, he looked a bit wet behind the ears. I'm not sure how much he knows about our type of business.'

'You'll find out when he takes over. Don't worry, Fred. You know your job and how the place should work. You also have a get-out clause.'

'In my bones, Lucy, I think I might want to use it.' Lucy went over and gave Fred a hug and a kiss. She then went to complete the evening meal. She noticed that Fred didn't have his usual appetite, though.

The cleaning of the house and its operation was working very well and Lilly Young seemed very happy with her job. It was a surprise one morning when Lilly asked if she could have a word with Lucy as soon as she arrived for work. Lucy asked her to come round to the office in ten minutes as she wanted to make an early call to Eva Benfield.

When Lilly came into the office, dressed in her cleaning attire, Lucy was relaxed, having made an appointment to meet with the Benfields. Eva had been surprised at the request and seemed to want to ask questions, but Lucy had put her off with a general comment that the meeting would be a routine review.

'Now then,' began Lucy. 'Have you got a problem, Lilly?'

'I'm worried about David, Mrs Platt.'

'In what way are you worried, Lilly?'

'He's swotting hard for his O-level exams in a few weeks time, but he seems to be struggling with his maths. He comes down, after puzzling with a problem for an hour or two, and says to me, "I just don't get it." As you know, I never got anywhere near as far as him with my studies, so I can't help him.' She cast her eyes down and there were signs that tears might be imminent. 'I feel that I am a complete failure, Mrs Platt. I don't know what to do.'

'You need some help, Lilly, and I will sort it out.'

Lilly looked up with surprise and hope.'How will you do that, Mrs Platt?'

'David needs some private tuition on his maths syllabus. Once he understands how to sort out his maths problems, he will gain confidence with his other subjects.'

'How do I arrange private tuition?'

'You don't have to do anything, Lilly. I will arrange it. It might be easy.' She rang through to Margaret in the general office. 'Margaret, where is Mavis?'

'She's out on a taxi booking to the airport. She should be back shortly.'

'Ask her to come in and see me when she gets back, please.'

'I'll do that, Lucy.'

'I think Mavis may be able to spend some time with David,' Lucy said to Lilly. 'I know she did well at school with maths. If he needs extra tuition in addition to Mavis, I think I will also be able to arrange that. You go back to your work in the house and I'll speak to you after I've seen Mavis.'

Lilly stood up to leave. 'That''s a great relief to me. Thank you very much, Mrs Platt.'

'Lilly, I wish you would call me Lucy. Everyone else does.'

'I'll try, but it just doesn't feel right Mrs.....Lucy.'

Lucy met Mavis and explained the problem. Mavis agreed to visit David for an hour or so on the next two nights and give him some help. The proposition was very attractive to her. 'I always loved maths at school,' said Mavis. 'It will be a great pleasure to get my brain in gear again with some mathematical questions.'

Lucy popped around into the house to give the news to Lilly. She found her in one of the bedrooms, on the floor, cleaning under the bed.

Lilly was delighted with the plan, but she raised the question of payment. 'It will cost you a cup of coffee each night, and Mavis likes it strong. All the rest is paid for.'

'Oh, you are so kind,...' she hesitated and then added, 'Lucy.'

'That's better, Lilly,' replied Lucy, with a grin, as she went back down the stairs.

Mavis had a quick tea when she got home, as she had been delayed sorting out a staffing problem for the drivers' rota with Margaret. She then went round to Lilly's house where she was immediately impressed with the neatness and tidiness of the rooms. David was upstairs doing his homework, so Lilly called him down and introduced him to Mavis. He was very shy but he held out his hand so Mavis shook it and said how pleased she was to meet him.

'Where do you want to work, David?' asked Lilly. 'You have the choice of your bedroom or the front room. Whichever you choose, I will keep out of your way.'

'It would be better to use my bedroom, because I have all my books there,' said David.

'That's fine by me,' Mavis confirmed.

'I hope that it's tidy,' said Lilly. 'You can take the chair out of my bedroom for Mavis.'

Mavis gave Lilly a smile as she followed David up the stairs to his bedroom. They settled together at his desk and he showed her the maths exam papers that he was going through. Very quickly Mavis realised his lack of understanding of certain basic principles of mathematics.

She therefore spent the next hour slowly explaining and developing his knowledge. They then went back to the exam papers and David quickly showed that he had understood what Mavis had explained to him.

'I think that's enough for tonight, David,' Mavis said. 'If you like, I can come tomorrow night for another session on any other aspect of the syllabus that's worrying you.'

'I would be very pleased if you could spare the time,' David replied politely, with a smile.

They went back downstairs.

'I think I've cracked it, Lilly,' announced David. 'Mavis is very good at explaining the principles to me. We're going to have another session tomorrow night.'

'Are you sure you can spare the time, Mavis?' asked Lilly. 'I've got a cup of coffee ready for you before you go home. I hope it's strong enough.'

'I suspect that Lucy has been spilling the beans,' said Mavis, with a smile.

Lilly produced a cake from her pantry.

'You must try a piece of this as well, Mavis. Are you going to be sociable and have a piece of cake, David?'

He was about to go back upstairs but he realised that he had better be sociable with his new friend who held the key to his exam results. The three of them talked together for the next half hour until Mavis left. She was satisfied with her teaching success and was impressed with the little household of Lilly and David. When she saw Lucy in the office the next morning she told her about her session with David.

'He's a lovely young man, Lucy. And he was very appreciative of my help in explaining some basic principles to him. I'm going to have another session with him tonight.'

'Thank you very much, Mavis. I'm glad you've been able

to help him. Lilly was very worried.'

'She shouldn't be worried. The house is a credit to her and she is certainly filling the roles of sister and mother. I met them both at the Grimethorpe Band concert and I was intrigued by their life together.'

'Keep your eye on things this afternoon, will you? We have a meeting with Paul and Eva Benfield. It might go on for quite a while. Bob will be with me.'

'Is there some problem with them? I've heard rumblings.'

'There won't be any problems after this afternoon's meeting. I've got a very clear objective.'

The meeting took place in Lucy's office and it was all friendly at the start. Margaret brought in a tray of tea and coffee, with a plate of biscuits. The Benfields had brought no papers with them, which contrasted with Lucy, who had a file in front of her which obviously contained numerous papers. Bob, as pre-agreed with Lucy, opened the meeting

'We think it is important to review the way our agreement is working and to sort out some issues that we think have arisen. Are you happy to do that?'

'We are happy to discuss the position,' replied Eva. 'We have no problems with the way the agreement is working, so we have no issues to raise.'

'Well, that is surprising,' said Lucy, with a look of shock on her face. 'I have had reports from my staff which tell us that there are significant problems as far as you were concerned.' Lucy paused, waiting for a reaction.

Eva Benfield again was the one who replied. 'I am baffled here. Can you tell us what these significant problems are, that we apparently have?'

'I received a report that your husband told some of our drivers that he was not happy with the way the agreement was working and he might have to renegotiate it, or pull out.'

Paul Benfield had his head down and his hands clasped in front of him. His wife was looking daggers at him.

'Is that true?' she asked.

'I might have made a comment like that, one day, about the agreement.'

'You silly bugger,' said his wife as she lifted her arm in despair and banged it down on the table. 'Where do we go from here?'

'Now you see the true position, Eva,' said Lucy. 'We took the matter very seriously. We couldn't understand the reaction of your husband. We've monitored the payments made each month under the agreement.' Lucy passed over a paper which showed all the figures. 'From these figures we think that your income is now about four times what it was last year. You should be very happy with the change in your fortunes.'

'Yes, we are pleased with the way it's working out,' said Eva Benfield.

'But why then was your husband passing on to our drivers his intention to renegotiate the deal or pull out?'

'I don't know,' Eva replied. She turned to her husband and put the matter in his court. 'Come on, explain what made you say that.'

'I can't explain what I said,' said Paul Benfield. 'I know I was feeling upset that day,' he said, with a shrug of his shoulders.

'But we had to take the issue seriously,' repeated Lucy. 'We couldn't take it as a 'bad day' comment. Our future bookings through the rest of the summer are very good and on many days all ten coaches will be out on the road. So I will tell you what we have done.'

She took out the letters that she had sent to the other coach company and the reply she had received, and placed them on the desk. She carefully covered the part of the letter that showed the other company's name and logo.

'We have made a proposal to another coach company to hire some spare coaches from them in place of the Benfield coaches. They have replied that they are willing to make an agreement with us and we are now at the point of finalising that option.'

Lucy paused, observing both Paul and Eva Benfield turn very pale.

'Don't throw us out, Lucy,' immediately pleaded Eva. 'It was a misunderstanding. We are very sorry for it.' She looked across at her husband.

'Yes, I'm very sorry. I should not have said what I did that morning.'

'Please give us another chance, Lucy,' pleaded Eva. 'If you throw us out now that will be the end of the company. We will have to declare bankruptcy.'

'Eva, we had to react on the information passed to us and cover ourselves. You should know, as well as we do, that running a coach company is a serious business. We could not risk being left without spare coaches to fulfil our bookings. We did wonder if you had made a deal with another company to lease coaches to them or sell out to them?'

'No, we had no plans to change from our agreement with you,' said Eva.

There was a silence in the room and the Benfields were looking at Lucy to hear what their fate was. Bob also looked across at Lucy.

'Can I make a suggestion?' continued Lucy. She paused to gather her thoughts. All eyes were on her. 'I think that there are three things we must do. Firstly, we must make a record of this meeting as a general review of our agreement. We will record that the agreement is working well. Secondly, I think that Paul should have a three-month sabbatical from driving to allow him to recover his health. From what I have heard, I am assuming that he made his statement when he was stressed. Thirdly I will write to the other coach company and tell them that we have decided not to proceed, at this time, with the expansion of our business, but we might want to work with them in the future. We must all sign the minutes of this meeting. Can you agree with these proposals?'

'Yes, we can agree with your proposals Lucy,' said Eva. 'Thank you very much for taking this approach. I am sorry for the problems my husband has caused you.' She looked across at her husband. He hurriedly joined the discussion.

'Yes, I'm very sorry for what I said and the trouble it has caused you.'

'It did cause me a lot of extra work,' said Lucy, 'but we will draw a line under that. I will get Margaret to replace you on the drivers' rota,' she added, looking directly at Paul. 'We will review the situation in three months time.'

The meeting closed with the Benfields shaking hands with Lucy and Bob as they left the office, and again thanking them for agreeing to continue the operation of the agreement. Paul knew that he was in for a major torrent of abuse from his wife when he got home. In fact, it started in the car as soon as he drove off the forecourt.

'You are a stupid fellow,' said Eva. 'We have escaped from bankruptcy by a hair's breadth. You saw that she had an agreement there with another coach company to hire coaches from them. She will keep that company in reserve in case she has any more trouble with us.'

'I'm sorry for what I said. I was just feeling, on that

morning, that Maxwell Motors have a very good deal using our coaches.'

'They may have a good deal, but I don't give a damn how much money they make with our coaches, we have a lifeline now for our business. We shall lose quite a bit of money in the next quarter with you not doing any driving, but we will have to accept that. We have got to be as helpful as we can be to Lucy, so that she lets you get back driving after the three months.'

'In what way do you mean?'

'I don't know at the moment, but I will keep in touch with Lucy to see if there are any problems that arise where we can help.'

Lucy had a short meeting with Mavis and Margaret and instructed them to take Paul Benfield off the driving rota for the time being. She assured them that the agreement with Benfield Motors was to continue and she dictated to Margaret the minutes of the meeting which had just finished. Underneath the text was a block to be signed by both parties. She also dictated a letter to the other coach company.

Back in her office, she had a coffee with Bob.

'I don't think we will have any trouble with the Benfield agreement as we go forward,' she said.

'I think you put them in a corner, Lucy. They were relieved to get another chance and they know that they are lucky to have escaped bankruptcy.'

David Young took his O-level exams a few weeks after Mavis had tutored him on his maths syllabus. Mavis arranged with Lilly that she would go over and see David to find out how he had got on with the exams. When she arrived, David was up in his room swotting for some other exams and Lilly called him down.

'There's a lady to see you, David,' Lilly shouted up the stairs. 'Please come down.'

David came down the stairs in leaps and bounds, obviously very keen to talk to Mavis. He brought the papers down with him and they spent twenty minutes discussing the answers. David confidently explained the answers he'd given. When they'd finished their survey, Mavis concluded, 'I don't think you need worry about the results from those papers. You should get good marks.'

'I felt hopeful that I should have passed,' replied David.

'Well, we must celebrate with a coffee and a piece of cake,' said Lilly, who went into the pantry for the cake and to put the water on to boil.

'What are you going to do over the holidays, David?' asked Mavis.

'I don't know. I have no plans.'

'Would you like a part-time job at the garage?' asked Mavis.

'What sort of job?' asked David, who'd clearly never thought about work.

'We have fuel pumps and we serve a lot of petrol and diesel to the public. I know that the young lad who normally does that job is away on holiday in August, and I think it is the same time that Lucy's son, Richard, will also be on holiday. The job is simply working the pumps and taking the money. I know that you're good at maths now, so working out the money will be easy for you.'

'It would be a good chance to earn some pocket money,' suggested Lilly, to encourage him.

'I would be interested,' replied David. 'I suppose there will be some training in how to work on the site.'

'Everyone at Maxwell Motors has to undergo training, whatever they do. I'll have a word with Mrs Platt and get back to you,' said Mavis, as she accepted her cup of coffee from Lilly.

When Mavis left, Lilly gave David a hug and explained to him how wonderful it would be for him to work for Maxwell Motors.

The next day, Mavis had a word with Lucy and suggested that David Young might be a young person who could look after the fuel sales, particularly during the holiday period.

'That's a good idea, Mavis. Arrange for him to come down and see us. Lilly will no doubt be very pleased for him to earn some pin money with us.'

'She thinks the world of him, Lucy. I had a lump in my throat when I was with them and saw how she lavishes love on him. No mother could give him more than Lilly does.'

On 1 August the Wilkins engineering company where Fred worked was taken over by a mining machinery company, Optinum Mining. The company manufactured conveying equipment for the coal industry and its main factory and head office was on the outskirts of Birmingham. It placed a young mechanical engineer in charge of the Yorkshire operation. He spoke to Fred, who explained the work in progress and the future orders. By the end of the first day the changes began to emerge. Fred reported to Lucy when he got home. 'It is that young man, Bob Green, who is to be in charge. He's made one big mistake already, on his first day. He's sacked our marketing chap. All the sales are to be handled by the Birmingham sales team. I explained to him that our marketing fellow has very good relations with the mechanical engineers at many pits in Yorkshire and we get jobs on short delivery times. That is our bread and butter. But he says that all orders will be cleared and priced in Birmingham. He did say that the main company might give us some fabrication work to do when they get a large conveyor order. According to the office staff, he went out for a two-hour lunch and came back smelling of alcohol. I'm not feeling happy about my job now.'

'Don't worry, Fred, Just do your best and see how it works out.' Lucy gave him a cuddle as they went into the lounge to watch television. She would have to give some time to support Fred in the coming months.

Fifteen

David Young was dressed in his Maxwell Motors outfit for his first day on duty at the fuel pumps. Lilly called on him when she arrived to do her cleaning job. She didn't speak to him, as he was cleaning the windscreen of a car he had just filled up and a lorry was parked waiting to be filled with diesel. She was confident that he'd do well. Mavis had told him that he would be needed every week throughout August, on the fuel pumps, as Brian Hunt was covering for other people who were on holiday.

Lucy was very busy making detailed plans for a family holiday in the last week of August, as Fred's engineering works was scheduled to be closed down for that week. She knew that Fred needed to have a holiday this year, more than ever, as he was not happy with the way Wilkins was being managed. She had made a deal, through Mavis, to go to the hotel in Brighton that Maxwell Motors used on their south coast tours. Lucy and Fred had a suite booked in the hotel and the room for the Richard and his friend Matthew Senior was on the same floor. Richard checked the first-class County Championship fixture list and identified that Sussex were playing Middlesex on Saturday 27 August and Monday and Tuesday 28 and 29 August, at their Hove ground.

'What a pity we can't travel down on the Friday, and then we could go to that match,' said Richard, at the breakfast table one morning.

'If you want to go to that match we'll travel down on the Friday and add an extra day to the holiday,' Lucy had said.

So it was agreed that Fred, along with Richard and Matthew, should spend three days watching cricket. Lucy telephoned the Sussex County Cricket Club and obtained tickets in the members' stand for the three days. She knew that Fred would be shocked when he saw the price of the tickets.

Having sorted out the tickets for the cricket, Lucy had a chat with the boys and Fred about food at the match. They agreed that they didn't want to buy any food at the ground, and that they would prefer to take sandwiches and drinks that they could eat while they were watching the cricket. Lucy rang the hotel and discussed with the head chef whether he could provide food and drinks for the match. She emphasised that the boys and Fred liked plain sandwiches, with a selection of savouries, and some cakes.

Telling them of the arrangement, she said to Fred and the boys, 'But you can't eat it like tramps. You are, after all, sitting in the members' stand. We need to organise something to carry the food and you will need cutlery and crockery so that you can eat with elegance.'

'Elegance?' blurted out Richard. 'Is this an exam, Mum?'

'No, Richard, it is not an exam. But I want you to be noted

for your knowledge of cricket and also for your eating manners. You never know who might be in that stand.'

The next morning Lucy went into a department store in Leeds and bought two impressive picnic baskets. One was to carry the food, the other contained a full range of crockery and cutlery. She opened them out on display when she got home.

'They'll fit under your seats while you're watching the match. You won't have to carry them far, as I will arrange that you will go to the match each day in a taxi. You'll need to arrange with the taxi driver what time you want picking up at the end of the day's play, so that you're back in time for dinner in the hotel.'

August was a busy month for Maxwell Motors. There was wedding business booked on every Saturday of the month, which tied up both Mavis and Elsie. Wedding contracts were becoming a significant earner, and an added bonus was that they offered new, free advertising as almost every week there were photographs of the new Maxwell wedding taxi in the local papers. Bookings for the wedding taxis were exceeding availability and more drivers were needed, as Mavis and Elsie could not be expected to work every weekend.

Bookings for the coaches were better than in the previous year, and on many days every coach was in use. There had been some shuffling of drivers to take over the coach that Paul Benfield would normally drive, and the pool of reserve drivers had been increased. The hire of the mini-coach for day-trips to the seaside had increased and many of these bookings were now covered by a male driver to allow Elsie to have some time in the office.

Lucy was having one of her regular chats with Bob Maxwell.

'Bob, we're doing quite well. The Benfield issue is resolved and they have signed the minutes of the meeting we had with them. But we have one problem —a problem of success — but we need to think about it.'

'What's that, Lucy?'

'We've significantly increased our wedding business. It can only get worse as more and more people get to know about our wedding service from the photographs of the wedding taxis in the papers each week.'

'Yes, I've seen these reports. What do you think is the answer?'

'We need another driver to help out. I think we should stick to female drivers as they have more affinity with the bride, and I think we have the answer already working for us. Lilly is old enough now to have a driving licence. She's a smart young woman and would look very good in the driver's wedding outfit. I have a great respect for her, Bob, and I think we should offer to get her trained as a driver.'

'You go ahead, Lucy, and see if Lilly wants to drive for us. I too like her very much, and her brother also seems to be a responsible young fellow.'

Two days later, after having discussed the matter with Mavis, Lucy asked Lilly to come into her office to see her. Lilly dropped everything in the house and came into the office in her cleaning outfit. She was apprehensive, thinking that something must be wrong. Surely, she thought, it couldn't be about David? He seemed very happy with his work at the fuel pumps. She sat down opposite Lucy who was at her desk.

'You look a bit worried, Lilly. Is something troubling you?'

'I'm afraid that you want to see me because I have made a mistake and done something wrong.'

'You are a worrier, Lilly,' replied Lucy, with a big smile. 'Of course nothing is wrong. I want to put a proposal to you. We want to send you to a training school so that you can get a driving licence. You will then be able to drive the taxis. When you get some experience we think you'll be able to drive at some of the wedding bookings. How does that grab you?'

'Are you sure, Lucy? I've never thought about driving. Do you think I will be good enough?'

'Once you get used to it, Lilly, you'll find that driving is as easy as walking. You've seen Elsie in the taxis and the mini-coach; we have no doubt that you could become just as good as Elsie.'

'Wow, I wonder what David will think when his sister becomes a driver!'

'He will be very impressed, I'm sure. I'll make arrangements for your lessons then. If I can, I'll arrange an intensive course, so you may find you have a lesson every day, so you might have to cut back a bit on the cleaning.'

'I'd better get back into the house, then, and get in front.'

Lilly didn't actually go straight back into the house. She went to David who was reading a book as he had no customers. He was surprised when his sister entered the kiosk.

'David, you will not believe this piece of news. I can't understand it myself yet. Lucy is going to arrange that I have driving lessons, so that I can drive the taxis. What do you think to that?'

'I'm very impressed. I suppose it will make a change from driving the Hoover around the house. I actually think you will make a good driver, Lilly.'

'I hope that you're right.'

Lilly went back into the house and intensified her

cleaning work. Later in the afternoon Lucy brought in the schedule of her lessons. The first one was in two days' time and lessons were every day for three weeks. Lilly had no time to get used to the idea.

In the third week of August, Fred received a telephone call from the mechanical engineer at one of the large pits in Yorkshire which had used his company in the past.

'Can you help me, Fred? I've been trying to get in touch with your sales fellow, but he doesn't seem to be available. We want a hundred-ton bunker making and installing for our Coal Preparation Plant. It's a straightforward job, but we want it in a rush.'

'As you know,' responded Fred, 'we've been taken over by the Optinum Mining Company and there are a few changes taking place. They want all the sales to be handled by the sales team in Birmingham.'

'That's no bloody good, Fred. You know they'll be pissing about for weeks. They'll want drawings and site visits, and they won't strike a blow until we sign a contract with them. I've agreed with my manager that I would give the job to you and that you would manufacture and install it by the second week in September. Can't you sort it out, Fred? You know it's a straightforward job. You've made these bunkers before.'

'I'll have a word with our new manager, but he's not used to the type of work that we do. I'll get back to you when I get his reaction.'

Fred asked to see his new manager, Bob Green. His secretary said she would let Fred know when he was back in the office. 'Tell him it's a substantial order from one of the pits, which will be good for us.'

He was kept waiting for two hours before Bob Green was

available, and that was after he had been out to a long lunch.

'Now then, what is it, Fred?'

Fred explained all about the request and its implications, but Bob Green was sceptical.

'We need the expertise of the Birmingham team involved. They will know if the profit margins are right. We can't take on jobs that don't show a profit.'

'We did an identical bunker for another pit about six months ago. Tell your secretary to get the file out for that job. I know it made a very good profit.'

'Yes, but did it cover all the overheads?'

'Of course it did. Optinum wouldn't have paid the price they did for this company if we hadn't been making real profits.'

'Tell me the name of the engineer and the pit and I will get our sales team to go and see them.'

'That's no good. The engineer has told his colliery manager that we will manufacture the bunker and install it by the second week in September. I know that we can achieve that. But to do it on time I'd have to get the plans out and start organising the steel so that we can start manufacturing the bunker frame tomorrow. I'll ring the engineer up and tell him we can't do it.'

'That's a bit drastic, Fred. We need jobs to keep our order book full. But you don't want to be living off rush jobs all the time.'

'Rush jobs are our life-blood; that is what this business is. We're used to doing jobs for the pits faster than they can do them in their own workshops. We have a reputation of doing the impossible and still delivering on time. Our orders will dry up unless you pull your finger out.'

Fred marched out of the office. It crossed his mind that

he might get dismissed, but he realised that the firm would go under if Bob Green carried on as he had started. He was in a blazing temper when he got home.

He discussed the incident with Lucy and he was pleased that she agreed with what he'd done.

'So did you ring the pit and tell the engineer that you couldn't do the job?'

'No, I thought it was too late after I'd had finished with Bob Green. I'll ring him in the morning.'

'Can I make a suggestion?'

'Of course you can, Lucy. I'm open to any ideas.'

'I think you should see your new boss first thing in the morning and tell him you want to put your notice in. Tell him you see no future for the business with him in charge, so you want to get out. Tell him you have another job lined up. He might realise that if he makes a mess of his job in the first few weeks, his future could be at risk. You'll be giving him a choice — he either goes for that order for the bunker, or he loses you. That will test him.'

'I think I might try that approach, Lucy.'

Next morning, at breaksfast, Fred had a positive look on his face. He had a final comment for Lucy before he left for work.

'I might give you a ring and let you know how I get on.'

'Good. I expect to be around all day.'

Fred was waiting at Bob Green's office so that he could see him as soon as he arrived. Surprisingly, Bob Green arrived early, even before his secretary, who usually opened up the office.

Fred quietly explained his position. He noticed that Bob Green turned very pale. Lucy could have been right in her diagnosis of the new manager's position.

'I don't want you to leave us, Fred. We can't manage without you in the fabrication shop.'

'It's no use me being in the fabrication shop if we have no orders. My old boss always told me to be sniffing about for new orders every day. I could have gone to that pit yesterday afternoon and had an order for over £15,000 in my pocket. But you don't think like me. You are a big company man. You expect somebody else in the system to get the orders. But it won't happen. We deal with people we know and they trust us to deliver.'

'I've been thinking about what you said last night, Fred. We need that order. Can you get it for us at the same price as you did the last one? I checked the files yesterday evening and you were right, it did make a good profit.'

'I'll get out the plans for the previous bunker we made, and then we'll both go to the pit and see the mechanical engineer. I'm on holiday next week, but I know two men who will work so that all the steel is cut ready to be welded-up straight after the holiday. You need to understand these engineers at the pits, Boss. They work under immense pressure and the trouble is that most of their equipment is spread out underground in many miles of roadways and multiple coalfaces. Some of it is hellish difficult to get at.'

Lucy took a telephone call at lunchtime from Fred.

'You were right. He was worried. We've been to the pit and got the order. I'll be late home tonight, as I'll stay on sorting out the steel so that we can start work on it tomorrow. We need to work on it next week. Can you manage without me in Brighton?' he asked, though he was laughing as he said it.

'Fred Platt, you wouldn't dare!'

'Don't worry, Lucy, I've got two men laid on for the holiday week and they'll know what to do. I think my new boss learned a lot this morning. I'll try him for a bit longer.'

David Young had a word with Mavis to see if it was possible for him to have two hours off the next day to go to school and pick up his exam results.

'I'll fix it, David,' said Mavis. 'I am as keen as you are to know how you got on with your exams. I'll arrange for Elsie to man the fuel pumps. She's around tomorrow. Tell her what time you want to leave.'

The next day David went to school as planned. He came straight back to the garage and immediately went back to his job, without saying a word to anyone. When Elsie returned to the office from the kiosk, Mavis asked her about David's results.

'He didn't say. He just got on with his job as there were two pumps being used and one was a big fill-up for a lorry.'

'But this is important. I'll go and have a word with him.'

Mavis found David sitting in the kiosk looking at a sheet of paper with the list of his results.

'How did you do, David? Are you satisfied with the results?'

'I think I did pretty well,' he said, as he passed the paper over to Mavis. A car drove up to the pumps and David went out to fill it up. Mavis worked her way through the list. The results were good throughout, but the maths result was top grade. She went out to David.

'David, these are excellent! I'll deal with this customer, you go at once into the house and show your sister. She'll be thrilled.'

Mavis completed the fill-up.

It was a day of rejoicing at the garage. Lilly was dancing around and went immediately to see Lucy with the news. Lucy passed it on to Bob and she explained that David would be able to go into the sixth form and do any A-level subject he wanted. David was embarrassed with all the fuss, though he was extremely impressed when Elsie went round to the kiosk to offer her congratulations. She squeezed his arm and placed a quick kiss on his cheek before she dashed out.

In the afternoon, when Lilly went for another driving lesson, she still had a smile from ear to ear. She had an intensive hour of driving, with three-point-turns and emergency stops. Then she had a drive through Horsforth town centre, with lots of turns against oncoming traffic. She survived and she was starting to relax a little at the wheel.

'You did well today,' said her instructor when they finished. Lilly gave him a big smile. It had been a red letter day all round.

It was the day before the family holiday and Lucy was in her office having finished making the arrangements for her absence from Maxwell Motors. Bob called in and told her to go and get packed.

'You need this holiday, Lucy. Just forget about us for a week and enjoy yourself. How is Fred fixed for the holiday?'

'He's alright. He's been working late the last three nights. They got a rush job for one of the pits. He's not sure yet about his new boss, but we will see.'

Lucy was tidying up her desk when Mavis asked her to pop round to the general office, where the driver who covered the colliery bus service was waiting to see her.

'I'm sorry to bother you, Lucy, but Bill has been called in to have an operation next week on a serious hernia. He might be off two or three weeks.'

'Have we any driver who usually covers this job?'

'Yes, but I have another idea.' Mavis turned to the driver. 'You go now, Bill, I'll let you know who's going to cover your job next week.' When he had left, Mavis explained her idea to Lucy.

'What I wondered, and this is why I wanted a word with you, was why don't we ask Paul Benfield to do this job for a few weeks? I know he has not had his full three-month sabbatical; but this will test whether or not he is interested in the company. I really don't think he dare say no. What do you think?'

'I think it's a good idea, Mavis. Tell Bob I agree with Paul being approached. Get him to come and see you on Monday morning. If he says yes, arrange for him to have two days with the regular driver so that he understands the routes and the timings. We have had no complaints at all about that contract and we want to keep it that way.'

'That's fine, Lucy. I'll see Bob and sort it out.'

'It's all yours now, Mavis. I'm going to get my packing finished. We're going on an early train from Leeds station in the morning.'

'Elsie will take you to the station. Have a good holiday.'

Lucy relaxed when they were on the train from Leeds to London. She was in charge of the group and had all the tickets. She was dressed in a new outfit, but she was just carrying her handbag, as all the luggage was handled by Fred and the boys. She noticed the looks from other passengers who obviously saw her as a very smart, well-dressed lady who was being supported by a man and two boys. She reflected that it had been a good year since last year's holiday. Richard's school report had been good and his position in the form guaranteed that he would remain in the top stream in his third year. He was also due prizes for his performances for the rugby and cricket teams. Maxwell Motors was continuing to increase its performance and its profits. The only problem was Fred's job. In a way she would like Fred to be in charge of the maintenance of the Maxwell buses and coaches and she knew that he would be completely reliable in that role. Relaxing in her seat she closed her eyes and was soon asleep. Fred looked at the boys and motioned to them to talk softly so that Lucy could sleep peacefully.

Mavis saw Bob and he agreed that they should ask Paul Benfield to take over the colliery bus for a few weeks. The meeting with him lasted only a few minutes. When Mavis put the proposition to him, he just shrugged his shoulders and said,'Yes, that's okay.' Mavis then made arrangements for Paul to spend the two days with the regular driver so that he knew the routes and the times of each journey. Mavis looked across the office at Margaret and smiled.

'You have to remember to book him driving days from tomorrow, Margaret. I think he's come back into line very quietly.'

That was the start of a very busy week for Mavis. She was determined to take on Lucy's role fully and efficiently, but there were daily challenges. A spare driver had to be fetched into the garage in a rush to drive the double-decker service bus when the driver was taken ill. Elsie rang in from Harrogate to say that she had a puncture on the mini-coach. She was trying to change the wheel but she couldn't move two of the wheel studs. Bob went out to help her change the wheel and he took David from the fuel pumps with him to help. On the Wednesday a passenger on the south coast tour collapsed in the hotel. She was attended by a local doctor and when she had recovered he gave her medication but said she should rest and take it easy. Marion Stead rang Mavis and reported that the woman and her husband wanted to go back home to Leeds. They agreed that Marion would drive them back to the half-way service garage. Mavis gave Elsie a flask and some sandwiches and sent her in the taxi to bring the passengers home. Mavis herself took on Elsie's afternoon booking to take a group in the mini-coach on a shopping trip to York. On the Thursday morning mavis checked that Paul Benfield was carrying out the colliery service to the planned timetable, as it was his first day on that job. When she was preparing to go to the bank, later in the morning, she was surprised at the amount of cash to deposit. Margaret explained that it had been a very busy time on Wednesday afternoon with people booking tours and trips. A Club secretary paid in cash for three coaches to go to the illuminations in Blackpool.

'It was hectic, but we got through, Mavis,' concluded Margaret.

'Well, it was a real emergency yesterday, with the woman taken ill on the south coast tour. Elsie didn't get back until very late last night. She said that the clients were very appreciative of what we did to get them back home. She said that the woman didn't look well when she dropped them off at their house, so she thought they had done the right thing to get back home. Poor Elsie has had an early start as well this morning, with two taxi runs to the station.'

'Lucy will be pleased with us, I'm sure. I hope she's having a good holiday.'

Lucy was impressed with the hotel and the service her group received. They had an excellent table on the Friday night in the dining room. Fred thought it was a bit posh, but he liked the choice of food on the menu. Richard and Matthew seemed very relaxed and ordered their food from the head waiter without any guidance from the grown-ups, which impressed Lucy.

On the Saturday morning, Lucy saw off Fred and the boys in the taxi to the cricket ground, with their hampers. She'd briefly had a look at the food and thought it would be meet their approval, and there was plenty of it. The rest of her morning was spent touring the shops and spotting things to buy. After having a nice lunch, she returned to the shops to buy clothes for herself, two shirts for Fred and ties for the boys. She had really enjoyed herself. She also felt virtuous at being able to spend some money. She was amazed at how little of their income they were spending. The savings account at the bank was growing very quickly.

She packed away her clothes and decided to have a bath before the rest returned. She knew that Fred would be excited by a nightdress and some glamorous underwear she had bought.

On the train back to Leeds, Lucy wondered who would pick them up at the station, as she was aware that both Mavis and Elsie would be tied up at a wedding. When they got to the station entrance it was Bob who was waiting for them. He had brought the mini-coach, as the taxis were engaged.

Once they were on the road, Bob asked 'So how was the holiday, Lucy?'

'It was truly magnificent, Bob,' she replied. 'We lived in luxury and we've all had a memorable time. Fred and I have danced on four nights and that reminded us of our early days together. He's had to work hard to remember his old dancing skills, but he got quite good by the end of the holiday!'

'I think it was Lucy who had to work hardest,' replied Fred. 'She made a right mess of a tango on the first night.'

'The boys had an exciting week as well, didn't you?' she turned to Richard. He was glad to give his own view.

'We had three days at the Hove cricket ground watching the Sussex– Middlesex game. We saw two centuries scored and we got autographs of quite a few players. My mates in the cricket team at school will be jealous. The Members' pavilion, where we sat, had some famous old cricketers sitting near us, and there was a radio cricket commentator from the BBC there. It was quite something.'

'Dare I ask about Maxwell Motors during the last week?' asked Lucy, tentatively.

'You won't get an answer from me,' replied Bob. 'As far as I'm concerned you're on holiday until Monday morning. All I will say is that your team in the office has worked very well and that there have been no catastrophes.'

When they got out of the mini-coach they were met by Lilly. She'd made sure that the house was immaculate for them and she had the table laid for tea.

'What are you doing here, Lilly?' asked Lucy.

'David is on duty all day on the fuel pumps, so I came down to be a bit of company for him and I brought him some sandwiches. I wanted to check that the house was all in order for you.'

'You are spoiling me, Lilly. I've got to get back in harness on Monday morning.'

'Well you can leave all the clothes washing for me to sort out on Monday. I've finished all my driving lessons now, and my instructor helped me to fill in the application form for a test.'

'That's great news, Lilly. We'll have to arrange that you get some extra driving practice in, while you're waiting for your test. We'll put some L-plates on the van. I'll arrange for a few people to take you out for drives around the test routes.'

Both Lucy and Fred were in for a period of intensive work when they resumed their jobs on the Monday morning.

Fred got involved with the bunker manufacture and he stayed overtime with his men to complete the assembly in the workshop. When it was all marked-up and assembled he called the engineer at the pit and invited him to come and inspect it. He brought the colliery manager along with him. They were very impressed and assured Fred that the site was ready for the bunker installation. Fred arranged the strip down and transport it to the site where there would be a crane available to assemble it from the large sections. He was sure that this would allow them to beat the agreed completion date.

Lucy had to arrange the management committee meeting and then the board meeting in the first weeks of September.

The management committee noted the growth of the business reflected particularly in the increase in the number of passengers from the Harrogate area and bookings for the wedding taxis, which were exceeding availability.

At the board meeting, after noting the results, a discussion took place on the intensity of operations on the site now that there were ten coaches, two double-deckers, the colliery bus, the mini-coach and two taxis. It was agreed that the physical resources were now the limiting factor on expanding operations.

Bob led the discussion. 'When we built the new garage, which holds just eight buses or coaches, we thought it would be plenty big enough for all our needs,' he said. 'But now we have a much bigger fleet, and we also have more people using our fuel pumps. It all adds to the pressure on the site. I agree with Lucy, that our aim is to become more efficient with what we have, rather than thinking of expansion at this time. Any major expansion would really need a bigger garage and that could mean a new site.'

Mike Best advised that the company was accumulating quite a sizable investment portfolio from the operational profits and that while this would be available to fund expansion if it was thought desirable, it did make Maxwell Motors a financially attractive proposition for any company in the travel business seeking to expand. It was the first board meeting which offered no guidance on a strategic plan for the future.

Lucy set up a rota of people who could take Lilly out on the road to get experience in driving. One driver on the books had been an examiner for driving tests and knew the routes and the way of testing the applicants. Lucy made sure that he had a couple of sessions with Lilly before the test at the end of September. Mavis did a few runs and she was very confident that Lilly was making a good driver. She also tested her on the content she would be asked in the theory questions. By the time she took her test, Lilly was driving with confidence and assurance. She was able to give her examiner a charming smile when he joined her in the car. She passed without any problems, and the news was met with much rejoicing on the garage forecourt.

Sixteen

It was an exciting time for Lilly Young. David moved up into the sixth form, studying Chemistry, Physics and Mathematics. He had an intensive timetable with few free periods and lots of homework, but he seemed very happy. For herself, life was full of new challenges. Mavis was taking her out on a few occasions with taxi runs, emphasising to Lilly the importance of parking properly and the best way to welcome her passengers and take their bags or cases. She was fitted out in her driving outfit and her peaked cap and, looking in the mirror, Lilly had to admit that she looked quite smart.

Lucy had a word with Mr Higson and briefed him on Lilly's background. He was happy that Lilly would be allocated as his driver. Shortly after she started driving him, there was one week when he had three separate days in London, each requiring Lilly to take him for the early train in the morning and pick him up when he arrived back in the evening. Lilly blushed when a spray of flowers was delivered to the garage for her at the end of the week.

Lucy also arranged that Lilly should spend half a day each week in the office with Margaret, getting to know the office systems so that she could help out if it got very busy. After a very busy week, Lilly was amazed when she drew her weekly wage.

'Just look at this, David,' she said on the Friday night. 'Could you ever believe that I could be earning £30 in one week? We're getting rich now.'

'You're putting a lot of extra time in, though,' he replied, wisely.

'But my life is much more interesting now. It's still a thrill for me to drive the taxi. I think they've picked some of the best passengers for me.'

'Will you be driving one of the taxis for the weddings?'

'That's the idea, but nothing has been said about it up to now.'

'Mavis has sent me a note to see if I can do some Friday evenings and extra hours on Saturdays and Sundays on the fuel pumps. I've replied that I'll fit in with her needs. I like the extra pocket money.'

Lucy went to a home game for Leeds Grammar School Colts team on a Thursday afternoon. Fred couldn't get time off work as he was involved in a rush job in the fabrication shop. Lucy took her place on the touchline, having travelled there in the Maxwell van. She hadn't told Richard that she'd be watching the match. She was dressed in her boots, her warm coat with a fur collar, and a fur hat which she pulled down over her ears. She walked up and down the touchline to keep her feet warm. It was a surprise when Dr Poxon came up and joined her.

'I thought that you might be here, when I saw the

company van. We haven't seen you at matches so far this year, Lucy.'

'To be honest, as you learned at the board meeting, we're very busy at Maxwells and the more Mavis and Elsie are tied up with bookings for the taxis and the mini-coach, the harder it is for me to get away. Fred gets to some Saturday fixtures, so I do know how Richard is playing and how the team is performing.'

'Yes, they're doing very well. They've won every match so far. Richard is making a good captain and I think he will feature in rugby and cricket throughout his school career.'

The teams ran out onto the field and Richard was visibly surprised to see his mother on the touchline. She waved to him and he acknowledged it with a quick nod of his head. He then got down to the business of marshalling the team and directing the tactics. The two teams appeared to be equal in size and strength in the scrums; but the organisation and rugby skills of the teams were very unequal. The Leeds team knew what they were going to do and they carried out their plans with clinical precision. They'd soon scored two well-worked tries to give them a commanding lead. Richard kept pressure on his team and they continued to add points to their score. Near the end of the second half an infringement in a scrum near the Leeds line led to the opposition scoring a penalty kick. The final score was 46—3 for a Leeds win. Dr Poxon summed up the match to Lucy.

'I expected a win, but I was impressed with the way it was done. The boys are really working as a team and they help each other. It was nice to see you here, Lucy.'

'It's been a welcome break. I've really enjoyed it and I appreciated your company on the touchline. It can be a bit lonely for a fond mother to be cheering on her own '

She had a smile on her face as she drove back to the

garage, leaving Richard to travel back on the service bus. As captain, he had a job to do entertaining the opposing team to tea in the refectory.

In the general office, Margaret reported that everything appeared to be working to plan, so Lucy was able to review the bookings for the next few days. There were mid-week bookings for trips to the Blackpool Illuminations beginning to feature in the programme. One or two had originated from the agent in Harrogate, so Lucy decided to pay a visit to the agent, as she felt there was more potential business there.

Paul Benfield came to see Lucy in the middle of September.

'I've finished my stint on the colliery and school bus as the regular driver is starting work again next week. I wondered if it was possible for me to return as a regular driver?'

'Have you got into the swing of things again?' asked Lucy.

'Yes, I'm much happier driving rather than sitting around.'

'Can I take it that you're happy with the agreement between Maxwell Motors and Benfield Motors?'

'Yes, I signed the minutes of our meeting. Both Eva and myself appreciate that you've given us a second chance. We're now beginning to appreciate the financial benefits of the agreement.'

'We have plans for our business that require the full support of our staff at all times. I want you to be positive with the other drivers. Can I rely on that in the future?'

'Yes, Mrs Platt, you can. I will give my support at all times.'

Lucy gave him a long, hard stare before she replied. She wanted to be sure that this change of heart was permanent.

‘I will arrange with Margaret that you are back on the drivers’ rota from the first of October.’

‘Thank you.’ He was relieved that he had some good news to take to his wife. Eva had checked the money transferred over to Benfield from Maxwells each month and she’d shown him how much their finances had improved. Her views were clear.

‘We have to stick with Maxwell Motors, Paul’ Eva had said. ‘We can’t afford to leave them. You must get back driving and show them that you’re all for the agreement we’ve signed. No more slip-ups.’

Well this was a start, Paul thought, as he drove home.

Two days later, Fred came home with a warning message. Bob Green had been called down to the head office of Optinum Mining to see about some new plans for the Leeds site. He hadn’t arrived back when Fred reached the end of his shift and came home.

‘I just have a feeling, Lucy, that they’re going to make some big changes. We’ve been doing quite well in the fabrication shop, but I’ve heard that the casting business is short of orders.’

‘Don’t worry, Fred,’ replied Lucy. ‘You know that you can get out and work for Maxwell Motors at any time. We might need you because I’ve had another problem with the maintenance company. It may have just been a clerical error, but they included a claim on an invoice for work on a coach that was in Scarborough all day. Their manager rang me and apologised, after Mavis had rung up and refused to pay the invoice. I left him with a clear impression my patience was running out.’

The next day, Fred was called into Bob Green’s office to be briefed on the changes that were to be introduced.

Optinum Mining had obtained a large order for conveyor equipment for a coal mine in South Africa. It had been agreed to let some of the casting work be carried out at the Yorkshire site, but all the assembly of the equipment was to be done in the fabrication shop. It would give three months' work for the shop. When Fred asked how they would carry out their normal work for the Yorkshire mines, Bob Green said that they would fit it in if they could. However that wasn't the main issue, as far as Fred was concerned. It had been decided to send an engineer from Birmingham to have responsibility for the conveyor assembly contract.

'We do not want to lose you, Fred," Bob Green had stated, but he knew that Fred was being by-passed. Fred surmised that it was also likely that the specialist jobs for the coal mines would be abandoned and his response to Bob Green was simple.

'We'll see, but I think it's unlikely that I will be working here much longer.'

When he got home he had a long talk with Lucy. She was quite clear in her mind that Fred should put his notice in and she would arrange that he would be employed full-time at Maxwell Motors, with responsibility for maintenance work on all their fleet. By the next day, Bob was in full agreement with Lucy's plan. He said he would seek out all the maintenance documents for the different buses and coaches.

'I've suspected for a while that we were not getting everything done by the young lads who did the work,' said Bob, when Lucy told him of Fred's new role. 'I have an oil can in the garage for oiling some of the doors and catches that were squeaking for want of oil.'

'You should have told me, Bob. I enjoyed leaning on their manager. I am sure when Fred gets settled down he will do a first-class job. He'll be useful for looking after other equipment on the site.'

'It sounds like you have plenty of plans to keep him busy.'

'He likes a challenge at his work. I'll let him work under you on all the maintenance work, Bob. It will be better if you are his boss.'

That night Lucy took home a number of maintenance books for the buses, coaches and taxis and she explained that there were more to follow.

Fred put his notice in and left Wilkins two weeks later. When he started with Maxwell Motors he studied the reports for each vehicle in the maintenance records before preparing a schedule to have each vehicle out of service for a day or part-day so that he could work on it in the garage. Margaret marked in her forward diary which day each vehicle was required for maintenance.

'We now have a system of planned maintenance,' she reported to Lucy.

'For some time I've been sure that the servicing of our fleet was a weak part of our operations,' replied Lucy. 'That might all change now.'

As expected, Fred got involved in other aspects of the garage operations. He stripped down the hoses and filters on the pressure sprayer used for cleaning the vehicles. It was much more effective after that service. Bob suggested that Fred should train Brian Hunt on some aspects of the maintenance programme as the lad was showing great interest. When Lucy heard this she told Fred that if Brian showed genuine interest, she would pay for him to go to nightschool and get some qualifications. When Brian was told of this proposal his eyes were wide in shock.

'But I was no good at schooling. I don't think I could do

the studying,' he said with a despairing look.

When Lucy heard this, she had a word with Mavis. 'You have a word with him, Mavis, please. I'll bet he had a bad teacher at school. Spend a bit of time with him, and give him some tuition in reading and writing.'

So Mavis took on another teaching project. She invited Brian to her house to have privacy with no competition from brothers and sisters or parental opposition. He needed help with spelling, and more practice at expressing his thoughts in words. Over a period of two months she met him and left him with writing exercises to complete. She always gave him them in an envelope and asked him to return them to her in the general office in the sealed envelope. At the end of the period she reported to Lucy that she thought Brian would be able to enter a Technical College course with reasonable confidence in the next academic year.

Lucy visited Leslie Fortune, the manager of Priestley Travel Agency which was marketing Maxwell Motors tours in Harrogate. It was a small office in a back-street of the town, run by a young man with three female assistants. Lucy had never been in the office before. She noticed that the posters for the Maxwell Motors tours needed updating. Her main concern, though, was that the office was really too small and there was not enough room for the girls to talk to the customers with any element of privacy. She spoke to the girls and found them keen, with the right charm for dealing with customers.

She went into Leslie's very small office to extend her discussions.

'I think that you've done a good job for us in starting to extend our business into this area, but I think we can grow much more in Harrogate and Knaresborough. However I'm sure you would benefit from a bigger office and a smarter one. I want you to come over to our office and bring one of your girls with you.'

'I know we could do with a better office, but the owner of the travel agency doesn't have the financial scope for us to move to bigger premises.'

'Just come over and see us, and we'll be able to discuss the options.'

They arranged for the visit to Horsforth in two days' time. Lucy had a word with Bob as soon as she returned to the garage.

'I think I see an opportunity to expand our business.' She explained that Priestley's office needed to be more central in the town and much bigger and more luxurious. To achieve this it would need Maxwell Motors to take the initiative. 'I'll let you know how I get on.'

Leslie Fortune and one of his staff came over to the garage and Lucy gave them a detailed brief about the company. She showed them one of the coaches and the two wedding taxis which were parked there. They visited the general office which was the nerve centre of the operations and introduced them to Margaret. She took particular care to show them the area adjacent to the general office, where people making bookings could sit and have a cup of coffee while someone was sorting out the details.

'This is where we can treat customers as someone special, and make them confident to travel with us. I think that you need the space to allow you to do the same. You should have a bigger unit and it should ideally be nearer the town centre. It needs to be designed to attract some of the more wealthy folk of Harrogate. I'd like you to bring your owner here so that we can talk about some form of joint venture.'

'We know that we're bursting at the seams in our present accommodation and your tours have been a welcome addition to our range of UK holidays, but when I've discussed new premises, our owner has no interest, as he doesn't have the capital to expand.'

'Please bring him here and let me talk to him. We have the capital to work with you, and we know how to manage expansion in our tourism field.'

The travel agent owner and Leslie Fortune came over to see Lucy and Bob a week later but it was an inconsequential meeting. The owner wasn't prepared to take any financial risks at all. He wanted to hang on to what income was coming from the agency and he showed only little concern when Lucy said that if he was not interested, she would seek an agreement with another travel agent in Harrogate. Leslie whispered in his ear the drastic effect such a move would have on their business.

Lucy decided to play a waiting game. She told Bob she would look at properties of the right size and in the right location in Harrogate, and she would come forward with a design and a financial proposition. She set herself the task of having a detailed proposition available by Christmas.

At the management committee meeting in November the agenda was more varied than usual. Mike Best gave detailed figures for the wedding business. 'The wedding service is a significant business in its own right, now,' said Mike.

'I didn't realise you were charging as much as that for dressing-up in your fancy outfits, Mavis,' said George Clay, with a smile.

'There are surcharges for glamour and style, as well as the driving,' responded Mavis.

The maintenance of the fleet and all the garage equipment by Fred was highlighted. and George Clay added his views on that. 'I can tell you that the drivers are all in favour of this change. They know that they can now report any minor problems with the coaches or buses and it will be sorted out straightaway. They were never sure about the old system of leaving written notes.'

Lucy used the meeting to explain her policy of developing staff. 'It's my aim to develop all our staff so that they can take on more responsibilities which will benefit both them, and Maxwell Motors. We did it with the drivers so that quite a number of them have become driver/managers on our tours. Mavis has been trained so that she can take over from me when I am away. Running this company is a complex job and it needs a lot of detailed planning; Margaret does a lot of that in the office. But when things go wrong someone has to make quick decisions to take action to get things back on plan. There are thousands of people who travel with us now, so we need to communicate well with them, as we're trying to extend that number.'

Lucy went on to explain her meeting with Priestley's travel agency in Harrogate. She was asked some questions, but she wouldn't expand on the details, though she promised to brief the management committee at its next meeting.

The final item on the agenda was the Christmas bonus for all employees. Bob proposed that the bonuses should be the same as the previous year and this was agreed unanimously. Lucy said that she didn't mind if this information was passed on to the workforce, as she wanted their full co-operation in the busy Christmas period.

Lucy had spent several visits to Harrogate touring the town and looking for a suitable site to establish a travel agency. Eventually she found one. It was on a main shopping street, near the railway station. The advantage of the location, she saw, was that many people arriving by train would pass the travel agency as they walked towards the town centre and Betty's famous teashop. The building extended well back from the street. She contacted the estate agent and expressed an interest. She then visited the property with a specialist in shop design. She explained what she had in mind and sent him away to prepare a schematic picture of his proposal within the next week.

When Lucy received the illustrations she was thrilled. There was a room at the back which could be used by the manager; there was also a kitchen, where tea or coffee could easily be made; the open-plan office was laid out with luxurious seating and the positions of the agents were separated from each other by glass partitions, which gave an intimacy between themselves and the clients. Along one side of the office were display boards to hold brochures about holidays and tours and the window at the front was large and would allow space to display special offers. Lucy showed the illustrations to Mavis and to Bob and they were just as impressed as Lucy had been.

'How do we proceed, from a business point of view?' asked Bob.

'We have two options,' she replied thoughtfully. 'We could establish it as a travel agency under the Maxwell name. If we did that, I would have to recruit some experienced staff. That might not be diffifficult as the staff in the travel agency we are working with would probably jump at the chance to work in premises like these. The other option is to offer the existing travel agency owner preferential terms for his staff to move in and carry on expanding their business. I would prefer the second option, but I would want the owner to show a bit more enthusiasm than he did when I met him last time. I'll go over to Harrogate and show these illustrations to Leslie Fortune and his staff to get them excited at the thought of such a move.'

'We can leave it to you to get the best deal for Maxwell Motors, Lucy, using your extensive skills of pressure and persuasion,' concluded Bob with a knowing smile.

'I'm not keen to take on a new business like a travel agency,' said Lucy, quite seriously. 'We are good at running a bus and coach business. I would like us to stick to that.'

The week before Christmas there was a large wedding for the daughter of a wealthy Leeds family and the logistics for transport were extensive. It involved the two taxis, the mini-coach and a coach. The reception was in a large hotel on the outskirts of Leeds and a significant number of guests were staying in the hotel overnight. Maxwells had to provide transport from the hotel to the church, and then, after the wedding service, transport back to the hotel. A full-sized coach was provided to take most of the guests but, to transport some senior family members, the mini-coach and the two taxis had to do a run each way as well. It was an ordeal for Lilly who, for the first time, would be driving the number two taxi. Mavis was on the number one taxi, Elsie on the mini-coach and a normal driver on the coach.

Lilly had done a practice run between the hotel and the church and between the bride's house and the church, but she was still nervous on the Saturday morning and expressed her reservations to Mavis and Lucy.

'Don't worry, Lilly,' said Lucy. 'Mavis is very experienced at wedding arrangements. She'll look after you.'

'Just keep that gorgeous smile on your face and the passengers will fall in love with you,' added Mavis.

'I'll try,' replied Lilly.

'You look wonderful in your outfit,' said Elsie. 'I'll have the difficult job of getting fat ladies with big hats into their seats on the mini-coach without them spoiling their outfits! You won't have that problem with the taxi.'

In the end, the plan worked very well. The bride arrived at the church an acceptable three minutes late and all the transport arrangements worked as planned. At the end of the evening, when the bride and groom returned to the hotel dressed to leave on their honeymoon, all their guests gathered outside to wave them off. The best man went up to Mavis, who was at the taxi door, and slipped ten pounds into her hand.

'You have done us all a great service. Everything has gone like clockwork.'

'Thank you,' replied Mavis. 'I've just to get the bride and groom to Manchester airport. They will be able to have a nap in the car going over the hills.'

'Just keep your eye on the groom. He's a bit of a lad. He might not want to have a nap on the journey.'

Mavis closed the door and took her place at the wheel. She drove off and the groom gathered his wife into his arms for a long cuddle. Mavis concentrated on the road. It had been a long day.

The Christmas break was a relief for Lucy and for Fred, too, this year. He often went into the garage to check that the buses and coaches were leaving on time. He was trying to give Lucy some practical support so that she could spend more time in the house. Lucy had begun to wonder how she had managed before Fred left his job.

Maxwell Motors was busy over the Christmas period, 1966. They ran a limited bus service on Christmas Day, starting at nine o'clock and finishing twelve hours later, with the last double-decker bus from the centre of Leeds. On Boxing Day there was a full programme of football matches and entertainment, so both double-deckers were in use all day. Lucy was amazed when she counted the money taken on the service buses on Boxing Day. There was no doubt that the service by Maxwell buses was appreciated by the local population, as some other companies ran only limited services.

There were also several bookings for both the taxis. Elsie covered the daytime bookings for the number two taxi on Christmas Day, while Lilly covered the bookings on Boxing Day. Some wealthy young people specifically booked the wedding taxi to take them to night clubs and fetch them back in the early hours of the morning. Mavis always took these bookings, as she didn't want Elsie or Lilly to have to face up to passengers who had been drinking heavily. She always inspected everyone getting into the taxi for the return journey to identify anyone who looked as though they might be taken ill on the way home. If this was the case she sent them back to the toilets, accompanied by another member of the party. Lucy was apprehensive of these bookings but Mavis justified them by the very high charges they were able to make.

Lucy laid on a Christmas Day lunch for eight people: Mr and Mrs Senior and their son Matthew, her own family of three and then Lilly and David. Lilly was strictly a guest, but she was there all morning helping Lucy prepare the food. It was a standard Christmas meal, with all the trimmings, timed so that they could watch the Queen make her speech at three o'clock. There was a lot of talk about the success of the three boys in their studies, and then Richard had to answer questions about the success of the Colts team at the Leeds Grammar School.

The afternoon ended with a tea of ham and pork pies, with a tomato salad, followed by trifle with cream. The

Seniors left after tea, and Lilly and David left after Lilly had completed all the washing-up. Soon Lucy fell asleep in front of the television, so Fred turned the sound down and Richard went up to his bedroom to read. Lucy woke up after over two hours' deep sleep. Fred suggested that they go to bed and Lucy didn't argue. She snuggled up to him in the new nightdress that Fred had bought her for Christmas.

'I am so fortunate,' she said. 'I have so many people to support me. And you, Fred Platt, are a wonderful husband. You keep me going and lift me up when I get tired.' He cuddled her until she went back to sleep.

'What a woman,' he thought to himself 'And she is my wife. Surely life can't continue as good as this.'

In the first week of 1967 Lucy arranged a meeting with the owner of Priestley Travel Agency. She knew that the Harrogate staff were thrilled by the proposals she'd shown them, but she wasn't sure if the owner would be interested.

The meeting took place in Lucy's office. She was surprised when the owner appeared with his wife, as well as Leslie Fortune, the manager. Lucy was supported by Mavis, as Bob was out driving. She began by laying out the schematic pictures for the shop. The owner's wife was very impressed with the ideas and spoke positively. So Lucy moved on to the financial options. She looked straight into the eyes of the owner.

'You are no doubt wondering about the commercial possibilities?'

'Yes, I am. It will cost some significant money to set this up.'

'This development will be financed by Maxwell Motors so we will own the lease on the property. We will require you to pay the same rent as you are paying now with your existing shop. So you are getting a bargain. Our objective is to expand the Maxwell business in the Harrogate area, so our payback will be in the agency fees for the business you sell on our behalf. In each quarter of the year I will want twenty-five percent of the business free of agency commission.' She saw a look of horror on the owner's face. 'But for the rest of the business in each quarter we will pay you one percent more than our current agreement with you. So if you expand our business you will not lose out. Can you accept this proposal for the first year? We can then review it.'

Lucy noted that Leslie gave a small positive nod of his head to the owner. The owner's wife was interested in the timescale of the development.

'When do you think the conversion will be complete?', she asked.

'All the plans are ready and an experienced builder has been briefed, so I would expect the changeover to take place by early March. I must tell you that Maxwell will go ahead with this project irrespective of yourselves. We are sure that we can get a deal with another travel agency if you aren't interested.'

'Oh, but we are interested,' the owner's wife jumped in. 'We see this as giving us a chance to expand our sales significantly.'

'We will need the Maxwell business to do that,' chipped in Leslie. 'But I see very large opportunities to increase the Maxwell commissions in the future.'

'So you're happy for me to get an agreement drawn up on the terms I have quoted?' said Lucy. The owner agreed.

The following day Lucy gave instructions to the architect to commission the work, and to the Maxwell solicitor to finalise the lease of the building. She then had a meeting with Bob and Mavis.

'I want to discuss with you a new initiative that I think is available with the Harrogate travel agency. We have a chance for a new type of tour, centred on Harrogate clients. It will be an all-inclusive luxury tour. We need a coach, Bob, with around forty luxury seats and facilities for a courier to serve refreshments to the passengers. They will have the best rooms in hotels and visits to exceptional homes and gardens, preferably ones not open to the public. My idea is to set up the first tour to Edinburgh in April.'

Mavis was dispatched to Edinburgh to plan a detailed, all-inclusive, six-night, weekly tour. It would offer a significant booking for a hotel to have a regular weekly commitment from Maxwell Motors and Mavis said she would investigate using the same Edinburgh hotel for the mini-tours, but using cheaper rooms and alternative restaurant facilities. Mavis had evidence of hotels on the south coast successfully carrying out such an arrangement.

The management committee meeting in late January had a long agenda with several items of new business. Bob spoke about the improvement in the maintenance work since Fred had taken it over and George Clay agreed with this report on behalf of the drivers. Lucy described the improved facilities for people visiting the garage to make bookings and that the office had been redecorated by Fred. Lucy displayed the plans for the travel agency in Harrogate and outlined the commercial agreement with the current travel agent to use the facilities.

Lucy also introduced the concept of a new grade of luxury tour starting in April. It would be for six nights, in Edinburgh, leaving each week from Harrogate on Saturday morning and returning on Friday evening. Mavis took up the explanation with the details of the all-inclusive tours.

Bob showed the layout of the new luxury coach which would have only forty seats, each with lots of leg room and a table to hold drinks and refreshments.

'It seems to me that these tours are designed for wealthy folk who want to put on weight,' quipped George Clay.

'That might be true, George,' replied Lucy. 'And there will be a courier on each coach to make sure every one has an unforgettable trip.' She added that the charge for each place on the tour would be determined after all the costs were known, but it would be significantly higher, as a rate per day, than the other Maxwell tours. However, she quoted the rates per day charged by other up-market tours run by some coach companies and she said she expected to be competitive compared with their rates.

Over lunch after the meeting, Mike Best asked when the new Priestley's travel agency would be in operation.

'I visited it yesterday and the work is well advanced,' replied Lucy. 'I expect the staff to move to the new site by the end of February and be fully operational by the first of March. We've already discussed an advertising campaign, in March, about these luxury tours, and the coach should be delivered in March.'

'You don't waste much time when you get a new idea, do you, Lucy,' said George Clay, who was listening to the conversation.

'You're right, George. We want to get established in the market before another Yorkshire company comes up with the same idea.'

After lunch, the committee went to the general office and inspected the new decorations and furniture. They didn't stay long, as Elsie was discussing a booking with a client for a south coast tour in March, for four people. They returned to Lucy's office before they dispersed.

'That was an interesting conversation you might have overheard in the general office,' said Lucy. 'Last year we had waiting lists for any cancellations on many tours which became fully booked. We've been trying to get the message around this year for people to book early to avoid disappointment. It's obviously working because Margaret tells me that we have many more firm bookings this year than we had at the same time last year.'

'She never misses a trick,' said George Clay to Mike Best.

'You're quite right,' replied Mike.

Seventeen

It was the last week in February, and Lucy decided to go and check on progress with the new travel agency. She'd approved a new display sign over the premises, reading 'Maxwell Motors and PRIESTLEY TRAVEL AGENTS'. She conceded the capital letters so that customers realised who was running the travel agency.

The final touches were being made to the furnishings and the telephones were being connected to the four sales positions. Staff were filling the racks of travel books and brochures along one side of the office. Leslie Fortune's room at the back, and another side office, provided the option to invite clients to move there if the main room became crowded. The development was creating significant interest to the passing public, with many people stopping to peer through the window.

Leslie arrived to meet Lucy, as she had requested. He was also excited by the public reaction. He explained that all the office equipment would be moved over so that the agency was fully operational by the following Monday.

'That's good,' said Lucy. 'Why don't you put a big notice in the window stating the opening day and your office hours?'

'I'll arrange that straightaway,' he replied enthusiastically.

'It should encourage some of these passers-by to drop in on your first day.'

On the Monday morning, Lucy was challenged by Richard.

'Mum, I was hoping that you'd be supporting me next Saturday.'

'Is it a special match, Richard?'

'It's a needle match. We're playing Bradford Grammar School, in Bradford. We've won every match so far this season, and so have Bradford. So this will be the deciding match that shows which team is the best. Can't you drive the coach, so that you're working at the same time as you're supporting our team?'

'If you want me at the match I'll arrange to drive the coach, and we'll make sure that Dad is also there to support you.'

'Thanks, Mum. We usually win when you are on the touchline.'

Lucy went to work conscious that she had a problem to resolve. She was sure that both Mavis and Elsie had a wedding on Saturday, so they couldn't cover the garage and the general office. The final solution was that Margaret covered the office, Bob would be available around the forecourt and Lilly would cover the fuel pumps. This meant that Fred could take David Young with him to the match in the Maxwell van.

Lucy left it until Monday afternoon before going over to Harrogate to see how the travel agency's first day was progressing. Two of the girls had clients, so she went through into the Manager's office.

'How are things working out, Leslie?'

'Very well,' he replied. 'We've had far more customers today than we did in the old office on a Monday.'

'Yes, but have they been buying, or just looking round?'

'Oh, they've definitely been buying.'

'Have they been buying any Maxwell tours?'

'They have, for sure. I know of one booking for six people on a south coast tour, and another for four people on a mini-tour. There might have been others that I don't know about yet.'

'How do you tie in with Margaret to avoid over-booking on tours that are nearly full?'

'I'll ring her every day and she'll tell me which tours are nearly full. We'll then give the staff a list of these tours and before they finalise any booking they'll ring Margaret to confirm that there are still places. Margaret really knows her job.'

'Yes, she's very good. When we launch the luxury tours centred on Harrogate, you'll control the lists for each tour. So Margaret will need to ring you on any tour that is getting fully booked. Have you had any questions about the luxury tours today?'

'Yes, the girls have had a few queries. They've handed out the fliers detailing when the tours will be on sale.'

'So I can go back to Horsforth and report that the agency is in business?'

'You certainly can,' Leslie concluded.

On the Saturday afternoon Lucy parked the coach at the school in Leeds. There was a crowd of players and masters milling around, before Dr Poxon, who was in charge, gave instructions to pack players onto the seats. In the end, there were several players crouched on the floor of the aisle. Lucy realised that she would be carrying nearly seventy passengers on the coach.

As soon as she parked at the Bradford playing fields she got out and went round to wish Richard 'good luck' as he went to the changing rooms. As the last of the passengers were leaving, Fred drove up in the Maxwell van and parked behind the coach. Dr Poxon suggested that they sit and wait in the coach as it would be half an hour before the teams came out onto the field. Dr Poxon chatted with David about his O-level results and the subjects he was taking in the sixth form. Lucy chipped in that David also worked occasionally at the Maxwell garage on the fuel pumps.

'You seem to employ all your friends in jobs at the garage, Lucy. Is that your policy?'

'Yes it is. I like to encourage young people to work in their spare time. I think it helps them to focus on the hard work that's necessary to make a success of their studies at school.'

When the teams came out onto the field, it was surprising to see how many supporters for each side had gathered at the field being used for the Colts' match.

The game kicked-off and, from the start, it was clear that neither team was prepared to concede any ground to their opponents. Every attack by either side was stopped by fearless play and not one player hesitated before throwing his body into tackles, regardless of the bumps and bruises that they might receive. Much of the game was played, backwards and forwards, in the middle third of the field. It looked as though there would be no score as the game approached half-time, but then a Bradford player missed a tackle on the Leeds winger and he advanced thirty yards towards the Bradford line. He was backed up by his forwards and they managed to score a try in the corner. It was not converted, but the Leeds team was in the lead at half-time.

During the half-time break, the masters in charge of both teams encouraged the players to continue playing with complete commitment. The game would be settled by the team which had the strength and discipline to play at full power through to the final whistle, they said.

In the second half, the game followed the same pattern of solid defence that had applied in the first half. But then the game changed and there was a period of intense pressure by the Bradford team in the Leeds half and, with only a few minutes to go, Bradford scored a try. It wasn't converted, so the scores were level.

'It's all to play for in the final minutes of the game,' said Dr Poxon, looking at his watch.

Two minutes later, Richard tackled a Bradford player and, while he was laid on the ground, another Bradford player, following up, stuck his boot out and caught Richard on the side of his head. The contact was clearly seen — and heard— by all the spectators. There were cries of foul from the crowd, and the referee blew his whistle to stop the game. Richard lay on the ground and didn't move. The first-aid staff from both teams ran onto the field and immediately a doctor supporting the Bradford team on the touchline was called onto the field. He took one look at Richard and called for a stretcher. Two staff members ran to the pavilion and returned as fast as possible with the stretcher. A crowd was gathering around Richard, so the spectators couldn't see clearly what was happening. Lucy was in shock and desperately she turned to Fred.

‘Richard is badly injured. He’s not moving. What can we do, Fred?’

‘Come here, Lucy,’ he said, taking her in his arms and holding her so that she couldn’t see onto the field. ‘Just stay calm. The experts are on the job. We have to leave it to them.’

Fred saw that they lifted Richard onto the stretcher very carefully. The doctor crouched down again by the stretcher, examining Richard. Presumably Richard started to come round for, after another two minutes, the doctor looked across at the crowd and gave a thumbs-up sign. They lifted up the stretcher to carry it across to the pavilion. The match referee gave a big blast on his whistle to indicate full-time, having decided it wasn’t appropriate to resume the game. So the final result was a draw, which most spectators considered a fair result.

Fred took charge of things. He asked Dr Poxon to take Lucy back to the coach while he went with David across to the pavilion to see Richard. He promised to send David back with a message as soon as he got the latest position from the doctor. Dr Poxon took Lucy’s arm and slowly walked her across to the coach. He was concerned that she looked very pale and frightened.

‘Will you be alright driving the coach back to Leeds, Lucy?’ he asked.

‘I’ll certainly be alright if Richard is recovered enough to be able to travel.’

They’d been sitting on the coach for ten minutes when David came running over to them, gasping for breath.

‘Mr Platt says I’m to tell you that Richard is slowly coming round. The doctor has examined him again and thinks he will be alright, but he’ll need to rest overnight. He also said that he’ll need a further examination by a doctor tomorrow. Mr Platt is going to stay and help Richard to get cleaned up and changed. He might decide to take Richard straight home in the van.' He paused for breath. 'I'm going back to help.'

'Thank you, David. That is good news. I feel very relieved now.'

'Well, what you need now is a drink of tea, Lucy,' said Dr Poxon. 'Come on, we'll go across to the dining room.'

This time they walked much faster and in the dining room Dr Poxon gave a sign to the staff and two cups of tea were immediately brought over to them. The colour slowly began to return to her face once Lucy had drunk her tea. When the first members of the Leeds teams started to leave the dining room, Lucy and Dr Poxon went back and Lucy open up the coach. It became clear that there would be fewer passengers for the trip back to Leeds as several players were travelling home with their parents. The coach party was nearly complete when they saw Richard slowly coming towards them. He was helped by Fred on one side and David on the other. He looked quite weak and very pale. Lucy went to meet them.

'I am taking Richard straight back home, Lucy,' said Fred. 'I want to get him settled in bed where I can keep an eye on him. You take the coach back to the school and then come and join us. I'll look after him. I'm sure he's going to be alright.' Richard didn't speak as they manoeuvred him carefully into the van. Lucy was relieved that they had both been present at the match.

She parked at the school and the teams got out and collected all their kit. Dr Poxon had a word with her before she drove away.

'Well done, Lucy,' he said as he squeezed her arm. 'You have been very brave. Richard is a strong lad, and I am sure he will be alright.'

Back at the garage Lucy had a quick word with Margaret

and Bob. They'd already seen Fred and David helping Richard out of the van, so they knew that something was wrong. In the house, she went straight up to Richard's bedroom. He was already in bed and Fred was attending to him.

'I'd like him to have a drink of tea, but he says he feels sick,' said Fred. 'So I've put him a bowl on the chair beside the bed.'. Richard had his eyes closed and he was still very pale. There were the first signs of a bruise and swelling on his head and one of his eyes.

'We'll have to keep a close watch on him through the night,' said Lucy.

Lucy took on the major part of that watching role. For most of the time Richard was asleep, but on two occasions he became very agitated. Lucy held his hands and tried to calm him. She wondered if he was re-living the incident. Fred took over from Lucy in the very early morning and they were both impressed by the improvement in Richard when he eventually woke up. He had a light breakfast but Fred and Lucy insisted that he stay in bed until the doctor had examined him. The doctor came just before lunchtime and he gave Richard a thorough examination before concluding that there were no serious problems. He said that Richard would be sporting an ugly lump on his head, and a black eye, for a few days. When Richard got up he looked at himself in the bathroom mirror and was quietly impressed by the angry look of his injuries. He hoped that they would look the same when he went back to school on Monday morning. His parents insisted that he had a quiet day on the Sunday and David Young did his planned time on the garage fuel pumps.

Lucy returned to her duties with a sense of relief that Richard was alright and back at school. Maxwell buses and coaches were busy and the reports from the travel agency were very positive, with a big increase in business compared with their old office. Lucy reflected that prospects were good and her only pressing priority now was to finalise the launch of the luxury tours from Harrogate for when the new coach was delivered. She couldn't have been further from the truth.

Lucy received a telephone call, from Bob, late on Tuesday evening.

'Lucy, we need to meet first thing tomorrow morning. I don't want to discuss it now, but something has cropped up which could have a major effect on Maxwell Motors.' She detected that Bob was stressed and didn't want to say any more.

'Right, Bob, we'll meet in my office first thing tomorrow. Goodnight.'

'She turned to Fred, who was watching television.

'That was strange. It was Bob on the telephone and he sounded very upset. He says that something's cropped up which could have a major effect on the business.'

'It might be that someone has put a bid in and is trying to buy Maxwells. Come on, Lucy, turn the television off. Let's get you to bed to have some sleep so that you're fresh in the morning.'

'Okay, Fred,' she replied, but she knew that her sleep would be affected by her thoughts about what Bob might tell her in the morning.

Lucy was settled in her office early and she told Margaret and Mavis that she would be having an important meeting with Bob. When Bob came into her office ten minutes later, he looked tired as he sat down opposite her and held his head in his hands. Lucy didn't say anything to him, but waited for him to speak first. After a few moments he lowered his hands and looked straight at her.

'This is a very terrible situation, Lucy. I'm finding it very difficult to decide what to do. I need your help.'

'Tell me what has happened, Bob, and of course I'll help you if I can.'

'I had a visit yesterday evening from an old friend of mine, Joe Lidgett, who set up Lidgett Motors. They run the service from Otley into Leeds city centre. He's now a shadow of the man he was. He has not been involved directly in the company for a few years; it's been run by his son and daughter-in-law. The company is in serious financial trouble and the police are involved. His son and his wife are likely to be charged with misappropriation of funds, and could go to jail. It's a messy business.'

'What did Joe want you to do?'

'He needs £50,000 to put into the company accounts to replace the money that's missing. And he needs that money within the next forty-eight hours to prevent legal proceedings. He would sell us the company for the £50,000, plus another £15,000 to be paid later.'

'That's a tall order for us to arrange. But what do you want to do, Bob?'

'I would like to help Joe, if we can. You see, Lucy, Joe started with buses – charabancs, in fact — before we did. I knew him fairly well in those days. He saw us and persuaded us to buy our first charabanc to replace our horse-drawn carriages. He was so confident that this was the right thing to do that he lent us £1,000 to get us started. That was a lot of money in those days, and we paid him back without paying any interest. That was really the start of Maxwell Motors.'

'Why has his business gone so wrong?'

'His son and daughter-in-law have lived the high life. They've spent freely and milked the bus company of its cash. Joe is heartbroken by what has happened. It really hurt me to see how he was affected.'

'Tell me about the Otley route. Could it be a profitable business for us?'

'It could be, Lucy. It really runs parallel to our route into Leeds, pasings through Bramhope, Adel, Weetwood, Headingley and Woodhouse, and then on to the city centre. It goes past the university, and several of their halls of residence are on the route. Some of the route is covered by other bus companies, but Lidgett are running a half-hourly service.'

'What does the company consist of?'

'They have a garage in Otley, which is big enough to hold their fleet of four double-decker buses. I think they're old buses, not like ours.' Bob could see that Lucy was turning over in her mind the possibility of buying the Lidgett company.

'Bob, if you feel that we should help your old mate, I think we should go for it. But we have to make a plan. Firstly, we need to go and talk to our bank manager. I'll ring him in a few minutes.' She rang Mavis and asked her to come into the office.

'Mavis, I want you to drop everything to do a bit of research for me. It's very confidential, but I want you to go into town and travel out to Otley on the Lidgett bus service. Then ride back on a different bus. I'll want to see you this afternoon with your impressions.'

Lucy rang the bank and asked to speak to the manager. She was told he was tied up in meetings all morning, but she switched on her charm and persuaded his secretary to re-arrange his diary so that they could meet for half an hour immediately after lunch. Lucy stressed that it was a significant opportunity for Maxwell Motors.

Lucy then set out, with Bob, to plan a positive approach with the bank manager.

'We know that we have a successful route with our Horsforth service buses. If we adopt the same standards with the Otley route we should be able to repeat that success.'

'Yes, but we have new double-deckers on the Horsforth route, Lucy. They don't.'

'We'll need new double-deckers on the Otley route,' Lucy immediately replied.

'That will be a big investment.'

'That is why we are seeing the bank manager, Bob. We want a cheque for £50,000 from him tomorrow and we will need an agreement to borrow the cost of the new buses.'

'But what about our garage capacity, Lucy?'

'I don't think we should raise that with the bank manager at this stage. That investment can follow later. If we decide to close the Otley garage we could always use the Benfield garage to take the overflow. The Benfields are now settled and supportive of the Maxwell business. I am just thinking aloud, though, Bob.'

Lucy informed Margaret that she would take all the cash and cheques to the bank and hand them over before the meeting. As Bob left the office he looked more relaxed. He'd clearly been infected with Lucy's positive approach.

When they arrived at the bank, the manager welcomed them with the expected question.

'I don't usually get requests for an urgent meeting with Maxwell Motors. Is something wrong?'

Lucy got straight to the point. 'No, nothing is wrong, but

we have been offered a business opportunity that could have a far-reaching impact on us. And we have to make an immediate decision which has financial implications. That's why we have come to see you first.'

'When did you learn of this opportunity?'

'Yesterday evening. Bob was approached by an old friend of his.'

'Why do you have to make an immediate decision?'

Lucy explained all the details of the present position of the Lidgett Bus Company and the need to provide an immediate payment into their accounts to avoid bankruptcy and possible prosecution.

'Do you think expansion into this additional route would benefit the Maxwell operations?' asked the bank manager.

'I am sure it would,' replied Lucy. 'We would apply the same system that we operate on the Horsforth route. And we see no reason why it shouldn't be just as successful. That is why we need your support, as we will have to buy some new double-decker buses.'

'Well you are set well financially, and your reserves are building up.' He opened his drawer and pulled out a file. 'You have approaching £40,000 in your deposit account. How much will you need?'

'We need a cheque for £50,000 tomorrow morning. We will hand this over to go into the Lidgett accounts and have an immediate transfer of ownership to us. As we go forward we'll need to invest in the new buses and there will be a further payment of £15,000 to finalise the acquisition of the company. In total, it might mean we need to borrow an additional £40,000 from the bank.'

'I will have to clear such a loan with my superiors at head office.'

'But it's not an immediate loan, and I think my figure will

be on the top side,' said Lucy. We only need an additional loan of £10,000 to finance the cheque for tomorrow morning.'

'Yes, I understand that. But I will need a business plan to pass to headquarters to cover the additional loans.'

'If I get the cheque from you tomorrow morning, to effectively seal the deal, I will see you on Tuesday next week with our business plan for the Otley route.' Lucy could see that she was going to get what she wanted.

'I can accept that timetable. You have a track record of delivering successful expansion plans, and I fully expect I will be able to recommend this one to head office.'

They left the bank manager with the usual courtesy of handshakes. As they were driving back to the garage, Bob commented to Lucy, 'You have set yourself a major challenge to prepare a business plan to hand over to the bank manager next Tuesday.'

'That is true, Bob. But my mind is already working on that and we shall only be replicating what we've already done. I'll get Mike Best involved with the finances over the weekend. Our immediate challenge is to get your old mate Joe to see us this afternoon. Can you fix that up? I'll also need to get our solicitor involved in the discussions with the Lidgett team.'

When Lucy got back to her office, Mavis had just returned from her travels on the Otley route and was ready to report.

'Be brief, please, Mavis. We're making progress and we have the bank manager backing us, but we have several other people to see this afternoon. My aim is to settle the deal tomorrow. So what did you find out?'

'The buses are all quite old, and I have to say that they were clean inside. But the staff will need significant additional training. One conductress called everybody 'Duckie', and at the terminal she couldn't get off quick enough to have a cigarette. They didn't seem to have any concern about old or disabled passengers. And their timetable is strange: their first buses in a morning start at seven o'clock from the town centre and also from Otley; on an evening, the last bus from the town centre is at nine-thirty. A lot of passengers are from the university. On both my journeys there were plenty of passengers travelling and the buses became quite full. Due to traffic, the journey time both ways could stretch to over half an hour on some parts of the day. The way they cover this is to run three buses, and they all park up and spend any spare time in the town centre. It appears to work alright, and the staff have a rest period each cycle.'

'Did you see any potential for improvement?'

'In simple terms, Lucy, lots. New buses, better-trained staff, and an extended running time throughout the day. That's just three, for starters!'

'That's very helpful. Thanks, Mavis. Just keep Lidgett Buses under your hat for the time being.'

Joe Lidgett came in to Lucy's office, with Bob, later in the afternoon. Bob whispered to Lucy as he took his place at the table opposite Joe. 'I've not said anything to him, Lucy. He doesn't know what to expect.'

Lucy looked at Joe. His head was down and he was obviously fearful of what he might be told. He was ashamed at having to beg for help. Lucy decided to give him the good news first.

'Joe, we have made progress. We will have a cheque for £50,000 to hand over to you tomorrow. It will be made out in your name.' Joe heaved a great sigh of relief.

'Oh, thank God for that,' he whispered. He looked across at Bob. 'Thanks Bob, you have saved me.'

'Don't thank me, Joe. Thank this lady; she's the one who's working miracles.'

'We need to agree what happens next,' said Lucy, not responding to the compliment. 'Firstly, what is your position in the company, Joe?'

'I am President; my son is Chief Executive and his wife is Company Secretary.'

'We will need to meet tomorrow, at our solicitors, but I haven't made the arrangements yet. I'll let you know the time when I've fixed it. Do your son and his wife realise that when we hand over the cheque, we will immediately be taking over the company?'

'I think they will get the message when they are with me at the meeting.'

'Where does your son live?'

'In Otley. It's a nice, big house, but the site is not special. It's alongside the garage.'

'Who does the house belong to?'

'It belongs to the company. He does have another house of his own, in Scarborough.'

'So when we get the company, we get the buses, the garage, your son's house and the licence to run the route between Otley and Leeds.'

'Yes, and we do have the right to pass on the licence to another reputable bus company.'

'I think we can fulfil that criterion,' replied Lucy with a smile.

Lucy rang to talk to Maxwells solicitor, but he'd left the office to go home early. She turned on her charm with his secretary and persuaded her to pass on his home telephone number. Lucy knew that she'd have to use all her charm treatment. She'd met James Low on a couple of occasions, but had not got to know him well. She rang the telephone number and it was James who answered.

'Good afternoon, James,' she began. 'I am Lucy Platt, from Maxwell Motors. I'm very sorry to trouble you at home, but we need your services for an urgent meeting tomorrow morning.'

'I remember you, Lucy. It sounds like a rush job. Can you tell me what's going on?'

Lucy gave him a brief rundown of the situation and stressed that the matter had to be resolved very quickly.

'I need to know a lot more than that, Lucy. I think you are holding something back. When did you get to know about this?'

'Only yesterday. There are financial implications and we tackled them first, but we have now got an agreement from our bank manager about the necessary finance. I can tell you the full story if you like.'

'I require the complete story if I'm to do my job properly and cover the legal aspects.'

Lucy very slowly explained all that had transpired between Joe Lidgett and Bob Maxwell, and the investigations that she'd carried out about the company. She also told him about the meeting at the bank and the agreement for the bank to provide a cheque for £50,000 to hand over tomorrow. When she paused, James Low gave his reactions.

'So, what you are saying, Lucy, is that you are prepared to hand over a cheque for £50,000 to a company that is likely to go bust anyway. You have decided to do this without doing a due diligence investigation. Surely you would be better to wait until the company goes bust and then you'll be able to pick it up for a song?'

'But in that situation there might be other companies keen to get that route, so it could cost more,' Lucy quickly responded. 'The real reason for us going forward in this way is that Bob wants to help his old mate to avoid the shame of a criminal investigation and possible prison for his son and his daughter-in-law. It might not appear to make sense, but I know that we will be able to run that route and make good profits for Maxwell Motors, when we apply our organisation and introduce new buses.'

'I know that you have done very well, Lucy, for your company in the past, but this whole issue smells of a panic job. What do you want me to do?'

'I want you to chair the meeting for us tomorrow. I have told them that when we hand over the cheque we get immediate possession of the company, so we will need a document for them to sign signifying this. Tomorrow afternoon I want access to their site, and possession of all the documents relating to the Lidgett Bus Company. There will no doubt be a more detailed legal document, later, to cover the full takeover, when we will pay the remaining £15,000.'

'You don't want much, Lucy, do you! But I can understand where you're coming from in that you want to get your hands on the company before the financial situation gets any worse.'

'James, you have got our position spot on. Can you deliver it?'

'I'll try to get you what you want, Lucy. I'll do some preparation tonight.'

'Can we meet in your conference room, at eleven o'clock tomorrow morning?'

'Yes, Lucy, but I want you in my office at nine thirty so

that I can go through the format of the meeting with you. I will want to check all the facts that I intend to use. I can tell you now that I will open the meeting by saying that I have advised you not to proceed at this time with the takeover, but to wait until the company goes bankrupt.'

'I can understand that you feel you must make that statement, but I will be happy when we get our hands on the company tomorrow afternoon. Thank you very much, James, for allowing me to talk to you this afternoon at home. I'll see you tomorrow.'

'I'll see you tomorrow, and I hope we can deliver what you want.'

Lucy's last job that afternoon was to arrange with Mavis to meet her at eight-thirty the next morning in her office. Mavis was booked for a taxi service to the station at that time and Elsie had a booking for the mini-coach, so Mavis arranged for Lilly to cover the taxi booking. Thank goodness Lilly was available now to cover for taxi bookings, thought Mavis.

The next morning, Lucy launched straight into explaining to Mavis a major change in the organisation. 'I expect us to acquire the Lidgett Bus Company later today. It will clearly be a priority job to integrate and reorganise that operation and make it a successful part of the Maxwell company. I feel that I must concentrate my efforts on that objective and all the ancillary business and legal implications related to it, so I want you to take on the introduction of the new coach and the start of the luxury tours centred on Harrogate. Those tours have to be very special, Mavis. From the time they make the booking to the time they get off the coach at the end of the tour those clients should be delighted and impressed.'

'I know what you have in mind, Lucy, and I'll sort it out. I've identified a woman with the right experience to be courier for these tours. She's called Audrey Worth.'

'You interview her, with Margaret, and I'll agree her terms. We then want the tours to sell themselves on personal recommendations. That is your objective, Mavis. It's a major challenge. While you're working hard in the luxury field, I'll be slogging away in the mundane bus business.' Lucy gave Mavis a big smile.

At the solicitor's office Lucy had an hour-long intensive discussion on the format of the meeting and the way James Low intended to handle it. James showed Lucy the agreement he'd drafted for signature by all the parties. He made a list of all the matters he would raise to clarify the position of the Lidgett Bus Company, and then the offer from Maxwell Motors. After he was satisfied, he talked to Lucy about Maxwell Motors and the way the Company was performing. Lucy described all the different elements of the business and how they contributed to the profits of the company. She referred briefly to the luxury tours.

'Really, the Lidgett opportunity has arisen at the wrong time for us. However I've given the responsibility for launching and developing the luxury tours to my side-kick, who is an expert in the tours business. So I will be able to concentrate on integrating and upgrading the Otley route.'

When they assembled in the conference room, James Low sat at the table flanked by Bob on one side and Lucy on the other. Opposite them sat Joe's son, in the middle, with Joe on one side of him and his wife on the other. Lucy couldn't help but notice the appearance of Joe's son: he was restless and his eyes wandered about the room and he didn't focus on James at all. Lucy concluded that he was afraid of the meeting and its consequences. By contrast, dressed in a smart, two-piece suit, and with skilful make-up to obscure any fear or tiredness in her eyes, his wife sat up straight in her chair.

James Low commenced the meeting.

'This is an important meeting for both parties — Maxwell Motors and the Lidgett Bus Company.' He looked up, and and his look required agreement by both parties with his statement. He paused until he got nods from the Lidgett team.

'It is an unusual business situation. I have to tell you that I have tried to persuade the Maxwell team not to proceed with their offer at this time. It seems clear to me that the Lidgett Bus Company, if it continues, will go bankrupt and it would then be available to be bought by Maxwell Motors for a much cheaper price.' Again he paused to get general agreement with his statement.

'However, Maxwell Motors have decided to continue with their bid and it is my job to establish the details of how this can proceed.' Again, he paused to get agreement to continue. He then established the roles of the three persons from the Lidgett Bus Company before moving on.

'Maxwell Motors is prepared to pass over a cheque for £50,000, to go into the Lidgett balance sheet, which will allow last year's accounts to be finalised. Do you accept that the cheque will be used for that purpose?'

Joe's son agreed to this with a shrug of his shoulders. The other two gave a clear 'yes' as their answer.

'The basis of this is that when the cheque is passed over, the Lidgett Bus Company is immediately transferred to Maxwell Motors. Do you accept this?' Again, there was agreement from the Lidgett team.

It took quite some time for James then to itemise in detail what was included in the transfer: the buses, the route, the garage, the son's house, all cash balances, and all relevant papers, documentation and records pertaining to the company. He itemised each one separately and got agreement to that item being a part of the deal. He then discussed the house in particular and said that it should be vacated in the near future. He looked to Lucy for a definition of 'near future'.

'As the occupants own another property, I think that the period should be set at two weeks,' she said.

There was a sign that this might be challenged, so Lucy decided to add, 'I understand that many of the records and papers of the company are in that house and it's my intention to take a team there this afternoon to remove everything relevant to the company. Therefore the occupants will have no need to stay on the site, as far as this deal is concerned. All they have to do is prepare to move out.'

James noted that this was the reality of the deal, as far as Lucy was concerned, so he required agreement to the timescale.

The next item for discussion was notification to the Lidgett staff of the transfer of ownership. Lucy said that she would deal with that and she intended to visit the site tomorrow, Friday, and have a word with all the staff. She then asked an important question.

'Have the wages for the staff been made up for this week?' She looked across at Mrs Lidgett to answer this question.

'No, as we didn't know what was happening.'

'Has the cash from the operations been paid into the bank this week?'

'No.'

'Where is the cash, then?'

'It's in the house.'

'So I assume there will be enough cash to pay the wages.'

'Yes, I would think so.'

'We might need your assistance to make up the wages this afternoon. If there is a significant amount of cash in the house I shall have to request that you do not return there until I am present with my team. We should be there by two-thirty.'

James Low sought their agreement to this request and there were reluctant glances between Mr and Mrs Lidgett which indicated that they had no choice but to accept. James Low then passed around the draft document, to be signed by both parties, agreeing the handover. He took them through the text, sentence by sentence, checking that they understood the meaning. When he'd finished, he adjourned the meeting so that he could get new copies that included the time the document was signed. When he returned a few minutes later, the signing took place by both parties.

'In conclusion, I have to tell you that this is one of the most benevolent commercial deals that I have ever been involved with. I hope that it will not impact detrimentally on the Maxwell business. The cheque can now be handed over.'

Bob Maxwell took the cheque out of his pocket and passed it over to Joe Liggett and they shook hands. The participants then left the conference room with no chat between the parties. Mr and Mrs Lidgett went off with Joe to have lunch. Lucy hurried back to the garage to organise her team for the afternoon visit to the Lidgett's house in Otley. Bob told her that he didn't want to join the salvage party, and that he would leave it to Lucy. She arranged that Fred would go with the Maxwell van, and Elsie would take the mini-coach. Their instructions were to collect all the documents about the Lidgett company, and pack them for transport to Horsforth. Lucy also arranged that Mike Best would be there to concentrate on the financial information. When the Lidgetts arrived back there after their lunch, they had to park in the road as their drive was full of Maxwell vehicles.

When they entered the house it became clear to the Maxwell staff that Mr Lidgett intended to play no part in the proceedings. He went into the sitting room and settled comfortably on a settee for an afternoon of smoking and drinking. In answer to a question from Lucy, Mrs Lidgett said that most of the documentation for the company was upstairs, in a bedroom that she used as an office. She led the way upstairs and the team followed. Fred and Elsie began to empty a cupboard filled with files. Lucy asked where the cash was and she directed Mike Best to extract it from the safe. After he'd counted all the cash from the safe he told Lucy that, in his opinion, there must be some more cash elsewhere to equate to a full week's operation on the buses. After questioning, Mrs Lidgett said that there could be some cash in the bedroom and she led Mike and Lucy there. They found two carrier bags in one wardrobe, full of cash that had not been counted.

'You do realise that we will have to undertake a thorough search throughout the house, to be able to identify what rightly belongs to the company, and which we need to remove?' said Lucy. Mrs Lidgett agreed.

'We will do that search later, but we would appreciate your help in sorting out the staff wages that are due to be paid tomorrow.'

Mike retired to another bedroom where Mrs Lidgett had a machine for preparing the information on the wage slips. From the cash collected, Mike filled the envelopes with cash to match the wage slips.

Lucy spoke to Fred and Mike.

'We must now do a full search of the house, looking for cash and for any other files or documents relating to the company. This will be the only chance we get, so it has to be done right.' She informed Mrs Lidgett what they intended to do.

Lucy went into a bedroom with Fred and watched him open a drawer and look inside. 'Don't just look, Fred, but feel about under the clothes to make sure nothing is hidden there. The next drawer he opened was full of Mrs Lidgett's underwear. He blushed as he lifted out some of her flimsy silk and satin knickers and bras, but that drawer yielded nothing suspicious. In Mr Lidgett's suit, a wallet contained over fifty pounds. Lucy took a view that this was personal property and did the same when Mrs Lidgett showed Lucy the contents of her handbag, which also contained cash in a wallet. In a drawer in the sitting room they found two files about the company. One of them contained letters from the auditors, explaining why they could not sign the annual accounts. Lucy showed them to Mr Lidgett, but he just shrugged his shoulders.

'You might as well take them. I've finished with them.'

It was while Lucy was in the hall that she noticed a door which she'd not used. She opened it and saw steps down into a cellar. She spoke to Mr Lidgett again in the sitting room.

'We need to check the cellar.'

'You'll not find anything down there. It's full of junk. I suppose we'll have to sort it out before we leave,' he replied.

It was as he'd described — full of old furniture and other household articles.

'I don't think there'll be anything here, Lucy,' said Fred.

'No it doesn't look promising,' replied Lucy.

But then they came to a large pile of curtains, heaped up

on top of some old carpets.

'Just lift those curtains and pile them somewhere else, Fred.'

In total, he lifted three arms-full of the curtains and then exposed a small case. Lucy picked it up and tried to open it, but it was locked.

'This looks interesting,' she said. She took it into the sitting room and showed it to Mr Lidgett who feigned surprise.

'That is private property,' he said.

'How do I know that?' replied Lucy. 'It's not too heavy, but it could contain paper money. I need to have it opened.' Mr Lidgett didn't move.

'I suppose if you do not open it for me, I could take it to the police and ask them to investigate it.'

'Don't kick us in the teeth. You know we can't go to the police.' He stood up and took a key out of the cupboard and passed it to Lucy. She opened the case and found it was stacked with bundles of pound notes. She passed it over to Mike and he quickly determined that each bundle was one hundred pounds. There were thirty-one bundles.

'That means that we've found over £4,000 in the house this afternoon, Lucy,' Mike said.

After a final look around, Lucy dispatched Elsie and Fred back to the garage. Mike stowed away all the spare cash, and the wage envelopes, into Lucy's taxi.

'Thank you, Mike, it's been a good afternoon's work. I shall need you on Monday to help me prepare my business plan to keep the bank manager happy. I'm going over to the Lidgett garage now to make sure that Mr and Mrs Lidgett are not allowed access to the site any more.'

Across at the garage, Lucy spoke to the woman in the office.

'You are now a part of Maxwell Motors. We've been over at the house this afternoon, removing everything relating to the company. Mr and Mrs Lidgett will be leaving the house during the next fortnight and they have no right of access to this garage site. You'll be glad to know that I will be paying out all the wages due to the staff tomorrow. I have one question to ask you. How do you deal with the cash collected from the conductors during the afternoon shift?'

'I am here to meet the bus crews and I take the cash and put it in the safe. On some nights Mrs Lidgett comes over and empties the safe, but she often collects the money the next morning.'

Lucy realised she had to make changes immediately.

'In future, I want you to count the money from each conductor, record the amount on a slip of paper, with the name of the driver and the conductor. Don't use your safe any more, as there could be the risk of Mrs Lidgett using her key to get at the money. Can you get me the Maxwell office on the telephone please?'

It was Mavis who answered the 'phone.

'Mavis, you'll recall that we installed a bigger safe in the office about a year ago. What happened to old safe? I think it might be stored in the garage. Get hold of Bob, please, and ask him if he can bring it, with the keys, to me at the Lidgett garage. If the safe is missing, ring me back as I shall have to think of something else.'

Lucy talked to the clerk and asked her lots of questions about the Lidgett operations. She obtained the names of all the staff — a total of seventeen full-time, but there were others who could be called on in an emergency. Ten minutes later Mavis rang her back.

'We've found the safe and the keys. Bob's on his way to deliver it.'

Bob arrived, with Fred, in the Maxwell van, which they backed up to the office. As well as the safe they had a pair of wheels from the garage.

'It might be a small safe,' said Bob, 'but it's still very heavy. Just show us where you want it.'

They lowered it onto the wheels and carefully manoeuvred it into place. It needed two extra men from the Lidgett staff to lever it into its final place. They handed over one of the keys and the clerk tried the lock and the door. It worked easily as Fred had put some thin oil into the lock mechanism. Bob travelled back with Lucy in the taxi and she gave him a blow-by-blow report on the afternoon's work. He was duly impressed.

'At least we have foiled the plans of Mr and Mrs Lidgett to escape with a few thousand pounds of cash that didn't belong to them,' Lucy concluded.

Eighteen

On the Thursday evening, after the busy day taking over the Lidgett Bus Company, Lucy fell asleep on the settee, exhausted by her day's work. Fred watched over her and then gently woke her up and helped her upstairs to bed where she fell straight back asleep. When he woke up in the morning she wasn't there. He later learned that she'd risen at five o'clock and was preparing notes for her meetings with the staff of the Lidgett Bus Company.

Lucy was on the Otley site before noon, to see the teams coming on for their afternoon duties. As each one arrived, Lucy met them with a handshake and presented them with their weekly wage packet. She welcomed them to Maxwell Motors but didn't offer them other details of her plans. She did offer to answer any questions they might want to raise, and was pleased that her offer was taken up.

'What's the involvement of Mr and Mrs Lidgett, from now

on?' someone asked.

'They have absolutely no involvement in Maxwell Motors, they have no right of access to this site, and I expect them to be leaving their house, which now belongs to us, within the next two weeks.'

'Will you continue to use this garage?' asked another driver.

'We have not made a firm decision on that, at this time. We'll want to use the facilities we have, in our garage in Horsforth, for cleaning and servicing these buses.'

'Is there any chance of getting some new buses, because ours are crap?'

'I can be very positive about that. Yes, we will be getting new buses to the Maxwell specification as soon as possible.'

'Will we get some new uniforms? These are a bit tatty.'

'I would expect you to be measured for the Maxwell-coloured outfits within the next week.'

When Lucy met the second set of teams, who had covered the day shift, the meeting followed the same format. Some of the questions were the same but one was different and Lucy couldn't resist replying to it.

'Might you consider altering the times of our services?' asked one of the drivers.

'I have to say that it's likely that we will. At Maxwell Motors we take the view that we're in business to provide a service to our passengers, and they appreciate our early-morning and late-evening services. We will evaluate what we think we can achieve, and then discuss our plans with you.'

'If we work longer hours, will we get more pay?'

'You will be paid the same way as the Maxwell drivers and conductors are paid. In time it's very likely that all our drivers and conductors will operate as a single pool, to cover both the Horsforth and Otley routes.'

'So you'll be offering us a job on the same basis as the Maxwell staff?'

'Exactly.'

'Can't complain on that basis, then.'

'I have to add that I intend to arrange a meeting with you all at the end of next week. I'll want to know then if any of you want to leave your jobs at this stage. That will allow me to recruit new drivers and conductors if we cannot provide them from our reserve staff. I would expect to be able to tell you when the new buses will be delivered, what hours the Otley buses will operate throughout the week, and where the buses will be garaged. It will be a very important meeting.'

Lucy was confident that she had broken the ice with the Lidgett staff. She could sense that they had little respect for Mr and Mrs Lidgett, and some of them were pleased to be picking up a job with Maxwell Motors. She collected the envelopes, with the cash from the previous day's operations, from the safe. It would be interesting to get Mike Best's views on the cashflow from this route.

On the Saturday morning, Lucy sat down in her office with Bob to review the situation.

'We've moved a long way in the last two days, Bob. There is a lot still to sort out, but I'm confident that we can make a success of the Otley route. The most important question to answer is when we can expect to get the new double-decker buses. Have you anything to report on that?'

'I've had two discussions with the manufacturers, and I am hopeful of having a firm delivery date on Monday. I told them that we'll be ordering three double-deckers to the

Maxwell specification but that delivery is critical. I think they're keen for the order, so they will be trying to meet our needs.'

'What would your best guess be for delivery?'

'I'm hopeful for three weeks, but it might be four weeks from this weekend.'

'Three weeks would be brilliant, but four would still be okay.'

'What are you going to do about garaging the extra buses? I just can't see how we could run this site with four more double-decker buses parked here.'

'You're right, Bob. I've thought about this and I intend to use the Benfield site to park the Otley Buses. Their site is nearer the Otley route than Horsforth. We could agree to the day shift staff picking up their buses from the Benfield site and the afternoon shift would park their buses back at the Benfield site at the end of their shift. Eva Benfield would collect all the money and shuffle the staff around during the day. Joe North could collect any bus that needs cleaning and refuelling, and bring it to Horsforth to service it. He could then return the bus back to the Benfield site ready for the next day's operation. I'm sure Joe would be able to work out the best way to organise this, and it would avoid this site getting bogged down.'

'I'll leave you to sort all that out, Lucy.'

'If we can do that, Bob, we'll not need the Otley site. My aim will be to sell the house with vacant possession, and the garage site for development. That will get us some cash back.'

'Have you any other plans for the Otley route?'

'Yes, I have. I think we should extend the operating hours of the service as soon as possible. We should start the first services from Otley and from the town centre at six o'clock each morning, and the last service at night should be at eleven o'clock. When people get familiar with these new times our passenger numbers should grow.'

After Bob left, Lucy started drafting her business plan to present to the bank manager on Tuesday. She would show it to Mike Best for him to prepare the financial figures to include in the report.

Mavis came in to see her.

'I just want five minutes to show you what I've prepared for the advertising campaign for the luxury tours, Lucy. The new coach will arrive on Tuesday, so I have arranged for it to be photographed to illustrate the adverts.'

Mavis showed Lucy a series of sketches she had prepared. Some were to use on the service buses, some to display in the travel agency, and some to be used for commercial advertising. They were very impressive and Lucy was thrilled.

'I think they're excellent, Mavis. Which publication are you going to use for the press adverts?'

'I was going to use the Harrogate Advertiser. I've invited one of their reporters to take a look at the coach here, on Tuesday.

'I think we might splash out into a wider field, Mavis. I suggest you also arrange an advert in the Yorkshire Post. That has wide coverage in Yorkshire, but it goes across the Pennines and even into London. That would register Maxwell Motors in the minds of many new people.'

'It will be expensive, Lucy, but if you want, I'll arrange it. Should you tell Bob?'

'Not especially, there's so much taking place on the Otley route, and Bob is fully involved with that. He'll get to know about it when I report to the management committee and the board meeting.'

On Monday, Lucy worked in her office with Mike Best, finalising the business plan for the Otley route, to present to the bank manager. Mike had analysed the cash handed in for Friday and Saturday from the Otley buses. It was interesting that one team was consistently lower than the other teams operating on the same shift, but the total takings were higher than Lucy had expected. With the new timetable, and then the new buses and additional staff training, Lucy was confident the revenues would increase. Her objective was to achieve the same income per bus journey as on the Horsforth route.

'If you can achieve that, Lucy, you'll have a real cash cow,' concluded Mike.

'Put that as an objective in the report to the bank manager,' she replied. 'That is what I will be aiming for.'

The report included the plan to sell the house and the garage site at Otley for building development. When the business plan was finished in the afternoon, and typed up, Lucy showed it to Bob, saying, 'I have not noted it in the conclusions, but this plan will allow us to make this merger at much lower cost than we stated in our discussions with the bank manager. Not only that, but if we can get the income that Mike has predicted from the route, we will repay any loans very quickly.'

Bob read through the report and was surprised at the figures included. 'Are you sure that these financial projections aren't too optimistic, Lucy?'

'I can assure you that Mike hasn't included all the increases in income that we identified, but I accept that we have a lot of changes to make and then we have got to make them work.'

'Well, that's very good, Lucy. I can also give you some good news. Two new buses will be delivered in three weeks' time, and the third, the week later.'

'That's excellent, Bob.'

On Tuesday morning, Lucy had a meeting with Eva Benfield at which she went through the new business plan. Eva would be in charge of collecting and recording all the money from the conductors on the Otley route. Once each day she would transport the cash over to Horsforth, with the records of each team's results. Lucy agreed with her the rate that she would be paid for this responsibility. It was a seven-day responsibility and special arrangements would have to be made when Eva was not available.

The following day Lucy met with the bank manager, accompanied by Mike Best, as Bob was tied up with Mavis and the new coach delivery. They worked through the business plan in detail, with Mike justifying his calculations. When they'd finished, the bank manager presented his thoughts. 'As I see it, this business plan represents a more favourable situation than you described when we met last week about this merger, Mrs Platt. Is that true?'

'Yes, it is,' replied Lucy. 'Not only that, but we shall only need the loans for shorter periods.'

'That's good news. I am sure that I shall have no difficulty in my discussions with headquarters.'

'However, we are getting the new buses earlier than we expected, so we'll need finance to pay for them in three weeks' time,' said Lucy.

'That will be no problem,' he assured her.

Her final task for the day was to inspect the new luxury coach parked on the forecourt in Horsforth. It was impressive and very luxurious, with its plush seating and air-conditioning. Audrey Worth, recruited to be courier on the luxury tours, was there and she expressed her view that anyone travelling on that coach should be able to relax and enjoy the comfort of a journey in total luxury.

'It will be your responsibility, Audrey,' said Lucy, 'to add the little details throughout the tour which ensure your passengers wallow in a memorable experience, so much so that they can't stop talking about it when they get back home. We're trying to establish a new brand of our tour business here. I don't want this to be a one-off example.'

'I will be trying to achieve that, Lucy. I understand what your vision is for this new Maxwell business.'

The planned meeting with all the Lidgett staff took place on Thursday morning, in the committee room of a working men's club in Horsforth. In total there were eighteen people present. Maxwell staff were operating the Otley route this morning to allow all the Lidgett staff to be present at the same time. They were somewhat apprehensive, as nothing like this had ever happened to them before. All week there had been new initiatives either introduced or talked about. They'd been told that there would also be visits to the Benfield site, to meet Eva Benfield, and to be briefed on the use of that site and collection of all the cash. They were getting the idea that they were to be subject to major changes to their working lives.

Lucy mingled with them before the meeting started. Then she addressed them. Firstly, she welcomed them and spent fifteen minutes showing them slides with key facts about the Maxwell operations.

'You are joining an organisation that has grown quickly over the last few years and is now a big business. I am proud to show you the financial results for last year and how that is built up from the different business units we run.' There were some surprised looks when they saw the financial results from the taxis and wedding taxis.

'Obviously, the income from the bus routes will be substantially higher with the Otley route added to the Horsforth route. Starting in April, we will also have a new development as we'll start running luxury tours.' She described the tours and what they included, ending by saying that if they were successful they would be extended to other towns and cities to give more choice for passengers.

'Why has Maxwells been so successful in expanding its business?' she asked, somewhat rhetorically, before going on to answer the question. 'The main reason is that we have developed our staff to be the best in the field. They all know their job, and they want to turn in top-class performances every day. They are proud to work for Maxwell Motors. They work hard; we all work hard for the company. The company looks after us. Each Christmas all our staff receive a Christmas bonus, which is significant and means all their families can afford to have a good Christmas.'

'So how will you be affected?' she went on. 'We will give you all additional training to help you to be better at your job. Your working life will become more varied. We will mix you up so that you are working on the Horsforth route one week, and on the Otley route another week.'

'Let me tell you of other changes that will affect you. Firstly, two new double-deckers will be delivered and put into service starting a fortnight next Monday. On that date we will introduce additional services. The first service will leave Otley and the town centre at six o'clock in the morning; the last service from Otley and the town centre will be eleven o'clock at night. Notices of these new timetables will be displayed on the buses from next Monday.'

'After this meeting you will be visiting the Benfield site, where the buses will be garaged overnight and where you will pick them up on a morning. This means that we will cease to use the Otley garage.'

'I know that I've given you a lot to take in, but I'm keen to get this merger resolved so that we can all settle down. The final thing I want to raise, is your decision whether you want to work for Maxwell Motors, or whether you will take this opportunity to move off to another job. I will answer any questions you want to raise now but, while we all have a bite and a drink together, I want you to tell me what your decision is.'

There were a few questions, but they were mainly to clarify the changes proposed rather than to bring up new issues. Lucy had a list of all the staff and she was able to give them a tick or a cross when they each gave her their decision about working for Maxwell Motors. They were all ticks except the clerk in the office, the lad who cleaned the garage, two drivers and two conductors. Lucy saw them as a group when the meeting closed and she gave them the choice of leaving straightaway or in two weeks' time. She told them she would pay them one week's wages for every full year they'd worked for the Lidgett Bus Company. When she later reviewed the records of the six who wanted to leave, she found that they'd had limited time in their job, so she didn't have to pay out much severance pay. She actually welcomed the vacancies that this created, because it allowed some reserve staff, who had experience with Maxwell Motors, to be offered full-time appointments.

On Friday, Lucy had an intensive day in her office catching up with paperwork. Mavis came to see her in the afternoon and showed her the report in the Harrogate Advertiser and the advert for the luxury tours. The advert in the Yorkshire Post was arranged for the Saturday edition and Mavis was visibly excited. 'It's worked, Lucy! We already have six places booked on the first tour and I'm told by the travel agency that several other people have been in the shop and taken away details of the luxury tours. There's confidence among the staff there that they'll have other confirmed bookings over the weekend.'

'That's good news, Mavis, but I want to see how many of the forty seats are filled when the bus leaves on the first tour at the beginning of April, before I get excited.'

March was a busy month for Lucy, with a management committee meeting in the second week of the month, and then a board meeting during the last week of the month.

The management committee meeting was more intense than the usual. Mike Best's presentations about the annual results and the improved profits were accepted with no questions, but then Lucy described the location of the travel agency in Harrogate, and gave figures showing the increase of bookings compared with the old office. On the commercial arrangements, the puzzled looks were resolved by Mike Best when he showed that it was in the interest of the travel agency and Maxwell Motors that more passengers were sold tours. The concept of luxury tours centred on Harrogate was presented by Mavis and this elicited a question from George Clay.

'Suppose these luxury tours become very popular. Will you have to buy more of these special, up-market coaches?'

'The answer to that question is, yes,' replied Lucy, confidently. 'But we will want to have results that demonstrate that they are as profitable as other parts of our operations, before we do that.'

Lucy reported on the Otley route, including the use of the Benfield garage site, and including the purchase of new double-deckers and the integration of drivers and conductors into a single pool.

Mike Best spoke on the financial impact of all this. 'We anticipate that the Otley route will deliver more cash than the Horsforth route. But, of course, there are three buses on the Otley route compared to only two on the Horsforth route.

The management committee concluded with a sandwich lunch over which Lucy took the opportunity to talk informally to the committee members. She picked up that they were keen for the Lidgett staff to be trained up to the level of Maxwell staf and that the luxury tours were creating a lot of interest among the staff.

Lucy' focus was on the Otley route. She travelled on two occasions on one of the services to see how the staff operated. When she joined the bus on her first trip, the conductor spoke to her and explained what was happening as the bus covered the route. She was told that there was occasionally exuberant behaviour by university students who preferred to travel on the upper deck and that they had been known to stamp on the floor when they got excited. 'That upsets the other passengers,' said the conductor.'

'Hopefully, they will treat the new buses with a bit more respect,' replied Lucy. 'It's only a matter of a few days now until we'll have the first two buses delivered.'

On Lucy's second trip on the service she had a different driver and conductor. The driver was friendly enough when she spoke to him while the bus was parked in the town centre, but the conductor just ignored Lucy throughout the journey. Her approach to all the passengers was cold, distant and uncommunicative. Lucy saw her need for training in communication and the way to approach her passengers.

Much to Bob's and Lucy's delight, the two new double-decker buses for the Otley route were delivered on the Friday morning of the board meeting. They looked splendid parked up on the forecourt. The board members had a good look around them before they had their sandwich lunch in Lucy's office. They were impressed by what they saw and by what Bob told them about the technical specifications. When the lunch was cleared away there was a joint effort by Lilly, Mavis, Elsie and Lucy to convert the office into a meeting room. It was converted in five minutes.

'That was an impressive transformation, Lucy,' said Dr Poxon. 'Do you tackle all jobs with that speed?'

'It's our speciality, Dr Poxon. You will hear of a more dramatic success in the meeting.'

The board meeting concentrated on the financial results for the previous year. When Mike Best concluded his detailed report, he suggested that the board should agree a dividend of seven percent. This was accepted by the board with no hesitation. Lucy then led a discussion about the takeover of the Lidgett Bus Company and Mavis gave her presentation on the luxury tours. Lucy reported that the travel agency exercise in Harrogate had resulted in significant increases in bookings for Maxwell tours and she took care to point out that it was Bob who'd suggested seeking clients in the Harrogate area.

The meeting ended with its members assured that Maxwell Motors was in a very good shape.

That evening Elsie and David Young went to the pictures together in Leeds. Mavis saw them in the queue, shyly holding hands. Mavis was thrilled at the sight. It was a surprise to her, but she remembered that Elsie had seemed on edge during the afternoon, and she'd left to go home as soon as possible. Mavis hurried past the cinema queue, on the opposite side of the road, with her head down so that they did't see her. She thought to herself that it was just what Maxwell Motors needed — a bit of love and romance. She must mention it to Lucy. On reflection, she contrasted it to her own life. She had a good job, with lots of job satisfaction and excellent pay, but she had no men friends to take her out. Her one real relationship had withered and died as she pursued her career. Might she explore a new relationship? It seemed unlikely, what with the intensity of challenges on the go at Maxwell Motors.

On the Monday morning, Mavis mentioned to Lucy what she had seen in the cinema queue. Her reaction was very supportive.

'How wonderful,' she said, with a great smile on her 'We must quietly support them. You can't tie Elsie up every Saturday with weddings from now on, Mavis. And we mustn't have David covering the fuel pumps if Elsie has an evening off.'

'You can't run Maxwell Motors and manage everybody's private relationships at the same time!' laughed Mavis.

'I know I can't, Mavis. But they are both so sweet. I want to help their relationship develop if I can. That's really cheered me up. I'm going to do a couple of trips on the Otley route to see how the new buses are being received. It will be interesting to see how the public are reacting to them.'

It was one of the new buses that was parked at the stand, waiting to leave on the half hour, when Fred dropped Lucy off. Lucy spoke to the driver and conductor.

'How is it running this morning?'

'It's like a Rolls Royce, compared with our old tanks,' replied the ex-Lidgett driver.

'It's caused some comments from the passengers,' said the conductor. 'One or two have said. "Posh now" and

“Going up-market”. And “Will the fares be going up?” is a typical Yorkshire question. I think a few more passengers have got on our bus rather than the competition. It does feel nice for us to be up front instead of tagging on behind.’

‘That’s a really good start. How about the new timetables? Have you had some passenger reaction on the early-morning slots?’

‘A few have asked if it would be a regular service at that time,’ replied the conductor. ‘We pass one or two works that start around seven o’clock, so their workers could get to work on one of the early buses.’

‘So you two are happy with the new buses and the new timetable?’

‘Yes, we have hope now,’ replied the driver. ‘With the old set-up, for the last two years, we were always fearful that it might be coming to an end.’

‘What we want now is a bit more cash flowing into your money bags,’ said Lucy.

‘I think that’s starting already,’ replied the conductor, as she climbed onto the bus behind Lucy and to start collecting the fares. She cheerily addressed the passengers with: ‘It’s a bonus for you today — no increase in price and a seat on a brand new bus.’

‘Not before time,’ replied a grumpy old lady. ‘We were sick of waiting for some better buses. Bumping up and down on those old crates; I’m sure it’s knocked my arse out of shape.’

‘You’ll be alright after this week,’ said Lucy. ‘They’ll all be new buses from then on.’

‘How do you know that, Mrs?’ asked the old lady.

‘Because she runs the company!’ said the conductor, helping Lucy out.

‘Bloody hell, what’s the world coming to!’

Lucy smiled broadly at that remark, but she concluded that her trip so far had gained only positive reactions.

Her return trip back to the town centre was with a Maxwell driver and conductor and she noticed the more professional, respectful approach to passengers. The conductor helped an old lady and her husband to get off the bus and start walking on the footpath.

Later that week Lucy reviewed the forthcoming weekend. There were two coaches leaving on Saturday morning for south coast tours, both fully booked. Also on Saturday, the first luxury tour was leaving Harrogate for Edinburgh, and this had thirty-three passengers on board. Mavis and Audrey North would be on the coach as couriers. And also on Saturday there was a coach leaving on a mini-trip for four nights to Scarborough, leaving one hour after the south coast tours. And there was a wedding booking for the two taxis, covered by Elsie and Lilly. Lucy organised Fred and Brian Hunt to be on the forecourt with her to handle the luggage and make sure all was well with the south coast tours. She worked out that they could then provide the same service for the start of the mini-tour to Scarborough.

On the Saturday morning there was a complication when a couple weren't ready for the pick-up with the mini-coach. Elsie was driving it and she decided to go to their home to check on the passengers. They were bleary-eyed, suggesting to Elsie that they'd been out drinking the night before. Elsie told them that she would delay her departure, but they had to be ready in fifteen minutes. There was a scuffle by the two of them, despite their hangover, because they didn't want to miss the coach. Elsie watched them from the mini-coach, parked outside their gate with the engine running. As they struggled out to the mini-coach, shielding themselves from the angry looks of the other passengers, Elsie gave them a little advice.

'I'll be in trouble with my boss for waiting for you; but I'll make an excuse that one of you was taken ill, which delayed you.'

'Thanks,' said the woman. 'I hope this makes 'im behave himself during the rest of the holiday.'

The south coast tours left fifteen minutes late, but the driver/managers were sure that they'd be able to make up that delay before they reached the hotels. The mini-tour to Scarborough left on time, with the coach full except for two spare seats. Later in the morning Lucy inspected the two taxis before they drove off to the wedding. She commented how impressed she was with the smart appearance of Elsie and Lilly.

'You two will get some admiring looks from the wedding guests. Just take care of each other. I don't want either of you stolen by a young man who needs a partner.'

'There's no chance of that happening,' said Elsie. Was she referring to her friendship with David, Lucy thought, but kept that thought to herself.

There were other coaches booked for trips to the seaside. Only one coach was left in the garage by mid-morning.

Lucy and Fred went into the general office to have a coffee break.

'Lucy, I worry about you,' said Fred. 'Can you keep up with all this pressure? Maxwell Motors is such a big company now and there's so much happening every day. How do you feel about things now?'

'Fred, I am proud of what we are achieving with this company. Aren't you also excited to be involved with Maxwell Motors?'

'I am, Lucy. I accept that it's exciting. But I don't want

you to push yourself too far, that's all.'

'But I have you, Fred, and our Richard. You both inspire me. And then think about the team we have here. What could be more inspiring than the support I get from all of them? It's a great privilege to lead this company. I couldn't ask for anything more satisfying in my life.'

She leaned over and took Fred in her arms. They clung together in a long hug. Then the door opened. It was Richard who was doing a few hours on the fuel pumps.

'What on earth is this carry on? In office hours as well!'

'It's called team—building, Richard,' said 'We were just considering how lucky we are to be involved with Maxwell Motors. Come here, you can join us.' She put her arms around Richard and gave Fred a sign to join them. The Platt family clung together in a symbolic hug. They'd never done it before, but it seemed to reinforce the family bond. When they broke up, Richard brought them back to reality.

'I just came in to tell you that we'll need a delivery of fuel from Shell in the next two days.'

Lucy kept her eyes on the Otley route during the week. She studied the takings recorded by Eva Benfield on the operations by all the teams on the route and as she wrote down the results she noted the signs that the takings were increasing. She asked Mike Best to design some graphs of the results so that she could see clearly the trends.

Mavis rang on the Tuesday afternoon to report to Lucy on the Edinburgh luxury tour. It was good news: the passengers were satisfied that they were getting first-class treatment at the hotel, both with their rooms and in the restaurant, the trips had all provided access to the best private stately homes in that part of Scotland, where the owners were happy to explain the history of their homes and display their family treasures.

'I think we have cracked it, Lucy,' concluded Mavis. 'There hasn't been one word of complaint so far, and I am being asked if we have plans for other venues for this type of tour.'

'That's great, Mavis. Well done. How is Audrey Worth performing?'

'She's doing very well. She has the right manner to deal with this type of client. She shows them great respect.'

'Do you think she could face the next tour without you, Mavis?'

'At a pinch, I think she could. Why do you ask Lucy?'

'I need you here. We've made a good start with the Otley route, and we've got the extended timetable operating, but we urgently need to put the drivers and conductors that have joined us from the Lidgett Company through a training course to get them operating to the Maxwell standard. There are some good people who have potential. But we need to get them sorted out before they settle down.'

'That will be alright with me, Lucy. You can arrange for me to lead a course next week. Let Margaret work out the rotas to manage without eight staff for that day. I'll talk to Audrey and prepare her to take on next week's tour on her own.'

'Good. So we'll plan one course next week, and one the week after.'

Lucy decided to make a quick visit to the travel agency in Harrogate on Wednesday afternoon. She was pleased to see that the place was busy, and that the three agents on duty had clients at their desks. They all spoke to Lucy and said 'Good Afternoon' as she went through to Leslie Fortune's office.

The manager gave Lucy an update on the operation of the agency. Their total business, in financial terms was up by thirty-five percent, but the bookings for Maxwell tours were up by thirty-eight percent

'That sounds impressive,' Lucy said, 'but can you give me more details about the forward bookings for the luxury tours?'

'We are watching these carefully. We have thirty-five passengers on the next tour, starting on Saturday. We need feedback from the passengers on the first tour that we can distribute to people who are showing an interest.'

'You'll get that very soon, and from what Mavis told me yesterday, it will be good news.'

'My boss was actually showing an interest in the tour. He wants to know about the passengers' reaction.'

'I'll tell you what to do. Tell him he can go on the tour with his wife, free of charge, as a gift from me. The conditions are that he goes within the next few weeks, while there are still spare places, and that he remains incognito as far as the other passengers are concerned. I will expect him to write a report when he gets back, describing the trip, which we can use as publicity material.'

'I think he'll jump at that. Well, he might not jump at the offer, but I know his wife will. I'll ring him this evening.'

'You need to brief Audrey Worth when your boss is on the passenger list. She will be the courier on her own for the trips from next Saturday as I need Mavis back in Horsforth.'

Lucy left the agency, having refused a cup of tea, accompanied to the door by the manager.

She was in Harrogate again on Friday afternoon, to meet

the return of the first luxury tour from Edinburgh. She mingled with the passengers as they sorted out their luggage before being taken on home either by relatives or taxis that they had organised. She noted their words of thanks to Mavis and Audrey. The bus driver touched his hat to them when they handed over tips. It was all very positive, thought Lucy. Mavis carried a number of slips of paper that had been handed to the passengers to complete, evaluating the services on a scale of one to five. The top grade was five, and almost all the ratings were at that level. There was a paucity of suggestions for improvements.

'I've looked through these Lucy,' said Mavis, 'and I could not have wished for better scores or comments. I've also spoken to one couple and one lady travelling on her own and asked them to write a short report on the holiday and I think they'll do this. We should be able to pick out some phrases to use in publicity for the tours.'

'I want to have a chat with you and Audrey, in my office, when you get back. I assume you will be travelling back in the coach? I'm in the van and will drive myself back to Horsforth.'

Both Mavis and Audrey were hoping to get back home and have a night with their feet up, but they knew that Lucy wanted to have more details about the tour.

Back in the office, Lucy opened the discussion.

'Have you a feel for the financial outcome for the tour Mavis?'

'We've had some incidental expenses smoothing the way for the first trip, but I don't think that we will have lost money overall.'

'I'll get Mike Best to analyse the figures in detail early next week. Of course it should be less costly for the tours in the future, as we will have only one courier from now on. How do you feel about running the tour on your own,

Audrey?'

'Since I knew that this was a possibility, I've spent some time with Mavis, and she's given me lots of tips. If the passengers are similar to the ones we had on the first trip, I feel confident that I'll be alright. Also I'm sure that I will have the full support of the driver, who is very good and attentive to the passengers' needs.'

'We picked the driver out carefully, as he'd gained a very good reputation on the south coast tours,' added Mavis.

'We need you to start work on planning more of this type of tour, Mavis. If there is a demand we need to be able to satisfy it. I'm not sure when we'll be able to buy another specialist coach, so we may have to use the one coach but going to different locations each week. As you start researching new locations, keep Audrey in the picture so that she effectively becomes the expert on the luxury tours.' There was a smile on Audrey's face when Mavis agreed to that suggestion.

'I would welcome that role,' she said.

'Well, I think we can be satisfied that we've taken another step forward for Maxwell Motors. You'd better get off home, Audrey, and get some sleep. You'll be off on the road again tomorrow with a new set of people to coddle and charm. I'm leaving it to you to be on show to welcome the passengers in Harrogate, Mavis. I'm hoping that the third new double-decker will be here tomorrow so that we can get it on the Otley route on Monday. It's all go at present.'

'We can agree with that!' said Mavis.

Mavis and Audrey left the office somewhat amazed at Lucy's unstoppable drive and energy.

Nineteen

Lilly drove the taxi into the forecourt at seven-thirty on Saturday morning. It was raining. She parked up carefully, as there were coaches parked everywhere. Two coaches for the south coast tours and the luxury coach at the front as it was departing shortly to go to Knaresborough and Harrogate en route for the Edinburgh tour. Mavis and Audrey were there talking to the driver.

'Where have you been, Lilly?' asked Mavis.

'I've taken Mr and Mrs Higson for the early train to London. They're there for the weekend. I have to pick them up tomorrow night.'

'Can you do me a favour? I'm going with this coach to welcome the passengers for the Edinburgh tour and Audrey is the courier in charge. When the coach has departed from Harrogate I want to get back here as soon as possible. Can you pick me up and drive me back?'

'I'll gladly do that, but I have the taxi to clean and trim

up for a wedding. Will it be alright if I fetch you in the van?'

'Yes, that would be fine.'

'I'll have a word with Lucy to explain what I am doing. The housework will have to wait a bit.'

At that moment Lucy and Fred came onto the forecourt and Lilly got agreement to fetch Mavis from Harrogate. Fred took the taxi into the garage to clean it so that Elsie could trim it up under cover.

For the next hour it was hectic. Driver/managers were collecting the names of their passengers from Margaret in the office, passengers were arriving and had to be directed to their particular south coast coach, the luxury tour coach left but was replaced by the mini-coach, which arrived loaded with passengers and their luggage. When the mini-coach was empty, Elsie took it out onto the road. It allowed four coaches to get through for a club trip to Bridlington. At nine o'clock the two south coast tours left, on time, to go to their different holiday towns and a great silence descended upon the garage. The only activity was at the fuel pumps, operated by Brian Hunt. He was facing a long day as he was on duty until nine o'clock that night.

Mavis arrived back at ten o'clock and settled down in the office ready to take over at lunchtime when Margaret left. She noticed that there were bookings coming in for the luxury tours at the Horsforth office. Margaret explained how she had been marketing the luxury tours to clients who seemed to be looking for something different. She explained that her records identified those clients who were well-travelled and obviously had plenty of money. So she'd used her initiative and given them information about the new luxury tours.

'That's a clever move, Margaret,' said Mavis.

'It's not clever,' replied Margaret. 'It's just good marketing. You have to help some people spend their money.'

Elsie and Lilly worked in the garage to trim up the taxis, after Fred had cleaned and polished them. They then brought them out and parked them on the forecourt as it had stopped raining. They went into the house to get changed into their wedding outfits. It was an early wedding, at one o'clock, so they had to be at the bride's house for midday. The reception was at a hotel in Horsforth and the last duty for the wedding taxi was to drive the bride and groom to Leeds station for the five o'clock train. Elsie asked Lilly to do that, as she wished to go out in the evening. Lilly agreed without comment. Elsie wondered to herself when David would tell his sister about their friendship.

Lucy came into the office from the forecourt.

'There's no sign of the new double-decker,' she said. 'It's supposed to be delivered today. I wonder if Bob has got any late information about it? Do you know where he is today?'

Margaret provided the answer. 'He's doing this morning on the Number two double-decker on the Horsforth route. He should be here by two o'clock.'

'Why does he keep driving on the service buses?' asked Mavis.

'He asks for slots,' replied Margaret. 'He says he can leave the planning of operations to us.'

'I have to admit that it helps him to keep his ear close to the ground,' said Lucy. 'He picks up if there are any problems brewing in the ranks.'

At that moment a couple of women came into the office to make a booking. Also Lilly and Elsie came in to announce their departure.

'You have to agree that they look smart, Mavis?' said Lucy, and everyone in the office looked at the young ladies in their wedding gear.

'You' right, Lucy, they do. I think that I might lose my wedding job. I'm too old to compete with them.'

'That's not true, Mavis. You are not too old,' said Elsie. 'We need you on the weddings. Lilly is taking the bride and groom to the station on the start of their honeymoon, so that I can have a Saturday night out.'

'Is it something special?' asked Lucy.

'No, just a trip to town with one or two of my girl friends,' was Elsie's reply.

Mavis looked at Lucy. Neither of them believed Elsie's story about girl friends.

When Bob arrived back at the garage, he spoke to Lucy. He'd received a phone call from the bus manufacturer saying that there was a delay, but they hoped to deliver the new bus some time on Sunday.

'Will you delay putting it on the Otley route until Tuesday, Lucy? It seems to be a bit of a rush.'

'If it gets here tomorrow, I think we should go ahead as we've planned,' replied Lucy. 'I want to get that route settled down with the new buses. I'll get some figures from an exercise Mike Best is doing next week, but I'm confident that the passenger numbers are increasing on the new buses. Mavis is doing two training courses, one next week and one the week after. I'll be interested to see how the Lidgett staff perform on their jobs after the courses.'

'Mavis has certainly made some improvements to the staff as a result of her training sessions,' replied Bob.

'We need her to start planning some more luxury tours. The passengers on the first tour were asking what our plans are to extend the range. I've asked her to keep Audrey in the picture as she develops her plans. We need someone else who understands that part of our business, besides Mavis.'

'You're not thinking that Mavis might leave us, are you Lucy?'

'Certainly not; she has a very good job, which is well paid. But there are no men in her life, so she must be lonely at times.'

The two south coast tour coaches pulled into the forecourt at the end of their week. The holidaymakers had happy faces, and the drivers had big smiles as they gathered the tips from their passengers. Lucy did a quick inspection of the coaches as they were both needed on a five-coach booking for a club trip to Morecambe the next day. The drivers were keen to get home to get some sleep, as they had to leave the garage at seven o'clock

Fred was up early on the Sunday morning and he talked to the five drivers of the coaches booked for the trip to Morecambe. There were one or two comments from drivers who had been on the same club's trip the previous year to Scarborough.

'We'll have an exciting day,' said the first driver, sarcastically. 'There will be bloody kids everywhere. Some of the parents are determined to enjoy their day, so they give their kids some spending money and tell them to bugger off. It's only at the end of the day that they seem to remember them again. There are bound to be some that have got lost. It will be a mad search, then. It's not uncommon for some of them to have joined their mates on the wrong bus. Then it's punishment time. A few kids get slaps and the language that some of the women use with their kids makes my hair curl.'

'The women are bloody tight with their money as well,' commented another driver. 'They think that a shilling is a big tip for a woman and five kids, after having a free day out.'

'Maxwell will pay you well for the day, anyway, you know that,' said Fred with a smile.

'You have to realise that for many of these kids it's all they will see of the sea for this year,' said another driver. 'I'm glad we take on these bookings.' On that comment the drivers got into their coaches and drove off in convoy.

Fred went back into the house and quietly went up to the bedroom to see if Lucy had woken up, as he'd left her fast asleep when he got up. She was sitting up in bed with her eyes closed.

'You stay in bed, Lucy. I'll get you some breakfast. Everything is sorted out in the forecourt. The service buses have left, and the five coaches for the club trip to Morecambe have just left. Who's on the fuel pumps this morning?'

'It's Richard this morning, and David Young for the afternoon.'

'I'll get Richard up, then, and give him some breakfast. What do you fancy?'

'You're not serious, are you, Fred? I'm not used to having breakfast in bed.'

'Of course I'm serious. There's no reason for you to get up yet, so have a lie in this morning.'

'Well, if you insist, I would like cornflakes, followed by poached eggs on toast. Do you think you can manage that?'

'Of course I can. You just lay back and enjoy it.'

Fred made sure that Richard was awake before going down to get the breakfast ready. When Richard came into the kitchen he saw the tray with the cornflakes in a dish.

'Where's Mum?'

'I have persuaded her to have the morning in bed. Elsie

is covering the office and I will be around in the yard. The only thing of consequence today is the delivery of the new double-decker bus, if it comes.'

'Is she alright?'

'Yes, she's fine, but a little tired after the last few hectic weeks. You can see for yourself. I'll take these cornflakes up and then you can take her the poached eggs on toast that she has ordered.'

Lucy was very pleased to see Richard when he went up with the poached eggs.

'Two men looking after me! How lucky I am. Just put the tray here on the bed, Richard. I have a special job for you. Pass me those keys on the dressing table.' Richard passed her the keys and she held them up for him.

This is the key to my office,' she said,'and this one is the key for the top left-hand drawer for my desk. In that drawer are two files — a pink one and a blue one. I want you to get them and bring them up to me here. I can have a quiet two hours studying them while I relax in bed. Don't let your Dad see you.'

'Mum, he'll kill me if he finds out.'

'No he won't, Richard. If it keeps me in bed all morning he will understand. But your test is to get those files to me without him seeing you. You need do it as soon as possible, before Elsie starts in the office.'

'Mum, do you always have to set impossible tasks for the people who work for you?'

'Richard, we are investing in your education so that you can face challenges.'

Richard concealed the keys in his pocket and went downstairs.

'I'm going out to open up the fuel pumps, Dad.'

'You're a bit early, but I suppose that doesn't matter. I'm going to wait until Lilly comes in. I'll get her to make the Sunday lunch so that your mother doesn't need to get up until lunchtime. I've a job to do in the garage on the pit bus.'

'Right, Dad, I'll keep in touch.'

Richard went out to see to the fuel pumps. Elsie hadn't arrived in the general office, so he quickly went into Lucy's office and collected the two files. He took them into the fuel kiosk and hid them under the desk, wrapped in his old jumper. The first car arrived at the pumps, somewhat surprised to see them already manned. Elsie arrived on site and gave Richard a wave. A few minutes later, when he had no clients, he slipped into the general office and spoke to Elsie.

'My Dad will be coming out to work in the garage this morning. Will you tell me when he does, as I have something to do in the house?'

'Yes, I'll do that, Richard. How long are you covering the pumps for today?'

'Up to lunchtime, and then David's taking over.'

Half an hour later, Lilly arrived, and Fred told her that she wasn't to do any cleaning upstairs, but to take Lucy a coffee at eleven o'clock, in her bedroom. She was then to prepare Sunday lunch for five people, as Lilly and David would be able to join the Platt family for the meal. Fred then went into the garage.

In the next lull of customers, Richard rushed into the house, with his jumper covering up the files, and went upstairs.

'All quiet on the forecourt. I've come in to change my jumper,' he reported.

'Well done,' said Lucy, holding out her hand for the two files.

To justify his visit to the house, Richard went into his bedroom and selected a distinctly different coloured jumper. It was a busy morning at the fuel pumps and it was only near lunchtime that he again saw his Dad, who was washing oil from his hands and arms.

'We're having lunch with Lilly and David at one-thirty,' Fred said. 'Mavis is covering the office, as Elsie has a booking for the mini-coach, so Mavis will watch the fuel pumps while we all have lunch.'

'How is Mum? Is she up yet?'

'I've not been in the house. I've been busy in the garage. I think she'll be up by now.'

Lucy supervised the lunch, full of praise for Lilly's cooking. In the conversation while they were eating, Lilly explained that she would be staying at the garage until the evening, when she was to pick up Mr and Mrs Higson from the London train. She therefore offered to do all the tidying up after lunch. Richard looked around, but he couldn't see any signs of the files anywhere. So the subterfuge had worked.

It was teatime when the new double-decker bus was delivered. Lucy and Bob gave the bus an inspection. Bob was impressed with its specification and he knew that Maxwell Motors could be proud of its fleet.

'We'll get it filled up with fuel and take the paper covers off the seats. It can go into service as the number three bus on the Otley route tomorrow.' Lucy wrote a short message to the driver and conductor requiring them to pick up this new bus at the Horsforth garage in time to form the six-thirty bus service from Otley to Leeds and Lilly hand-delivered the messages.

On the Monday morning Lucy signed the contract to market

the old buses to a company in Manchester. They planned to collect them on Wednesday morning, from the Benfield site. Eva Benfield was briefed and provided with all the relevant papers, to supervise the handover.

'It seems to me that there's more money coming in from the Otley route, now,' said Eva.

'So there should be,' replied Lucy. 'We've spent a lot of money on the three new buses and we've extended the number of services we offer. We've still a long way to go until the Otley route gives us the same performance as the Horsforth route, though.' Eva Benfield was somewhat surprised by Lucy's push for improved performance from the new Otley service.

Lucy did a full circuit to Leeds and back as a passenger on the new bus. She rode on the upper deck into Leeds and on the lower deck back out to Otley, listening discreetly to passengers' conversations. Upstairs, a student commented on the bus service. 'This Maxwell Motors must be a progressive firm,' he said. 'I think they now have three new double-deckers on this route; they must have access to a fair bit of capital to do that.'

'It's a bloody lot better service than those old bone-shakers that used to be on this route,' replied his mate.

On the lower deck, the passengers were generally older people and mainly ladies, but they, too, clearly appreciated the new buses.

'I refused to travel on those old buses,' said one woman. 'They were so uncomfortable. I travelled on the Corporation buses. But these are better buses and more comfortable than the Corporation buses.'

Her neighbour added her comments. 'I think that the conductors and drivers are better on these buses. One of the conductors helped me get off the bus last week, when I had a lot of shopping. I'm a bit wobbly at times, so the bit of help was appreciated.'

In the bus station, Lucy spoke at length to the driver and conductor and they were confident that the service would grow in popularity. The conductor asked her a question.

'I've been notified that I have to go on a course next week. What's that all about?'

'They are not really courses, they're briefing sessions about the company. But we also explain how we think our staff should operate so that they do their job better and get more respect from our passengers.' She turned to the driver. 'How did you find the sessions?'

'They were very good, I felt. We all thought that they might be a waste of time, but we were wrong.' He looked at the conductor. 'You'll learn some interesting stuff about the company, and you'll pick up a lot of tips on how to do your job better. Mavis is a very good teacher, with a lot of experience.'

'Okay, I'll look forward to next week then.'

On the Wednesday, Lucy had three separate meetings in her office with three estate agents. To each one she showed details of the house in Otley, and plans of the garage site. She explained that she was looking for a deal with an estate agent to sell the house with vacant possession and then market the garage site to a building firm with outline planning permission for houses on the site.

In the first meeting the general manager of an agency expressed how large and successful his company was and he assumed that Lucy would benefit by choosing a large company like his. He was taken aback when Lucy asked what terms he would charge. He gave a percentage that he would expect to receive for handling the sales.

'I don't think we need to extend this meeting,' said Lucy. 'I'm confident that I shall be able to negotiate a significantly lower rate with one of the other agencies that I shall be seeing today.'

The man was flustered and tried to explain that he was not aware that this was a competitive tender exercise, but this just played into Lucy's hands. 'Maxwell Motors operates to the highest commercial standards. We're careful to make sure that we are not taken for a ride by anyone we deal with. I'm afraid that you have blown it, Sir. I'll bid you good morning.' Lucy stood up and offered her hand. Head bowed, he shook it and left.

The representative of the second company was better prepared. He was fully briefed about Maxwell Motors, and knew that they had taken over the Otley route, which now had new buses. Lucy warmed to him, and was impressed with the questions he asked. When he quoted his price as a percentage of the total sales she smiled to herself that it was significantly lower than that of the first company.

A much younger man represented the third estate agency and he also knew about Maxwell Motors. In answer to Lucy's questions it became clear that his was a smaller company, though he did have a specialist on his staff who covered the sale of sites for development with the planning authorities. When he quoted his terms for handling the contract he quoted one percentage for selling the house and a different percentage for the sale of the development site. Lucy quickly did some calculations and she was pleased with the estimates. She decided to accept his offer. He agreed to send Lucy a detailed proposal for her approval. Lucy was so pleased by the young man's manner and approach that she offered him a cup of coffee, which he accepted. They spent twenty minutes drinking and talking, during which Lucy picked up the latest position in the housing market and the representative gained information about Maxwell Motors. Lucy was sure that she had chosen the estate agency to bring the best financial return on the property.

David Young had a request to make of his sister.

'Would it be possible for us to invite Elsie to have tea with us next Sunday? We've been out together a few times, and I like her very much.'

Lilly was surprised by the request and didn't immediately know how to react.

'I did wonder if something was happening, as you seemed to be going out more. I didn't think it would be a girl friend, though, and certainly not Elsie! She must be a bit older than you.'

'Yes, she's nearly three years older than me, but we get on very well. She's a very nice young woman. I would rather bring her to our house than visit her house. She has a sister and two brothers and I don't think I would be comfortable in a crowded house.'

Lilly quickly decided that she would prefer to entertain Elsie for tea rather than let David go into a strange house.

'Okay, we can have her to tea next Sunday, but we'll have to check that none of us are affected by commitments at the garage.'

'That's why I'm asking you now. I might be on the fuel pumps for Sunday morning, but not all day. I think Elsie will be free, because she has a big wedding on Saturday which will prevent us going out on Saturday night.'

'I know it's a big wedding on Saturday, because I'll be driving the number two taxi.'

Lilly asked to have a word with Lucy about a family matter. Lucy agreed, not having any idea what it was about.

'I wasn't aware of what has been happening, but David has asked me if he could bring Elsie to tea on Sunday. I wonder what you think of this, Lucy? She's older than David, but he says that they are getting on well together.'

'I think it's a wonderful idea, Lilly. They are both very nice young people. I don't know much about Elsie, or her family, but she was the first person I recruited for Maxwell Motors. She's fulfilled all the promise that I saw in her and she's also flexible and can take on responsibilities in the office.'

'I do like her very much and I've done some driving with her on the weddings, but it's just that David seems so young. He's not quite seventeen, and he's never had a girlfriend before...' Lilly's voice died away as though she might have more to say.

'I know it's a challenge for you, Lilly. After all, you yourself are only a little older than Elsie. But think of all that David has gone through, with losing his mother. He needs a friend, as well as your support, Lilly. We'll all have to encourage them to enjoy their time together.'

'I don't know how serious they are, but David has a lot of education in front of him before he can think of settling down. I suppose that's what's worrying me, Lucy.'

'Don't think about wedding bells and things like that, Lilly. That's well into the future. Relationships between young people can be exciting and wonderful when they first start, but when they go wrong they can be heartbreaking and desperately cruel. I think David and Elsie are just at the start. Let's just give them a helping hand.'

'You don't have any need for me on Sunday afternoon, then?'

'Certainly not; you have some catering to do at home. And let them have a bit of time together on their own. You want them to spend time in your house rather than on the streets or in dark corners.'

Lucy didn't say so, but she was challenging herself to think what she would do if she had a similar request from Richard in a couple of year's time.

Lucy spoke to Mavis and told her that Sunday afternoon was not a time to tie up Lilly, Elsie or David at the garage.

'Do I detect that the young lovers have a date?' questioned Mavis.

'I couldn't possibly comment,' replied Lucy, 'but I'm confident that it will be a distinctive afternoon tea.'

Lucy spent some time with Bob, going through the contract that she'd received for the sale of the house and the garage in Otley. They then went on to discuss the report Lucy had received from Mike Best, about the progress with the Otley route. As she'd asked, he'd prepared the results in graph form. These showed that the income on the route was increasing on a week by week basis. At the end of his report he'd written a positive conclusion: 'If the trend can continue, and there is every indication that it will, then the income from the Otley route will be much bigger in total than the income from the Horsforth route.'

Lucy then presented Bob with some figures for the luxury tours to Edinburgh. The passenger numbers were creeping up. Lucy explained that she had arranged for the owner of the travel agency to go on the tour and write about his experiences and that she hoped to be able to use his comments to advertise the tours. She also explained that Mavis would be going on tour, to plan in detail two more luxury tours — one to the Lake District, and one to Chester.

'We are doing well, Lucy,' said Bob. 'When I asked you to expand the company, I never thought it would be to its present size. Where do you think it will end?'

'I have no idea, Bob. I just keep taking the opportunities as they arise.'

The Saturday wedding was the biggest ever serviced by Maxwell Motors. The bride lived in a large house on the outskirts of Yeaden, the wedding service was in St Margaret's, the big Anglican church in Horsforth, and the reception was in a hotel on the outskirts of Ilkley. This all presented logistical problems to be sorted out for the two taxis, the mini-coach and a standard coach. They were transporting guests between the bride's home, the church and the hotel, all afternoon and evening. Some guests also travelled to Leeds station to wave off the bride and groom on their honeymoon. The final transport duty was to take the parents of the bride and groom back to their respective homes when they thought they' had enough of the entertainment at the hotel. This meant that Mavis and Lilly didn't get back to the garage until after midnight. Throughout the evening Lilly had been thinking about the tea that she'd planned for the following afternoon, so her driving passed in a haze.

On Sunday morning, Lilly got up feeling tired. She made breakfast for David before he went to the garage to work on the fuel pumps from eight o'clock to two o'clock.

'You got in late last night from the wedding, Lilly. Did it go off alright?'

'Yes, it was well after midnight when we got back to the garage. Mavis dropped me off here. It was a big do and there'll be some thick heads for the wedding guests this morning. Shall I bring you a sandwich to the garage for lunch?'

'You can if you like. I've arranged to meet Elsie after lunch and we'll arrive for tea about five o'clock.'

Lilly went to the garage with sandwiches and shared them with David. He was disturbed during his lunch by two customers who pulled in to have their tanks filled up.

'This place seems to me to get busier and busier,' replied Lilly. 'Both Lucy and Fred put a lot of hours in these days.'

'Yes, it's lucky that they live on the job,' replied David. 'It was a clever move by Bob to offer them this house. At least he gets a bit of peace now.'

Back home, Lilly tried to rest during the afternoon, but she was thinking about the tea and how she would get on with Elsie away from the garage. At four o'clock she went to her bedroom and got changed into a white blouse and a pale-blue skirt. She was relieved when it got to four-thirty and she could set to work to lay the table. She was using a new, clean tablecloth and the best crockery. The main course was ham and pork pie, with a salad of lettuce, tomatoes and cucumber. The bread was white teacakes, which Lilly had baked herself. With all the food on different plates, the kitchen table seemed crowded. She decided against serviettes, as David would say that she was making a fuss. The dish of tinned peaches for sweet was chilling in the fridge and the final item was a chocolate cake that Lilly had made.

Just before five o'clock David and Elsie arrived. Elsie looked very smart in a flowery dress, which Lilly thought was a little short, but it did show off her legs and her high-heeled pink shoes.

'It is so kind of you, Lilly, to invite me to tea,' Elsie said as they walked in. 'I appreciate the chance to see your house. David is always talking about the house and the way you live.'

'We've been for a walk, and we need to have a wash before we have tea,' said David. 'I'll take Elsie upstairs so that she can use the bathroom.'

'That's fine. I won't mash the tea until you come down,' said Lilly. It all seemed very relaxed, which was a relief to Lilly.

Upstairs, when they had both used the bathroom, David showed Elsie into his bedroom, which was very tidy.

'After tea we'll come back here and I'll show you the studies that I'm doing now at school. Just because I don't have a regular job like you, I don't want you to think that I'm not working. I also need a kiss before we go downstairs.'

'Okay, but just be careful. Don't disturb my hair, and I don't want you to smudge my lipstick.'

David took her in his arms and looked into her eyes. She felt so soft and inviting. As he bent to kiss her she closed her eyes and sighed. What a feeling she aroused in him.

The tea passed in a relaxed and friendly atmosphere, with Elsie talking freely about her family. Hers was obviously a crowded three-bedroom house. Her father worked as a police constable and was a strict disciplinarian with his family. She suggested that her brothers went out drinking at night simply to keep out of their father's way. She finished off her family resumé with a comment about herself. 'I can't believe how lucky I am to have met Lucy Platt. I was drifting to the end of my schooling, when a teacher told me that Maxwell Motors were looking for a young girl. I didn't think I had a chance, but Lucy was very kind when I met her. She asked me a lot of questions which I couldn't answer, but I said that I could promise to work hard for her and do anything she wanted me to tackle. When she sent me for driving lessons my family was shocked, but my Dad was proud of me. When I called with the mini-coach and parked it in our street, all the family came out to have a look. My brothers were speechless.'

'We are all very lucky to work for Lucy,' said Lilly. 'I was very down and depressed when I first met Lucy, and I didn't know what to say, so I asked her to come and see my little house here and how I kept it. She came and then offered me the job, and we've never looked back. When she sent me for driving lessons David was a little sceptical, but it's made my life very interesting.'

'I don't think I was sceptical,' queried David. 'I seem to remember saying that I thought you would be a good driver. And I have been proved right.'

When Lilly produced the chocolate cake to finish off the tea, Elsie was full of praise 'Oh, Lilly you are such a clever person. It's been a wonderful tea, and the chocolate cake just caps it. I'm going to have a big piece, please, even if it does spoil my figure.'

'With all the work you do, Elsie, you'll never get fat at Maxwells,' joked Lilly.

'I've promised to explain to Elsie all the school work that I'm now doing in the sixth form,' said David, just a little hesitantly. 'We'll be in my bedroom, but we won't be too long.'

'I have given instructions that I have to be home early,' explained Elsie. 'I have a booking in the morning to take a team to a course in Manchester, so I have an early start.'

'You two carry on. I'll be tidying up here,' replied Lilly.

In David's bedroom, Elsie was genuinely impressed by the books David showed her. She asked some questions and he answered them seriously, as he wanted to impress her. After half an hour he closed his books and changed the subject.

'Come on, Elsie, we've only another twenty minutes before we have to leave. Let's enjoy that time here together and have a cuddle.' He left his desk and went to sit on the bed.

'Will your sister come and disturb us? I don't want to offend her.'

'She wouldn't think of coming up here. This is my private territory. She'll trust us to behave ourselves.'

'That's alright David, but you know how you turn me on. I don't trust myself not to want you to do more than just cuddle.'

Elsie sat beside him on the bed. He put his arms around her and laid her down. His kisses were answered by Elsie putting her arm around his neck and pulling him towards her. Her kisses became passionate and David couldn't resist running his hand along her legs and feeling the soft, exposed flesh above her stocking tops. Elsie didn't object, so he also stroked her breasts through her dress.

Lilly was sitting in the kitchen wondering what was keeping them so long upstairs. But she recalled Lucy's instruction to let than have some space and time together.

David was driven to more exploration, and Elsie moaned softly and whispered to him how much she liked what he was doing to her. He raised his head and looked down at her laid beside him. Her dress and underskirt were around her waist. He'd never seen anything so beautiful and sexy in his life. He bent down to kiss her again, but Elsie had other ideas.

'Stop now, David. I don't want you to go any further. It was wonderful, but I have to tidy myself up. It's going to be a real challenge not to show Lilly how excited I've been.'

'You are very beautiful, Elsie. I think I need a wash in cold water to calm down myself.'

As they went into the kitchen, Elsie reported calmly on their discussion.

'David is a clever fellow, and he's convinced me he's working hard at school.'

'I'm sure he is," replied Lilly. 'It's been lovely to have you here, Elsie. You must come again.'

'That would be wonderful. And next time I'll insist on doing the washing-up and helping you get the tea ready, Lilly. My mother would have a fit if she knew that I've been treated like a lady this afternoon.'

'Don't worry about that. You get off home and have some sleep. It will be a busy day for you driving to Manchester.'

David held Elsie's hand as they walked to her house. In the street before hers they paused in a driveway and had a goodnight kiss and David had the last word.

'Do drive carefully tomorrow, Elsie. I shall be thinking about you, my dearest.'

David wasn't sure how he'd be able to concentrate at school the next day. The visions of Elsie, laid on his bed, kept coming before his eyes.

'You've not been to see me play cricket this term, Mum,' said Richard. 'I know you're very busy on a Saturday, but we have a game next week, away at Ripon Grammar School, on Thursday afternoon. Is it possible for you to drive the bus for that game?'

'I'm glad that you've told me, Richard. I'll put myself forward for that driving job. I'll see if I can get your Dad to have the afternoon off, as well. We could have a picnic.'

'You should enjoy it. Now that we have moved into May the weather is getting better for cricket.'

Bob was available on the forecourt that afternoon, so Fred joined Lucy on the coach to Ripon. He stowed the picnic equipment in the luggage compartment, including excessive quantities of food. It was a beautiful summer afternoon when the coach parked at the school.

Lucy and Fred set up their site on the boundary of the Colts match. The Ripon team batted first and had some capable batsmen. They'd reached thirty-five for two wickets when Richard was called up to bowl, but he had no luck. Two catches were dropped and he was replaced after bowling four overs.

'That's the first time I've seen him replaced before he got a wicket,' said Fred, disappointedly. 'He's having an off-day.'

'Everybody has off-days from time to time,' said Lucy. 'But he does look a bit angry.'

When the score was 110 for four wickets Richard was brought back into the bowling attack, but from the opposite end of the wicket. Richard had inspected the wicket and thought there was a bit of rough ground just short of a full-length ball. He decided to aim for that rough patch and when he hit it there was a sharp turn of the ball. There was a parade of Ripon batsmen to the crease and quickly back to the pavilion. They were all out for 131 runs, with Richard taking five of the wickets.

Fred fetched the picnic over from the coach, and Lucy invited Dr Poxon to join them.

'I suppose that I should really have tea with the teams,' he said, 'but I'll leave that to my colleagues as I can't refuse your invitation, Lucy. It will give me a chance to catch up on what's happening at Maxwell Motors.'

Without being prompted further, Lucy gave a full description of the latest happenings.

'We're still increasing the income from the Otley route. We realised two weeks ago that cricket matches at

Headingley are good for business when Yorkshire are playing. It will be even better when there's a test match there, so we will deploy an extra double-decker from the Horsforth route then. All the tours are fully-booked, with waiting lists, including the luxury tours to Edinburgh. We've plans to introduce luxury tours to Chester and the Lake District later in the year, using just the one luxury coach. We've extended the range of mini-tours and they are doing really well. The wedding business goes from strength to strength and we get far more requests than we can accept. There are also a lot of additional bookings through the travel agency in Harrogate. In a word, Dr Poxon, things are very good. We are squeezing our assets flat out.'

'You can say that again,' said Fred with feeling.

'Fred Platt, don't you complain! I know that you enjoy working for a successful company.'

Dr Poxon laughed out loud at Lucy's sense of humour.

The cricket match didn't last long after tea. The Leeds batsmen were able to knock the runs off for the loss of three wickets, so Richard didn't get to bat. The first team match lasted nearly an hour longer than the Colts match, so Richard had a leisurely chat with his parents, sitting on their picnic chairs by the coach.

Bob wanted a word with Lucy about the management meeting due in May. 'We have a driver, John Bright, retiring in May, who's had a long period working for Maxwell Motors. He also had a distinguished career in the Second World War and I think it would be worth making a fuss about him.'

'Tell me more,' said Lucy.

'Well, John started working for us when he left school, in 1913. It was all horses and carriages in those days. He was good with horses and when most of them were commissioned in the First World War we kept him on doing all sorts of jobs with the remaining horses and carts during the war. He was too young to be called up. After the war, when we moved to charabancs, he showed that he understood the motors if they broke down and he was a good driver. He couldn't avoid the Second World War, so he volunteered for the army and got involved with a tank regiment as a driver. He was deployed to France and he managed to escape back to England from Dunkirk. He was then in the Eighth Army to the Desert campaign, with Montgomery. He survived that and then fought in Sicily and Italy until the end of the war. He was mentioned in dispatches several times, and awarded a number of campaign medals. He came back to Maxwells and he's been driving since the beginning of 1946 to the present time, on the service buses. He's proved an excellent driver of our new double-deckers. To my knowledge, he has never had an accident of any type. Goodness knows how many thousands of passengers he's transported into and out of Leeds. He's just a quiet, reliable fellow, who likes his job. I don't think he would be retiring now, except that his wife has a debilitating disease and she needs him to look after her.'

'Wow! That is some story, Bob. We have to give him a good send off.' Lucy paused to gather her thoughts before continuing. 'What I suggest is that we invite him, with his wife, to come to the garage for the end of the management meeting, which will be in the last week of May. Assuming it's a nice day, I'll get Lilly and the ladies to lay out a buffet in the yard. If it's raining we'll have to lay it out in the garage. I'll get Fred to smarten up an area, just in case. We can invite a lot of his mates, and I'll get some reporters from the Leeds papers to be here. We'll need one of our double-deckers to be on show, so that they can get photographs of him in the driving seat. You can make a presentation to him and we'll get a bouquet of flowers for his wife. I suggest you give him a big cheque, say £500? What I think we should also do is write up his history and print it off so that the press get some easy copy. It might avoid the reporters making mistakes and spoiling a good story.'

'I'll leave it with you, Lucy, but I like your suggestions.'

'I appreciate you telling me about this fellow, Bob. I think we can pay due respect to John Bright, and at the same time get some good publicity for Maxwell Motors.'

The management committee meeting was opened by Bob, who explained what was to happen after the meeting to recognise the retirement of John Bright. George Clay stated that he thought the plan to recognise John's retirement at the garage had been a brilliant idea, and had the full support of the staff. He gave his view that John was a true gentleman and the very best example of a loyal member of Maxwell staff.

The agenda was quickly covered, as Lucy effectively repeated the items she had raised with Dr Poxon on the Ripon School cricket field. In addition, she reported £1,300 income from the sale of the old Lidgett buses, and a similar figure for the sale of the house which was included in the Lidgett takeover. These figures meant that the cost of the merger was much lower than the first estimates and had undoubtedly been a good deal.

The committee members went out onto the forecourt to mix with the staff who were gathering for the ceremony. John Bright was there, with his wife, so the committee was able to meet them. The weather was fine, so Lilly, Elsie and Margaret were laying out the buffet lunch on two tables set up at the side of the forecourt. It was an impressive spread of sandwiches, nibbles and cakes.

As soon as Lucy came out, she immediately went over

and welcomed Mrs Bright. She took her and found her the seat which had been placed by Fred near the refreshment table. Lucy stayed by her side and she called Mavis across and asked her to look after the press reporters and the photographers who were hovering in the crowd.

When the tables were covered with cloths, Lucy gave a sign to Bob and he brought John Bright over to stand in the front of the refreshment tables. They were both delighted by the number of friends and colleagues who had gathered. Bob took some notes out of his pocket, which Lucy had prepared, and spoke of John's career in the early days of Maxwell Motors, his army life and his subsequent time as a driver with Maxwell Motors. Lucy noted that two of the reporters were following the text with the notes that they had received. Bob spoke with great feeling for his final words. 'This is what I would like you to remember from today. John Bright is the example of what is best in Maxwell Motors, and what has made this company so successful. He is a gentleman, he is completely reliable, he has no edge at all and he is the same as he was in the war. He drives his double-decker bus, like he drove his tank, to provide a first-class, complete service for his passengers. John, we wish you and your wife all the very best for the future. I have two gifts for you: one is a check for five hundred pounds and the other is two cards, one for you, and one for your wife. These cards allow you both free transport on Maxwell buses and coaches, for the rest of your life. Use the cards, John, and let someone else drive you, for a change.'

There was loud applause from the crowd of spectators. Lucy watched the reactions of people: the press reporters were making additional notes and Maxwell staff were marvelling at the generosity of the gifts. Lucy was pleased that the free travel for life, which was a late idea of hers, was being recognised as a generous award.

The photographers encouraged John to take his place in the seat of the double-decker bus to give them some pictures. The staff took advantage of the buffet and Lilly, Elsie and Mavis were kept busy providing fresh tea and coffee. Lucy looked after Mrs Bright, who was very pleased when Elsie presented her with a large bunch of flowers after she had finished her refreshments.

There were many handshakes and good wishes from members of the staff to John, whose wife stayed in the background with Lucy by her side. Mrs Bright confided a comment to Lucy about her husband. 'He has always been a wonderful husband through our married life. I was afraid, on many occasions during the war, when I was left on my own; but he was a very brave soldier and he came back unscathed. I've always stayed in the background because I knew that he would always do what was best for us. I hope I can keep going for a bit longer and that I don't become too big a burden for him. He deserves a happy period of retirement. I'll do my best to make sure he gets it.'

At the end, as the staff drifted away, Bob and Lucy bid farewell to John Bright and his wife. Lucy clung to his wife in a hug and she kissed her. There were tears in Lucy's eyes as she realised that it was a celebration of a distinguished past, but also a welcome to a limited future in very changed circumstances. Lucy summed up her emotions when she spoke to Bob in her office.

'I'm so glad that we arranged that celebration, Bob. But talking to Mrs Bright, I think that their future together might be short, with a lot of suffering. I hope John has some help in the caring that he will have to undertake.'

'I am not sure that they have any close family around,' replied Bob, a note of sadness in his voice.

Twenty

One evening at the beginning of June, Lucy, Mavis, Margaret, Elsie and Fred met to review the forward operations programme for the company.

'How do things look, Margaret? said Lucy to open the discussion. 'I know we are very busy, but can we cope through this summer period?'

'In simple terms, Lucy, you could say that we are 'full up'. There was a time when we were fretting about having tours leaving with empty seats, but it's not like that now. The tours are full and we're juggling waiting lists to fill any seats that become available. I don't think we realised how much business would be provided by the travel agency in Harrogate.'

'Have we enough staff to cover everything without excessive overtime?'

'We've increased the number of part-time drivers but we could do with one or two more conductors. Some of the women have family and just can't do more than eight hours.'

'We will fix that up, Margaret. What about the wedding bookings, Mavis?'

'Our bookings are completely full through to the autumn. We're using Lilly a lot now, but we really must get another female driver, because so many weddings want the two taxis and the mini-coach.'

'I expected you to say that, Mavis. We are open to suggestions for a young lady that we can train for the glamour brigade,' said Lucy with a smile.

'What about your field, Fred?' she continued.

'As you know, we've acquired equipment so that we can change the bus and coach tyres when they get punctures or are worn out. It means that I'll be using Brian more and more, as it's a two-man job to change a tyre. I think we need another young lad in the yard.'

'Have a word with George Clay and see if he can come up with a young lad who'll be as good as Brian Hunt.'

The meeting continued, discussing other details of the administration of the company and little issues that needed sorting out to increase efficiency. Lucy then brought the discussions to a close.

'I think that this has been a useful get-together, but we haven't finished yet. I've invited Bob to join us for a few minutes and to have a drink with us.' She turned to Mavis. 'Will you tell Lilly that we are ready now, and then fetch Bob round, please?'

Lilly came into the room carrying a tray of glasses and two bottles of sherry; she passed the glasses around and then, before she could leave, Lucy told her to stay and take a place at the table.

Mavis returned with Bob, who took a seat at the table

and looked around.

'I knew that Lucy was holding this meeting and so I asked if I could join you when you'd finished your discussions. I just wanted to say to you all a very big 'thank you' for what you are doing to make this company operate so efficiently. The organisation of all our fleet, and the drivers and other staff is excellent. Everyone who works here relies on you to plan their shifts fairly for them to do their job and several drivers have expressed their appreciation of the way you operate. The people who worked for the Lidgett Bus Company knew what it was like to work for poor management. We know that our management team is the very best. So fill your glasses and relax as we drink a toast to Maxwell Motors.'

They all clinked glasses with Bob and there were smiles all round. They enjoyed a further ten minutes of friendly chat.

Fred was the first to leave the room to go into the yard. He needed to see Joe North about the vehicle cleaning programme for that night. He then went into the kiosk and collected all the receipts and cash from the fuel pumps and locked them away in the safe.

In bed that night, Fred asked Lucy a question.

'Was it your idea to ask Bob to close the meeting tonight, and to share the drink with us?'

'Yes, it was. I know Bob relies on the team to organise and plan the operations and I thought we should recognise all your efforts. Any objections?'

No, I thought it was a good idea. We do need a bit more strength in one or two places, though.'

'I knew we did, but I wanted other people to propose the recruitment.'

There was a rush of efforts to get the additional recruits needed for the company. George Clay suggested three names of young lads that he thought might be suitable and Mavis and Fred interviewed all three. One very capable lad explained that he was a good football player and that he was to have a trial with a football league club. He was quickly ruled out. Another lad completely failed on the mathematics of adding up the charges at the fuel pumps, so he too was rejected. The third lad was very quiet and shy, but he answered all the questions correctly. He even impressed Fred by saying that he was familiar with car engines as he helped his father servicing cars. To ensure that he was a possibility, Mavis took him into the general office and asked him to answer the telephone, having first asked Lucy to ring the general office with some questions. His answers were in a quiet, shy voice but they all made sense. Margaret observed him in the process and saw the beads of sweat on his brow. When he put the phone down she spoke to him.

'You did well, but you'll have to develop your voice so that you sound confident on the phone.' The phone rang with an outside caller. 'Like this,' said Margaret.

'Maxwell Motors, this is Margaret speaking. How can I help you?'

Fred took the lad across to the garage to show him the coaches and discuss maintenance with him. Fred was impressed. Margaret spoke to Mavis when she came back into the office.

'He seemed to be a nice young man,' she said. 'I don't think he's ever answered a phone before and he needs a bit of voice coaching. Has he been successful?'

'Yes, we think he will be alright. His name's John Wall. He lives in Rawdon but he has a motorbike so he'll be able to get here quickly any time we want him. When he starts, you can train him to answer the phones with a confident voice.'

On the question of an additional office worker and taxi driver, Lucy had a word with Mavis.

'You remember when we appointed Margaret, we interviewed a smart young woman called Pearl Featherstone. We were both impressed with her, but we thought that Margaret suited our needs better at that time. How about seeing if she might be interested?'

'It's a thought, Lucy. She would certainly make an impact in the glamour brigade, driving the wedding taxis. As I recall, her bust was bigger than any of the current staff.'

'Do I detect a note of jealousy, Mavis?,' Lucy laughed at the description Mavis had used. 'I'll contact her and ask her to call in to see us. I shall want you there, Mavis.'

'You could ask her to send us her vital statistics before the meeting!'

Two days later, when Pearl Featherstone entered Lucy's office, she was wearing a black skirt with a clinging red jumper. Lucy and Mavis exchange glances and smiled at each other. There was no doubt that the tension in the wool jumper verified Pearl's ample bust proportions. Lucy asked Pearl what progress she'd made since that first interview.

'Not much, to be honest,' Pearl replied. 'My boss was shoved out in a reorganisation, so I have been filling-in since then. I was hoping that something might turn up to offer me a new challenge.'

'Well, you've come to the right place,' said Lucy. 'What we require is an all rounder who can take on a range of jobs, in the office and on the road. The needs change from day to day, so whoever gets the job will not be bored but will be continually challenged. Are you interested?'

Pearl confirmed her interest and also that she had a

clean driving licence. She added another clinching comment.

'I've always fancied getting a PSV licence.'

'Now that, too, can be arranged,' said Lucy. 'I have a PSV licence.'

Lucy reported to Bob on the success of appointing John Wall and Pearl Featherstone.

'I was wondering,' Lucy said,'if we should place an advert in the local paper to get one or two drivers and conductors. What do you think?'

'I'm not in favour of that, Lucy. We've never advertised for staff; we've always been able to get the type of person we wanted by using personal contacts. After all, Lucy, we didn't advertise for your job, and we got the right person.'

'I hear what you say, Bob, and I agree with you.'

'How many people are we lacking?'

'Margaret thinks we need a couple of spare conductors and possibly another spare driver.'

'You leave that to me, Lucy. I'll get Margaret the right sort of people that she needs.'

'Thanks, Bob.'

Lucy was cross with herself for misreading the situation on recruitment methods.

July brought several changes in staff. Bob presented Margaret with the names of another spare driver and two spare conductors.

John Wall started work on the forecourt, looking very smart in his Maxwell outfit, but Fred gave him an old boilersuit to wear when he was working on maintaining the buses and coaches. Fred quickly realised that he understood engines and the work necessary to keep them operating.

Fred knew that John Wall would become an important member of the maintenance team.

Pearl Featherstone made an instant impact on the office operations, and as a support for Margaret. She also went out with Mavis in the taxis and the mini-coach to get the feel of them on the road. Mavis reported to Lucy that she would be an excellent addition to the wedding team. 'Though we will need to purchase a larger size blouse and jacket in the Maxwell colours,' added Mavis, with a grin.

The management meeting in July reported the staff changes which reflected the increase in operations throughout the company. The financial figures were also improved in line with this. Bookings made through the Harrogate agency were just under thirty percent of the total, but were still increasing. The level of income from the Otley route was higher than the Horsforth route, and significantly better than the projections at the time of the merger. It was also reported that the arrangements for John Bright's retirement had had a very positive impact on all the staff.

A week later, Margaret asked to see Lucy in her office to discuss a confidential issue.

'There's something happening with Paul Benfield, Lucy. His wife rang me yesterday and asked me to replace him on all his driving slots for the time being. I think he must be ill. She didn't tell me what the trouble is, but she said they would need some time to sort it out.'

The next morning, Eva Benfield rang Lucy.

'Paul is not well at all, Lucy. It's all happened very quickly. He was his normal self three weeks ago, but since then he's lost his appetite, he can't keep food down and he's really weary. We've been to our doctor and he has referred us to the hospital as an emergency case. We have an appointment tomorrow. Our doctor explained that they may need to keep him in for a day or two to do some tests to get a diagnosis. It's so strange for us. He has never been ill and was always critical of people who were continually going to the doctor with supposed health problems.'

Lucy expressed her concern and told Eva to concentrate on her husband and forget about Maxwell Motors. She assured Eva that she would arrange for someone to take over her responsibilities on the Benfield site.

'That would be a great help, Lucy. I think Paul is very frightened and I just don't know how to help him. I've never been in this position before, right through our married life.'

'Just hang in there, Eva. Let me know how you get on at the hospital, tomorrow. I'll come over then and meet you and we can discuss anything that we can do to help.'

Lucy arranged that Pearl Featherstone should divide her time between the Horsforth office and the Benfield site. She would receive all the cash from the Otley route and transfer it to the Horsforth site on a daily basis.

Paul Benfield stayed in hospital for two days and was then sent home. The consultant asked to see Eva. He spoke to her very quietly and explained all the tests they had done. He tried to prepare her for bad news. Then he gave her the diagnosis. Paul had an aggressive form of cancer and it was already affecting several of his main organs. With this type of cancer, he said, Paul could be expected to decline quickly and his life expectancy would be measured in weeks rather than months. He would discuss the position with Paul's doctor who would be able to prescribe drugs to limit the pain and reduce the mental stress for Paul.

Eva immediately burst into tears and the consultant called in his senior nurse to help him to calm her down. She had a range of questions that she wished to raise — questions that had never crossed her mind before. Through her tears she blurted them out.

'How can I help him? What do I tell him? We have no children and we've lost touch with both our families. Who will help me to help Paul?'

In response to Eva's obvious panic, the senior nurse, who had seen people in this position before, advised her to contact any friends she had and discuss the situation with them. The senior nurse also thought that Eva should see their doctor, with her husband, to get some advice on how to give Paul guidance on the seriousness of his position.

Eva didn't drive straight back home, but instead decided to call in Horsforth and see Lucy. When she was shown into Lucy's office it was clear that she was very disturbed. Lucy asked her to sit down.

'Just relax as much as you can, Eva, and then we'll talk. I'll arrange for us both to have a cup of tea first.' She asked Elsie to bring in tea and biscuits.

Both Elsie and Margaret, who had seen Eva when she entered the general office, realised that something was seriously amiss. Lucy fussed around and distracted Eva from talking until the tea was available. After she had served both of them a cup of tea, she sat beside Eva and took her hand.

'Now, Eva, tell me your news.'

'It's the very worst news, Lucy. I'm on my way back from seeing the consultant. He suggested that I should talk to any friends to get their support. So I decided to call in and see you, Lucy. I hope you don't mind. But I'm desperate and don't know what to do next.'

'You have done right to call and see me, Eva. I will do all I can to help you. What did the consultant say about Paul's illness?'

'It's cancer, Lucy. The consultant says that it's a very aggressive form of cancer, for which there's no treatment. He says that Paul can expect to live only weeks rather than months. What can I do, Lucy?' Eva burst into tears and leaned her head on Lucy's shoulder. Lucy comforted her and then helped her dry her tears.

'The first thing you must do, Eva, is forget about Maxwell Motors. You have to be available constantly to help Paul in whatever way he needs you. I've already organised that Pearl Featherstone will take on all your duties at the Benfield site. You will still get paid, so you mustn't worry about the money side. I'll also arrange that Paul is paid just as though he's working.'

'Thank you, Lucy. But it's not money that's worrying me; it's how to handle Paul. He is not the easiest husband to deal with, but he looks really afraid now, Lucy. The nurse in the hospital suggested that I should talk to our doctor and get him to visit Paul and explain what can be done to help him.'

'In that case, Eva, I think you should ring your doctor from here and talk to him and arrange when he'll visit Paul at home.'

There was a delay until Lucy obtained the telephone number for the doctor. Lucy went round to her desk and listened to Eva's conversation with the receptionist and then with the doctor. Eva was calm and explained what the consultant had told her. From the snatches of conversation, Lucy gathered that the doctor and the district nurse would pay a call the following morning, at around eleven o'clock, to examine Paul and discuss with him the diagnosis and the medication that would be prescribed.

'Did Paul know that you were going to the hospital this afternoon?' asked Lucy.

'No, he thinks I was going into town to do some shopping.'

'In that case I feel it might be better for you to go home and say nothing about the diagnosis. Let that come out in the discussions with the doctor tomorrow. You could tell Paul that you've called to see me and that you're both free of any responsibilities for the Benfield site. It's a big challenge for you, Eva, but you have to be positive and normal tonight. Try to relax him with love and tender care.'

'I'll try, Lucy, but Paul might reject me. What he wants is some reassurance that his illness can be cured. When he gets the truth he will be shattered.'

'We will try to help you when he's in that state. Let me know how you get on with the visit from the doctor tomorrow.'

Lucy spent some time during the following day thinking of the implications for Maxwell Motors that would follow from the death of Paul Benfield. She decided to keep the diagnosis of Paul's illness to herself, so ignored the questioning glances in the general office.

That same night, David Young and Elsie had another night at the pictures in Leeds. Unlike their normal routine, they'd arranged to call back at David's house to have a cup of tea with Lilly before David took Elsie home. Lilly had the kettle boiling and served the tea quickly. There was a short chat about the film, and then David asked to discuss an idea with Lilly. Elsie took up the conversation.

'What I would like to do is to prepare a meal here, next Sunday afternoon, Lilly. There would just be the three of us, but I would like to be in charge. David says that you are always providing food here, and at Lucy's house, so you deserve a change. What do you think, Lilly?'

'That's very kind of you, Elsie, but putting on a meal is no problem for me. I wouldn't know what to do if I wasn't in charge.'

'I'll tell you what to do,' replied David. 'You can relax in your bedroom and then get dressed in your new outfit and come down when we call you.'

'Oh, so it's a posh do then!'

'It certainly is,' replied David.

So the plan for Sunday afternoon was agreed. That night, when they got near Elsie's house, even though it was not really dark, David gave Elsie a passionate kiss. He was thrilled that their relationship was moving forward and he had every confidence, from their discussions, that Elsie would provide an impressive meal.

The following afternoon Lucy took a call from Eva Benfield to report on the visit by their doctor to examine Paul and discuss medication with him.

'How did it go, Eva?' she asked.

'It went quite well. The doctor was very good and he has clearly had similar cases to deal with in the past. He explained how serious the situation is, but he also concentrated on the medication he will be prescribing for Paul. He gave Paul plenty of chances to ask questions but Paul didn't have any questions. That seemed a bit strange to me. I asked Paul if he was clear what was going to happen and he just nodded and said he was in the picture.'

'That does seem strange, Eva. How is Paul generally now? Is he less stressed?'

'He's different from what he was before he went into hospital. You might say he's more laid-back and less edgy than he was, though I suppose it could be the medication. The doctor has certainly given him a range of pills. But he is not as restless as he was. He keeps going out for walks around the garage and looking at the buses parked here.'

'Do you think it would help if I called in to see him, with Fred or Bob?'

'I'm not sure about that, Lucy. I am more in control than I expected to be, and Paul is not bitter and angry about the prospects, which is what I feared most.'

'We'll leave it for a day or two, then. Just you keep me briefed on what is happening, Eva.'

Elsie and David discussed Sunday tea as they went for an evening walk on Friday night.

'I know what I'm going to do for the tea, but your job will be to do the shopping tomorrow morning,' said Elsie. 'I will be in the office at the garage all morning, and through the afternoon and into the evening I'll be driving at a Harrogate wedding. So, I've made a list and indicated where in Leeds you can get the items I need. We shall be having prawn cocktail for starters, and then smoked salmon with salad for the main course. For the sweet, I've decided to have profiteroles with chocolate sauce. You'll have to buy the profiteroles and then carry them very carefully in a separate bag from town. Don't let them get crushed! I shall bake some bread at home on the Sunday so that we can have fresh brown and white bread.'

'It sounds like a bit of a posh menu.'

'It's the sort of meal you would get at a big hotel in Leeds. Your sister deserves a treat. I'm sure you agree with that.'

'Yes, I do agree. I want you to impress her, and I hope we can have a bit of time together in the evening, on our own, before I take you home.'

'Don't build up your hopes too high. There'll be the washing-up and tidying up to do after the meal, and I'll want your help. I might be too tired for any frolicking after all my efforts through the day. I hope Lilly likes fish?'

'Yes, she does. And she'll want me to show you her appreciation for your efforts. I'm sure you'll relax and let me do that.'

'David, I'm wary of relaxing too much because your wandering hands can't be trusted to behave themselves!'

It was half past five on Saturday morning when Lucy heard the telephone ringing and jumped out of bed to answer it.

'Lucy, this is Pearl. I am at the Benfield site. Can you come over quickly?' Lucy heard panic and trembling in Pearl's voice. 'There's a major incident here. I am afraid Paul Benfield has hanged himself at the back of the garage. I saw him when I came in here to get something for one of the conductors. The three bus crews have gone, but none of them saw Paul swinging on the end of the rope. I let them go, as I didn't want them to get involved. But it was a real shock for me. I've rung the police, and requested an ambulance as well, but I'm sure he's dead. Eva doesn't know yet and I'm assuming she's still asleep in bed. I'm trying to stop shaking so that I can concentrate on doing the right thing. I could do with some help.'

'I'll be there, with Fred, as soon as possible. If you can, don't let Eva see him while he's still hung up.'

Fred drove the taxi at speed and they were there in ten minutes. They parked at the entrance to the garage and saw Pearl taking two policemen to the site of the suicide. There was no sign of Eva.

When Pearl saw Lucy, she came over to her and fell into her arms.

'Thank God you've come, Lucy.' She was shaking violently. 'I don't think I could have handled it on my own for much longer.'

'You have been brilliant, Pearl,' said Lucy. 'We will take over now. Come and sit in the office here and calm down. You can't see Paul from the office.'

Fred was with the policemen, discussing what should happen next. One policeman was taking notes and Fred was answering his questions about names and the use of the site for Maxwell buses.

'Surely we should get him down?' said Fred. 'We don't want his wife to see him strung up there.' Near to Paul was a tall stool, laid on its side, that he had obviously kicked away when he was ready with the rope round his neck. At that moment an ambulance arrived. Fred met the two medics and took them into the garage. The senior ambulanceman said that, in his opinion, Paul had been dead for a while. He added that a doctor needed to come to certify the death and that the body would have to be removed for safe-keeping, as this was a case for the coroner. Fred asked the policeman to call for a doctor so that the body could be removed.

When Pearl had calmed down a bit, Lucy came over to Fred and suggested they went over to the house to see Eva. They told the policemen that they'd try to stop Eva coming into the garage. The policeman said he would have to interview her at some stage, and he would also want more details from Pearl. They found the house door unlocked and entered quietly. They went to the bottom of the stairs and then they heard movement above, so they stood and waited. Eva appeared at the top of the stairs. She was dressed in a white, satin nightdress and she had a dressing-gown over her arm. She looked dishevelled, as though she'd just woken up. She looked down at Lucy and Fred.

'What are you doing here?' she called out, with trepidation in her voice 'I'm looking for Paul. He wasn't in bed with me when I woke up just now.'

'Come on down, Eva. Let me make you a cup of tea. Then we can have a talk,' said Lucy.

Lucy went into the kitchen to make the tea while Fred waited for Eva to come slowly down the stairs. He took her arm and led her into the lounge. Eva gave Fred a strange, perplexed look. 'Where is Paul? Do you know where he is?'

'Yes, we know where he is. We'll explain it to you while we drink the tea.'

Fred was hoping that Lucy would have some ideas on how to break the news to Eva. Eva said she needed to use the downstairs toilet and when she returned Lucy had poured the tea.

'Lucy, tell me where Paul is.' Eva seemed to be waking up, but she still had a worried look on her face.

'He is in the garage, Eva. He's had a very serious accident.'

'Is he badly injured? I wonder what he was doing in the garage in the night?'

'You have to prepare yourself for very bad news, Eva. Paul was killed in the incident. The police are there and an ambulance team. The police will want to talk to you.'

'How did it happen?'

'I'm afraid Paul made it happen. He clearly didn't want to carry on living the final bit of his life, tortured by the cancer. He hanged himself.'

'Oh, Lucy, are you suggesting he planned this?' Tears were pouring down Eva's face. 'I now know why he changed his attitude when the doctor had told him the truth. I've failed him, Lucy. He should have told me what he was planning.'

'No, you didn't fail him, Eva. You did everything you

could to help him. Come on now, let me take you upstairs so that you can get dressed. There's a lot for you to do. I'll stay here with you today, Fred will check things in the garage and then he'll go back to Horsforth.' She turned to Fred as if to confirm the arrangements. ' I'll ring you when I want fetching, Fred.'

'Can you spare the time to stay with me, Lucy? I would appreciate it if you would. I'm so shocked that I can't think straight.'

'I will be around today and as much as you need me,' replied Lucy.

Fred went back into the garage. The ambulancemen had got Paul down and laid him on a stretcher to be examined by the doctor. Fred spoke to the police and they agreed to interview Eva in the house. They also agreed that the rope could be taken down from the beam in the roof. Fred found a long ladder and unfastened the rope from the beam. From the way it was tied it was clear that Paul knew what he was aiming to achieve. The police told Fred that they'd taken a full statement from Pearl before she'd left the site.

When Fred returned to Horsforth, he immediately sought out Pearl to ensure that she was recovering from her traumatic experience. He spoke to Margaret, Mavis and Elsie, and explained what had happened. They needed to watch Pearl throughout the day to see if she was affected by delayed shock. He then arranged to see Bob, when he returned from his morning shift on the Horsforth route.

Fred then got changed and went into the garage to join John Wall who had already started work servicing a coach. He was pleased with John's work in the garage.

Later, when the post came into the general office there was a large envelope addressed to Fred. It contained detailed drawings for the steel work and foundations to construct a garage extension alongside the existing garage. It also showed another access road, beyond Bob's new bungalow at the back of the garage. This extension to the garage facilities might be needed earlier than anticipated, with the death of Paul Benfield, thought Fred.

In Lucy's absence, Fred inspected the two taxis and the mini-coach as they departed for the wedding in Harrogate. Mavis was glad that she was on duty, having noticed the shocked faces of Elsie and Lilly as they spoke about Paul's suicide. She would have to make sure that they could produce their wedding smiles by the time the taxi convoy got to Harrogate. In the afternoon, Fred had a session with Bob, who was shocked by the news, and then mumbled that it could mean some more forced changes to Maxwell Motors. Fred decided not to show Bob the plans for the garage extension at this stage.

Lucy was picked up by Fred in the late evening. She explained what had happened since Fred had departed. Eva had been interviewed by the police and she'd given a full description of Paul's illness and the discussions with his doctor. She'd explained how Paul was calmer after he'd received the diagnosis from his doctor. The police had said that there would have to be a post-mortem before the body could be released for burial. Eva had indicated that it would be a cremation. Lucy's final comment to Fred was about the implications of Paul's death.

'I think Eva will be alright after the next week or two. She was much more settled when I left her. There are some interesting issues for Maxwell Motors, depending on what Eva decides. We might not have continued use of the Benfield site.'

'We have an alternative option,' Fred said, quietly. 'I've received the plans for a major garage extension today. It will allow us to handle all the buses and coaches on this site.'

'That won't be a quick fix though, Fred,' responded Lucy.

The calm atmosphere David and Elsie had experienced on the Friday night changed on the Sunday afternoon, at Lilly's house. They were all affected by the suicide of Paul Benfield and Lilly was the first to speak openly of her shock.

'I can't stop thinking about him doing that. I know he was very ill, but to take his own life by hanging himself sends a shiver down my spine. I spoke to Pearl and she described what she saw. It certainly upset her. It wasn't easy to get into the spirit of the wedding yesterday, with thoughts of Paul's body swinging on a rope.'

'We've got to try and put it behind us, Lilly,' said Elsie. 'Life must go on.'

'Yes, Lilly, let's think of other things now,' said David. 'Off you go upstairs and get changed. Elsie can't wait to see your new outfit. We'll give you a shout when the tea is ready.'

'Are you sure that I shan't be over-dressed?'

'No, it's a posh meal. We've got serviettes —so that you won't slop on your outfit!'

Lilly went upstairs where she'd already laid out her new clothes on her bed. She had a pale-blue, two-piece suit, with a white blouse. She also wore a new bra, with matching knickers, and a new suspender belt with pale-blue stockings. The skirt was tightly shaped around her bottom and showed off her shapely legs and her pale-blue high-heeled shoes. When she inspected herself in the mirror she wondered if she had gone a bit too far. Though she did consider that she looked smart. Would Elsie agree?, she thought.

Before they started to finalise the tea, David took Elsie in her arms for a passionate kiss. 'I want to have a kiss now, just in case you're too tired afterwards,' he said.

'Oh, well, that's the passion done with! We have only to concentrate on the meal now,' said Elsie, breaking free from his embrace.

Within half an hour, all was ready. David shouted up the stairs and called Lilly. She came down the stairs with careful steps as she didn't want to trip with her new shoes. She entered the room and did a swirl, for effect. Both David and Elsie gasped with amazement.

'Lilly, you look fabulous,' said Elsie. 'The outfit fits you beautifully, and it looks as if it was made especially for you. Where did you find it?'

'I was told by David to go into Leeds and buy myself a smart new outfit for my birthday. He even produced some of the money for it. I saw it in the first shop I went into. The shop assistant said I looked just right in the outfit, but I took a while to steel myself to buy it.'

'I told her she needed something for special events,' added David.

'Have you seen it before, David,' asked Elsie.

'No, but I did see it on the hanger and thought it looked good. But it looks a lot better with Lilly inside it.'

'Well, I am not wearing the jacket to eat tea,' said Lilly. She took it off and put it over a chair in the lounge. 'Now for the food. I'm really hungry, having got through the clothes show.'

The meal was a great success and every course worked perfectly. Lilly was full of praise for Elsie's skill in preparing such a meal. There was a contented atmosphere of satisfaction all round. David insisted that the tidying up and washing-up was for Elsie and himself and Lilly was excused to go back into her bedroom and get changed into more relaxing clothes. When she came back down, and the tidying up was complete, David said that he and Elsie were going up to his bedroom for a short while, as there was something that he wanted to show Elsie.

When they were laid on his bed, David reflected on the meal. 'You were brilliant, Elsie. That meal was top of the range. Lilly was very impressed, I'm sure. I'll bet she talks about today's feast in the office next week.'

'I'm glad it went well. I like to succeed. By the way, what's the thing you said you wanted to show me?' David hesitated, and seemed reluctant to answer the question.

'I'm a bit embarrassed to tell you, Elsie. Are you sure you want to know?'

'Now I'm really intrigued. You have to tell me.'

'Well it's in my trousers. You excite me so much that he gets very big and wants to get out.' Elsie reached over and touched the front of David's trousers.

'I can feel what you mean. But you can tell him he will have to stay locked up tonight. I deserve some kisses and a cuddle, but not too much excitement.'

She pulled David down onto her and wrapped her arms round his neck and kissed him greedily. It was a short session, but David made her sigh and gasp.

When Elsie was leaving, Lilly was effusive in her thanks to her for providing a tea that had taken their minds of the tragedy of Paul Benfield's suicide.

Lucy settled in the railway carriage seat with a big sigh.

'I am relieved, Fred, that we have made it to the start of our holiday. I never thought we would, when there was the delay of the post-mortem for Paul Benfield. It would have been impossible to leave Eva to go on the holiday before the funeral.'

'Lucy, just relax now. You really need to unwind. Nobody could have done more than you did to help Eva.'

'But we have left lots of ends to sort out regarding the Benfield site, and finding out what Eva wants to do.'

'But we're only away for a week. Eva has taken over running the Benfield site again, so that's a good sign that she doesn't want to pull out straightaway.'

'And I'm feeling guilty that we have not got Richard with us on this holiday.'

'Lucy, you know why he didn't want to come. He wants to play in the cricket matches for the local team this week. He's going to revel in the time we're away. He has David and Lilly staying in the house with him, so he'll get fed morning, noon, and night. He's sharing the fuel pump duties with David, so he'll be getting bags of money. He's on to a good thing!'

'He is growing up so much now, Fred. Do you think he'll want to move away from us soon? I don't want to lose him.'

'You won't lose him, Lucy. He knows that we're proud of him. He has done brilliantly on the sports field this last year and his academic results have also kept up.'

'It will be an important year for him when he goes back to school in September. He'll have his O-level exams next July. We'll have to support him through that, Fred.'

'We'll support him like we have always done. Now, concentrate on this holiday, Lucy,' he finished. 'That's an order.'

'I will, Fred. Mavis assured me that we'll have the best of everything in the hotel in Torquay. I think that for the first couple of days I'll just want to chill out and sleep. But I have a list of events taking place in the town while we're there.'

'Make a start now, and close your eyes. We might get more passengers in this compartment when we get to Doncaster.'

Bob had relinquished his driving slots for the week and said he would be around on the forecourt to support Mavis. There was a puncture on one of the wheels of a double-decker on the Otley route on Sunday afternoon, so a coach was put into service to allow the double-decker to be withdrawn. Bob called out John Wall and Brian Hunt to change the tyre. They had a spare wheel, and all the equipment available when the bus was driven into the garage. Under John's instruction they had the bus jacked-up and the wheel changed in just under half an hour. The driver took the bus to the town centre to replace the single-decker coach.

'That was pretty slick, lads,' said Bob, as the two young men tidied themselves up and cleared away the equipment they'd used on the job.

'We'll change the tyre on that wheel in the morning,' said John.

Richard was doing the afternoon shift on the fuel pumps. They were quite busy when he took over from David, and it continued like that through to teatime. Richard had played a full game of cricket on the Saturday, when he had taken three wickets and scored thirty-five runs. He was hoping to have a quiet evening resting after he closed the pumps. He was just settling down to do so when he got a phone call from Lucy.

'I'm missing you here, Richard,' she said. 'How are you getting on?'

'I am fine, Mum.' he replied. 'Are you having a rest and a

change?'

'Yes, your Dad and the hotel manager are cosseting me night and day. I'm perking up already. Here, have a word with your Dad, who wants to know how you went on at the cricket yesterday.'

Richard gave a report on the match and then he gave his Dad clear instructions. 'You have only to answer yes or no to these questions,' said Richard, and then he asked lots of questions to ascertain if Lucy was really relaxing on her holiday.

'How is your mother, then?' asked Lilly, when Richard put the phone down.

'I think she's getting a rest and a change, if I can trust Dad's answers.'

'Can I get you a scone, or a piece of cake, with a drink for your supper?'

'That would be nice, Lilly. I think I'll have a piece of your chocolate cake. You are spoiling me. I think I'll go to bed then.'

'I'll wait up for David. He's gone out with Elsie, so he could be late.'

Lucy and Fred came back from their holiday fully refreshed. They'd enjoyed their week in Torquay and Lucy was tanned from her time in the sun and her eyes had their sparkle back. She agreed with Bob that she would tackle the main issues facing Maxwell Motors, starting with the garage extension.

Fred had called in a builder friend of his, who had prepared the plans, which were now laid out on the table in Lucy's office. Fred explained that the design would provide sufficient garage capacity so that the company could operate from one site. The fleet was listed down the side of the plan; five double-decker buses, ten coaches (including the three Benfield Coaches), one luxury coach, one mini-coach, one mine bus and two taxis. Fred explained that the plan utilised the existing wall of the current garage, so the new garage would only need one side wall building. The builder showed an elevation of the new garage, which would be slightly higher than the existing garage. This allowed the rainwater from half the new garage roof to be collected into the existing water channel of the old garage, which would need to be enlarged.

There was a long discussion about the new access road from the main road round to the back of the garages. This would become effectively a one-way entrance to the main garage site. All the vehicles would leave by passing through one or other of the garages and then the forecourt onto the main road. Behind the garages there was a maintenance bay and a cleaning bay. It was the cleaning bay and the maintenance bay that defined the need for additional land to be bought. The total capacity, at eighteen vehicles under cover, meant that there was room for all the operational vehicles on most nights.

Fred explained another concept of the design. It was planned that, before being parked for the night, all vehicles would be filled with fuel for the next day. It was thus desirable to have a separate fuel pump, behind the garages, in addition to the existing fuel pumps.

At the end of the meeting it was agreed to appoint a project manager who would take the concept through the planning process and draw up detailed specifications to appoint a contractor for the work. As a separate exercise, Bob would have a plan prepared to approach the owner of the land that was required at the back of the garages.

'When do you think we can expect to have the enlarged facilities operational?' asked Lucy straight to the point as usual. Fred looked at his builder friend to give a reply.

'Planning permission will be the critical issue,' he said. 'Then I would expect the actual building work to take around six to eight months.'

'So I can plan on working with the existing arrangements for the next year.'

'Yes, I think that's a fair assumption, Lucy,' replied Bob.

On the Tuesday after returning from holiday, Lucy, accompanied by Mavis, had a meeting in her office with Eva Benfield. Her first concern was to see how Eva was coping with her new situation after the death of her husband.

'Let me say at the outset, Eva, that I was most impressed by your guts in getting back into harness last week, looking after the Benfield site. I was away on holiday but I can tell you that everybody was thrilled to see you back. How are you feeling now?'

'I am slowly getting back into the real world. I think it was the best thing for me to resume my duties on the site, rather than sitting around brooding about the changes to my life.'

'Good. What I want to do now is discuss the plans that we have going forward,' began Lucy. 'We will continue to hire Benfield coaches, for which you will get paid at the daily rate, and you will also get paid for your supervision of the site and the Otley buses. So you will thus have a significant income and no financial worries.'

'That is fine by me, Lucy. It will keep me busy while I settle down.'

'And I expect that arrangement to continue for the next twelve months. We have started planning for a major extension to our garage facilities, which will allow us to operate all our fleet from this Horsforth site, in due course.'

Lucy laid out the plans and explained them to both Mavis and Eva.

'It seems a good scheme, as far as I can make out,' concluded Eva.

'We have one extra suggestion to make, in the short-term. We think that we should withdraw the three Benfield coaches from use, one at a time, and send them away to be re-sprayed in the Maxwell colours, and also have the seating refurbished. How do you feel about that Eva?'

'I've no objections to you doing that. I assume it will be paid for by Maxwell Motors?'

'Yes, it certainly will be paid for by us. When we have the new garage facilities, and we're operating from the one site, we would expect to buy the three coaches from you at their valuation at that time. You will then be able to sell your garage site for whatever value you can get for it. You will be rich then, Eva.'

Eva smiled at Lucy's last comment. 'I know it's in the future, but what if I wanted to keep working in some role with Maxwell Motors. Would that be a possibility?'

'With your knowledge and experience of the way we operate, I can assure you that we'd be able to find you a role in the Maxwell organisation.'

'I would like to have that option as a possibility.'

'That is no problem, Eva. I will give you a letter spelling out what we've agreed.'

Eva left, seeming quite relaxed about her role in the future.

Lucy had made arrangements for Pearl Featherstone to have lessons to get her PSV licence, so she could expect to do more driving. Lucy was sure that there would be slots to fit Eva Benfield into a role in the future.

Lucy met Bob and explained what she'd negotiated and

he started the ball rolling with arrangements for the Benfield coaches to be withdrawn and re-branded. He also explained that he was going to see one or two of his friends on the Council to explain the garage plans. He intended to make the point that the garage plan would devalue his bungalow, with the new access road going around his property.

'You can also tell them that it takes all the land from our garden,' said Lucy. 'But neither Fred nor myself will lose any sleep over that. And just think what a difference it will make to the efficiency of our operations.'

Twenty-one

September saw the introduction of a new programme for the luxury tours. The monthly cycle consisted of three tours to Edinburgh and one tour to Chester. Mavis was confident that she'd organised a six-day tour that visited excellent locations and properties in the region around Chester. The five-star hotel in the city centre was steeped in history, with large rooms incorporating the latest luxury fitments.

The Chester luxury tours had been advertised to everyone who'd travelled on an Edinburgh luxury tour, and flyers had been distributed on the passenger buses and coaches. Mavis was pleased at the numbers booked on the September and October tours. Audrey Worth was grateful that her role of courier would now have some variety, with there being two luxury tour locations. She'd asked Mavis if the policy was for more luxury tours in the future.

'Yes, I have ideas for developing more luxury tours, but they are on hold. The priority for the company seems to be to do a major expansion of the garage so that we can operate everything from the Horsforth site.'

Lucy was very proud in September when Richard returned to school for his fourth year culminating with the O-level exams. He was a confident young man, who knew that he could achieve good results in his studies as he was rated now in the upper half of the top stream. Both Lucy and Fred had encouraged him to regard the academic performance as his main objective for the school year, however, after his first few days of term, he came home with the news that he would be vice-captain of the school second team at rugby. He confided to his Dad that he might even get a run out with the first team before the end of the season.

'Don't mention that to your Mother, Richard. She worries about you playing rugby, and she's enough on her mind with Maxwell Motors.'

The bi-annual board meeting took place in September. The financial report was very positive and emphasised the increased results from the Otley route. The importance of the bookings that now came through the Harrogate travel agency was noted and the new luxury tour to Chester was described in detail. The plans for the garage extension were tabled and explained. The death of Paul Benfield was noted and the future use of the Benfield site and its eventual disposal was explained. The forward objectives for the Company were distributed in a brief written report by Lucy. It stated: 'We plan to keep our programme of operations working flat out for the next year. We will continue to develop our staff so that they are given the skills to perform with confidence in a busy company. We want them to be able to cope with the challenges that arise in the day-to-day operations of our business. Their performance in the last year has played a major role in ensuring the success of Maxwell Motors.'

The board unanimously accepted the reports.

Dr Poxon asked to have a word with Lucy, in private. He stayed behind until Lucy's office was cleared of all the remaining food and crockery, and then he raised his question. He was confident in his approach to her.

'Lucy, we want to arrange a repeat of the Grimethorpe Band concert that the school put on two years ago. It was a major event for the school and it was a great success. Will you be prepared to sponsor it, like you did last time?'

'The answer to that is quite simple; yes, we will sponsor the concert. When are you planning to arrange it?'

'I understand that there have been initial discussions with the band and the date will be in March next year, before the Easter holidays.'

'That is an ideal time. We have an interest in the exams next year, as Richard will be taking his O-levels. We're encouraging him to concentrate on his academic studies for this academic year.'

'I think you'll find that he can cope with his sport commitments and his studies. He's a mature young man, now. I think he must take after you, Lucy.'

'My sporting achievements as a young woman were zero, so he must get his sports skills from his Dad.'

'I think he gets from you his commitment to work hard at whatever he's doing, whether it's sport or studies. You don't have anything to worry about, Lucy.'

Lucy was pleased at that evaluation of her son.

'Mavis had a meeting with Lucy about the future of the

luxury tours.

'I am not clear what to do about developing new luxury tours, Lucy. The tours are very profitable, and there is a lot of interest by our clients. But with just one luxury coach available, there is no room for more destinations. I have ideas for an additional tour, centred on Cambridge, and one centred on Cheltenham. What should I do?'

'You should quietly phase in your work on those tours during the next nine months. As soon as the new garage project is completed, I am confident that we'll want to purchase another luxury coach. Of course, that is confidential between me and you, Mavis. I don't think I could get agreement for such a purchase at the present time, with either Bob or the board.'

Lilly was having a half-day at home doing her weekly clean through the house to keep it in its pristine condition. She had just David's bedroom and the bathroom to clean and tidy. David's bedroom was fairly neat, but she found a pencil and a paper under his desk. She picked them up and opened his desk drawer to put them away. At first she was surprised, and then shocked. In an open box were several packets with pink things in them. Lilly picked one up to examine it and then dropped it as she realised that it was a condom. She felt her face flush and she gasped.

What did this mean?, she thought. Was David having sex with Elsie? She knew that they were very fond of each other, but had it progressed to full sex? What could she do about it? She couldn't discuss it with David, because he would know that she'd looked in his desk.

Lilly felt very insecure. She had never had a boyfriend of any consequence. Her contact with boys had dried up when her mother became ill and she'd been confined to the house looking after her. But Elsie was only a little older than

Lilly. She sat down on the bed and realised that she was missing out. Would she be left on the shelf? Then she thought of Mavis, Margaret and Pearl. They were all smart women, but none of them were married.

Lilly then had another thought. It might be that David and Elsie were being very sensible, by taking precautions. Lilly quickly replace the pencil and paper on top of the desk, to remove any evidence that she had seen inside it.

Lucy met the luxury coach when it returned from the first tour to Chester. She had received a mid-tour report from Mavis, who was acting as courier alongside Audrey Worth, to say that it was going well. Lucy chatted with the passengers and she was delighted with their comments. They had really enjoyed the trip. Mavis said that she was confident that they had another tour that would be well supported due to word of mouth recommendations by passengers.

In October, Bob made one of his fairly infrequent requests to sit down with Lucy for a chat. He told her that he had reached an agreement to buy the additional land needed for the garage extension. He'd bought more land than had been initially planned, but it gave a significant advantage for the operations. It allowed the new access road to be moved further away from Bob's bungalow and there would be a double-width road, allowing ten vehicles to be lined up there, waiting to be cleaned or serviced, before passing through to the garages.

When Fred saw the revised plan he was over the moon.

'That extra standing space had made this an absolutely cracking scheme now, Lucy,' he said.

'Bob must be a good friend of the owner of that land,

because he's got it at a reasonable price,' replied Lucy. She had spoken to the bank manager that afternoon and arranged to have money held in the current account until the solicitors had finalised the contract for the land.

'We are doing very well at the moment, Fred. Money is flowing in as never before. I hope it will continue.'

'We'll be able to get the plans for the new garage finalised now,' added Fred. 'It's an excellent scheme and I don't see why the planners should raise any objections.'

'They will have to consult the two properties that will be affected. Do you think they will object?'

'I doubt it,' said Fred.

Bob came again to have a word with Lucy after he'd met one of his Councillor friends.

'I was casually talking to him about Maxwell Motors, with a view to mentioning the garage extension, when he said that the Councillors didn't know anything much about us. He said that some companies meet from time to time with Councillors to brief them about their business and in his view the Councillors find such meetings helpful. I think he was hinting at what we should do. We have to lay on a presentation, Lucy, to a selection of Councillors.'

'I agree. That might be a good idea, Bob.'

'Right, I want you to prepare a presentation, Lucy. Then I will arrange for an invitation to a select few Councillors to come for an evening with us.'

Lucy set to work collecting photographs she could use to demonstrate the different aspects of the Maxwell business. Her collection was completed by a photograph of the lady drivers in their wedding attire, for special comment. All these pictures were made into slides to illustrate the text.

The next section of the presentation demonstrated the

growth of the business. Illustrations showed the impressive rise in the financial turnover and the increase in personnel. One slide showed Mavis delivering a staff training session.

Lucy concluded her text by pressing the publicity factor for the community.

'Nobody asked us to do it, but I want to assure you that Maxwell Motors operates around the country and we are always promoting Leeds and Yorkshire. People want to do business with us, and they know that we are fair and use good, honest, Yorkshire standards. They trust us, and because of the way we work, they will be glad to trade with other local companies.'

When she'd completed her text and the illustrations, Lucy ran through it with the office team and Bob. They had one or two ideas for changes, which she readily accepted. It was then agreed that Fred should do a very short presentation outlining the concept of the garage extension, showing how all the operations could be concentrated on the one site.

After the presentations, the proposal was that the councillors would see how the operations were planned when they visited the general office where Margaret would show the schedules she prepared for the allocation of the coaches and drivers. They would then inspect a coach on the forecourt, and the wedding taxi. Then it would be back to Lucy's office for a top of the range buffet.

Lucy said that Lilly would prepare the buffet and the food but that the conversion of Lucy's office between the presentation and the buffet would have to be done by the whole team with military precision, in a matter of just twenty minutes.

Lucy had several more practices with her presentation, but she also had meetings with the team, and Lilly to agree the menu for the hot and cold food and the logistics of getting it laid-out. Bob reported that seven Councillors would be attending, so Lucy's office would be at full capacity. Lucy imported an extra small table for the screen so that her slides could be seen by everyone in the room.

All the planning and hard work paid off. The presentation went well and the questions, after Fred's short outline of the garage extension plans, were sympathetic and easily answered. The visit to the forecourt and the office was very successful and the food was ready before the party came in for the buffet. They were attracted by the smell of the hot food and they all enjoyed the food and drink. Discussions after the food lasted for half an hour and then the Councillors expressed their appreciation for an informative evening by a very successful Leeds company.

When Lucy and Bob had seen their guests off the site, they came back into the office to thank the team for their excellent work and they all tucked into the food that was left. Lilly took on the job of tidying up the food and returning Lucy's office back to its normal role.

'I think that's been a good night's work, Lucy,' commented Bob.

'It was your excellent idea,' replied Lucy. 'And, yes, we had a good story to tell.'

The same evening had been an exciting and passionate time for Elsie and David. They'd planned to meet at David's house as soon as Elsie returned from the mini-coach trip to Manchester. Because of the uncertainty of when exactly this would be, she wasn't to be involved in the Councillors' visit. She'd brought a change of clothes, which she left at the garage, to avoid her having to go home. David agreed to provide her with tea and sandwiches. In fact, her day finished earlier than expected and she arrived at David's house at seven o'clock.

'What do you want to do, Elsie? Have tea first and then we can go upstairs? Or do you want to have a wash and get changed first, and then have tea?'

'I'm keen to have a drink and a bite to eat first. I have only had one drink of tea at lunchtime. I'll go upstairs for a quick wash, and then we'll have the food.'

'It will be ready for you in five minutes, madam,' mocked David.

He'd prepared a large plate of mixed sandwiches, followed by scones with jam, and then some chocolate cake that Lilly had made. They enjoyed the meal together and were able to chat about various things, mainly Maxwell-related.

'Would it be like this if we were married?' asked Elsie, with a big smile.

'Yes, every day,' replied David, reaching across the table and squeezing her hand.

While David tidied up in the kitchen, Elsie went back to the bathroom to get changed. She'd brought a skirt and blouse in place of her Maxwell outfit. She also changed into a new bra and knickers and some black stockings. She applied liberal cosmetics to her face and painted her lips with a new, bright-red lipstick. Finally she sprayed perfume to her body and clothes. She inspected herself in the mirror and hoped that David would approve.

When she walked into David's bedroom, he welcomed her with a cuddle and complimented her on her appearance. 'Elsie, you look ravishing, and your perfume makes you smell absolutely irresistible.'

They fell into a passionate embrace, laid on David's bed. There was kissing and stroking, and Elsie was gasping with pleasure. David decided it was time to ask the vital question.

'Elsie, you're very excited. Just pause for a minute and answer this question. Would you like us to go all the way? You can if you like. It will be safe for you. I've got some protection.'

'What do you mean by protection, David?'

'I have some condoms in my desk drawer. Let me show you.' He reached over and passed the envelope over to her. She had never seen anything like this before. She took out one of the packet and examined the pink condom.

'They feel very strange, David. Have you used one before?'

'Of course not, Elsie; you're my first girlfriend.'

This was indeed true, but David had established a close friendship with the school Romeo. He was the year above David, but took the same subjects. He was drooled over by the girls in the sixth form at the High School and he took on the role of mentor to the younger boys, happily briefing them on his theories of good sex, in the privacy of their lunch breaks. His main contention was that young boys, fired by their hormones, couldn't wait to get into a girl's knickers, but that this was the wrong approach, in his opinion. Instead, they should first concentrate on making sex exciting and satisfying for the girls. He gave lots of hints on how to achieve this. David had memorised these and he wondered if this was the night for him to apply some of these techniques on Elsie. She seemed to be issuing the right signals.

Elsie opened up the condom and stuck her thumb in it.

'It seems too big, David.'

'You obviously don't know how big our 'John Henrys' get when they're excited, Elsie. Now you must make your mind up. If we're going to have sex we must do it right; we're not going to be fighting with lots of clothes. As a first move, I suggest we should strip down to our minimum underclothes.' Elsie didn't answer his question but her actions showed she had made up her mind. She jumped off the bed and headed for the bathroom. David was slightly disappointed by this move. He had anticipated the titillation of seeing Elsie stripping off. However, he complied by removing all his clothes apart from his underpants. When Elsie came back into the bedroom she was dressed in her bra and knickers, her suspender belt and the black stockings.

'I left my black stockings on as they are supposed to excite young men like you, David.'

He clasped her in his arms.

'My dear, Elsie, you don't need black stockings to excite me. Just being with me, as you are now, is all I crave for.'

This set off another period of kissing and stroking. David unclipped Elsie's bra and gently kissed her nipples and held her breasts. They stood up firm, proud and sexy. He then removed her knickers and stroked between her legs. She was hot and moist. She looked at him.

'Come on, David, remove those underpants and let me see him in all his glory.'

David removed his underpants and his swollen penis sprang up, relieved from the constraints of being locked in his underpants. Elsie said nothing, but she was surprised at its size.

'We have to dress him now,' said David. 'Just give me a hand.'

He started it off and Elsie then unrolled the condom down the full length of his penis.

'You were right, David, it's not too big.' She lay back down on the bed.

‘Just a minute; let me put a pillow under your bottom. It will make it easier for me to enter you.’

‘You seem to know a lot about this, David. But I do want you.’

‘All I’m concerned about is that it’s a good experience for you, Elsie.’

He crouched over her.

‘I am going to enter you now, Elsie. I’ll do it slowly. Just yell out if I hurt you.’

Elsie looked up into David’s eyes as she grasped his bottom.

‘That’s it, Elsie; you guide him in as you want him.’

‘I’ll want all of him, David; but a bit at a time.’

Once or twice Elsie blinked, as though there was some pain, but she slowly applied pressure to keep him going deeper.

‘You’ve got him all now, Elsie.’ David lowered himself down and kissed her. ‘Let’s just stay like this for a minute or two. I’m desperate, but I’ll wait until you’re ready. You are a wonderfully brave lover, Elsie.’

After a few moments Elsie moved her position.

‘Come on, David, move him. I want to feel you explode.’

David knelt above her and started thrusting in and out. He was trying to do it gently but his body told him to accelerate to a climax. Elsie kept her eyes on him and also started to move with him.

‘Go on, my darling. David, make it happen.’

David let out a yell as he exploded. He fell on top of her and they clung together until they had both calmed down.

There was more cuddling later, and when David was taking her home, she clung onto his arm with a sense of achievement.

‘It can’t be wrong to do what we’ve done tonight, David. It was so wonderful. And you were very gentle with me. I was a bit afraid at the start. I’d heard some stories of how painful it is first time.’

‘It will be better for you in the future, Elsie. I’ll make sure of that.’

There was a meeting in Lucy’s office with the designer of the new garage extension and the project manager, James Green, along with Fred and Bob. Lucy watched and listened quietly as the architect and project manager explained the scheme in detail. After discussions on the materials to be used, and on the signage at the entrance to the new access road, to indicate that it was Maxwell Motors’ property, Bob agreed that the plans should be submitted. James Green said he would arrange to meet the planners to introduce the project to them and answer any initial questions they might have.

Lucy suggested that there should be another meeting with James Green as soon as he had had met the planners. She emphasised that this was a major initiative to increase the company’s efficiency. The project manager looked at Lucy and realised that she would be pushing him to get planning permission and complete the project in the minimum timescale. He also reckoned that Lucy would be prepared to spend some extra money on the contract in order to get it finished earlier. He’d need to consider the best contractor to achieve that objective.

David and Elsie had a few opportunities to have passionate cuddles in his bedroom in the next few weeks, but any thought of sexual intercourse was out of the question with Lilly in the house at the same time.

‘When will we be able to try making love again, David?’

asked Elsie, 'I'm ready and keen to do it again.'

'I am as keen as you are, Elsie,' replied David. 'But we'll have to wait until we have the house to ourselves. I'm sure there will be a chance soon, but you seem to be doing a lot of evening bookings with the mini-coach these days.'

'Yes, the bookings have increased. We now have several groups of ladies who plan nights-out to shows, or to go on shopping excursions. I know Lucy is pleased by the growth of this part of our business, but it does tie me up on many evenings. On the plus side, I usually get some good tips, so I turn on the charm, to encourage them to make further bookings.'

Elsie's involvement with Maxwells came to a dramatic halt at the end of October. She was making her way home through Horsforth, in the late evening, after a shopping trip in the mini-coach. She was walking on the edge of the footpath when there was a collision between two cars, one of which was trying to overtake the other along a narrow stretch of road. The inside car was pushed from the side, and, as a result, it bounced onto the footpath and knocked Elsie down. She was badly injured and the car ran over her right leg, clearly breaking it.

Fortunately, there were other pedestrians on the footpath and they called for an ambulance and for the police. One person had first-aid experience and he knew how to look after Elsie until the experts arrived. He covered Elsie with a coat and lifted her head slightly to put a pad under it. He ascertained that she had no external bleeding from a lump on her head, but he was worried about internal bleeding. Elsie was initially unconscious, but she did recover and the first-aid person kept talking to her until the police and ambulance service arrived.

The police took statements from the witnesses and the

two drivers involved. Elsie was carefully loaded onto a stretcher and driven away in the ambulance, with lights flashing, to Leeds General Infirmary. Other than bruises, the main problem was the break to her leg. The doctors assured Elsie that they would be able to repair the break, but they insisted on keeping her in hospital, under observation, to ensure that there were no complications from the lump on her head. The doctor in charge was hopeful that she would be alright when she told him about her job.

'I'm on the staff of Maxwell Motors, and I drive the mini-coach and the wedding taxis. You have to make a good job of the repairs to my leg, as my right foot operates the accelerator.'

'Young lady, I can assure you that your right foot will be able carry out its duties. But you will be out of service for a few weeks. You will need to be patient.'

Elsie was relieved when she was transferred to a bed on one of the wards. Her mother arrived, after eleven o'clock at night,accompanied by Elsie's older brother. She'd been in bed when the police knocked on the front door. They were both shocked by the Elsie's appearance; the lump on her head looked angry and was swelling and turning yellow. It was clear she would have a black eye by morning. Elsie was suffering from shock and she was trying to hold back the tears. She was beginning to realise that her injuries were serious, but that they could have been worse.

Her mother held her hands and tried to comfort her. She asked Elsie what she could do to help her.

'You must ring Lucy, first thing in the morning, and tell her what has happened. She'll have to arrange someone to cover all my bookings for the next few weeks. I was due to be very busy, so I don't know what she'll do.'

'Don't worry about Maxwell Motors,' said her brother.

'When you finish late at night you shouldn't have to walk home.'

'But I like the walk home. It's so nice to be out in the fresh air after I've spent most of the day in the driver's seat.'

The night nurse came and suggested that Elsie's mother and brother should leave and let the patient settle down for the night.

Lucy was surprised when the telephone rang next morning even before she'd started on her breakfast. It was Elsie's mother, who described what had happened and which ward Elsie was in at Leeds Infirmary. Lucy was very concerned when she learned of the injuries and immediately said that she would visit the hospital during the day and discuss the plans for Elsie's treatment. She promised to talk again to Elsie's mother so that they could ensure that Elsie had the support of plenty of visitors during her stay in hospital.

Lucy explained the position to Fred and, after grabbing a light breakfast, she went over to the general office to look at the bookings which Elsie was planned to cover for the next few weeks. When Mavis and Margaret arrived she explained what had happened to Elsie and they discussed how to cover Elsie's job. Mavis was quite clear that the best way was to move Pearl Featherstone over completely into Elsie's programme. Pearl had driven the taxis and the mini-coach, so she would also be able to take over a role with the wedding taxis, and she had received her new wedding outfit. Mavis added a personal comment.

'I was amazed at the shape of her blouse and jacket. No doubt the male wedding guests will enjoy the sight of her at the wheel.'

Margaret then raised the issue that she was planning to take a week's holiday in a fortnight's time, and she had expected Pearl to cover for her.

'What are your plans for the next few weeks, Mavis?' asked Lucy.

'I'd plans to do more work on the new luxury tours, but that isn't critical, so I could cover for Margaret on her holiday week.'

'Right, that's fine. We need to get Pearl in to talk to her.'

'I'll see to that, Lucy,' offered Mavis.

'My priority is to go to the hospital and see Elsie. Then I must have a word with Lilly, as I am sure that her brother David will be upset to hear of Elsie's accident.'

Lucy saw Lilly when she arrived and explained about the accident.

'Oh, dear. David will be very shocked,' said Lilly, with a worried look on her face. 'Nobody has let him know, and I think he was planning to meet her tonight.'

'Well, we will have to organise for him to see her tonight in the hospital at visiting time. You'll have to tell him what's happened when he gets home. I'll get him some flowers which he can take for her, and I'll have a word with Mrs Brown and see if she can go at visiting time this afternoon.'

Later in the morning Lucy went to the hospital and went up to the ward and spoke to the ward Sister. She explained who she was and the concern that she felt for Elsie, who had been walking home from her work when the accident happened. The Sister explained that Elsie's leg had been set in plaster and she was back in the ward. The wound to her face had been cleaned, but it looked quite ugly and she had a black eye. The Sister advised that Elsie would be in hospital for a few more days. Lucy used her charm with the Sister to get permission to spend a few minutes with Elsie. When she saw Elsie she was concerned at her appearance. Elsie tried to smile, as she was pleased to see Lucy.

'How are you feeling now, Elsie?,' Lucy asked as she took hold of both Elsie's hands.

'I'm feeling a bit better than I felt last night. My leg is set now and they tell me it will be alright. I took a look at myself in the mirror in the bathroom this morning and I know that my face looks a real mess.'

'It will get back to normal, don't worry about that. Is there anything you need?'

'I need my mother to bring me a spare nightdress.'

'I'll arrange that,' replied Lucy.

'Does David know where I am?'

'He'll know this afternoon, and I'm arranging for him to come and see you tonight at the visiting time. Your mother will be visiting you this afternoon. All the team in the office send you their best wishes and we'll do everything we can to help you make a full recovery and get back with us as soon as possible.'

'I'm sorry to be letting you down, Lucy. I think it will take a few weeks to get this leg back to normal.'

'You are not letting us down, Elsie. I have put Pearl Featherstone onto your bookings, and Mavis is going to spend more time in the office helping Margaret. You've built up a very good set of bookings for the mini-coach and it will be there for you when you get back to us. Just relax and get your strength up. I'll have to go now or the ward Sister will be cross with me. I'll be coming to see you again, though.'

'Thanks for coming to see me.'

Lucy gave her a wave as she left. She thought about how best to prepare David for Elsie's damaged appearance. She decided that she would take David to the hospital herself and she would prepare a box of cosmetics and perfume so that Elsie could make up her face to disguise the injuries. After she'd handed over her gifts she would leave David there to spend the time with Elsie.

Back at the house, Lucy briefed Lilly and made arrangements to pick up David to take him to the hospital.

'Is she going to be alright, Lucy?'

'Yes, I'm sure she will be fine and make a full recovery. But David might get a shock when he sees the damage to her face. I think she's just relieved that she was not killed by the car.'

That afternoon Lucy had a meeting with the manager of the travel agency in Harrogate. He'd asked to see her. Lucy went through to his office and the assistants at their desks all greeted to Lucy as she passed.

The manager had a tray with tea, coffee and cakes on his desk, to welcome Lucy.

'How are things in your business now,' she asked.

'Very good, Lucy, and as our overall business expands, the bookings for Maxwell Motors also expand at the same rate. But I have a new development to discuss with you.'

'Now I am all ears. I'm glad I've come.'

'We have had a breakthrough with an American firm which plans holidays for their clients to York, as part of their English tour. They've indicated that they would like to advertise your luxury tours to Edinburgh as an extension to those holidays. We need to agree the financial arrangements.'

'Okay, what has been agreed so far?'

'We've only discussed the transport of their clients from York to Harrogate and back.'

'That is no problem, and we will be able to use our mini-coach for those journeys. What about the price for the trips?'

'I think we'll be able to agree a figure, in dollars, similar to the normal price that you charge in pounds. They're aware that their clients will be having a top-class experience on these tours and they're flexible in programming the Edinburgh tours — they're offering them either before or after the stay in York.'

'Have you got any idea how many Americans are visiting York each year?'

'Yes, they had over a hundred last year, but the number is increasing this year.'

'It will be just a trickle, as far as we are concerned, but we'll have to try and grow it. In time there will be other luxury tours. I think we could afford to offer a 10% discount on the tour charge for next year. The Edinburgh tours are making good profits for us. It will be interesting to observe the interaction between the American guests and the wealthy Yorkshire folk on the tours. I'll get Mavis to tweak the tour programme to incorporate little bits which will be of special interest to the Americans.'

Lucy left the travel agency confidont that it was now an essential part of the Maxwell business.

When Lucy picked him up in the Maxwell van, David was clearly shocked at the news of Elsie's accident. Lucy used the journey to calm him down and emphasised that his job was to support Elsie, and build her up, so that she didn't get depressed. She explained that she would go in with him for just a few minutes to hand over her box of useful items that she had got together for Elsie. She would then wait in the car park to take him back to Horsforth.

'It's very kind of you to transport me around, Lucy. I'm dreading this visit, as I don't think I'll be very good as a sick visitor.'

'You will be fine, David. Just hold Elsie's hands and look

into her eyes and cover her with your love. That is what she needs right now.'

Lucy gave Elsie the box of goodies and explained what there was. David handed over the flowers and Lucy went to find a vase so that the flowers could be put on display beside her bed. When she returned, with the flowers in a vase, she noticed that David was holding Elsie's hands and looking into her eyes. Elsie was near to tears, but Lucy was fairly sure that they were tears of relief and hope. David had a major role to play in the recovery of Elsie in the next few weeks.

When David got back home, Lilly was waiting for him, anxious for news.

'How was she, David?

'She was quite tearful. Her face is badly bruised and she has a lump on her head. Her leg is now set in plaster up to her thigh, so she's struggling to move about. They're going to help her to use crutches tomorrow.'

'When will she be coming home?'

'She thinks it will be in a few days. She wants me to go and see her each day while she's in hospital. Lucy agrees that I should go, and she is going to agree this with Elsie's mother. I told Lucy that I would go by bus tomorrow, and she's arranging a pass so that I get a free ride. I'll go on my own tomorrow, but if Elsie is still in hospital the day after, you could come with me, Lilly. She's missing the team at Maxwells.'

'I'll do that, David. I can take her a cake from her friends at work to cheer her up.'

'She's not looking forward to getting back home. She thinks she'll be very lonely there.'

'I'm sure Lucy will want to make sure Elsie gets visitors

from work every day when she's back at home.'

The management committee meeting in November followed the normal format. The finances were good and all the individual businesses were playing their part profitably. The deal to offer the Edinburgh luxury tours to the American clients visiting York was explained. These would be advertised in the American company brochures for next year. The accident to Elsie was recorded and it was hoped she would be back at work by Christmas. A report was given on the successful meeting with Councillors, to brief them on Maxwell Motors. On the garage extension scheme it was planned to make the formal submission within days to try to get planning permission before Christmas. It was stated that the majority of the cost of the garage extension should be covered from revenue streams of the current operations. It was agreed to give Christmas bonuses to staff at the same level as the previous year.

David was pleased that Elsie was getting lots of visitors each day once she was home. The Brown family had taken a positive approach to Elsie's recuperation: her eldest brother was effectively carrying her down the stairs each morning and then back up at night; she was able to meet visitors in the front room and use her crutches to get to the kitchen for her meals. Lilly decided that the family couldn't be expected to provide tea and cakes for all the visitors, so she sent David every other day with a large cake that the family could also enjoy.

Most evenings David was able to spend time with Elsie in the front room and they weren't disturbed by the rest of the family. He concentrated on holding Elsie's hands and looking into her eyes and he became expert at stealing a few kisses. The treatment was working, as Elsie's face began to return to normal and she became more cheerful as she gained confidence that she would make a full recovery.

In the second week of December the plaster was removed from Elsie's leg and she began the slow process of getting her leg muscles back to work. David took on the task of getting her to take a walk each night to build up her strength. After a few nights it became possible for them to walk as far as David's house, where they spent time in his bedroom. Elsie was a little concerned at the disfigurement of her right leg from the wounds she'd suffered. She removed her stocking to show them to David.

'I'm sorry to be soiled goods, David. I used to be proud of my legs.'

'They are still lovely legs, Elsie. In time the marks will disappear. I like them as they are. They show how bad the accident was and how brave you have been.'

He sealed these remarks with some passionate kissing.

Lucy had kept in touch with James Green, the project manager, to know where the garage scheme was in the local authority planning process. She'd left him in no doubt that she was hoping that it would be approved before the Christmas holidays. He used all his contacts to try to achieve that result, as he was getting concerned that Lucy was questioning his ability to handle the project effectively. He was relieved to be able to ring Lucy and report that the Maxwell Garage extension would be on the agenda of the last planning meeting before the Christmas break.

'Can I assume that it will go through?' she asked.

'I hope so, as I've answered all the questions that officers have raised with me. I am assuming that there are no Councillors that have a grudge against Maxwell Motors?'

'I think we'll be alright on that score. As soon as you

know the outcome from the council, I want to know. We shall need a meeting to agree the contractor for the job and when they can start. I want this job all settled before we eat our Christmas dinners.'

'Bloody hell! What a woman!,' James Green muttered to himself as he put the 'phone down. He was planning to have an extended break over the Christmas period, but he might as well abandon those plans now, he thought. It obviously wouldn't be right for him to be away, whether the scheme was approved or rejected.

When Lucy put the phone down she was thrilled at the prospect of another major move forward for Maxwell Motors.

Twenty-two

Lucy was chairing a meeting in her office about the garage extension, with the project manager, the project architect, Bob and Fred. It was five days before Christmas Day.

'We now have authority to proceed with this scheme,' she announced 'We need to agree the contractor and get the work started. Are all the detailed plans ready to issue to the contractor?' She looked at the project architect.

'The working plans will be finalised in the next two days. I am aware that you wish to proceed as a matter of urgency.'

'Have you got a contractor in mind for this job?' She looked at James Green.

'I have contractors that I know who could do the job.'

'And have you approached them?'

'I've discussed the job with two of them.'

'So what is your next move?'

'We could issue both of them with the necessary

documentation and get them to quote a price for the job.'

'How long would that take?,' asked Lucy, not letting up the pressure.

'We could ask them to return their quotes by the end of the second week in January. That doesn't give them much time to work out their prices to get a good quote.'

'The most important information we want from the contractor is the end date that they see for the project. Wouldn't it be better for you to get both the companies on site, so that they can see what has to be done and they can then evaluate the options for how they organise the work to get early completion?'

'Yes, we could try that. However there might be delays in getting the materials for the job, particularly the steel girders.'

'There is no need for any delay there,' Fred interjected. 'If you can give me the drawings for the steel work I can arrange for it to be made locally. And the price will probably be lower than you would get from a main contractor.'

'I want you to realise that we want this job done very quickly,' continued Lucy. If I could spare my husband from his duties within Maxwell Motors, I would get him to go back to his old job and manage the project. We don't want fobbing off with any excuses from a company that's out to exploit us rather than getting the job done.' Lucy gave James Green an icy look.

The meeting went on for another hour before agreement was reached on the actions to be taken: the architect would complete the drawings to go out with the tender requests in the next twenty-four hours; the project manager would get senior managers from the two possible contractors to visit the site within the next three days; Fred would be given the drawings for the girder work and would arrange delivery on site by the middle of January; and the tenders, with prices and completion date, would be requested by the end of the first week in January.

'That has set the short-term programme, then,' concluded Lucy. 'If there are any problems, then I want to know so that we can convene again and resolve them. Fred will be available to meet with the contractors when you bring them on site,' Lucy said to James Green.

'I think you gave them something to think about, Lucy,' said Bob, when James Green and the architect had left the room.

'I was determined that they realised that we know what we're talking about, and that they will be under pressure if the job does not proceed efficiently.'

'It's a straightforward job, really,' said Fred. 'The only problem could be the weather — if the site gets waterlogged, or we get heavy snow, before the roof's on.'

'I'm going to hand out the wage packets this week, which will include the Christmas bonus. In this pay packet the staff get a share of the success of the company. It has been a very good year, this year.'

'It certainly has, Lucy,' said Bob.

'It hasn't been good for Elsie, though. She's coming in to the office for a few hours tomorrow. I want you to fetch her in the van, Fred. Then I'll take her back in the afternoon. I want to make a fuss of her. She's been very brave.'

Fred picked up Elsie at her home at eight-thirty. She'd been looking out for him. He helped her down the steps and into the car. She was limping, and using her right leg with care. Fred wondered if it was right that she was coming back to work.

'It's great to be getting back in harness,' Elsie said, when she was settled in the car. 'I shall only be able to help in the office for the time being, not with driving.'

'There'll be plenty for you to do, there,' replied Fred.

Lucy was there to welcome Elsie, and both Margaret and Mavis gave her a hug. Elsie was smiling and clearly relieved to be in familiar surroundings.

'I want you to go with me down to the bank, Elsie, to pick up the payday money. Then you can help me set up the wages, which include the Christmas bonus.'

Pearl Featherstone came into the office and greeted Elsie.

'The mini-coach and the taxis are still running okay, Elsie,' she said. 'You certainly have some right clients, with these women's groups who like their shopping trips. There's another one today, this time it's Christmas shopping in Manchester.'

The telephone rang and, as Mavis and Margaret were sorting something out together, Elsie answered the phone.

'Maxwell Motors, Elsie speaking. How can I help you?'

It was a significant order from the secretary of a working men's club. He wanted to book four coaches for a children's trip to Scarborough, in March next year. Elsie took down the coach booking folder and checked availability. There were just four coaches available.

'Yes, we can do that. I'll put Margaret on, who will agree the price and how you will pay for the trip.' She passed the phone to Margaret, who rattled off all the details. She said she would prepare a contract and send it with an invoice to the secretary.

'Well done, Elsie. That's a good booking. We are glad to get you back.'

Later, Lucy came round with the taxi and waited until Elsie got in beside her.

'How is the leg now, Elsie?' Lucy asked, as she drove out of the forecourt.

'It's getting better, Lucy. It just seemed so weak when they took the plaster off.'

'You need to keep exercising it every day. We'll want you fully fit when you start driving. There's plenty of work around the office, in the meantime, though.'

'David is insisting on us going a walk whenever we can, to build up my muscles.'

When all the wage packets were completed and checked, they were stored in the safe until the next day.

'I shall want you with me tomorrow, Elsie, when I hand out these wages. The staff will be glad to see you.'

Lucy then drove Elsie back home, even though it was only three o'clock in the afternoon.

'You've done enough for today. I'll get Fred to pick you up again in the morning.'

'I can walk to work, Lucy, 'I don't need a lift.'

'Oh no you can't, Elsie!' Lucy replied, forcibly.'You need to go steady for a bit longer. We're going to get you fully recovered, without any setbacks.'

The next day, Lucy got a schedule of where every member of staff was working before setting off with Elsie, in the taxi, to intercept them as they did their job. Elsie was impressed with how pleased everyone was to receive their packet from Lucy, along with her good wishes for the Christmas holidays. Lucy knew which members of staff were operating buses and coaches over the Christmas period and she thanked them personally for taking on these extra commitments. Some of the staff looked at their pay slips and realised how much money was in the packet, with the additional bonus. They were especially thankful and some shook Lucy's hand.

Lucy's final task for the day was to meet the team which was on duty cleaning and re-fuelling the buses and coaches on the nightshift. She gathered them together and had a chat with them before handing out their pay packets. In each case she wished them a happy Christmas before she gave them their pay. In one or two cases the young lads and young women were shy and embarrassed to be greeted individually by Lucy. Joe North stayed behind a couple of minutes to thank Lucy for seeing his team.

'We have a good set of folk in this team now, Lucy. When do you expect the new garage extension to be available? I hope we can keep most of this team on the cleaning job.'

'It should certainly be in operation by next Christmas, Joe. The cleaning operation will certainly be more efficient than the current system, but we should be able to adjust the staff numbers with natural wastage.'

Lucy went into the house and joined Fred.

'The two bosses of the firms in for the garage contract are coming tomorrow morning,' said Fred. 'One is coming at nine o'clock and the other at eleven o'clock. I'll join them, with James Green. In the afternoon I've arranged for an old mate of mine to come in to discuss the manufacture of all the steel work.'

'I assume James Green will stay over for that meeting.'

'Yes, I've arranged that. I'll fix him up with a sandwich so that he can stay on the site.'

'I've arranged for Lilly and David to join us for the Christmas Day activities. Lilly says she'll come early in the morning to help with cooking the lunch. I've also invited Elsie to join us, and she agreed when she realised that

David and Lilly were invited. I've told them all it's a 'no presents' invitation.'

The next day, Fred and James Green toured the site with the manager of the first company which was going to tender for the garage extension, Marshall Builders. Fred explained that he thought there were opportunities to have at least two teams deployed on site at the same time. One job was to make the access road from the main road round to the garages. The next critical job was to dig out the sites for the foundations on which the main vertical stanchions would stand. Getting the roof on was an obvious priority, to protect the site from any winter weather.

'When will the steel be available,' asked the company manager. 'I understand that it has now been withdrawn from the contract.'

'We have a meeting on that this afternoon,' replied James.

'I shall be organising that,' added Fred. 'I worked for a steel manufacturing company before I joined Maxwell Motors. I'm confident that the steel will be delivered to site by the end of the second week of January. I'd be surprised if you'd got all the bases concreted by that time.'

The company manager acknowledged that the site visit had been very helpful. He promised to submit a tender price for the job and he would give the earliest date that he thought the garage extension could be completed.

For the second company, Luke Construction, the manager had similar reactions to the first regarding the contract and the work involved. He confirmed that he'd be submitting a tender price and a schedule of work, phased over the contract, to achieve the earliest possible completion date.

While Fred and James had a sandwich lunch, provided by Lilly in the kitchen of the house, they reviewed the morning's work.

'Which of the two companies do you favour?' asked Fred. James paused to consider his answer before he replied.

'Well, they are both capable of doing the job. I tend to favour the second company, Luke Construction, as in my view they have sharper management who will plan the work more effectively.'

'You will have gathered that Lucy is a very thorough financial manager. She will ask us some detailed questions to make sure there are no financial loop holes in the tender documents. If there are any, it will be an uncomfortable period for the contracting company, and for us two.'

James noted Fred's comments and he was sure that Lucy would be quite capable of taking Fred to task if he failed with any of his responsibilities.

During the afternoon session, with the engineering firm, James Green realised that Fred know what he was talking about. He listened as the detailed specification of the steel and the welding methods were agreed. Fred also arranged that the A-frames for the roof should be assembled in the workshop before they were dispatched to the site. The manager of the engineering firm told Fred that he had already identified where he could obtain the steel for the job, and he also quoted a highly competitive cost per ton. After their discussions of the job, Fred passed over a letter instructing the engineering firm to proceed with the work. In answer to questions from Fred, the manager informed him that they'd picked up some work for the Yorkshire coal mines, as the firm that Fred had previously worked for had pulled out of their factory. Fred wasn't surprised to hear this. The engineering firm manager left with a positive statement: 'I'll let you know when we're ready to start delivery. You'll need a crane on site for unloading.'

When he left, James shook Fred's hand. He was happy that they'd made good progress that day. He also realised that Fred was going to be an asset on the project.

Christmas morning dawned with a sharp frost of the ground. Fred had to scrape the windscreen of the van to clear it. He was going out to the Benfield site to see the service buses away on the restricted timetable for Christmas Day. He spoke to the drivers and conductors and wished them a happy Christmas.

'I don't think it will too busy this morning,' replied one of the drivers. 'But I sometimes think that when folks see that the buses are running, they come out for a ride. If it's like last year, tomorrow will be hectic. Everybody seems to go out on Boxing Day, especially to football matches.'

'I'm sure you will cope,' smiled Fred. 'And you'll get premium rates for today.'

'That's why I'm here,' replied the driver. 'After what my wife has spent on Christmas I need some premium rates!' He gave Fred a wave as the bus drove away out of the garage. Eva Benfield came out of the house to greet Fred.

'All away to time, Fred?' she commented. 'We're lucky to have some reliable staff.'

'You're right there, Eva. Working on Christmas Day isn't a priority for most people. I might pop over tomorrow, Eva, so I will empty anything in the safe then.'

Lilly left her house to get to Lucy's for nine o'clock. David was still in bed as he'd been out to the picture with Elsie the night before. She reminded him not to be late arriving for the Christmas lunch. In response she heard a grunt from under the pillows and took this to be an agreement.

In fact, David had made elaborate arrangements with Elsie that she should visit him, at his house, mid-morning, so that they could spend some time together before going on to Lucy's. When Elsie arrived at ten o'clock David was up, breakfasted, dressed ready for the lunch, with his presents for Elsie wrapped and placed on the table. When he opened the door, Elsie walked in with a parcel in her arms which she immediately put on the floor before falling into his arms for a passionate kiss.

'We have time to exchange our presents and then spend some time together upstairs,' said David.

'I'm happy to do that, but we must be careful not to look guilty when we get to Lucy's. I wouldn't want to fall asleep during the Queen's speech,' she added with a grin.

'Right then, let's exchange presents,' suggested David.

'But we said just one present each. There are four there, David. Have you broken our agreement?'

'Just a little; but you have special needs after your accident. Just start at that end. Some of them are only small, as you can see.'

Elsie opened the first present, which was powder puff similar to one that Lucy had provided in the parcel which she'd given to Elsie in the hospital.'

'That is just the shade I use David; how clever of you.' She gave him a kiss.

The next one was a small pouch, suitable to carry in a handbag, with lipsticks and face cosmetics. That too had Elsie's approval, which earned David another kiss.

The next present was a bottle of perfume, which caused Elsie to say. 'David, this is very special, and must be expensive. You are naughty.'

'Just put a dab behind your ear and then let me kiss you.'

Elsie did as he requested and David held her tight and

revelled in the smell of her perfume.

'You are my darling,' he murmured to her. 'You are made for expensive perfumes and clothes. Now, open the last one.'

Elsie took the parcel and stripped off the paper to reveal a box with a cellophane cover. It contained satin underwear comprising an underskirt, knickers and bra, all in pale blue. Elsie held up the underskirt to check its size. It was clearly the right size. She held up the knickers; they were smaller than she would have chosen, but, trimmed with lace, she knew that they would provide a sexy appearance and obviously weren't intended for comfort.

'David Young, how could you go into a shop and buy me this underwear?'

'It was a challenging experience for me. I had two shop assistants helping and advising me. They even held up the various articles against their bodies to ensure that I got the right sizes. Do you approve?'

'It's a beautiful set. I will only wear it on special occasions. Thank you. Now, open your presents.'

David opened the parcel and saw that it contained a very smart, maroon, wool jumper and two ties.

'There you are, you've broken our agreement too. There are three presents here! But they're very beautiful. Let's go upstairs now and celebrate this Christmas together.'

As Elsie settled down on the bed with David, she said quietly, 'I feel so relieved and fortunate to be here like this today. I could so easily have been killed in the road accident. It's wonderful to be here in your arms, David. Do be gentle with me.'

'My dear Elsie, I will of course be gentle, and my only aim this morning is that you relax and I thrill you. Just slip your dress and underskirt off.'

'What about you, David?'

‘Forget about me, Elsie. Today is for you. It will satisfy me if I can make you explode.’

He kissed her passionately while she closed her eyes and sighed. Slowly he removed her clothes and she arched her back, encouraging him to continue. He did so, with a frenzy of stimulation and penetration with his fingers. Elsie moved with his strokes and became more and more excited, until she was gasping with pleasure.

‘Oh, David, what are you doing to me? Just do it a bit more.’ David was shocked and afraid at the effect he was having on her. Her whole body twisted and exploded and her hand grabbed his hand and held it.

‘Stop now, David, I can’t take any more. Oh, you darling. I’ve never felt like that before.’ She collapsed into his arms.

‘Just relax, my dear Elsie, and slowly cool down.’ David was very impressed that he’d achieved the effect he’d planned.

They had a long slow cuddle, with gentle kisses, as Elsie relaxed.

When it was time for them to get ready to go for lunch, Elsie gathered her clothes and her presents together, to go to the bathroom and get dressed and put on her make-up.

‘Would you like me to wear my new outfit, David?’

‘Yes, that would be good,’ he replied. ‘But I hope you’ll give me a preview so that I can check if I got the sizes right.’

Elsie came out of the bathroom in her underskirt and gave a twirl for David. His heart missed a beat when she lifted up her underskirt and showed her knickers and stockings.

‘I’ll have difficulty eating my food, with that picture of you coming up before my eyes. You look ravishing, Elsie.’

They left in good time to walk to the garage. Elsie clung to David’s arm to help her to walk with hardly any limp.

But really the smile on her face, as well as her confident walk, told the world how proud she was of having a boyfriend who loved her.

The Christmas lunch was a great success. Lucy welcomed David and Elsie and she asked Elsie how she was feeling. Elsie replied very positively, but, much to David's surprise, Lucy sought a second opinion.

'How do you think she's progressing, David? You've seen her quite a bit lately.'

'I can see a continuing improvement. We walked from our house down here today and I'm sure she was walking much better.'

'David let me link his arm and he shortened his stride so that we kept together. I think that is cheating a bit,' chipped in Elsie.

'It's not cheating, Elsie, 'that's what David has to do now. He has to offer you all the help and support you need.'

Lilly was embarrassed, shortly afterwards, with the fulsome praise that she received for all the work that she'd done in preparing the Christmas lunch. It was a feast which pleased everyone. Fred even gave both Richard and David a glass of wine during the meal.

There was inevitably some discussion about Maxwell Motors, as it affected everyone there, but that was cut short by the Queen's speech. After that Richard suggested that David, himself, and Elsie, were going for a walk to give them some appetite for tea.

'Are you sure you'll be alright to take another walk, Elsie?' asked Lucy.

'I'm quite sure. It will do me good. They've promised that I can walk between them and link both of them.'

'It will be like the front row of the scrum,' said Richard.

'If you feel a bit tired you'll just get carried along.'

'Just you two look after her. And don't go too far,' called Lucy to them as they left the room.

Lucy turned to Lilly. 'We are lucky to have two young men like those in our lives, Lilly, don't you think?'

'I agree with you,' replied Lilly.'"David has grown up such a lot since he became friendly with Elsie. She's a lovely young woman.'

'Yes, she's one of the very best,' Fred joined in.

Later that evening, after tea and watching some television, Lucy instructed Fred to take Elsie, Lilly and David home in the taxi. She didn't want them walking home through Horsforth when there might be revellers about. David was a little disappointed, as this removed his option for an extended goodnight kiss. Elsie was dropped off first, so David jumped out of the taxi and led Elsie up her garden path to the front door. Ignoring that fact that Fred and Lilly were looking on, he took her in his arms and gave her a passionate kiss and Elsie responded by putting her arms around his neck and giving him another long kiss. He ran back to the taxi and jumped into the front seat.

'Sorry for that short delay,' he apologised to Fred.

'No problem,' replied Fred. 'You have to finish the day off properly. Don't you agree Lilly?'

'Yes, I do Fred.'

When he stopped next, outside Lilly's house, Fred jumped out of the taxi and helped Lilly out of the back seat.

'Thank you again for all that you've done to make this a wonderful day, Lilly.' He took her in his arms and gave her a kiss. Lilly blushed and was a little shocked by his action, but then she thought that she did deserve to have her day finished properly.

Boxing Day was a busy one for Maxwell Motors. There were five coaches booked to take supporters to away fixtures for two Yorkshire First Division teams. There were also two other coaches booked for half-day tours. And there was also a full daily schedule on the Horsforth and Otley routes for passenger services. Fred was busy from early morning, checking that all the double-deckers and coaches left on time. Richard was on duty at the fuel pumps from eight o'clock in the morning. To complete the full commitment of the Platt family, Lucy decided to join a couple of runs on the Otley route, and then two on the Horsforth route, to support the staff who were on duty.

Lucy was pleased with what she saw. The drivers and conductors were all fully involved in providing a first-class service to the passengers, including helping those who were old, or disabled, and assisting them to get on or off the buses. All the staff welcomed Lucy onto their vehicle and greeted her as a friend, not a boss. Some commented on the bonus that they'd received with their Christmas pay. Lucy took the opportunity to talk to some of the passengers. She generally got favourable comments, although many of the passengers only got to know who she was after she had left, when they were briefed by the conductors.

Richard was very busy at the fuel pumps. He worked out that everyone must have emptied their tanks over the holiday and were taking advantage of the garage being open to fill up. Fred visited him mid-morning and found that Richard had been so busy that he hadn't had time for a drink. Fred took him a cup of tea and a large piece of Christmas cake.

'Thanks, Dad. Do I have to fill in a form to get a sandwich at lunchtime?'

'Mum should be back then, to sort lunch out. She's given

Lilly a day off today, after all the work she did yesterday. You'll not starve, though, as there are plenty of leftovers to eat up.'

'It looks like we'll have a very busy day here,' Richard added.

Not only did the fuel pumps have a record day, but when Lucy totalled all the income for the total operation, it was significantly higher than the Boxing Day of the previous year.

She showed the figures to Bob and he too was very impressed.

'I think our Christmas present has been an upsurge in business,' suggested Lucy. 'But it's going to be a challenge to keep the operations going flat out while the garage extension is built. I think Fred should concentrate a lot of his time on the extension, over the next few months.'

'I agree with you, Lucy. Fred will be able to get more work on repairs out of the two lads now. They've gained a lot of experience over the last year.'

Lucy's discussion with Fred, about spending a significant portion of his time on the garage extension, took place in bed on New Year's Eve.

'Haven't we got other things to concentrate on tonight, instead of the garage extension?' asked Fred.

'I don't know what you have in mind, Fred Platt, but the garage extension is the major challenge for this company for the next year. Your experience could make all the difference to getting the job done efficiently, without it affecting our operations.'

'I will do all I can to get the job done safely, and as soon as possible. But I can't do anything for another week, until we get the tenders in.'

‘I accept that, Fred. As it’s New Year’s Eve, and considering all that you have done to help me this last year, I think you deserve a cuddle.’

‘I wouldn’t say no to that,’ replied Fred.

He took Lucy in his arms in a gentle cuddle. She quickly fell asleep.

Lucy got a call from James Green about the tender documents on 5 January 1968.

‘I can confirm, Mrs Platt, that I’ve received the tender submissions for the garage extension from the two contractors.’

‘Good,’ replied Lucy. ‘At least they have stuck to the agreed timescale. Have you evaluated them?’

‘I’ve only had a preliminary look.’

‘Well, I suggest you don’t spend any more time on them yourself. Bring them over here and then Fred can help you with the evaluation. We need to make the decision within the next forty-eight hours. I’ll speak to Fred and get him to drop what he is doing here and work with you in my office. I’ll tell him you’ll be here in the next hour. I’ll arrange food so that you can both work through the evening.

‘Just as you say, Mrs Platt,’ he replied. He could have kicked himself for not ringing Fred direct, rather than speaking to Lucy first.

Fred was changed out of his working clothes and was established at the large table in Lucy’s office, equipped with a writing pad and an adding machine, and several pencils and rubbers. They agreed that James would have one contract submission and Fred would have the other. They’d work through the documents, item by item, and record the costs and the time involved. They also agreed to list any exceptional items in the submissions. Progress was slow as the sections were not in the same order in both the submissions. When Lilly brought them a tray filled with sandwiches and cakes they were relieved to have a break. James considered that they were about half way through the exercise.

They resumed after the refreshments and, by ten o'clock, they could see that they were nearing the end. It was nearly midnight when they completed the exercise. On the timescale issue, the second contractor was offering a programme that showed completion early in July, while the first contractor offered completion by the second week in August. On price, the first contractor was marginally cheaper, but their submission had more items listed for possible variation orders. Without any discussion they both concluded that the second submission, from Luke Construction, should win the contract.

'We've got the figures; what do we do next?' asked James.

'We need a meeting with the Managing Director of Luke Construction, as soon as possible. I'd like you to arrange that within the next forty-eight hours, in this office. We can give him a letter accepting his submission, subject to certain criteria. I'll list them out for you. It will mainly depend on how soon he can start and who he's going to put in charge of the site management.'

'I'll deal with that first thing in the morning and let you know what I have arranged.'

Lucy had observed Elsie at work after the Christmas break. She noticed that her walking was getting better, and that she was fully involved in the office work. Lucy asked her to drive her to the bank for her regular visits. On the first two occasions it was in the taxi, and then she suggested they use the mini-coach. Elsie realised that she was being assessed and decided to say how she felt.

'I'm feeling quite relaxed to be behind the wheel again, Lucy. My right leg is not complaining and it does what I ask it, as far as the driving is concerned. I'll be glad to go back to my old responsibilities as soon as you're happy.'

'I think you should revert to your full duties next week, Elsie. Your driving is back to normal, as far as I can see. I'll tell Margaret that you'll be back driving next week.'

'That will suit me, Lucy and I think it will give Margaret a bit more flexibility with the taxi bookings.'

Elsie was pleased to report to David that she was going back to her old job at the garage.

'Will you be doing weddings, and evening trips in the mini-coach again?' he asked.

'Certainly; those are the bookings that can give extra pay with tips. You needn't worry, David, this is the low season for weddings and shopping trips, so we should get plenty of time together, if you're up to date with your homework.'

James Green and Fred met Martin Luke, the Managing Director of Luke Construction, two days after their evaluation of the tenders. Martin was accompanied by his secretary, who was an efficient looking lady, dressed smartly with expensive clothes, but giving the impression that she had no time for trivialities. She opened her attaché case and laid out pencils and a notebook and sat down at the table beside her boss. He referred to her briefly when he said he was pleased to meet the Maxwell Motors team again.

'We have assessed your tender document,' said James, 'and we are prepared to accept your tender. However, Fred has some issues that he wishes to clarify.' Fred looked at the list of items he'd discussed with Bob and Lucy, which they agreed should be raised at the meeting.

‘Firstly,’ said Fred, ‘how soon can you get started on the site, assuming we place the contract with you today?’

‘Well, we were not expecting to get the order so soon, but I think we could get some men on site the week after next.’

‘That is not good enough,’ said Fred. ‘Let me explain why. The steel for the garage will be delivered to site at the start of that week. By that time, I would hope that you could have got the concrete bases in place for the steel stanchions. So my hope is that you will have some suitable steel men to build up the roof steel structure during the week that you are proposing to put the first men on site. Surely you can get the site pegged out this week, and have a machine on site to dig out for the bases so that they are concreted by the time the steel is delivered?’

‘You seem to be in a hurry to get this job done. I can understand that, but we need to sort out the right men for this work. However, I can arrange for our surveyor to be on site tomorrow and the next day, to get the site pegged out. We can then arrange a small team to dig out for the concrete bases starting next week.’ He looked across at his secretary who was furiously taking notes.

‘My concern is to get the steel structure up and the roof on before we have any spell of bad winter weather,’ emphasised Fred.

‘We will do everything we can to help you to achieve that objective.’

‘The next issue is who will be your site manager for this job, and will he be full-time here?’ asked Fred.

‘That hasn’t been considered, as we didn’t know if we’d succeeded with our tender.’

‘Again, I will explain,’ said Fred. ‘Maxwell Motors is a very busy company, and there are buses, coaches and taxis going in and out of this site throughout the day. This means that the delivery of materials will have to be organised so that the lorries are unloaded as soon as they arrive on site. Also, the stocking area is effectively the building area. I think you realised this when you visited the site.'

'Yes, I realised that. It's going to be a congested operation, I accept that.'

'Well, clearly it needs a site manager who has bags of experience. I wouldn't like us to be dealing with a young fellow who thinks he's good, but in fact he's wet behind his ears.'

'I will guarantee that you'll have a very good, full-time site manager and we will sort that out and introduce him to you before the start of next week.'

'There is one item that hasn't been addressed in either tender document,' Fred continued. 'We think you've assumed that you would have to assemble the roof trusses on site. I have now agreed that they will be assembled in the engineering works, ready to connect to the other steel structure.'

'I am not sure I can answer that question. I will have to get someone to check the tender,' Martin Luke responded.

'I am prepared to leave the money in the contract at this stage, on the basis that it will be used if there are any variation orders that we have to settle during the total work programme.' Fred sat back, satisfied that he had altered the approach of Luke Construction to this project. He whispered to James what to do next. He addressed Martin Luke and his secretary.

'If you will spend a few minutes having a cup of tea with us, and also meeting the main shareholder, Mr Bob Maxwell, and Mrs Platt, who is in charge of operations, I will get the letter accepting your tender typed up.'

James went out to Margaret to finalise the letter. Fred

called in Bob and Lucy, who were standing by, and instructed Lilly to deliver the tea and biscuits that she'd prepared.

Martin Luke looked at his secretary and raised an eyebrow. He was not used to dealing with a client like this one, but as he talked to Lucy and Bob he learned a lot about Maxwell Motors, and recognised the importance of the garage extension to the company. He was glad to receive the letter confirming the order for the garage extension. It was a sizable increase in his order books and as he was driving back to his office he made a few comments to his secretary.

'They are an impressive bunch. I've seen their buses and coaches around, but I didn't realise how big an operation it is. They know where they're going. We'll have to give this contract our best shot. If we make a success of it we might get some good publicity that could lead to other contracts.' His secretary agreed with him.

'It just shows what can happen when you have a woman in charge of operations,' she said with a smile.

The next day a surveyor and an assistant arrived on site with surveying equipment and a large box of white pegs. Fred introduced himself and kept an eye on them. Once they'd established a base point in relation to the other garage, with measurements and levelling adjustments, the outline of the new garage began to appear. They also marked out the position of all the concrete bases that were required. The surveyor saw Fred at the end of the day and advised that they would be back the next day to lay out the new access from the main road. Fred was pleased that Luke Construction was getting started. Martin Luke came to the site on the Saturday morning and introduced their site manager, Ken Straw, to Fred, Bob and Lucy. Ken was around Fred's age, and had managed a good number of jobs for Luke Construction. In discussions, it was clear to Fred that he had studied the plans and had a feel for the site restrictions. He agreed to install the Luke site cabin at the back of the site, where the maintenance building was to be built. He finally confirmed that he'd have a small machine on site on the Monday, with the requisite manpower, to start extracting the overburden for the concrete bases.

There was great interest among the Maxwell staff at the array of pegs defining the road and the new buildings, as well as the garage extension. It caused some comments, to Fred, such as 'It's going to be a bloody big set-up when it's finished, Fred,' from one of the experienced drivers, and 'It'll be like Piccadilly Circus on a morning, when all the buses and coaches are leaving the site. It's a good job it's a one way system.' from another.

'That was our main consideration in the design of the site — to make it simple for you drivers.'

Fred took Richard around to see the layout. Richard weighed it up and then, based on his experience at the fuel pumps, asked a question of his father.

'I can see the benefits of the new road, to give access to the garages, but I think there's one item missing. You should really have a new diesel pump installed on the entrance road, or in the area between the cleaning and maintenance bays and the garages. This would mean that the buses and coaches wouldn't need to come to the other fuel pumps. The existing fuel pumps are busy anyway and I can see it getting a real bottleneck at times, what with all the buses and coaches queuing up to fill up as well as the public vehicles.'

'We have discussed it,' Richard, 'but we thought it would be very expensive to lay a fuel line from the existing tanks up to that point.'

'So why don't you put a single tank up there, and one fuel pump? The Shell tanker could fill that tank up and then come through one of the garages to fill the other tanks. Is it too late to include that in the current contract?'

'I think you've made a good case, Richard. I'll think about it.'

Fred decided to convene an urgent meeting with Bob and Lucy and it took place on the Tuesday afternoon in Lucy's office.

Fred exposed Richard's arguments and his solution. He waited for the reaction.

'I have to say that I think Richard is right,' said Bob. 'It does get busy at the fuel pumps now, and when we have all the fleet on this site it's bound to get even worse.'

'We need to get Shell involved, to inspect the site and see what they think', said Lucy. 'Will you arrange that, Fred?'

'I'll get onto it straightaway. The underground tank needs to be big enough so that it covers all our needs for the buses and coaches. There's spare money in the existing contract to cover for the excavation for the underground fuel tank and the power supply to the pumps.

It was a hectic few days for Fred. He received a report from Shell confirming that it was indeed feasible to have the extra fuel tank and pump. They specified the size of the tank —it was a very big one — and they gave an outline cost for their part of the installation. Fred met with James Green and asked him to amend the project plans. They then had a meeting with Luke Construction and explained the change to them, and gave them a variation order to cover the work. It was agreed that the excavation for the underground tank and its installation would be done early in the project, even though the commissioning of the fuel pumps would be near the end of the project.

Fred was satisfied with the first week's work by Luke Construction. All the concrete pads were dug out and the first two were concreted. Also, a number of lorryloads of soil had been loaded and removed from the site to get the ground levels right for concreting the floor in the new garage. Fred and Ken Straw had visited the engineering works to see the progress with the steel work. They'd seen an impressive collection of girders cut to size, and others being drilled. The first two of the roof A-frames were assembled, and the rest of the steel was being cut and drilled. Back on the site, Ken Straw had marked the area where the different steel girders would be stacked.

Lucy had complimented Richard on his suggestion for the additional diesel pump. She remembered that Richard had told her that he'd been picked for the school second team game, at home, with Bradford Grammar School that Saturday. She insisted that they should go and support him.

It was a fine, bright day and Fred drove them to the match in the Maxwell van. Richard had warned them that it would be a tough match, as Bradford had a good team that were generally winning their matches. Before the match, Lucy was able to brief Dr Poxon on the progress at Maxwell Motors, and Fred gave him a detailed report on the start of the building works for the garage extension.

During the match, Lucy was able to offer strong vocal support for the Leeds team, who played well and had a 12—6 lead at half-time.

'Can they keep it up through the second half, Fred?' she asked her husband.

'The Leeds team don't looked stressed,' replied Fred. 'I've

been watching one or two of the Bradford team, and they are blowing hard. Mind you, the Bradford master seems to be grilling his team. He might have given them lemons instead of oranges to suck. We shall see what happens.'

The second half comprised more open rugby, and a couple of missed tackles by both sides led to four tries, meaning that Leeds kept their lead. However, in the last ten minutes, a Leeds move that was started by Richard led to another try, so Leeds won with the scoreline 30—18. Lucy had a word with Richard as he left the field and said that she would wait for him with the van. It was a squeeze for the three of them in the van, but Richard was pleased to get home for a soak in a hot bath.

While Richard had his bath Lucy reflected on the start for the New Year.

'We've made a good start to this year, don't you think, Fred. It's nice for Richard to have some success as well as Maxwell Motors.'

'Yes, I agree Lucy. But there' a lot of this year left, and I'm sure we'll have some big problems to sort out before we get to the end of it.'

'Sure, but we are good at solving problems, aren't we Fred?'

Fred just nodded. He had no answer to Lucy's confidence.

Twenty-three

Fred was pleased with the progress made by Luke Construction at the end of January 1968. The pads for the steel stanchions were all laid in the garage area and the steel had been delivered and laid out in piles that would make it easy to pick up for installation.

A new crane, with an extended jib, was delivered to site on Monday 2 February and then on the Tuesday, a team of three steel fixers and a crane driver reported for duty.

Ken Straw had explained that Luke Construction used this team of steel fixers on their key projects and that they were an efficient and safe team. They had no nerves about being exposed at heights, but blustery winds were their main hazard. Fred watched them at work. Piece by piece the structure was assembled. At the end of the day the first two sections of the steelwork were in place, giving Ken Straw and his surveyor the opportunity to check that the structure was exactly in position vertically and laterally.

Ken Straw reported back to Fred. 'We've made a good start, Fred. It should be straightforward now. I think they should be able to do about the same amount of fixing each day, so we should get the main steel in place in the next ten days. It'll look a lot different then.'

'I've been impressed with the way they work,' replied Fred. 'I've done my share of steel fixing on projects, but I wouldn't fancy some of the exposure that those lads have. They are a good team.'

'They've been working together for a long time, so they trust one another and they can rely on the crane driver.'

While the steel structure was being assembled another small team dug out the base of the new road and started cementing in the kerbstones and laying the hard core.

It took a total of nine days to complete the steel structure for the new garage. It looked impressive, but that was the end of things for six weeks, until the end of March. The north of England was subjected to a severe dose of winter weather, with temperatures recorded at minus fifteen degrees centigrade and thick snow closing roads and affecting the railways. After a few days trying to fight the conditions, Lucas Construction faced the inevitable and laid the men off until the weather changed. Everyone thought it would be a short, cold spell, but as the disruption continued people became convinced it would be a long winter. There was no work that could be done in those weather conditions. Luke Construction reported that they were stopped on several sites in the north of England. Fred was pleased when he learned that the company had an agreement with their men that compensated them for the weather conditions such that they didn't seek alternative employment. Ken Straw was confident that they would have adequate manpower to push the job forward once they could get back on site.

Fred used the bad weather period to try out his plan to change the engine in a coach that had done a very high mileage. He'd cleared this idea with Bob, and a new engine had been purchased for the trial. Fred was sure that if he could change coach engines, and then send them away for the seating to be updated and the bodywork re-sprayed, it would be much cheaper than buying new coaches.

His approach was to plan in detail, with Brian Hunt and John Wall, how the job would be done. He purchased an A-frame that could be manoeuvred into place to lift the old engine out and lower the new engine into place. They checked positioning the A-frame and agreed all the spares needed for hoses and connecting bolts. John Wall wrote notes of all their findings during the examination of a sample coach, and wrote out the method to be used to do the job. Fred was sure that the half-day spent on this planning exercise was time well spent.

It was very cold in the garage on the day they chose to do the job, and they had to keep warming their fingers so that they could grip the spanners and other tools. But it went well. By mid-afternoon they'd removed the old engine and replaced it, along with some new hoses. Fred started the engine up and it ran sweetly, as one would expect from a new engine. Because of the snow there was no chance to take the coach for a run on the roads. Bob was impressed when he saw the coach and 'engine change' became a part of Maxwell maintenance policy, representing a significant cost saving for the company.

It was the quietest time of the year for coach bookings, but many had to be cancelled, including bookings for school sports fixtures. The main aim of the company was to try to keep the service buses running on the Horsforth and Otley routes. With the continuing snow storms, and the winds causing drifting, roads which had been opened at one time could be closed a few hours later. There was no chance of maintaining timetables, and it was a success just to complete the journey. It was clear that some other bus operators were withdrawing their services completely. This meant that the Maxwell buses were operating at full capacity and the passengers recognised that on some days their only chance of getting to Leeds was to catch a Maxwell service. Both Lucy and Fred spoke to the drivers and conductors and encouraged them to keep going as much as possible. Lucy summed it up. 'Forget about timetables, just keep going slowly backwards and forwards along the route. I'll see you right for your efforts when we get back to normal.'

'We keep getting the thumbs-up from some of our passengers when we turn up. No bugger else is running buses on some days,' said one of the drivers.

However the operations were not without mishap. On one day a double-decker on the Horsforth route went into a skid down a hill and ploughed off the road and into a ditch. The bus keeled over and came to rest leaning on the packed snow heaped up at the side of the road. No one was hurt, but everyone was shocked and it wasn't easy to get them off the bus, due to angle it was leaning. Also the exit was blocked by packed snow. A man who saw what happened from a nearby house came to the rescue with a large shovel and cleared a way from the exit of the bus onto the road. Fred was advised of the accident and organised a coach to go to the site of the beleaguered bus to take the passengers forward on their journey. When Fred got to the scene in the relief coach, he saw that there were over forty people huddled together in the snow at the back of the bus. The police were there directing the traffic as the road was effectively reduced to a single carriageway. Fred spoke to the police and they agreed to let the passengers leave the site on the relief coach.

Fred discussed his plans with the police. 'I will ring for a rescue vehicle to come and pull the bus out of the snow drift onto the road, if you agree?'

'You go ahead; it's the only way to get this road back into two-way traffic,' replied the police sergeant.

Fred rang a company on the outskirts of Leeds and explained the problem. They had a large, four-wheel drive, vehicle available that they used on outcrop sites for loading coal. It had a winch that could pull the bus out of the snow drift. The police sergeant agreed to collaborate to get the rescue vehicle through to the site and control the traffic during the operation.

The rescue vehicle appeared out of proportion to the other vehicles on the road. It had huge wheels and a loading bucket at the front, and a winch mounted on the back. The driver parked and went to look at the double-decker. Fred showed him the place on the rear axle where he intended to attach the rope, emphasising that he hoped the bus would come back onto the road without falling over completely. The first move by the driver was to spin his machine round and, using the bucket, push the snow back over a fence into a field so that he could park at the far side of the road from the bus. He then placed his bucket onto the floor to gain extra resistance against the pull in the rope. The police sergeant saw how quickly the snow was moved and commented to Fred. 'The Council could do with this fellow shifting snow. He's more effective than the machines that they have.'

Fred took the rope and attached it around the back axle of the bus. By this time he was wet through and dirty with scrambling under the bus. When he was happy with the rope attachment, Fred gave the okay to the driver to tighten the rope. A crowd of spectators had gathered and they watched closely to see what happened. Very slowly the tension was applied and the bus gradually moved out of the snow drift and straightened up. The position of the rescue machine was such that the bus was fully onto the road by the time it was necessary to disconnect the rope. The bus driver got back in his cab and started the engine. Everything appeared to be operational. Fred thanked the rescue machine driver and the police sergeant, and joined the bus to go back to the garage. An inspection showed that there was no damage to the bodywork or its engine. So the driver and conductor drove back to Horsforth and resumed their tricky operations.

On another day, early in March, Elsie had taken the mini-coach out on a journey to York with a group of ladies. The journey to York was considered feasible as the roads had been cleared of drifts, but the road surface was packed snow. However, on the return journey, Elsie faced a further snow storm and it was a very treacherous operation. She negotiated it satisfactorily but, when she parked at the garage, she was in a state of exhaustion and shock. Margaret and Lucy supplied her with hot tea and wrapped her in warm blankets to stop her shivering.

'That settles it,' said Lucy. 'We are not taking any more bookings for your ladies, Elsie, until we are sure that the winter weather is over. When you've warmed up, Fred will drive you home in the van.'

There were no signs of an end to the bad weather, and conditions on the roads and railways got even worse. There was a series of calls from people cancelling their bookings on the various tours. Lucy called a meeting in her office with Margaret, Mavis, Bob, Fred and the manager of the travel agency in Harrogate.

Lucy opened the meeting. 'There seems to be no sign of an end to this bad weather and we've had numerous people cancelling their bookings. My view is that we cancel all tours for the next couple of weeks. We dare not risk having an accident where passengers get injured due to dangerous road conditions.'

There was agreement to the cancellation policy.

'But I think we need to try to offer the passengers some alternatives,' suggested Mavis.

'That's an idea, Mavis. Have you any suggestions?'

'Firstly, we should offer everybody who has paid for a trip their money back, straightaway. We could then offer them an alternative trip, within the next month, at a discounted price, of say twenty percent off the normal price. Are there any spare places on our tours at the end of March, or in April, Margaret?'

'Generally the tours are fully booked, as we're moving into the Easter holidays, which are the last weekend of March.'

The manager of the Harrogate travel agency confirmed that the luxury tours were also fully booked. Mavis couldn't accept that there were no alternatives.

'Well, could we double-up, and put two coaches on tours instead of one, for a few weeks? I'm sure I could get extra rooms in most hotels, or even use different hotels in the same town.'

'There will certainly be some coaches available on most weeks,' suggested Margaret.

'I think we have to go for this damage limitation policy, Lucy,' said Bob. 'We don't want to end up with a few hundred disappointed passengers. We need some creative thinking.'

‘We will cancel all our tours until the Easter weekend at the end of March. Surely, by then, there will be a change in the weather. Your job, Margaret, is to contact everyone who has made a booking. Ask them if they can call in for their money and, at the same time, see if they are able to take advantage of any of our extra tours with twenty percent discount.’

The manager of the Harrogate travel agency agreed to contact everyone who had booked on the luxury tours.

‘Fred, will you go through with Margaret and agree which coaches will be used to double-up on tours for the weeks of April? I’m hopeful that a lot of passengers will rebook with us. You’ll have to use your magical negotiating skills, Mavis, to get the necessary hotel rooms.’

‘There’s going to be a lot of people visiting us over the next week or so,’ Margaret pointed out.

‘You are absolutely right. I’ll make my office available for meeting people. We could carry out two interviews at a time if we used both ends of the large table. It needs at least three of us to be available, with half-hour slots, to meet passengers through this period. That’ll be me, Margaret and you, Mavis, but we’ll use Elsie if any of us are tied up with other matters.’

It was a hectic period, with sessions booked throughout the day and into the evening, for people wanting to collect their money. It soon became clear that everyone was tired of the winter weather and wanted to take any opportunity to get away for a holiday. The majority of cancellations were replaced by a booking on one of the discounted holidays. A major problem was that there were no spare luxury coaches. After much searching, Fred managed to find one with an specification much better than their standard coaches, though not as good as the Maxwell luxury coach. He hired it for the months of April and May, so that one extra luxury tour could be scheduled each week in that period. Pearl Featherstone was drafted in as second courier.

There were concerns that the weather might prevent the Grimethorpe Colliery Band Concert taking place as planned at Leeds Grammar School on Thursday 28 March. However the school, and the band, decided to let the concert date stand and the weather improved, allowing the band and the audience to get to the school.

The concert was a repeat success of the event two years earlier, however there was one particularly memorable item in the programme. A euphonium player at the school, called Les Jones, impressed the Grimethorpe conductor, firstly as a mischievous fourteen-year-old lad, and secondly by his playing of the euphonium. The conductor decided to let him play a solo after the school brass players had played an item with the band at the start of the second half of the concert. It was a virtuoso arrangement of the famous music-hall song 'My grandfather's clock was too tall for the shelf so it stood forty years on the floor.' The young lad was tutored by the conductor, and the band, to show his proficiency with his instrument and milk the audience with his fearless style. It was a triumph and achieved a standing ovation from the audience and the band players. The audience went away forgetting about the bad weather, but with the image of a young lad playing his heart out for their entertainment. Maxwell Motors reaped many plaudits in the press for their sponsorship of the concert.

With the change in the weather there was a return of Luke Construction men, in force, to the garage site. Fred assumed that the steel fixers would continue with the roof of the new garage, but Ken Straw explained the changed priorities.

‘I want to get the steel shell up for the maintenance building and the cleaning building. There’s a lot of complex equipment to go into those buildings, so we need to get them built to release them to the sub-contractors as a priority. It’s the best way to give us any chance of catching up some of the time we’ve lost with the weather.’

‘I am all for anything that regains us a bit of the lost time,’ replied Fred.

‘We have to complete the excavation of the hole for the diesel tank. We’ve hit some shale strata, so you’ll hear our compressed air picks at work, chopping out the last three feet of strata. As soon as that’s done we’ll get the tank delivered and fix it in place. That will be an interesting job as it must be a very large tank. We can get the bricklayers deployed, then, to complete the walls of the excavation and get the covers in place on the top.’

For the next three days the whole garage, the forecourt, the offices and the two houses vibrated to the sound of the compressed air picks at work. When they ceased a peaceful calm fell on the site.

Saturday 30 March was the start of the holiday season. Four coaches were scheduled to leave the Horsforth garage for south coast tours.

‘We’ve never had four coaches leaving at the same time, Lucy,’ said Fred. ‘It will be a real test of our organisation. I’ll park the coaches on the forecourt with space inbetween them for passenger to move about.’

‘I’ve arranged for a big notice to be displayed on the front of each coach, showing its destination. There will be myself, Margaret, Elsie and Lilly with lists, to make sure that passengers get on the right coach.’

‘I’ll have John Wall, Richard and Brian Hunt to deliver

the luggage and help the drivers load it. I'll keep an eye on things and try to sort out any problems.'

The problems arose when a service coach and the mini-coach arrived at the same time, delivering passengers they'd picked up. There was quite a crowd of people milling around and, it seemed, luggage everywhere. Once the passengers had identified the coach they were travelling on, they concentrated on ensuring that their luggage was loaded onto the right coach before they boarded it and found their seats. Due to the melee of people, the lads who were trying to handle the luggage just couldn't get through with their special luggage carts. Eventually, the four coaches left the garage fifteen minutes late, but the general mood of the passengers was a mixture of excitement and pleasure at being able to go away on holiday.

When the coaches had gone, Fred spoke to his team, who were sweating profusely from their efforts getting the luggage onto the coaches.

'Well done, lads,' he said. 'That was a real challenge, but we got the coaches away. We'll have it all to do again next week!'

'Surely we can have a different layout to the one today,' suggested Richard. 'It was chaos out there, we just couldn't move to get through with the luggage. There needs to be a different set-up for dispatching four coaches at the same time.'

Fred walked around the forecourt with Richard, them both silently trying to think of an alternative. Richard broke the ice.

'Can I make a suggestion?'

'Certainly,' replied Fred.

'The aim is to park the coaches so that other traffic can

get past them, into the garage area.'

Fred agreed with that objective.

'I think there is room to back the coaches up to the wall, on the same side as the fuel pumps. Can you get a coach out and try it?'

Fred brought a coach out and Richard directed him to park on the forecourt, near to the fuel pumps. There was plenty of room for other vehicles to drive past the coach to the garage. Fred got out and viewed the situation.

'As you can see, there's room to leave a gap between each coach, for loading the passengers and luggage, and there's room to park four coaches the same way,' concluded Richard, a sense of pride and achievement coming across in his voice.

'We will leave the coach parked there and show it to your mother and Bob to get their agreement.'

'We need to paint the parking bays on the back wall and along the tarmac. Any coach leaving this site should then park in one of the bays for loading and dispatched. It will be an efficient and tidy system, don't you agree, Dad?'

'Yes, I do, Richard. I think you may have cracked it.'

The meeting with Bob and Lucy resulted in full agreement to the change. Measurements were made to equalise the spacing between the coaches and the wall and tarmac were marked-up. Brian Hunt was given a large tin of special white paint to show the parking slots and to mark the places as 1, 2, 3 and 4 on the wall. When he'd finished, the system for parking coaches was clearly defined. Margaret was instructed to issue parking slots for all tours, no matter how many coaches were involved and drivers were instructed to use the parking bays when they returned from tours.

In the first week of April the large fuel tank was delivered to the site. Fred watched as Ken Straw took the low-loader slowly along the access road as he didn't want the kerbstones damaging. The driver parked his vehicle so that the crane could lift the tank and lower it into the hole. It took half an hour of small adjustments by the crane before the tank was settled into place.

'We'll be able to get that bricked up now, and the hole covered over,' Ken reported to Fred. 'There's a great deal of bricking to do on this job, so I want to get started.'

The next day a team of three men started to brick the walls of the fuel tank. Intensive work by the steel fixers established the steel shell for the cleaning building and the maintenance building. Their next job was to dismantle the spout and the fall pipes along the old garage and replace them with a much bigger spout and larger diameter fall pipes. Both the maintenance and cleaning buildings were tall, as they were designed to service the double-deckers. The steel work for each end of the buildings was a complex frame, surrounded by brickwork that was designed to carry the roller doors and so involved more work for the steel fixers. Fred wondered when the steel fixers would get back to the roof of the new garage.

The new arrangements for parking coaches on the forecourt met their first real test on Saturday 6 April, when there were four coaches to be dispatched on south coast tours. The system worked like clockwork. The four coaches departed on time, and there were no problems with people getting mixed up. In the afternoon, when the four coaches returned from the previous week's tours, the drivers reversed into the bays and discharged their passengers and their luggage, again with no problems. One driver, in fact, commented that this new arrangement made it easier for the passengers to pass on their tips to the drivers. Richard was playing cricket at school, so he wasn't available on the forecourt that day. When he was having a cup of cocoa at supper time, he casually asked about how things had worked.

'It was brilliant,' replied Lucy. 'The whole exercise in the morning, and when the coaches returned in the afternoon, worked very professionally. I shall note that it was your idea when I report the system at the management committee meeting next week. You'll probably get mentioned in the minutes.'

'Do you get a reward if you're mentioned in the minutes?'

'I don't think so. It's never happened so far in Maxwell Motors.'

'It was just common sense. You have to look at what is happening on any operation and think how it can be done better.'

'You have a very clever son, Fred,' Lucy said with a smile, looking across at Fred. 'Are you proud of him?'

'Of course I am. I've seen him organising his team on the rugby field. I know the way he thinks.'

The management committee meeting the next week started with a review of the effect of the bad weather on Maxwell Motors. The total income for the first three months of the year was fourteen percent down on the previous year. The results could have been worse but for the efforts of the bus drivers who had persisted against very adverse weather conditions. The number of tours that had been cancelled in March was noted, but sixty-four percent of the passengers affected had rebooked for a discounted tour. The new parking arrangements on the forecourt were explained. Five weeks had been lost on the garage extension project, so it would likely be completed in August not July. The negative effect of the weather on staff morale was discussed. Finally, it was predicted by members of the committee that the company would be performing at its normal levels of efficiency in the near future.

Lilly asked to have a word with Lucy, about a private matter. Lucy took her into the house so that the discussion was completely private.

'Now then, Lilly what is the problem?'

Lilly seemed reluctant to speak out. 'It's David. He's decided to leave school after he's done his A-levels in July. He says that he doesn't want to go to university and he doesn't think he's good enough for an academic career. I am lost, Lucy, and I don't know what to say to him. Can you advise me, or will you have a word with him, please?'

'What I can say, Lilly, is that there are other ways to become educated besides university. Take me and Fred, for example. What does he want to do?'

'That's part of the problem — he doesn't know. He says he'll look around when he finishes at school.'

'The main thing is for him to take his A-level exams and do the best he can. I will think about it, Lilly, and then I'll tell you if I have any ideas.'

'Thank you, Lucy. I'll certainly encourage him to work hard for his A-levels.'

Lucy was beginning to detect that there were problems arising with the bookings between the Horsforth office and the Harrogate travel agency. There seemed to be competition between the two offices for places. She discussed the problem with Leslie Fortune, manager of the travel agency, and following this she decided to have a meeting with all the Harrogate staff and Leslie, along with herself, Margaret, Elsie and Mavis from Horsforth. She arranged for the meeting to be in a private room in a Harrogate hotel, as an evening meeting, preceded by sandwiches. Lucy mingled with the six staff from the Harrogate office and detected an atmosphere of tension. She arranged ten chairs in a circle, and made sure that the staff of both offices was interspersed. She defined the objective of the meeting.

'Both the Harrogate and Horsforth offices appear to be getting an upsurge of bookings for tours. Whether this is a temporary reaction after the bad winter weather, or a permanent feature of our joint businesses, it is presenting us with problems. You might suggest that we increase the number of tours we offer. We did that, on a temporary basis, to compensate for those tours that had to be cancelled, but we're not able to do that as a regular arrangement. This meeting is to openly discuss all the problems that are arising and then we can agree how we are going to manage the situation. Please speak out and don't be afraid to give us your views.'

The discussion started slowly, and then more and more facts were exposed. It became clear that the Harrogate staff could satisfy their clients by redirecting them to tours other than the Maxwell programme. Lucy wished to avoid this and so, in the end, certain actions were agreed. The waiting lists for any tour would be restricted to a maximum of five people at any time and they would be put on the list in date order of their booking, as it was inferred that there might have been adjustments to some waiting lists as special personal favours in the past. The management of the luxury tours would be the responsibility of the Harrogate office and the Horsforth office would be responsible for all other tours. There would be a transfer of information each day between the two offices of those tours which were within six passengers of a full booking. Any requests for further bookings for those tours would have to be cleared with the responsible office. Lucy had a word with Leslie and he agreed that the actions proposed would increase the efficiency of the booking systems. He was sure that his staff were pleased that Lucy had arranged the joint meeting.

In the taxi going back to Horsforth, Mavis commented on the evening.

'I am sure, after this evening, we shall get a better working relationship going between the two offices. But we have another problem, Lucy.'

'What's that, Mavis?'

'I think we're putting too much work on Margaret now. She is getting less help from me, what with all my work on the new tours and solving problems with the old tours. And Elsie is doing more trips with the taxi and the mini-coach, so she is less help around the office. I think we are a person short in the office.'

'I have been thinking about that, too; I am glad you are raising it, Mavis. You are not saying anything, Margaret? What do you think?'

'I have to admit that, since the bad weather, life in the office has been hectic. It's also more tricky due to the increased number of bookings coming through the Harrogate office. There's more cross-checking to do to ensure that we don't double-book.'

'That's fine, Margaret. We'll discuss it in detail in the morning.'

The next morning Elsie took charge of the general office, while Margaret and Mavis met with Lucy in her office.

'If we assume we need another person in the office, who do you want Margaret?'

'I've been thinking about that one, Lucy. There are people who know the routine here, but I think I would be happier to have a young person who I could train up to do the job. I would be in charge then.'

'But you are in charge of the office, whoever we appoint,' suggested Mavis.

'You know what I mean; some strong characters have a different style to me. I like to get the job done with as little fuss as possible.'

'We do know what you mean, Margaret and I'll sort it out,' said Lucy.

She arranged another meeting that day, with Fred and Bob.

'We have agreed this morning that we need another person in the general office, to help Margaret. She says that she would rather have a young person that she can train, rather than shuffle current staff.' She paused, waiting for a reaction from Fred and Bob.

'I suspect that you have a solution to this issue that you would like to put to us, Lucy?' said Bob, with a wry smile.

'I happen to know that a young fellow, who works for us from time to time, has decided to leave school after taking his A-level exams and find a job. He doesn't want to go to university and he has no idea what career he would like to follow. I've been thinking about this and would suggest that we offer him an apprenticeship, so that in three years time he becomes proficient at all aspects of our operations. He would have to go to nightschool to study engineering and business management. He would also have to become familiar with every aspect of our business by moving around doing all the different jobs. By this I mean that he would have to get a driving licence and then his PSV qualification to be able to drive all our fleet. What do you think about this?'

'I am assuming that you are referring to David Young,' said Bob. 'I like the lad, and he seems to have the same work ethic as his sister. Do you think he would be interested?'

'We can only make him an offer, and then we shall see,' replied Lucy. 'Your job, Fred, is to sort out the courses at the Technical College for engineering studies and business management techniques. You will then have to draw it all together into a document listing all that is involved in his practical work and his studies to form the three year apprenticeship. It has to be in enough detail so that it can be registered as an official apprenticeship.'

'I'll do that, Lucy, but how are we going to keep it under wraps?'

'We will have to keep it confidential between the three of us. I will arrange for my friend Diane, the manager of the employment agency, to prepare the documentation. When we are satisfied with a final document, she can then deal with the necessary registration of this scheme as an apprenticeship for a bus and coach company. We won't say anything to anyone here about it, but we need to get it sorted out urgently. His first posting will be with Margaret, in the office, over the summer period. We'll want him to start as soon he has completed his last A-level exam in June.'

Fred concentrated on drawing everything together for the apprenticeship scheme.. After two weeks, he had sourced all the courses and discovered the qualifications they would give for successful exam results. He'd also obtained examples of other schemes and he took all this information over to the employment agency. Diane Rhodes agreed to prepare the final documentation within three days. She would see to the licensing of the scheme later.

When the documentation was returned to Lucy she set

up another meeting with Bob and Fred to go through the scheme in detail.

'Well, it's a very good scheme, Fred,' said Lucy. 'Anyone who gets through this programme will be an asset to any bus or coach company. There is only one thing missing. What are we going to pay him?'

'As he goes through this programme he'll do a lot of work for the company,' suggested Fred.

'He's a good lad, and I would like to encourage him,' said Bob. 'Can we put him on a salary rather than pay him on a time basis?'

'I agree with that,' said Lucy. 'And can I suggest £1,200 per year, paid monthly? And he should receive an increase when he passes his driving test and also when he gets his PSV licence.'

'That sounds good to me,' concluded Bob.

'I will have a word with my friend and get her to put these figures at the end of the document. I'll then write to David and ask him to come to see you and me, Bob, one evening. Lilly can deliver the letter, but it won't say why we want to see him.'

Two days later, Lucy gave Lilly a sealed letter to pass on to her brother. Lilly placed it on David's plate when he came home from school and sat down to tea.

'What's this about?' David asked, as he looked at the letter.

'I have no idea,' replied Lilly. 'Lucy passed it to me this afternoon and she made no comment.'

David opened the letter. He was surprised that it was written by hand, from Lucy. He read it twice and then looked up at Lilly.

‘It’s from Lucy. She wants me to go and see her and Bob tomorrow night, at seven-thirty. It doesn’t say what for. She’s written the letter by hand.’

‘You must go, David, and you had better look smart. It could be important.’

‘It’s very strange. It could be to give me the sack, but I can’t think I have done anything wrong on the fuel pumps.’

David sat opposite Lucy and Bob, across the big table in her office. He looked smart in his best school uniform, with a white shirt and the school tie. Lucy greeted him a warm smile.

‘We’ve asked you to come and see us on a confidential matter, David. We understand that you are planning to leave school after your A-level exams and seek a job. What sort of job will you be seeking?’

‘I am sure that I am not cut out for an academic career. I don’t know what line of work I want to follow, but I hope it can be interesting and challenging. I accept that I will have to do some more studying to get on.’ He paused for a moment. ‘I can’t add any more to that. I’m sorry to be so vague.’

‘That’s fine, David. So you have not ruled out any options at this stage?’

‘No, I’ve decided to leave those decisions until after the exams.’

‘Well, we might be able to help you.’

Lucy outlined the plan to set up an apprentice scheme within Maxwell Motors and she described the features of the scheme. Bob joined in by explaining the need for young people to gain skills in the company. They talked for about a quarter of an hour and then Lucy posed the question.

‘Might you be interested in entering into an

apprenticeship with Maxwell Motors?'

Without hesitation, David, said, 'Yes, I could be. I've enjoyed working here and I've gathered some impression of the size of the operation.'

'Well, what I suggest is that you take away this document and study it.'

Lucy passed the document over to David in a sealed envelope.

'It tells you all about this appointment. You'll note that we want the person appointed to start as soon as possible; in your case it would be immediately after your last exam. Thank you for coming to see us, David. You can let me know what your decision is when you have made it. We're not intending to interview anyone else at the present time, as we think you're the right person for this appointment.'

David went around the table and shook hands with Lucy and Bob before he left, carrying the large, sealed envelope.

Twenty-four

The management committee meeting was postponed by Lucy until the last week in May, and was held on Friday 31 May. She'd wanted to have results for the full month of April and the first three weeks of May, to get a measure of the level of operations since the bad weather problems. The notes of the meeting recorded the issues discussed.

The eight weeks to the end of the third week of May showed an increase of eight percent on the same weeks of last year. Committee members were reassured that the business was back to normal. The company was under pressure from passengers wanting to book holiday tours and an agreement had been made with the Harrogate travel agency to smooth out the booking systems. More multi coach trips were being undertaken, requiring the leasing of coaches from other companies, but boosting income. The plan was to refurbish some coaches with new engines after the main holiday season was finished. Work on the garage extension was progressing well, with an estimated completion for hand-over by the end of August. The new apprenticeship scheme was described and Lucy announced that David Young would be starting in the third week of June as Maxwells' first apprentice.

Back in the office, Mavis asked the question that she'd detected other members of the management committee would have liked to ask, but didn't.

'I was surprised to hear that David Young will be starting as the first apprentice. How did that come about?'

'It came out of our discussions about the need to give more help to Margaret. In talks with Bob we decided that we should bring in a young person to boost our numbers. We recognised the need to educate and train any young folk to cover all aspects of the business, so we drew up an apprentice scheme. It was then that we made a great scoop. We learned that David wasn't going to go on with his education after this year, so Bob and myself interviewed him and made him an offer, which he accepted.'

'Oh, I like David, and I'm sure he will do well. Are you planning to appoint any more apprentices?'

'Not at the moment, Mavis. We want to see how this appointment works out.'

Lucy went into her office and reflected on what had happened after David's interview. Apparently, he had gone home and read through the apprentice document in detail. He was amazed at what the document contained.

'I can't believe this Lilly,' he'd said. 'This scheme has everything I could wish for in a job. And I'm going to get paid!' He described all the aspects of the education and training. When he'd finished he looked at the clock.

'Do you think it's too late to go out to the phone box and

ring Lucy, now? I want to tell her that I accept this offer, before they change their mind.'

'Yes, I think it's too late to disturb her tonight. Ring her first thing in the morning,' Lilly had advised.

David was up early and rang up from the telephone box at eight o'clock the next morning. Fred answered the 'phone and he passed it over to Lucy at the breakfast table. David was stuck for words.

'It's David.' He paused. 'I just wanted a word about my interview.'

'Right, David, what do you think?'

'I am over the moon. I can't believe it. I do want to accept the offer, and I'll start as soon as possible. I have my last exam on the morning of Tuesday 17 June. I'd like to start work that afternoon, please.'

'Good. That's fine, David. I'll make a note of that date and have a word with you nearer the time.'

'Thank you very much, Mrs Platt.'

'That's your apprentice, Fred: he can't wait to get started.'

The very busy period continued for Maxwell Motors, but not everything worked out as planned. The day after the management meeting there was a problem with a south coast tour. Marion Stead rang Mavis to report that Maxwell passengers had been given inferior rooms in the hotel. The best rooms had been allocated to another premier tour company. This was a new hotel that Mavis had decided to use in preference to the normal one in the town, which had changed their manager and chef. Marion Stead had made no progress in resolving the issue with the hotel manager and she asked Lucy and Mavis to discuss the options.

'There is only one thing to do, Mavis,' said Lucy. Grab some clothes and get into the van and drive down there.

You know how to sort this out. We're not playing second fiddle to any other coach company.'

The outcome was an apology by the deputy manager, who had taken the decision on room allocations. Maxwell passengers were moved into the best rooms in the hotel, after two days when the other tour left. The hotel also reduced the charge to Maxwell Motors by twenty percent for the week, and Mavis and Marion were able to tell the passengers that they would receive a rebate of twenty percent of their holiday charge when they got back to Yorkshire. 'When Maxwell Motors agrees a contract with a hotel we allow no tolerance for any failure on what has been agreed,' Mavis told them. 'I am sure you will enjoy the rest of your holiday.' She set off back to Yorkshire once she had a note, confirming the discount, in her hand from hotel manager.

David was spending Sunday afternoon swotting for his exams. As Elsie had no driving commitments that afternoon he'd invited her over for tea. He'd received a letter confirming his appointment and how he would be paid.

'Have you told Elsie about your new job, David?' asked Lilly.

'No, I've been waiting to get the offer in writing,' he replied. 'I didn't want to jump the gun in any way.'

'Well, I think you should tell her this afternoon. I'm sure she will be as excited as I am.'

'You could be right. I'll think about it.'

Elsie arrived looking very smart in a new dress which was short enough to reveal her long legs. David realised that he couldn't see any signs of the wounds on her legs. She had her hair up on top of her head and her face was full of smiles, emphasised by her lipstick and rouge. He took her in his arms and hugged her. She allowed him a small kiss, but didn't want her lipstick smudging.

'You look, and feel, wonderful, Elsie,' he said. 'Come on and meet Lilly. I know that tea is ready.'

Lilly was bubbly and very chirpy, but she was sure that David had still not told Elsie his news. The chat over the meal was on a range of subjects — David's exams, Elsie's two full-day trips with the mini-coach, and Lilly providing a meal for Lucy to entertain some guests on the Wednesday night. When the conversation flagged Lilly couldn't hold her enthusiasm any longer.

'David has some wonderful news to tell you, Elsie. Go on, David, tell Elsie your news.'

'I have received a letter offering me an apprenticeship at Maxwell Motors.' He stopped and looked across at Elsie.

'What does that mean, David,' asked Elsie, who looked puzzled.

'I shall be leaving school as soon as I've finished my exams, and starting work at Maxwell Motors.'

'Oh, that is a surprise. What will you be doing?'

'Initially I'll be working with Margaret, in the office. But then I'll be training on all aspects of the business, and doing courses at the technical college. It's a three year programme. I'll show it to you when we go upstairs.'

'Don't you think that this is good news, Elsie?' said Lilly. 'Maxwell Motors is a very good company to work for.'

'I agree with you there, Lilly; they've been very good to me. I suppose I should congratulate you, David.' She reached across the table and squeezed his hand and gave him a big smile.

Later, David and Elsie went upstairs and he showed her the letter. She went through it carefully, reading all the details of the training scheme. She also saw the salary that he would be paid. She decided to be positive and show some enthusiasm.

'Wow, that is fantastic, David. You're going to be very busy to get through that lot.' She stood up and put her arms around him and gave him a passionate kiss. 'And we shall see each other as we do our jobs. That will be marvellous.'

'But we won't be able to give one another kisses like that at work.'

They spent an hour together. Elsie was shocked to realise that David would be starting his job within the next three weeks. As they walked back to Elsie's house she realised she couldn't put it off any longer. 'You never mentioned the job to me, David. Was there some reason to keep it a secret?'

'It's all happened in the last week, Elsie. I couldn't believe what was taking place. I didn't want to tell you anything until I received the letter confirming my appointment. Looking back now, I wish I had told you what was going on, but I was swept along by events. I'm sorry I didn't talk to you, Elsie.'

'David, I love you, and I want to love you more, but you have to trust me. I can keep a secret. If you have good or bad news, David, in future I hope you will confide in me.' David squeezed her arm.

'I promise not to keep anything from you in the future, Elsie.'

'Thanks. I can celebrate your good news now.'

Work on the garage extension continued at full speed during June. Near the end of installing the steel roofing sheets on the new garage there was an incident that could have been very serious. Fred saw it happen as he was walking across the forecourt to the office. There was a sudden gust of wind which took hold of one of the sheets and lifted it up and blew it off the roof. In flight. it struck one of the steel fixers and knocked him off the roof. Fortunately, he had his harness fastened to the roof truss, so he was left dangling. Fred rushed across, but Ken Straw was there first. He got on a platform and was raised up to where the man was suspended and assisted him onto the platform. He wasn't injured, but was obviously shocked. They lifted the platform up to the roof truss to disconnect the safety harness and then decided to fetch the other steel fixer down and have an early lunch break. Fortunately, the steel sheet which fell to the floor and was buckled didn't hit anyone or do any damage.

'That was a lucky escape,' said Fred to Ken Straw.

'Yes, it was fortunate that these lads are experienced and know how to use their safety harness. We'll get him back onto the job after lunch and keep an eye on him.'

By the third week in July the roof was on the new garage. It was clear then that the major effort was to complete the brickwork. Just two bricklayers placed the bricks at a very fast rate, serviced by several men mixing the plaster, distributing the bricks onto the platform and adjusting the height of the working platforms as the wall was raised in three foot lifts.

Unlike the existing garage, the new one had two large roller doors at each end, to provide improved security. A large section cross girder held the mechanism for the roller doors. Each end was completed by brickwork above the cross girder up to the top point of the roof. On the brickwork a major 'Maxwell Motors' sign was installed in the company colours.

In the service building a sub-contractor was on site at the beginning of July to install the girders along each side which would allow an overhead crane to travel the full length of the building. The height of the building was such that the overhead crane could operate above the top of the double-decker buses.

Also in July, sub-contractors came on site to install the pipework and control gear for the fuel pumps. Ken Straw arranged that on two days at the end of July the tarmac would be laid on the new entrance road. One of the last jobs would be to lay tarmac in the area around the service and cleaning buildings, and the connection through to the other garage. Laying the concrete floor in the new garage would be done by having ready-mixed concrete delivered to site and poured on a continuous basis.

On Friday 12 July, in the afternoon, Lucy came into the office to speak to David and Margaret. She'd observed David since he'd taken up his post in June. He always looked really smart in his sports coat, shirt and tie. Margaret was showing him all the systems and he'd gained confidence as he applied them. He frequently spoke to the manager of the travel agency in Harrogate about the bookings for tours, and handled telephone calls from potential clients with ease. He had a friendly style when meeting people in the office who wanted to book holidays. Whatever he was doing, Lucy had noticed, he was calm and assured.

'Now then, David, are you ready for taking over?' asked Lucy. 'Margaret is taking the next week off on holiday, so for a lot of that time you'll be on your own. Is there anything else that you want to know from Margaret?'

'No, I think Margaret has covered everything very well.'

'I am confident that David will be up to the job,' said Margaret. 'It's not just that he knows our systems now, he has actually been operating them since he came. He's also got some experience of the problems that can arise.'

'If there is anything that's way out of the ordinary, David, you know you can always ask me or Mavis for advice. I have full confidence in you David.'

'Thank you, Lucy,' David replied. The fact that he called her Lucy was a measure of his confidence in his role.

The next morning, his first day in charge, he showed his positive approach by being in the office at seven-thirty, before Fred came onto the forecourt from the house.

On Wednesday 17 July, Elsie had a full day in the office with David, after an early-morning taxi journey to Leeds station with Mr and Mrs Higson to catch the London train. Elsie was now very friendly with Mr Higson, as she often covered his taxi bookings, so they exchanged information about their lives. He'd told her that he had three meetings in central London during the day, associated with his engineering company. In the evening he was going with his wife to a dinner that would be attended by some senior politicians, so they were staying over in London. Asked what she would be doing for the day, Elsie explained that she had a quiet day, with no more driving jobs, so she would be in the office. She elaborated about David, her boyfriend, taking up an apprenticeship with Maxwell Motors.

'You sound very proud of him, Elsie,' said Mr Higson.

'Yes, I am. When he got the offer of this apprenticeship, I wasn't sure how he would take to it. But Mrs Platt seems to know how to spot people who will fit in with her organisation.'

'Yes, I have a great respect for Mrs Platt.'

It was a very busy day for Elsie and David in the office, with numerous contacts by clients and staff. They were so busy that they couldn't stop for lunch so had to grab a sandwich which Lilly brought over from the house. At the end of the day, Elsie had to state her respect for David.

'I've spent many hours, over the years, in this office, working with several other members of staff, but I have to say how much I admire you, David. You've handled so many issues today, but you never got rattled, you just calmly sorted everything out.'

'But I've had one great advantage today — I've had you helping me, Elsie. We're a great team.' He glanced around to see that no one was about before leaning over and giving her a big kiss.

'There you are, that's your bonus payment for today.'

As the building work visibly progressed in July, Lucy asked Fred to decide when it would be appropriate to arrange an opening ceremony for the new garage extension. He discussed this with Ken Straw in the Luke site cabin.

'Actually, the decision is yours, Fred. I can give you a pretty good estimate of the date we will finish, but that isn't really what you want. This job is loaded with technology, as you realise. Commissioning those systems is the last bit of the project and that element of the contract is the hardest to quantify in time. I don't think you'll want an opening ceremony with lots of equipment that isn't operational. You're pushing out the boundaries for garage systems and you have to be sure that they do what they're supposed to do. You want to have an opening ceremony only when you can demonstrate these new systems. That's the best way to impress the VIPs and the press.'

'You're right, Ken. You're really saying that the official opening ceremony should be in September.'

'Yes, I am, Fred. Lucy is a shrewd cookie, but I think she will see the sense of what I am saying.'

'I'll get back to you, Ken.'

Fred persuaded Lucy to have a meeting with Ken Straw,

in her office. She listened to his views and asked a few questions, but then she made the decision that the opening ceremony would be at the end of the first week in September.

The management meeting was slotted in at the end of July. It received good news of a successful period, both financially and operationally, for the company. The date for the opening ceremony for the garage extension was tabled.

After the meeting, Lucy spoke to Mavis and Margaret in the office.

'That was a really difficult meeting for me. At one time I would have given anything to have had a set of results like those to report, but today, I felt very insecure and a failure. I knew everyone was expecting me to tell them what our plans are for expanding our operations, but I didn't have any. I couldn't even tell them any details about the opening ceremony. I felt I was a real disappointment.'

'You mustn't feel like that, Lucy,' said Mavis. 'It's unfortunate that the garage extension is delayed, but I agree with you that we must get over that hurdle and then we can review the future. Have you made a final agreement with Eva Benfield?'

'No, but I've agreed with Bob that we must see her and take over their coaches when we have definitely finished with that site.'

Lucy had a talk with Bob in her office about the best person to cut the tape at the opening ceremony. 'Have you any idea of a famous person to feature at the opening ceremony, Bob?'

'I'm struggling, Lucy. I've thought about all sorts of

people, but most of them will either be on holiday or have full diaries.'

'I'd thought about TV, Bob, but with the collapse of the Emily Moor transmitter, they're only transmitting in black and white at the moment. With the colours of our coaches we want any record to be in colour. So, I've concluded we should fall back on Dr Poxon, deputy head of Leeds Grammar School. I know he would do a very responsible job and he is on our board.'

'I'll leave it to you, Lucy. I know that you'll organise a successful event.'

After much thought, she approached Dr Poxon. He accepted and he asked that the Headmaster should also be invited to the ceremony.

Lucy decided that the opening ceremony should be action-packed. She needed a meeting with her staff to decide on those actions and on the programme for the opening.

Lucy spoke with Bob, Fred, Mavis, Margaret and Elsie from the staff, but she also invited Mike Best and George Clay to a meeting, in her office, on the evening of Friday 2 August.

'We are here to decide the format of the opening ceremony for the new garage extension,' she began. 'It will be an important occasion for Maxwell Motors, so it needs to be organised on an appropriate scale. It will be opened by Dr Poxon, the deputy head of Leeds Grammar School, who is also a member of our board. In order that as many of our staff as possible can attend, it will take place on Friday evening, 6 September. It's Friday because Mavis and the wedding team have a big wedding on the Saturday. We couldn't run this event without our glamorous ladies present.'

'My view is that we want it to be a real experience for our guests, who can tour the facilities and see them in operation. We'll discuss that later. Let me spell out the rough timetable.

'Guests invited to assemble at six o'clock. They will be given a welcome drink. The Opening ceremony will be at six-thirty. It's assumed that there will be a tape across the new garage for Dr Poxon to cut. Guests will be invited to tour the facilities. A sit-down meal at seven-thirty in the old garage. Entertainment after the meal. The event should finish at around nine o'clock. Is everybody happy with that outline?' Lucy could see that there were questions pending. The first question was from George Clay.

'How many people do you think will attend, Lucy? It sounds like a big do.'

'Yes, it will be a big do, George. Let us cover that first then. I want as many of our staff as possible to attend. Obviously, a lot will be at work, but I suggest we put up a notice in the garages inviting all who want to come to tell us. They'll also be able to bring their wives or partners. There'll be a lot of other people invited, from the local authorities and the community and Bob will be in charge of those invitations. Anyone who agrees to come will be given a ticket and asked to present it when they arrive. There will also be some press people, who I will organise. They, too, will be given tickets. And there could be a TV presence. So, in answer to your question, George, I think we can expect around two hundred people, but it could exceed that figure.'

'What about catering, Lucy?' asked Mavis. 'These seem big numbers.'

'We shall employ professional caterers, but you've got yourself a job, Mavis. Can you please investigate the options and then recommend who you think we should appoint for that role. They have to be very good.'

‘The old garage area will need to be cleaned and smartened up, to be a dining area,’ suggested Mavis.

‘Yes, and that’s your job, Fred. You’ll need to partition off an area for the meal, near the entrance to the old garage. The floor should be covered with carpet, and the caterer will need a separate area for holding the food and all their ancillary equipment. All the tables and chairs will need transporting to the building and that will be quite a logistics exercise. You’ll have to plan the position of the coaches so that there is no need for any to be passing through that area on the Friday afternoon. There’s another requirement which I think you should sort out, Mavis. We need microphones and a loudspeaker system.’

‘Yes, I’ll fix that Lucy. I have a friend who specialises in that sort of equipment. He could also set it up to play music while the guests are arriving and having their welcome drink.’

‘That would be ideal, Mavis. You go for that.’

‘What have you in mind for the entertainment, Lucy?’ asked Margaret.

‘One option is to invite the Leeds Grammar School orchestra to give a concert, for about half an hour. We know that they have some very good musicians, and it would be nice to have some young people at this event. Do you feel I should put this idea to Dr Poxon?’ There was general approval from the meeting.

‘If they agree to come that will be another little problem for you, Fred. You’ll have to construct a stage near the dining area, and equip it with the required number of chairs.’ Fred made a note of that in his little book.

‘I now want to go on to the activities to be on show during the tour by guests. We need to have a coach being sprayed and cleaned in the cleaning building You need to organise it so that the guests can see enough without getting wet through, Fred!' This caused some real laughter.

'What do you suggest should be taking place in the maintenance building, Fred?'

'We could have a coach with the engine being maintained by Brian Hunt and John Wall. And of course, we'll be able to demonstrate the doors in operation as we go into and out of the buildings.'

'The final item, before people go into the dining area, should be on display as they leave the new garage,' said Lucy. 'What do you think we should display there, Bob?'

'What about our latest new coach? It could be manned by a driver who can demonstrate its features,' suggested Bob. 'We should also have the wedding taxi, fully decorated for the next day's wedding, and there should be a glamorous lady driver in attendance.'

'That role should be performed by Elsie,' immediately added Mavis. Elsie blushed, but she was thrilled to have a part to play in the opening ceremony.

'I think we should lay out a route that goes from the forecourt, along the main road footpath, and then follows the new road which will be used by the vehicles,' said Bob. 'The guests would then see all the special facilities and end up in the new garage.'

'I think that's the right route to follow,' said Fred, 'but can we expect two hundred people to cover that distance, and see the equipment being used, in the time allotted?'

'A good point, Fred, we'll need to carry out a time trial.' replied Lucy. 'We may have to drop the meal back by fifteen minutes. It's essential to let our guests see the systems in use and the photographers need to have the opportunity to capture the guests and the systems on show.' Lucy decided to conclude the meeting.

'Thank you, everyone, for your help in organising this

event. There will be a detailed plan prepared, showing everyone's responsibilities.'

Two days later, Elsie returned from another taxi run to the station with Mr Higson. Once she was back in the office she spoke to Lucy. 'Have Mr Higson and his wife had an invitation to the opening ceremony, Lucy? He's a regular user of our taxis and he gets all his company fuel from our filling station.'

'I will make sure he gets one, Elsie. And if you can think of anyone else who should be invited, please let me know.'

The invitations went out and there were mainly positive replies. Margaret kept a running total of the numbers, like she did with all Maxwell operations. It was clear that the grand total would be around two hundred and fifty guests. Lucy was thrilled that the Leeds Grammar School orchestra accepted her invitation to do a short concert. The music mistress rounded up her performers and had two special rehearsals during the school holidays.

The Platt family was having their evening meal together at the start of the second week of August when Fred decided to raise the subject of holidays.

'I know that it's not possible for us to have a family holiday this year, with all the activities happening at Maxwell Motors, but I think that we must plan a holiday before the end of September. You need a holiday Lucy.'

'Oh, I don't know, Fred. I'm alright.'

'You are not alright, Mum,' said Richard, quite vehemently. 'You need a clean break from Maxwell Motors.'

Lucy was about to raise an objection, but Richard raised his hand. 'You can't use me as an excuse. You and Dad go off together, without me. You need to get used to that when

I move off to university. I shall be fine here on my own. I would expect that you would plan for Lilly and David to live here for that week, so I will be well looked after, and certainly well-fed, with Lilly's cooking.'

Lucy gave way, with a smile on her face as she replied. 'I am overruled by my two men. I agree to your suggestion, Fred and I'll leave it to you to plan a five-star luxury hotel where we can relax for a week.'

'I'll do that, Lucy.' He delegated the task to Mavis, who arranged a week in Edinburgh, in a suite at a five-star hotel. She also booked first-class rail transport from Leeds to Edinburgh.

David was fully involved with his job assisting Margaret in the office, so much so that he regarded his A-level exam results as an irrelevancy. But when the day came for publication of the results, his curiosity was aroused. With Margaret's agreement he went to school after his lunch break. Some of his fellow students were more interested how he was enjoying his job, than they were about their results.

'What's it like to have a full-time job, David?' asked one friend.

'It's fine, never a dull moment.'

'What are you doing?'

David explained his role in the office and the range of his responsibilities. In answer to more questions he gave out facts and figures about Maxwell Motors.

'Goodness me,' said one of his close friends, 'I had no idea that it was such a big company and covered so many routes and tours.'

'I think you've hit the jackpot,' commented one lad. 'I wish I'd got an offer like that. Trouble is, I don't know what

I want to do.'

They went into the school hall, where one of the masters was issuing the letters which listed the results. David opened his letter and looked at his results. He'd passed in all three subjects, and had got an A grade in both maths and physics, and a B grade in chemistry. The group of friends re-formed and David was the last to share his grades, which were the best of that group. One of his mates stated his opinion.

'Bloody hell, David, you could go to university or college with those grades. Are you sure you want to stay at Maxwell Motors?'

'Yes, I'm quite happy where I am. I know I'll have a good job for the future.'

'I'll tell you what; I'll swap you for your results,' said another mate. 'With your grades I'd be able to go to college. With my grades I'll be lucky to get a job road sweeping.'

David wondered if he could get away without reporting his success back at the garage. He was soon disillusioned on this, though, as Elsie was waiting for him. When he showed her the letter she was thrilled and gave him a big hug and kiss. The message was out and his success was broadcast around the site. He was embarrassed by the fuss, but he was thrilled when Lucy came up to him and gave him a congratulatory kiss.

When it became clear when the new garage facilities would be available, Lucy invited Eva Benfield to a meeting in her office. Lucy was accompanied by Bob and Mike Best. The atmosphere was friendly as Lucy opened the discussion.

'We have to finalise the agreement with you to take over the three coaches and stop using your garage and forecourt for parking our buses. We think we can set the date as the end of September. We'd hoped to move off earlier, but we will pay you to the end of September. Is that date alright for you' Eva?"

'Yes, that's fine.'

'Have you decided what you're going to do with the site?'

'Yes, it's going to be a building site for houses. I've done a deal with a builder, and I've just to agree the handover date with him.'

'That's great for you, Eva. That deal should secure your finances for the future. So we've just to settle on the payment for the three coaches. We've checked the current market for coaches of that age and determined a valuation, however we've decided to offer a final settlement payment of four thousand pounds. This reflects our appreciation to you for what the use of your coaches has meant to Maxwell Motors.'

'Thank you very much Lucy. I have to say that working with you has been a blessing for Benfield Motors. It's just so sad that Paul didn't live to fully benefit from it.'

'We do sympathise with you over Paul's death. What are your personal objectives now, Eva?'

'I've been thinking about that, Lucy. I'm too young to start doing nothing and I suppose I could be attractive to some fellow searching for a woman with some money, but that doesn't appeal to me either. If it's possible, I would welcome a part-time role in the office here. If necessary I could move up to full-time for a week or two, but in general, I would prefer to work three full days each week. It wouldn't worry me if, on some weeks, the third day was a Saturday.'

'Well, that will be fine by us, Eva. Leave it with me and I'll get a formal offer to you. We'll be glad to have you.' Lucy went round the table and gave Eva a big hug.

Friday 6 September was a beautiful, autumn day, and the prospects were that the weather would stay fine throughout the evening. There was an atmosphere of expectation around the garage and on the forecourt. It looked very smart, with the tables and chairs in the fenced-off area for the meal. There were cables taped to the floor, for the microphones and speakers, and the site was provided with music in the afternoon as the sound system was tried and balanced. In the new garage, the latest coach and the wedding taxi were parked. These couldn't be seen from the selected area that was to be the feature for Dr Poxon to make his speech and cut the tape. David Young was to go in front of the leading group on the tour and open up the doors. The Maxwell Motors sign had been erected on the front of the new garage, as had streamers and flags. There was also a sign that stated that Luke Construction had been the contractor. There were streamers and ribbons alongside the office block and out towards the main road. Some of these were for decoration, but some were designed to make sure all the guests followed a prescribed route to the reception area.

Margaret and Mavis were positioned to collect tickets and direct the guests to Lucy and Bob, who were in position to welcome everyone and point them to the waitresses serving drinks.

Lucy looked across at Bob. 'This it, Bob, the big event. There's no going back now.'

'Just let it happen, Lucy,' he replied.

Twenty-five

The stream of guests started to arrive. After handing in their tickets and being welcomed by Bob and Lucy, they were served drinks near the entrance to the old garage. Lucy was looking out for her special guests in the flow and was relieved to see Dr Poxon and his wife, accompanied by the headmaster, Dr Adams, and his wife. She took them over to Pearl Featherstone, who was to look after them until the start of the formal procedures. Towards the end of the arrivals, Lucy was pleased to spot Susan Gray, in a wheelchair being pushed by her husband, Captain George Gray. Susan was looking quite weak, but when Lucy bent down to give her a kiss, she said that they were so pleased to have been invited. Lucy called Richard and he took the wheelchair to a place where Susan could see the tape-cutting and have a clear view of the speakers.

After the flow of guests died down, Lucy approached

Dr Poxon and asked him to go with her to the microphone and lectern to give his speech. She asked Pearl Featherstone to encourage the guests to assemble around the area for the tape-cutting ceremony. There was a general drift in that direction and the guests formed an arc around the speaker, five people deep in places. Fortunately, Fred had erected a stand approached by two steps and Lucy needed all that height to be able to see the crowd and make her introductions. She noted that there were three photographers also standing on boxes to get photographs of the crowd and the scene. When everyone was assembled, she spoke into the microphone, her voice amplified around the forecourt.

'I want to welcome you all here to this very special occasion for Maxwell Motors. The formalities will only take a short time, so we are asking you to take a walk around the new facilities to earn an appetite for the meal which is to follow. We hope that you'll get an impression of the new systems we've installed. But first, I want to introduce to you our chief guest, who will do us the honour of cutting the tape and opening the new garage extension. Dr Poxon is deputy headmaster of Leeds Grammar School, but he is also on our board of directors. Will you please welcome Dr Poxon?' There was a round of applause and Dr Poxon replaced Lucy on the platform.

'Distinguished guests, ladies and gentlemen, but most of all, members of the staff of Maxwell Motors, it is a delight that you are all here to celebrate this occasion. This is not a time for long speeches,' he waited for murmurs of approval from the crowd. 'But I must say just a few words of what has happened over the past few years to lead to this new garage extension. Maxwell Motors has grown quite quickly due to the public demand for their services. When Bob Maxwell appointed Lucy Platt to her role in the company she was given a strange title, Office Manager and

Operations Co-ordinator, but he told her that she had to grow the company. I think she still has that strange title, but she is really the chief executive of Maxwell Motors and she is continuing to grow the company. Over the last few years I have been able to see how she does it, and it's a very neat system: someone has a new idea; it's considered by the team and then, if approved, it's tried in a small way at first; if it succeeds, then the concept is expanded and exploited.'

'But the success has also resulted from the excellent performance, every day, of all the Maxwell staff. They are totally committed to being the best in their field.'

'Over a year ago it was clear that the company was bursting at the seams on this site, and some buses had to be garaged elsewhere. The need was for a garage extension so that all the operations could function from this one location. But this is not just a shed to hold more buses and coaches. As you take your tour around, you'll see that the project includes the latest systems for cleaning and maintaining buses and coaches.'

'I've talked enough. I now want to cut this tape and wish continued success for the future to Maxwell Motors and all its staff.'

Dr Poxon cut the tape and there was a round of applause. Lucy returned to the platform as he stepped down.

'Thank you, Dr Poxon. We would now like all our guests to please follow the guides on the route along the new access road to see the garage facilities?'

Fred led the first twenty guests on the tour. There were nine other tour guides, comprising Maxwell staff and key drivers. Lucy stayed on the forecourt waiting to greet the musical guests. When the Leeds Grammar School Orchestra arrived, Lucy welcomed the music mistress, who then directed the players to set up their instruments on the concert platform.

When the first guests returned from the tour Lucy showed them into the seating area for the meal. It was free seating except for three tables: one headed by Bob, for VIPs from the local authority and James Green and Martin Luke and his wife; Lucy's table was for her special friends Dr Poxon, Dr Adams, Mr Higson and George Gray and their spouses, and Lilly Young took the final table place and her role was to look after Susan Gray; Mavis's table was filled with Maxwell Motors staff, all dressed in their best outfits. The discussions at all the tables centred on what the guests had seen on the tour. The reporters from three local papers were making notes and jotting down the many superlatives that they could include in their articles about Maxwell Motors.

The photographers had had a field day on the tour, taking shots of the site and the guests. Their best selection had been photographing guests sitting in the seats of the wedding taxi being offered mock glasses of champagne by Elsie, dressed in all her wedding finery.

When everyone was seated, Lucy gave a signal to the head waiter to serve the meal. The first course was prawn cocktail or pate; the main course was a choice of beef or fish, served with hot vegetables and potatoes; and the dessert was fruit and cream or apple pie and custard. Lucy was impressed with the efficiency of the catering service, and even their ability to serve small portions or extra large ones. A glass of wine or beer was offered with the meal, but when the tea or coffee was served at the end of the meal, that was the finish of any alcoholic drinks.

As the guests were drinking their tea or coffee, and the noise of conversation was starting to rise, Lucy went to the stage microphone to call for order.

'Honoured guests, ladies and gentlemen, I know that we have given you plenty to see and to talk about this evening, but I would ask you to pause now in your discussions, for a special part of our programme. You'll get time for more talking later, but we are delighted tonight to have members of the Leeds Grammar School Orchestra here to entertain you with a short concert. Will you please welcome them onto the stage?'

Lucy stood down from the rostrum and the orchestra was applauded as the players took their places. The music mistress took her place on the rostrum and announced that it would be a programme of light classical music, with one very exciting feature item.

The concert opened with the Mozart overture to The Magic Flute. It was followed by an excerpt from the Eine kleine Nachtmusik and then a medley of tunes from the musical Oklahoma.

The music mistress then introduced the special soloist. 'We have been honoured to have had two concerts by the famous Grimethorpe Colliery Band at our school, sponsored by Maxwell Motors. At both concerts some school musicians had the thrill of performing with the band and at the last concert, the Grimethorpe conductor decided to use a brilliant young member of our orchestra as a soloist — a young lad who seems too small to be playing a euphonium. His solo is the theme and variations on the music-hall song, 'My grandfather's clock was too tall for the shelf so it stood ninety years on the floor.' We liked the result so much that we've adapted the musical accompaniment for the orchestra, so will you now welcome Les Jones and his euphonium.'

To loud applause the young lad came to the front of the stage, smiled at the audience and grinned at his schoolfriends on the stage. He looked at the music mistress and took up his instrument. There was quiet around the garage and even the waitresses stopped to listen to the music. Lucy looked across at Dr Poxon and smiled; they both knew what was coming. It was three and a half minutes of musical magic. The orchestra played quietly when the soloist was playing the variations, which included runs along the full range of his instrument with dozens of notes to each beat. When he hit the final high note his face might have been red with his efforts, but it wore a smile of triumph. The audience were on their feet, cheering and clapping for several minutes. After what seemed like an eternity to him, Les bowed several times and then went back to his place in the orchestra.

'I told you it was something very special,' said the music mistress. 'We will now close our concert with a new piece by Eric Coates, called 'The Dambusters March.'

Lucy had gone round to the rostrum and she took the microphone when the applause finished.

'Will you please give another round of applause to these wonderful young musicians?' There was further applause and the players and their conductor took a final bow.

'That marks the end of our event,' continued Lucy, 'but we don't want to stop you chatting to your fellow guests, and the waitresses will be coming around serving more tea and coffee. However in about an hour, our own team will be descending on this site to convert it back to a working garage. Tomorrow, over two hundred people will depart from this site on their holidays, and the whole of our fleet of buses, coaches and taxis will be on the road. Thank you all for attending and please have a safe journey home.'

Lucy hurried out of the garage and took a position near the office, where she and Bob could bid goodbye to the guests as they passed out of the forecourt. The staff passed through in a crowd, but one driver summed it up with a short comment to his bosses.

'A bloody good do, Lucy. See you tomorrow, when we're

back on the road.'

Lucy saw Lilly pushing the wheelchair towards her.

'Susan wanted to have a word with you, Lucy,' said Lilly, as she stopped at the side of Lucy, who got to her knees so that she could speak to Susan.

'It's been a thrilling day for me, Lucy, and I've been treated like a queen. How well you have organised this ceremony. Thank you for inviting us.'

'It has been my pleasure to have you as one of my special guests, Susan. Keep being positive in battling with your health.' Lucy hugged Susan and gave her a big kiss. She looked at George, who was waiting to take charge of the wheelchair.

'Thank you so much for thinking about us, Lucy. Today has been a memorable tonic,' he said. 'There might not be time for many more.'

Lucy squeezed his arm as he pushed the wheelchair to the exit.

Dr Poxon and Dr Adams left together and both shook hands with Lucy. Dr Poxon said, somewhat cryptically, 'Have you ever thought of running a restaurant as a sideline, Lucy? The meal was very good, and very efficiently served.'

'No, I'll stick to running a bus and coach company,' she replied with a smile.

As the guests drifted away, Lucy left Bob to say the last farewells and she went to find Fred, who was with the caterers.

'Well, done Fred, I think that went off very well. There's a lot of tidying up to do, though.'

'It's all organised, Lucy.' He saw Richard and called him over. 'You take your mother into the house and see that she goes to bed straightaway. When you're sure that she's safely in bed, come back and you can lend a hand here.'

'Come on, Mum,' Richard said, as he took her arm, 'Dad has spoken, and he's right. I don't want any trouble with you.'

'I am always obedient to the wishes of my men,' she said, admitting to herself that she felt very tired. She was happy to call it a day and get to bed.

When Richard came back out onto the forecourt to join his father, it was a hive of activity. Joe North had his full team deployed collecting all the cutlery, crockery and cooking equipment belonging to the caterers.

Fred instructed Richard, David Young, Brian Hunt and John Wall to strip down the dining area and fold and stack the tables and chairs.

John had adapted one of the luggage transporters, by fitting straps to secure the packs, for moving the tables and chairs to where they would be picked up the next morning.

Brian demonstrated his strength by the way he handled the packs and then almost galloped with the transporter. When the dining area was clear Richard asked his father what to do next.

'What are we going to do with the carpets, Dad?'

'They need rolling up and stacking at the side of the garage.'

Fred and the boys started on the carpets. The carpeting was in long lengths, twelve feet wide, so the rolls were very heavy and it took three of them to carry each roll to the stacking point at the side of the garage.

Joe came out and announced that his team were starting on the cleaning and re-fuelling process.

'You've done very well with the clear up,' Joe said, looking around the forecourt. 'I didn't think we would be back to normal as early as this.'

'I'm glad we won't be doing this exercise every few weeks,' replied Fred. 'We've just about finished, so we'll leave you in charge now. Off you go lads, you've done a great job today.'

As Richard and Fred moved off towards the house Richard turned to Fred. 'You'll have to think of names for the two garages, Dad. Calling them the old one and the new one is sure to cause confusion.'

'Point taken, Richard; I'll sort that out in the morning.'

Next morning, Lucy was still fast asleep when Fred got out of bed to oversee the start-up on the forecourt. He opened the office and greeted the five bus teams as they started to arrive. He then raised the roller door on the new garage, where the double-deckers were parked, all looking clean and smart and ready to go.

'Looks good, Fred,' said the first driver, viewing the row of buses. 'I suppose we just take the first one in line.'

'Yes, it should look like this every morning,' replied Fred. 'As planned, they're all cleaned and fuelled up for you.'

Over the next ten minutes the five double-deckers left for their route starting points. At eight o'clock the garage became fully alive: Margaret and David arrived in the office; Brian Hunt opened the fuel pumps ready for a long day dispensing fuel until nine o'clock; and two drivers placed their coaches in the parking slots for the south coast tours. Shortly after eight o'clock the luxury coach pulled out of the garage and drove off to Knaresborough and Harrogate to pick up its passengers. Elsie arrived and departed, with the mini-coach, to pick up passengers for the south coast tours.

‘Everything is working as it should,’ Fred reported to Lucy, when she came down to breakfast. ‘Mavis will be here to help with dispatching the south coast tours and I’ll have John Wall with me to deal with the luggage.’

‘I’ll come out to help with the two south coast tours. I’ll be glad to get back to normal, after all the excitement of the new garage and the opening ceremony.’

‘Dad can deal with them, Mum,’ suggested Richard, ‘You need to be planning for your holiday.’

‘It’s still two weeks away Richard! There’s a more important event before that. You will be starting back at school for your A-level year. That’s far more important than holidays. Are you feeling confident about the exams and what subjects you want to study at University?’

‘Yes, I’m set on doing an engineering degree, and I should get reasonable grades in my science subjects to allow me to do that. I’m planning to do an engineering degree course at a provincial university. Places like Birmingham, Manchester, Durham, Sheffield, and even Leeds, have some good degree courses.’

‘You keep researching what you want to do, Richard. You can always go and have a private talk with Dr Poxon. He’ll give you good advice.’

‘Everybody says that my sporting achievements will help me get an offer from most universities. I expect to be in the first team at rugby this year, probably as vice captain.’

‘Have you time for all that rugby this year, Richard?’ Lucy asked, tentatively.

‘Of course he has,’ put in Fred. ‘Over the last five years, he’s shown that he knows how to mix his studying and his sport and it’ll be the same this year, Lucy. You carry on as you have done so far at that school, Richard. We’ll support you.’

'We certainly will; you know that Richard,' concluded Lucy.

Richard came home from his first day at school and announced that he had been appointed a perfect.

'Goodness me, Richard,' said Lucy. 'That's another string to your bow.'

'Don't worry, Mum, I'll fit it in alright.'

The two weeks before her holiday was a busy time for Lucy. The company was doing very well, with just about all the tours fully booked and many with waiting lists. The buses continued to produce a very positive cashflow and there were times when all the seats were full. Mavis had completed four more mini-tours, so there was always pressure on the two coaches covering that range. Mavis had arranged luxury tours to Edinburgh, Chester, Alnwick in Northumberland, Cambridge, Cheltenham, Cardiff and Bristol.

'We'll have enough locations to have two luxury coaches next year Lucy,' Mavis reported. 'We might even be able to run some luxury tours right through the year.'

'I intend to review our programme for next year when we've resolved all the costs for the new garage, and see where we are,' replied Lucy.

Lucy had to sort out the final payment for the new garage with the bank manager by arranging a additional small loan. She hoped to be able to pay Eva Benfield the £4,000 for the purchase of the three coaches, at the end of October, from the revenue account.

David Young had now fixed up his courses at the Technical College so that he would have a full day at college every

Tuesday, and two other nightschool classes. Eva Benfield agreed to cover David's work in the office, with Margaret, every Tuesday throughout September. She would then do three days each week in the office, starting in October, as David was then moving on to cover the engineering part of his apprenticeship.

Lucy arranged the management committee meeting to take place two days before her holiday. Photographs of the opening ceremony were passed around the table. Dr Poxon was again thanked for his part in the ceremony and a cheque for £300 had been sent to the school for use by the music department, in appreciation of the concert by the school orchestra. The costs for the garage project would be finalised in the near future, members were told. It had been mainly financed from current income. Plans were being prepared for additional luxury tours and mini-tours to allow more options for clients in the future. The new garage arrangements were reported to be working well.

Outside the meeting, George Clay had a word with Lucy. 'Now we've got everything concentrated on this site, the forecourt is really busy, so there's no spare room for parking for visitors to the office. Also some of our drivers would like to travel here by car. We could really do with a car park. Has anybody thought of this, Lucy?'

'The simple answer is no, George, but it's a fair question. We'll look at it and get back to you.'

Lucy discussed with Fred what George Clay had suggested about a car Park. 'He is absolutely right,' agreed Fred. 'We need a piece of land, near the site, that we could use as a car park, so that no one parks on the forecourt. Every time we have a fuel delivery the site seems too small. I'll talk to Bob about it.'

'Try and have a word with him tomorrow,' suggested Lucy,'so that he can be thinking about it while we're away.'

Fred had a word with Bob the next day and discussed the need for a car park. 'I can see the need,' replied Bob, with a certain hesitation. 'But we need it to be near the office and the forecourt, to be ideal. The field just beyond the new access road is only down to grass, so I could try for a piece of that field. I'll have a word with the farmer.'

David was at home with Elsie and Lilly, explaining his schedule of studies at the Technical College.

'I had discussions with the senior lecturer today, to agree my courses. Basically, taking account of my A-level exam results, I'm skipping the first year of their four year course and starting on the second year syllabus. It will be quite tough. I'll be at college three nights each week, and on the other nights and at weekends I'll have to fit in some studying time.'

'That is going to be really tough for you, David,' said Lilly. 'Where are you going to fit Elsie into all this?'

'Don't worry about me,' said Elsie. 'I'm not going to be about very much either, looking at the bookings for the mini-coach and the taxis.'

'There's another thing,' added David. 'Fred has arranged for me to have driving lessons, starting next week, so that I can get a driving licence.'

'When do you start on the next phase of you practical training?' asked Elsie.

'As soon as Fred gets back from his holiday I'll be working on the maintenance side. I've got myself a new boilersuit and it will be oil and grease and dirty hands from then on. From what Fred said, there'll be a number of major repairs and upgrades of the coaches over the winter. I'll probably also be needed to help with the dispatching and receiving of tour coaches. Fred says he will try to allow me some time to fit my studies in.'

'I am always willing to help on the fuel pumps,' said Lilly. 'I spend a lot of time now at the house, as Lucy is so busy she has no time for housework or cooking.'

'Will you be moving in to live in the house when Lucy's away next week?' asked Elsie.

'Yes, we have to pack up tomorrow. It's good fun. Richard is a fine fellow and he's very appreciative of my cooking.'

'Lucy might ask you to move in permanently!' joked Elsie.

'There's no way we can do that,' replied David, quite forcibly.

Later, when they were upstairs in his bedroom Elsie asked David why he had objected so forcefully to a permanent move to Lucy's. David took her in his arms and laid her on his bed.

'Because there is no way that I would have a private room like this one, to do this to you.'

He ran his hands up her legs and kissed her passionately. She relaxed and looked up into his face. 'Go on then, touch me now. I might not be as keen when you have greasy and oily hands.'

In fact, both David and Elsie were looking forward to a hectic and thrilling future. Downstairs, Lilly was relaxed about what might be happening upstairs. She was content to be so close to the loving couple.

There were lots of changes happening at Maxwell Motors. While Fred and Lucy were away, Bob had a week without any driving slots and stayed around the forecourt. Mavis was unofficially in Lucy's place and spent quite a bit of time on administration in Lucy's office, and she did all the banking. The manager of the Harrogate travel agency asked Mavis if there was any possibility of an extra luxury tour in November, as a group of Americans wished to book then, and there were also people in Harrogate who had expressed an interest. Mavis discussed it with Bob, and they agreed the request. Notices about the tour were quickly on display in Harrogate and Leeds.

The Youngs' week in Lucy's house passed in a whirl. Lilly was at pains to cater for all eventualities and the range of educational commitments of Richard and David meant that every day was different. There were many moments of humour.

'I put my first pupil in detention today,' announced Richard, on Wednesday evening.

'What was he guilty of doing?' asked David.

'He was horsing around in the playground and being a nuisance. I told him to stop it and he ignored me. I think I did the right thing. I heard one of his mates say "he's a silly fool, serves him right for getting a detention, you don't fool around with Richard Platt." I must be getting a reputation among the junior forms.'

Lucy rang up twice during the week to see how things were in the house. Richard answered on both occasions and told his mother that everything was fine. He also spoke to his Dad and asked him questions about Lucy. Was she resting and relaxing? Was she enjoying the holiday? As far as Lilly could tell, he got positive answers.

David started his intensive programme of driving lessons. He seemed to be doing well from what he told his sister. Lilly did the afternoon shift on the fuel pumps on Friday and she was also called on to drive the number two taxi for a wedding in Leeds on the Saturday afternoon. This meant that she was very busy early on Saturday morning making sure that the house was clean and tidy for Fred and Lucy returning on Saturday evening. As she bustled around, Richard offered her his advice.

'They have been in a five-star hotel this last week, Lilly. Don't try to make this place into a five-star house. How can I bring my rugby kit home tonight if everything is so spic and span?'

Lucy and Fred had genuinely enjoyed their holiday in Edinburgh and Lucy had a sparkle back in her eyes. She had a couple of hours with Mavis in her office on the Monday morning, during which she approved the extra luxury tour to Edinburgh in November. When she saw the bank receipts for the money deposited, Lucy was in no doubt that it had been a bumper week, financially.

Bob came to see her about the car park, telling her that the farmer was prepared to rent a block of nearly two acres, adjacent to the access road. Bob had met one of the senior planners, to seek agreement for a change of use for the land. After an inspection the planner agreed that the parking at the roadside, which he observed, was a danger to the public. Bob expected to have a note from the planner agreeing to his request within the next few days. He'd also agreed with the farmer that Maxwell Motors would install a gate into the field from the access road and lay out a hard standing road and parking bays.

'Wow, that was a quick decision from the planners,' said Lucy.

'It was payback time, Lucy. He enjoyed the opening ceremony for the new garage and he was very impressed by what we've done on the site.'

The operation of the site was progressing very well. It had

been decided to call the old garage, the A garage, and the new extension the B garage. It was easier for Joe North to organise the cleaning and re-fuelling of the fleet, using two less staff and over a shorter timescale. Fred was also satisfied that the maintenance bay offered good facilities to carry out a full range of maintenance work on the fleet more easily than in the A garage.

Fred convened a meeting to explain his ideas for enhancing the cleaning process to Bob and Joe North.

'What I have in mind is to design a frame that can be swung into position to spray the coach as it's driven slowly forward. All that would be needed, manually, is to spray the front of the coach first, then the back, after it has been driven through the power spray. I think we should design a frame for the coaches first, but the main impact on efficiency would be to apply the system to our double-deckers.'

'Yes, if you could get a system for them it would be brilliant,' responded Joe. 'They take a lot longer to clean than the coaches, as we have to work at two levels and it's still difficult to spray the roof.'

'What do you intend to do next, Fred,' asked Bob.

'I've trailed through the technical press and I cannot find any system like I'm proposing. I think we should use a local engineering firm to design and make a frame to equip with the hydraulic system and the sprays. I can arrange a development contract with a local firm. If we make this system work, Bob, it could have wider application in our industry.'

'That sounds alright,' said Bob. 'We'll have another talk when you've made some progress.'

'Good luck, Fred; I think it's a brilliant idea,' said Joe. 'I can't wait to try the system.'

In October, the half-yearly board meeting took place, having beeng postponed from September due to Lucy's holiday. It was a low key meeting, with steady positive progress being reported rather than major new announcements. The positive publicity from the opening event was noted and the improved efficiency of the cleaning and maintenance buildings was described. A report on the cost of the garage extension was tabled and figures showing how it had been financed mainly from income flows. The plan to form a car park for the site was introduced and notice was given that a full review was to be undertaken of all services offered by Maxwell Motors and a strategic plan would then be made for operations starting in March 1969, matching resources to need. If it was agreed to have more tours next year then an investment plan for new coaches might be needed.

Fred selected a local Leeds engineering firm to take on the project for a pressure washing frame. They sent a designer to visit the garage and view the coaches and the cleaning bay. He took measurements and made sketches. Fred was very pleased with the competency of the firm he'd chosen and he reported the latest position to Bob when he'd received detailed design information.

By the end of October, both Richard and David had got their lives organised along new tracks. Richard was enjoying his role as vice-captain of the first fifteen rugby team and the side had managed to win its first two matches, despite Richard realising that there were some very powerful, fit players in the opposition teams. Academically, his courses were intensive, with practical laboratory work to complement the course work.

David had found his academic courses challenging, and the teaching at the Technical College different to the Grammar School. He'd found that students were given the outline and guidance on any subject, but then had to be prepared to find the rest in books and papers. He was relieved to pass his driving test in October, but he didn't expect to be asked to do much driving for Maxwells. He was thrown in at the deep end with the engineering training. John Wall was familiar with the planned maintenance schedule and set about it systematically, so John was really supervising David's training. They got on well together and John was very good at explaining how to do the work efficiently. He let David fill in all the reports on the maintenance work done for the company records, emphasising that these records were invaluable to demonstrate the high maintenance standards of Maxwells motors.

Twenty-six

Lucy called a meeting with her senior staff in the first week of November. Bob and Fred were there to cover all the operational side of the business; Margaret and Mavis to cover the latest information on tours; and Mike Best to cover the financial side of the business. Lucy set the scene.

'This is a confidential meeting. So the first thing we must all agree is that nothing discussed at this meeting will be passed on to anyone else in Maxwell Motors. Why am I saying this? Because this exercise will be different to any we have done before. Let me explain. We are going to agree at this meeting all the information we require to make our plans based on facts and trends. There is a lot of work we'll have to undertake to get all those facts. Let me give you an example. Margaret, I'm sure you keep a record of how many passengers go on each tour?'

'Yes, I do, Lucy, but I've never shown those figures in any report.'

'But you feel that there are more passengers on the tours now than there were last year?'

'Yes, I'm confident that is the case Lucy.

'Mike, you know how much money each of our businesses is turning over, and how much profit they are making, but can you relate that back to each tour?'

'The information must be there, but we've never analysed it, Lucy.'

'You might think I'm being a bit pernickety, wanting the detailed figures, but I have a hunch that in those details there are clues for our future plans. Are we charging the right prices for all our tours? Should there be more differentials in our charges? Each tour has incidental costs, but are they all valid? Would you like to comment on that, Mavis?'

'I can tell you that I always check the incidental costs when we start any new tour., but I don't do such an exercise on a regular basis.'

'On the vehicle use, are the maintenance costs split back to each double-decker and coach?'

'We record all the work done on each vehicle, and the costs of all spare parts,' replied Fred.

'What about major overhauls, such as an engine change?'

'We did do a financial appraisal, which Mike supervised, to get a comparison in the cost of major overhauls compared with buying a new vehicle. It was conclusive that one major overhaul for each vehicle was significantly cheaper, and after that it must pay to buy a new coach because there's then the benefit of any improvement in the new designs which appear every few years.'

'I agree with Fred's views, Lucy,' said Bob.

'On the service buses, we need to evaluate if we are running any unnecessary slots. I sometimes feel that we run the service buses with a minimum of managerial supervision. Is this right?'

There were nods of agreement.

'We have detailed information on the wedding service, as each wedding is an individual contract,' said Mavis, warming to Lucy's direction of questioning. 'As we're just about fully booked all the time, there might be a chance of an increase in our charges.'

'We must be careful not to be greedy,' said Lucy. 'I am rather surprised that no other company has set up to challenge us in that market.'

'No other company can possibly raise such a glamorous set of drivers,' said Mavis, with a smile.

'One service that does not have a future is the colliery service,' said Fred. 'I've heard that the pit has got only a limited future.'

'Have we done an exercise to evaluate the cost savings, and staff savings, from having all our services located on the one site?' Lucy looked at Fred.

'I've explained to Mike the changes affecting the cleaning system, where the process is done much quicker each night and there are staff savings, but there are other savings from not having to transfer vehicles and money between this site and the Benfield site.'

'Can you look at that, Mike, and get an estimate of the annual savings involved? It might really be much bigger than we think.'

The meeting continued with discussions of other factors, but Lucy brought the session to an end with two key actions. Mike Best would be responsible for co-ordinating all the statistical and financial figures and the next meeting would take place in November, but on a date after the management committee meeting. Lucy emphasised once more that this exercise would not be discussed, or even mentioned, at that meeting.

The last week in October was the first time for months that there was no wedding booked on the Saturday. Elsie therefore decided that it should be special weekend for her and David.

She agreed her plan with him a few days before the weekend. They would have lunch together at David's, where they would get changed. She would arrange the lunch as Lilly was on duty at the garage all day. They would then go shopping in Leeds, followed by a film and supper back at David's house.

The plan worked very well. They visited two large stores and looked at winter coats. It was the first occasion on which David had to assist in making the decision on Elsie's purchase. At the second store, the first coat that Elsie tried on was jade-green and fitted her perfectly. David duly gave his approval, but Elsie insisted on trying on two more to be sure. They left the store with the coat in a large bag proclaiming the name of the store.

The film was a musical which reflected in songs their happy relationship. As they sat together upstairs on the Maxwell service double-decker going home, they held hands and snuggled together, not caring if the conductor knew who they were. After a light supper they decided to go upstairs. Elsie asked David to let her go first, so that she could get ready. When David went up to his bedroom she was standing there in her new coat. When he approached her she let the coat slip open and he saw that she was naked.

They enjoyed over an hour of passion, ending in a joint climax. They collapsed into each other's arms, completely satisfied and peacefully exhausted. Elsie looked across at

David, her eyes partly closed and her lips bruised with the intense kissing.

'I do so love you, David,' she whispered.

'And I love you, Elsie,' he replied.

'I hope, in the future, it can go on being like today,' she sighed.

'I'm sure it can, if we work at it.'

David felt very grown up as he took Elsie home. He felt a certain possessive pride as they walked arm in arm. Back home he waited up for Lilly. He had the kettle boiling, and the table set for tea and cake, when she walked through the door.

'Oh, David,' she said, as she observed the table. 'Just what I need to wrap up a busy day; have you had a good day?'

'A very good day, Lilly,' he replied, and then he mounted the stairs, hoping he might dream of making love to Elsie.

Lucy agreed with Mavis a different format for the management committee meeting in November. She wanted it to concentrate on three items: the car park; a new cleaning system for the coaches; and the annual bonus for staff. Notes of the meeting were brief, but recorded that the new car park would provide parking for all visitors to the site and that there would also be arrangements for passengers on tours to leave their cars there for a minimal charge. Pictures were shown of a high-pressure frame being manufactured at an engineering factory in Leeds. It would be fitted in the cleaning bay and would significantly reduce the cleaning load, if it was successful. As a result of a record financial performance by the company it was proposed that the annual bonus for the year would be £200 and £100 in the two grades and this was approved by the committee.

Fred was involved in a series of visits to the engineering firm developing the high-pressure spray frame for the cleaning bay and when the prototype was ready, discussions took place on where to try it out. Fred weighed up the options. 'We've either to take the frame to the coaches or, for the trial, bring a coach to the factory.'

The engineering manager agreed to do the trial on his site, as he was thinking that the pressure frames might be a new product for his company.

So on a dull, damp day at the beginning of December, Fred organised that the colliery bus, which was well covered in dirt and grime, should be driven to the engineering site with Bob, Lucy, Joe North and John Wall on board to observe the trial. The track for the bus was marked on the ground for the driver to follow, and he was instructed to keep in low gear and follow instructions to adjust his speed according to the effectiveness of the cleaning process.

The pump was started and there was a haze of water spray from the frame. The bus moved forward, with its windscreen wipers clearing the view for the driver. It was obvious that the bus was being cleaned and as it moved out of the spray area, the success of the process was confirmed. Fred paid particular attention to the wheels and tyres, as they picked up most of the dirt from the road. He noticed that they were quite clean.

'As far as I see it, Joe, from the times I've recorded, you will need only just over five minutes to fully clean each coach,' said Lucy. 'Now that's real progress.'

'Yes, it's very impressive, Lucy,' replied Joe. 'But the real savings will come if we can get a frame to do the double-deckers. They are our biggest challenge and they tend to get very dirty on the roads into and out of Leeds each day.'

The manager of the engineering firm asked Fred if he would agree to leave the system on site for a week so that it could be demonstrated to other possible clients. Lucy agreed to this and also that the designer could start work on a frame that would clean the double-deckers.

Lucy reconvened her senior staff meeting to review the results of the investigations made into the current operations. She anticipated that it would be a long meeting, so she'd asked Lilly to provide sandwiches, which she was to deliver for the lunch break. The group looked at the many lists of figures which Mike had produced and he slowly took them through each page of statistics and then the financial implications of the figures. Lucy invited questions about the figures, but she deferred any discussion until later.

When it came to drawing conclusions, they started with the bus services which were a very positive cash cow and had to be retained. However Lucy felt that the service should be managed better and she suggested that Fred take responsibility for the service buses. She suggested also that the aim should be to get more passengers using long-term travel cards. It might be possible, she thought, to make an agreement for travel cards direct with the schools and the university.

'My view is that to exploit our services, we need an additional double-decker,' said Bob. 'It would allow us to double-up on services when there are special events. It would also cover us for any breakdowns.'

'I agree with that, Lucy,' added Fred. 'We have room now to cope with an extra double-decker.'

It was agreed to phase in a new double-decker, and for Fred to take over the management of the bus services.

A lot of statistics had been prepared about the coach tours, revealing that the luxury tours were showing a good profit and there were a range of destinations that would keep two coaches fully employed. It was therefore agreed to phase in the purchase of another luxury coach. The south coast tours were continuing to do well and Mavis suggested that one driver, who always incurred higher than normal incidental expenses, should be quietly transferred to another driving role. This met with no objection. On the mini-tours there was an increased number of destinations for the two coaches, and they were attracting capacity numbers on most tours. It was agreed there should be a marginal increase in the price of each mini-tour, so that the profit per day was comparable with the daily profit on the south coast tours.

'Our real problem,' said Mavis, 'is that we only operate through part of the year with our tour programme. Should we be offering some tours throughout the year?'

'Now that is a good question,' replied Lucy. 'Have you any ideas, Mavis?'

'Well, for a start, I think we could offer tours to Edinburgh right through the year. They could be a mixture of luxury tours or mini-tours. It's an attractive destination. Another option would be to develop London tours. There is so much going on there, all through the year. We might be able to offer a choice between a six-night tour or a three-night mini-tour.'

There was a full discussion on the London option, which they all thought could also help to extend the tour season throughout the year.

'How soon could you work up a tour programme to London, Mavis?'

'If I concentrated on it, I'm sure I would have one worked up by the end of January.'

'That would be in time for us to offer London tours in our programme starting in March or April,' said Lucy. 'You go for it, Mavis. What about our coach capacity for next year's programme?'

‘I think we need to buy two more coaches, Lucy,’ said Fred. ‘We need flexibility to double-up on some tours if demand gets very high. Do you agree, Margaret?’

‘Yes, I do. We’re getting more bookings from outside Leeds now — Huddersfield, Bradford, Ilkley, Wakefield, Pontefract, and even Barnsley. In some of the main holiday weeks we just don’t have the capacity to meet demand.’ So it was agreed to purchase two additional coaches.

‘Right, we’re making progress,’ said Lucy. ‘But we’ll break for lunch now. Can you go and help Lilly bring in the sandwiches and tea, please, Mavis?’

The team stretched their legs and were glad of the break. Margaret slipped out to check with Elsie how things were going in the office. Elsie had settled a major booking, by a club, for five coaches to take a day trip to Blackpool on a Saturday in July. Margaret reported this to Lucy when she returned and Lucy said it would come up later in the meeting.

‘Right, we can carry on, now that we’re refreshed. We’ve agreed to purchase one double-decker, one luxury coach and two coaches so far. Is there anything else affecting coaches that we need to discuss?’

Lucy got no response, so she continued. ‘That brings us, then, to the policy of tackling big bookings for trips, where we have to lease additional coaches. Should we continue with this? Elsie has taken an order this morning for five coaches to do a trip to Blackpool in July. It’s likely we’ll have to bring in at least two coaches to carry out that booking.’

‘If you can get coaches at the daily rate you paid this year, taking on these bigger bookings will pay off,’ affirmed Mike Best. ‘They’re big contracts, and the additional coaches do increase the profits.’

‘I feel that taking on these bookings might be paying off in another way,’ added Lucy. ‘It means that more people are getting to know about Maxwell Motors. So I’d like to continue with this policy.’ There was general agreement.

‘What about the wedding service? I know it’s been very popular, and this is because we have our special, glamorous, female drivers. Could we add a small increase to our prices, do you think?’

‘I am confident we could do that, Lucy,’ said Mavis. ‘In some cases we’re asked to do additional runs, that are not in the contract and we do this as part of the service. I think a four percent increase in our prices would not be noticed. After all, we are turning down a good number of weddings because we are fully booked.’

‘Right, we’ll do that. I think you should take this opportunity to design a new wedding brochure which includes the new prices, Mavis, though we’ll have to honour the prices quoted on those weddings already booked. How are the bookings going, Margaret?’

‘I would guess that over half our weekends are already booked for next year.’

‘Is there anything to say about the fuel sales?’

‘Yes, Lucy,’ replied Fred. ‘There are some clients who have their lorries filled up on our forecourt and they tend to block the fuel pumps when they call in. Should we give them the option to go round the access road and fill up at the diesel pump there?’

‘I’m not sure, Fred,’ Lucy replied. ‘Who will supervise them there? I’d prefer to keep that pump just for our fleet.’

‘I agree with you, Lucy,’ added Bob. ‘We need to keep that area of the site exclusive for Maxwell vehicles.’

‘I accept what you say,’ argued Fred, ‘but there is another issue I want to raise. What do we do if some operator asks us to do maintenance work on his bus or lorry? Also what do we say if a bus operator asks to go through our cleaning bay?'

'That's up to you, Fred. If you can fit it in, I'm not against it. But you must first agree the schedule of charges with Mike. The income for any of those services must be recorded as a separate account. I'm sure you'll agree with that, Mike.' Mike nodded.

Mike suggested that Fred might feel that there was another little business opportunity to be developed. He was sitting on the figures for the savings by operating on the one site. On an annual basis it represented a saving of over £10,000 per year. He decided to give Lucy the figures on a confidential basis, not raise them at this meeting.

Lucy thanked everyone for their contribution to the discussion and said she would work with Mavis to draw up the conclusions as a strategic plan for the company which would be kept confidential. There would need to be a special board meeting to agree the plan and the date of the next management committee meeting would be after the special board meeting.

Fred was determined to have the high-pressure spray frame installed in the cleaning bay before Christmas. He cleared with Lucy that she was happy to pay the engineering firm for the development work before Christmas, and so the frame, along with the high-capacity pump, was delivered and installed during the week before the holiday. The first night, Joe North had a queue of six coaches to clean, all lined up along the access road outside the cleaning bay. Fred looked at the assembled spectators: everyone from the office was there, and George Clay from the management committee was present with a group of drivers who were off-duty at that time. Fred positioned them well clear of the frame, to avoid them getting a shower.

Joe drove the first coach. Fred waved him through and then turned on the water jet as the coach approached the frame. It was an impressive sight, and the sound of the water jets increased the sense of power. The beating of the water on the coach made it sound as if there was a heavy thunderstorm. When Joe cleared the frame he increased his speed to go through the door and out onto the forecourt near the diesel fuel pump. The next coach was waiting ready so Fred signalled to the driver to go through the frame. Fred left the water pump switched on to give the effect of a continuous process, which might apply at busy times. The spectators filed through to inspect the cleaned coaches.

'Very impressive, Fred,' said Lucy. 'Have you got a name for this invention?'

'I suppose it must be called the Maxwell Jet Cleaner, if Bob agrees?'

'I'm happy to put our name to it, Fred,' replied Bob. 'It's an achievement to get this working so quickly from the design phase. It will do us a lot of good when Joe has a bigger fleet to clean.'

When they were in bed that night, Lucy turned to Fred. 'George Clay spoke to me after the demonstration. He said "Lucy, we're very lucky to have such a talented team in this company. Someone is always coming up with an idea or a plan to make things better. You can't beat that." And he's right, Fred. It's my job to keep inspiring the talents to show themselves.' She lay in Fred's arms and he cuddled her.

'You're very good at nurturing the talents, Lucy,' he whispered to her, as she fell asleep in his arms.

It was an exciting time for all the staff when they received their Christmas pay packet, which included the annual bonus. Lucy followed her traditional role of passing on all the wage packets personally and wishing each member of staff a happy Christmas. This year, her work was mainly at the Horsforth garage. Some of the staff ripped open the packets and their eyes shone with pleasure at the size of the total pay, knowing that they could organise a great Christmas for their families. Several came back to Lucy and shook her hand again to express their appreciation, although none of them seemed to know the right words to say to her.

One coach driver summed up his views when he saw his total pay.

'It's been a funny old year, this year, with the bad weather disturbance at the start, but we've certainly made up for it since. Most folks seemed to be picking Maxwell holidays.'

'That's why you're getting this bonus,' replied Lucy. 'We're presuming that you'll want to carry on in the same way.'

'We certainly will, Lucy.'

After the Christmas holiday, there was a bustle of activities in the office. Lucy and Mavis worked hard finalising the first draft of the new business strategy. After modifications, the final draft was typed up, in Lucy's office, by a temporary typist provided by the personnel agency. The plan had an impressive front page, with the title in bold, coloured type. 'MAXWELL MOTORS BUSINESS STRATEGY January 1969.'

Lucy had decided that the Business Strategy should be distributed to the Maxwell board members as a confidential paper, to be discussed and agreed at the special board meeting in the third week of January. It was a lively meeting, with the strategy being explained in detail, and lots of statistics presented by Mike Best. Approval was given for the purchase of a new double-decker, a luxury coach and two new coaches. Mavis was asked to explain in more detail her thoughts on designing tours to London and what would be included, before there was agreement that a six-night tour and a three-night mini-tour should be offered.

On the use of the new facilities for servicing buses and coaches from other companies, there were a number of questions, particularly on staffing levels to allow this to happen. Bob said that he expected another young lad would be appointed to train on the maintenance side of the business. On the washing facilities, he was sure that Joe North would be able to phase through additional vehicles with his existing staff.'

Lucy reported on a proposal that was independent of the strategy paper. Mike Best left the meeting while a discussion took place on the need for his appointment as financial director for the company. The board expressed the hope that Lucy would be able to arrange his transfer from his present employer to Maxwell Motors.

'I don't expect a problem,' she replied. 'If they won't agree to his move they'll lose their role as our auditors. I don't think they would want that to happen.'

After the meeting, Mavis left for London, to work out details of London tours. Her aim was to have the tours specified in enough detail to allow them to be advertised in brochures for a start in April.

Lucy completed the transfer of Mike Best and arranged for him to make an immediate start at the beginning of February. His accountancy firm were happy for the move as it would make their auditing process much easier, knowing that he was in charge of all the accounts.

Bob placed the orders for the two coaches, the luxury coach and the double-decker, having been assured of the latest specifications and that he was getting a discount for such a large order.

Fred decided to wait until Mike Best took up his post before pursued the sale of travel cards for school and university students. Adverts, though, were displayed on the service buses indicating that discounted travel cards were to be available. Margaret reported that there was a steady stream of a few people each week expressing their interest.

A short management committee meeting took place in the last week of January. It repeated the issues finalised at the board meeting.

January was a time of great debate, in the Platt household, about Richard's plans to choose a university course. Richard wanted to do mechanical engineering and his preference was a redbrick university, but he wasn't sure which one to focus on. Lucy insisted on getting expert advice and she invited Dr Poxon to pay a visit to their home on a Friday evening. Lucy had tea and coffee ready, with light refreshments. After the initial greetings it became clear to Richard that Dr Poxon had been briefed about the issues by his mother. He said that Richard should get good grades in his A-levels, which would allow him to get a place in a good engineering school at several universities. He then discussed with Richard whether he was interested in research or in joining an engineering company as a graduate, to progress in management? Richard didn't think he was interested in research. Dr Poxon gave him a list of redbrick universities where mechanical engineering courses were highly rated. The list comprised Manchester, Birmingham, London, Sheffield and Newcastle. He also named some large engineering companies who sponsored selected students through university courses. Some companies, he said, also offered vacation experience on one of their projects. If a student impressed a company, it often resulted in the offer of a permanent appointment after graduation.

Dr Poxon encouraged Richard, in his application forms, to record his work experience with Maxwells. Alongside his sporting achievements, he suggested that Richard would be able to assure any organisation that he had a commitment to hard work in whatever he was doing.

At the beginning of March, the new double-decker high-pressure washing frame was delivered. It was installed as a fixture, in a position near the entrance door of the cleaning bay. Again, a crowd of employees gathered to see it tried with the five double-deckers put through one after the other. Joe had a man with a hand-spray who did the front of the vehicle before the frame spray was switched on, and then did the back of the vehicle when the frame spray was switched off. Each vehicle passed through the whole process in about ten minutes. The results were impressive and the system was going to save many man hours in the cleaning process.

Lucy played her publicity card by inviting the press to see the cleaning process in action. Several local papers sent reporters and photographers and there were articles in several local papers, with photographs. The system was lauded as ground-breaking technology. One paper even reported the answer to a question by one of the reporters. 'Could this be used by other coach operators in the Leeds area?'

Fred had supplied the answer. 'If we were approached by some other company, we could come to an arrangement to put their coaches or double-deckers through, as we have spare capacity.'

Fred wasn't surprised when he had a call from a coach company in Leeds to ask if they could see the system in use. They were interested in using the system and asked to be sent details of the options. Fred asked Mike Best to follow through with the compan and Mike was confident that there was more business to be gained in this field.

In March, the wedding season was scheduled to start. Mavis had been away for nearly four weeks in London, and when she got back, her priority job was to design the brochure for the London tours.

'We will have to manage without Mavis for the first few weeks of the wedding bookings,' said Lucy as she looked at the order book with Elsie. 'It's critical that we have the publicity material finalised for the London tours. Can you take charge of the wedding programme, Elsie?'

'Yes, Lucy, I'll check what's involved. Lilly and myself will be alright if it's just the two taxis, but if we have a big wedding that also includes the mini-coach, we'll be a driver short.'

'Then we'll have to provide you with another driver,' replied Lucy.

'The trouble is that we've always had female drivers. The spare one is Pearl Featherstone and she has the wedding outfit.'

Elsie checked the book and saw that the second wedding was a big one requiring three drivers. Lucy decided to arrangeme for Pearl Featherstone to be in the Horsforth garage for at least two months. She contacted the manager of the travel agency in Harrogate and booked his staff member, who had covered as a luxury tour guide in the past, for the same period. Elsie decided she would drive the wedding taxi; Lilly would drive the number two taxi and Pearl would drive the mini-coach.

With the impending wedding season starting, Elsie and David had a Saturday night out in Leeds, going to the theatre, after a meal in a restaurant. They then called back at David's house to have a light supper with Lilly. As David walked Elsie home she clung to his arm and they felt extremely close after a very enjoyable evening. David said, 'It's been wonderful to be with you today, Elsie. I could have eaten you at supper time, and I'm sorry that we couldn't spend some time in my bedroom and have a grand finale to our day, but it wasn't possible.'

'It wasn't possible anyway, today, David, for me. But we've been together and shown our love for each other without the need for any sex. Don't you agree?'

'I do indeed,' he replied. Their parting kiss was long and tender, and very memorable.

The new luxury coach was delivered on Monday 17 March and the two new coaches and the double-decker on Friday 21 March. They formed an impressive sight parked on the forecourt. The luxury coach was immediately needed in service on the Saturday, as two luxury tours were booked. Lucy kept the rest on show as a backdrop for the start of the tour season.

There was an air of high anticipation on the forecourt on the Saturday morning. Fred and Lucy were there to supervise the dispatches, with Brian Hunt and David Young to handle the luggage onto the coaches. Margaret was in the office with all the lists of passengers for the couriers and drivers. The two luxury coaches left for Knaresborough and Harrogate to start the luxury tour season and there were two coaches parked up ready to start the south coast tour season. As the passengers arrived for those tours they looked across at the new vehicles and couldn't help but be impressed. One regular, who knew Lucy, went up to her. 'Spending again, Lucy?; does this mean that you're going to be doing more tours?'

'Yes, we have more plans to woo all of you. Starting next month we will be running tours to London. The brochure will be out next week, so I'll arrange for it to be available when you return from this tour.'

Later in the morning, a mini-tour left for the north east of England. Of the five coaches on tours, there was only one that had two spare seats.

'That is a good start to the season, Lucy,' said Fred, as they drank a cup of coffee in the office. 'Can we keep it up at this rate through the season?'

'From the bookings that are flowing in, I think the answer is yes, we can,' chipped in Margaret.

'All being well, Fred; there is no season now; it's all the year round.'

Lucy felt that Maxwell Motors could confidently claim its place as a substantial, diverse company in the travel business.

Twenty-seven

Easter was to be the first major holiday of the year which would stretch Maxwell Motors. Lucy had referred to this challenge at the management committee meeting held during the last week of March.

'We have accepted bookings over the Easter holiday period, 4 to 7 April, that are more intense than has ever applied before for the company. All our vehicles are committed, including the two new coaches and the extra double-decker. The new double-decker will be doubling up on the Otley run, as there are sports events at Headingley. The two new coaches are also needed as one will be doing the first London tour, which runs Saturday to Friday, and the other will be covering an extra mini-tour to Cheltenham and the Cotswolds. Not only that, but we've got two big trips on Easter Saturday and Easter Monday, where we are having to lease extra coaches. And our wedding team have big weddings on the Saturday and the Monday, using the mini coach as well as the taxis.'

‘Are you saying that every vehicle we have will be out on the road over that period, Lucy?’ asked George Clay.

‘Yes, I am, George. Just imagine how quiet it will be when they’ve all departed. The only traffic noise will be cars filling up at the fuel pumps. It will be a different story, though, at the end of the day, when the vehicles return, getting them all cleaned and ready for the next day. Thank goodness we have the new cleaning bay.’

There was tension right through the holiday period. Fred concentrated on being around all the time, either in the garage and on the forecourt, dispatching buses and coaches. Mavis had gone as courier on the first tour to London, and so, as this placed additional responsibility on Lucy, Bob was also trying to help out. It had been agreed that London tours would need a courier, as the drivers were challenged by the very complexity of driving in London and couldn’t be expected to have the dual role of driver/manager. So the aim was now to find one additional courier who could cover the six-night London tour one week and the three-night London mini-tour the following week. Lucy was relieved that there had been a very positive response from their clients to the London options, and the early tours were near capacity.

Lucy realised that it would take Mavis some time to identify and train a new courier, so she’d taken the option of retaining Pearl Featherstone to cover the London tours and kept the woman from the Harrogate travel agency as courier for the Edinburgh luxury tours.

At the end of the holiday week there was a feeling of relief around the site that there had been no calamities and everyone could settle down to a busy, but normal, operation. Fred summed it up in bed with Lucy at the weekend.

‘I think it’s been a remarkable achievement, to successfully complete our programme over the holiday period. You must be very pleased, Lucy?'

'Yes, I am pleased, Fred. We've only been successful because everyone has risen to the occasion and given that little bit extra. Take Lilly: she has taken on so much extra driving, at the weddings and with the taxi. And even Mike Best was out in the yard. He realises that the figures he sees in the accounts are only achieved by people doing work for the company.'

'We have a new development for next week,' added Fred. 'We have four coaches booked in, on the same day, to be given a full clean, and we've one coach booked in on another day for us to give it an engine service.'

'Are we right taking on this extra work, Fred?'

'Lucy, I can assure you that what we will be charging makes a nice profit. Mike Best has checked all the figures, and he is very happy.'

'It all sounds very good,' said Lucy, obviously reassured by Fred's words.

'Yes, it is all very good, Lucy. We've really arrived. You have made Maxwell Motors into a front-line company. Don't push yourself so hard, going forward. You have a good team who can deliver the success you have aimed for.'

On Saturday 12 April, Mavis went as courier on the first three-night London tour. Pearl Featherstone accompanied her to get the feel of the courier role on the London tours. When the tour returned on Tuesday afternoon, Mavis was available to help in the general running of the company.

'It will be a pleasure to get involved in the general operation of the company now, Lucy. I seem to have been out of circulation for quite a while.'

'I'm glad to have you back, Mavis. Last week was a great challenge, but I'm sure we will find it was financially a record breaker.'

'What's new then, Lucy?'

'There are four coaches booked in the cleaning bay tomorrow, and on Thursday one bus is booked in for a service in the maintenance bay. So this is the start of another business venture.'

'I'll look in on them, Lucy, and I'll be around to give Margaret a hand.'

'We need to give Margaret a few days off next week. She's been working flat out for six days each week for the last two months. I don't want her to break down because she's been under real pressure. And Lilly has been our real stop gap. She has done her full-time work in the house as well as driving the taxi many nights and she's done four weddings in the last ten days.'

'I'll drop into my old routines, Lucy. I'll certainly enjoy taking the lead in the wedding team.'

On Thursday morning Mavis and Margaret were on duty in the general office. Mavis decided to go into the service bay to see how the maintenance work was progressing on the coach that was booked in. John Wall was in the well, working on the engine and David Young was passing him tools and materials to do the work. David was also ticking off the work as it was completed on a schedule by his side.

'Is everything in order?' Mavis asked.

'Yes, we know what we have to do,' replied David. 'We've told Fred that we expect to complete the service by early afternoon, so that he can run the engine and park the bus on the forecourt.'

When she got back into the office Margaret looked at the clock.

'We've not heard from Lucy for a couple of hours,' she

said. 'I'll just pop round to her office and see if she wants a coffee.' A minute later Margaret burst back into the general office.

'Mavis, quick, come and help. Something terrible has happened. Lucy's collapsed and she's laid on the floor.'

Mavis ran into Lucy's office, took one look at the scene and turned to Margaret.

'You go and find Fred and get him to come here at once. If you can, see Bob and ask him to telephone his local doctor and get him to come as quickly as possible. I think you should also ring for an ambulance. Tell them it's a life and death emergency.'

Mavis knelt down beside Lucy. It appeared that Lucy had stood up from her desk and then collapsed. Mavis pushed her chair out of the way and then felt at Lucy's wrist. She could feel a weak pulse.

Margaret dashed out onto the forecourt. There seemed to be no one around. She ran through the new garage extension and saw Fred in the cleaning bay, attending to the sprays on the high pressure frame. She was gasping for breath.

'Quick, Fred; something has happened to Lucy. She's collapsed in her office. Mavis is with her. I want to find Bob to get him to ring for his doctor to come straight away. Mavis says we have to ring for an ambulance as well. She's sure it's a hospital emergency case.'

'Fred wiped his hands on a piece of rag and started running to Lucy's office, calling over his shoulder. 'Bob's in his bungalow. He went to have a coffee with his wife.'

Margaret ran round the access road as she thought it might be the quickest way to find Bob. She banged on the door and went in. Panting, she got out her message. 'Bob, we need you. There's an emergency. Lucy has collapsed in her office. Mavis is with her and Fred's on his way. Mavis thinks we need a doctor straightaway. Will you please ring your doctor and ask him to come? He's not far away. Mavis thinks we should also ring for an ambulance.'

Bob picked up his telephone and got through to the doctor's receptionist immediately. He knew her and explained what had happened, who was affected and how serious the situation appeared. He spoke a few words to the doctor who said he would be there in a few minutes. Margaret had slumped into a chair to get her breath back.

'You have a minute, Margaret, while my wife rings for an ambulance.' He passed the telephone to his wife. 'You know what to say. Stress that it's a serious emergency.'

Bob set off for the office. His wife rang for an ambulance and gave details of where the garage was and said that someone would be looking out for them. Margaret said she would go back and get Lilly into the office to release her and Mavis.

Fred rushed into Lucy's office after slipping off his working boots at the door. He knelt down beside Lucy, at the opposite side to Mavis.

'I think she's starting to come round,' said Mavis. 'Her eyes are flickering, but she hasn't opened them properly yet.'

Fred gently took hold of Lucy's head and turned it towards him. Lucy groaned as though this was painful.

'Come on, Lucy, talk to us. We're here to help you now.' Lucy tried to open her eyes but couldn't manage it.

'I think she has severe pain in her head, from the way she reacted to you turning it,' said Mavis. 'I wonder if she knocked it on the desk when she fainted.'

Fred gently ran his fingers around her head but he couldn't detect any lumps. He continued softly talking to her to try to get her to react. Bob put his nose around the door but didn't speak. Mavis stood up and went to the door. She explained that she was going to the office to get a wet cloth so she could apply it to Lucy's face and brow. Bob said that the doctor should be here within a few minutes. Mavis returned to Lucy's side and gently applied the cold cloth to her face.

When the doctor arrived, Lucy was showing signs of recovery. She had opened her eyes and looked at Fred, murmured his name and then closed them again. The doctor took over from Fred. He shone a bright light into Lucy's eyes and she flinched and tried to turn her head away. He also moved her head gently, and again she groaned with pain. He examined her neck and it was stiff. When the ambulance arrived the doctor spoke to the attendants and emphasised that she would have to be placed on the stretcher very carefully to protect her head and neck from any pressure. Fred and Mavis moved back and watched as the doctor and the ambulance team very gently manoeuvred Lucy onto the stretcher and transferred her into the ambulance. The ambulance left for Leeds General Infirmary, Fred having decided that he was not fit to travel in the ambulance. He asked the doctor what he thought had happened.

'She's had an incident that is serious. They'll have to do tests at the hospital to determine a diagnosis. I'll have a word now with the emergency unit to brief them about the case.' Mavis looked at Fred.

'Go into the house and get changed. Forget about everything here, Fred. We will run you into the hospital so that you can stay with Lucy.' When Fred left, Mavis spoke to Bob.

'We have to plan how we carry on. I think Lucy will be out of action for a while.'

'Yes, I agree with you, Mavis. It looked serious.' Mavis turned to Elsie, who was shocked at the reports she was hearing about Lucy.

'Elsie, you get the taxi out and park at Fred's door. Leave him at the hospital and tell him to ring when he wants fetching home. My guess is that he will be there until late tonight.'

Elsie left the office and Margaret settled back in her chair, with Lilly in the other seat to answer the phone.

'Did it look very bad, Margaret?' asked Lilly.

'I'm afraid it did, Lilly,' she replied. 'I'm still upset with the sight of her when I went into the office. I'll have difficulty concentrating on my job here for the rest of today.'

'I'll have to take over in the house completely, if she has to stay in hospital. How can we manage without her, Margaret?'

'I don't know, Lilly. It doesn't bear thinking about.' The phone rang and it was back to business.

When Elsie dropped Fred off at the hospital, they reviewed the situation.

'I'm going back to the office, Fred. If you want anything, just ring us there. I'll fetch you back whenever you want me, even if it's the middle of the night.'

'I am going to try to find out what is going on with her and what they think is the problem. If she's going to be in hospital for a while, I will want Richard to come and see her. I just don't know how serious it is.'

'If you want Richard to join you, just let us know. Mavis will fix it with the school, and I will fetch him.'

'Thank you, Elsie. I'll keep in touch. I just feel so helpless.'

In the hospital emergency unit Fred identified himself. The sister in charge asked him to wait in the annex, saying she would arrange for the doctor to come and speak to him as soon as he was free. She explained that Lucy had been examined and they were deciding what to do next. Ten minutes later the doctor came and took Fred into another private room so that they could talk confidentially.

'How is she, doctor?'

'She's stable at the moment, but I think she's had a serious haemorrhage. We have requested that our medical team comes to examine her. They will decide what tests they want done to determine the diagnosis.'

'How serious is it, doctor?'

'It's serious, Mr Platt, whatever the diagnosis. We will keep her under close observation here, and when she's moved to one of the wards she will have continuous monitoring in case there is a relapse.'

'Do you think I should send for my son, who's in the sixth form at the Grammar School?'

'Yes, I think you should. Anything can happen in the next twenty-four hours.'

Fred went out to find a telephone and he rang the office and asked for Mavis. She was in Lucy's office, with Bob. Fred briefly explained the situation as far as Lucy was concerned.

'I think we should send for Richard to come here. Can you please ring Dr Poxon and ask him to release Richard? Don't tell him too much; I think I will be able to cope better if I have Richard with me.'

'I'll fix it, Fred." Mavis turned to Bob and asked him to send Elsie to the school to pick up Richard. She then rang the school and spoke to Dr Poxon, choosing her words carefully.

'Dr Poxon, this is Mavis at Maxwell Motors. I need your help please. Lucy has collapsed in her office this morning. She is now in the hospital being examined. Fred is with her, but he has asked that Richard joins him. I have sent our taxi to the school to pick up Richard and take him to the hospital. Could you extract him from his class, ready to be picked up?'

'Yes, I'll arrange that, Mavis. It sounds to be very serious. Can you tell me any more?'

'I'm afraid I can't tell you any more details. I'm relieved that she's got to the hospital. We're waiting for more information from them. I'll keep you informed when we know.'

Mavis went back to join Bob, in Lucy's offic, where they resumed making plans for operating the company in the short term.

'You will have to cover for Lucy full-time now, Mavis,' said Bob.

'Yes, I'll do that, but we have the board meeting next week. You'll have to chair it. I will be secretary, as the lady from the solicitor's office is away on holiday, so I can't do all that Lucy usually does. We'll have to get Mike Best to play a bigger role.'

'I've already discussed the annual dividend with Mike, and we've agreed to keep it at seven percent. In the circumstances, we can make it a short meeting.'

'There's the possibility that Fred might not be there, if Lucy is still in hospital. The most important information will be about Lucy. I hope we have some good news by then.'

When Elsie drove into the Leeds Grammar School yard, she saw Richard at the main door, accompanied by

Dr Poxon. Richard opened the door of the car and jumped in, giving Dr Poxon a short wave as the car swung round to the school gate.

'Thanks for coming for me, Elsie. Did you see my mum before she left for the hospital?'

'No, I was in the main office. The ambulance was parked outside your mother's office. Your Dad was with her, and he spoke to the local doctor after they had lifted the stretcher into the ambulance. I drove your Dad to the hospital after he'd got changed. I agreed to fetch you if he thought it would help to have you with him. Mavis fixed it up with Dr Poxon.'

'It must be very bad for Dad to fetch me out of school. I hope she will be alright.'

Elsie didn't know how to reply to that, so she concentrated on the driving. When she pulled into the hospital entrance she saw Fred standing waiting for Richard and she wondered if this meant very bad news. Richard also gasped when he saw his Dad, obviously thinking the worst.

'I'm going back to the garage. Ring when you want me.'

'Thanks, Elsie.'

Richard got out of the car and went over to his father. Elsie looked in her rear mirror and saw them clasped in a big hug. They broke apart and she could see Fred talking to Richard as they went into the hospital. She was sure then that there must still be some hope for Lucy.

As they walked into the casualty section, Fred explained to Richard what was happening. Lucy was still in a cubicle in the reception and the medical team was expected to be examining her within the next few minutes. The doctor in the casualty department had promised that he would ask the senior doctor in the medical team to speak to Fred after the examination. It was likely that Lucy would be transferred to one of the wards while the tests were organised. Once she was in a bed in the ward, Fred would be able to visit her.

'Have you been able to see her in the cubicle?' asked Richard.

'Yes, I've spent some time with her.'

'How is she? Is she able to talk to you?'

'No, she's not talking. She's sort of wandering in and out of consciousness.'

'It's not good, Dad. It must be nearly three hours since it happened. She ought to be recovering by now.'

'I know, Richard, the symptoms are worrying. That's why I wanted you with me. If we can get her settled down, though, we will support her and pull her through.'

Richard admired his Dad's positive approach. He walked around the room, deep in thought. About twenty minutes later the senior medical doctor came and shook hands with Fred, who introduced Richard to him. He explained that he'd examined Lucy. He'd found neck stiffness and photophobia and said that Lucy had either suffered a brain haemorrhage or she had meningitis. He needed to have tests done to allow a firm diagnosis. He said she was being transferred to the ward and she would have a lumbar puncture as soon as possible, to take a sample of fluid from around the spinal cord, for immediate analysis.'

One hour later, Lucy was established in a ward for patients with serious conditions. When she'd been made comfortable, Fred and Richard were allowed to visit her. They talked to her quietly and squeezed her hands to try to bring her out of her semi-conscious state. There were times when they felt some response from her hands, and there were also times when her eyes flickered as though they were going to open, but they never did. A nurse came every half hour or so to check Lucy and take her temperature and pulse rate. After Fred and Richard had been there nearly two hours, the nurse and the ward sister asked then to leave, as Lucy was going to have a lumbar puncture. It was suggested that they went down to the hospital café for an hour and had a drink.

Richard said that he had no appetite, but Fred said that they should eat something as they'd got to keep their strength up.

'What are we going to do about the house?, asked Richard. 'Mum is clearly not going to be around in the short-term. Why don't you get Lilly and David to move in, like they did when you went away on holiday. That worked perfectly and I'm sure Lilly won't mind.'

'If you think that's the right thing to do, I'll ring her up and ask her now,' replied Fred. 'I can't think straight about anything though, except poor Lucy.' Fred's voice cracked and tears appeared in his eyes and ran down his cheek. Richard reached over and clasped his hand.

'Hang in there, Dad. I'm here to help you. We've got to be brave and positive together. Mum needs us to inspire her. She's a fighter, you know that. She'll do everything in her power to get better.'

They each had a cup of tea and a biscuit, and then went down to the public telephones. Fred dialled the garage number but then he handed the phone to Richard.

'You do the talking, Richard. I can't face answering questions. I might break down.'

Richard asked for Mavis, who of course asked him what the latest position. Richard explained that they'd taken Lucy to do the first of a series of tests.

'What I have rung for, Mavis, is to see if Lilly and David will move into our house like they did when Mum and Dad went on holiday. It's clear to me that Mum won't be around for a while.'

'Lilly has already been suggesting that might be needed. So leave it with me. I'll get her to move in this evening, so the house will be ready for you when you want to leave the hospital.'

'I'm not sure if Dad will agree to leave the hospital tonight. I think he'll want to stay with Mum until she has shown some signs of recovery.'

'Well, all you have to do is ring your home and Lilly or David will fetch you in the taxi. How is Fred?' Richard looked at his father, who'd moved away from the phone.

'He's fine,' he lied. 'We're helping each other to stay positive. I'm glad that I'm here to support him.'

'Tell Fred we're all thinking about Lucy, and both of you.'

'Thank you Mavis.'

Back at the garage, the news of Lucy's collapse and transfer to the hospital began to leak out. When John Wall and David Young had finished servicing the coach, they came out to find Fred and explain their progress. Bob saw them and told them about Lucy. He offered to move the coach onto the forecourt and suggested that they sort out the job Fred was doing in the cleaning bay.

Bob realised that he would have to take on Fred's responsibilities, so he would need to tell Margaret to cancel any driving slots she had booked for him. Life was going to be very different, for a lot of staff, until Lucy was back in her post. Mavis met Bob later in the evening and discussed the situation with him.

'We've two issues to consider, Bob. Firstly, what we tell

the staff about Lucy. I suggest we circulate a short note, tomorrow morning, with the latest position that we get from Fred at the hospital. We don't want to leave the information to leak out through the rumour machine. Secondly, I need to urgently recruit another young lady as a courier, so that Pearl Featherstone can be around to help here. I will be tied-up full-time covering for Lucy.'

'You'll definitely need to have all your time covering for Lucy,' agreed Bob. 'One thing I think we could do is get Mike Best to take on additional roles.'

Lilly and David had a quick meal when they got home before packings up their clothes and toilet things to move into Lucy's house. Lilly was keen to get established as soon as possible, so that she was available to do the run to the hospital. They travelled in the pick-up van. The evening dragged on and it was not until ten-thirty when Richard rang asking to be picked up. He said his Dad was staying on with Lucy, but he had insisted that Richard came home to get some sleep.

When Lilly picked up Richard at the hospital, she was hesitant to ask about Lucy. Richard realised this and so volunteered the latest position.

'I think she's slightly better. The outcome of the lumbar puncture will be available in the morning. The ward sister, who had come on for the nightshift, told Dad she was hopeful that Mum might recover some consciousness during the night. That's why Dad is staying on. I think if she can see Dad when she wakes up it will inspire her to fight to get better.'

'Oh, I'm glad there is some progress. We're all thinking about her, and wishing her well. I've got some food ready for you when we get home, if you can face it.'

‘I might manage a snack, but I want to get to bed as soon as possible. Dad has promised to ring me first thing in the morning to tell me how she is, but he wants me to go to school.’

‘I am sure your Mum would want you to go to school, too. There’s a lot going on at Maxwells, to cover for your parents.’

‘I don’t think Mum will be back in the short-term. What has happened so far?’

‘I don’t know all the details, but Mavis is working in Lucy’s office and I know that Bob has cancelled all his driving slots. He’s been talking to John and David about the maintenance programme. Mavis said she was glad that I’d be around all the time for any extra taxi bookings.’

When they got home Lilly showed Richard the fish pie she’d made, which was keeping warm in the slow oven of the Aga. He didn’t want to refuse the food so he took a large spoonful, which he ate with a cup of tea. David had left a note for Lilly saying that he’d gone to bed as he was wanted to be on duty at five-thirty in the morning as dispatcher of all the double-decker buses and coaches, so he would see them at breakfast time.

Richard was up early to get ready for school. He was on edge, waiting for his Dad to ring with news of Lucy. The phone call came just after eight o’clock and Richard grabbed the phone.

‘How is she, Dad?’

‘It’s better news. She improved in the night. She was obviously in pain, but she was able to talk to me between times when she faded into a disturbed sleep. I’ve been told that they plan to do more tests during the day which will take her from the ward. The day sister has suggested that

I go home when this happens to get a few hours sleep. I'll get back during the afternoon. Can you get somebody to fetch me?'

'I'll fix that, Dad. Just ring the office here when you're ready. I'll aim to come to you in the hospital as soon as my classes finish this afternoon. If you need me earlier, just let Mavis know. She's already in the office.'

'We've got to be independent of the team arranging transport for us, Richard, so I will go back to the hospital in our own car. They will have a lot on, without me and Lucy around.'

'Dad, don't worry about the Maxwell team. They all want to help us. They're sorting themselves out so that you can forget about the firm and concentrate on getting Mum better.'

In Lucy's office, Mavis was with Bob, finalising a note to pass out to all staff. It was kept short, as an initial statement.

LUCY

We would like to inform all staff that Lucy collapsed in her office yesterday morning, due to a major haemorrhage. She is in Leeds General Infirmary and Fred is with her. She has shown signs of improvement overnight. The hospital is planning to do tests to determine a diagnosis for the incident.

In the meantime, Mavis is taking over Lucy's responsibilities and Bob is covering Fred's role in managing the fleet and the operations at the Horsforth garage.

Further information will be passed to you about Lucy when we receive it.

Bob and Mavis.

‘We’ll get copies run off straightaway,’ said Mavis.’“Then we have to distribute them. I wonder what’s the best way to do that?’

‘I would make David responsible for organising the hand-outs to everyone. If he goes to the bus station this morning he’ll be able to see all the staff on the two service routes in a couple of hours.’

‘I think you’re right, Bob, I’ll arrange that.’

When David handed out the slips of paper he was surprised that some of the staff had no knowledge of Lucy’s collapse. He explained that Fred was staying at the hospital with Lucy, so there would be more information passed out in the future. After he’d covered all the service buses, he went back to the garage. He put on his work clothes and spent time with John Wall, servicing one of the Maxwell coaches. He went to meet the afternoon-shift teams when they changed over at the bus station. This time he was accompanied by Mike Best, who was handing out the weekly wage packets.

Lilly worked quietly in the house during the morning, after she had fetched Fred back from the hospital. After he’d had a cup of tea and some toast, Fred went to bed but he insisted that Lilly should wake him at one o’clock, so that he could return to the hospital. Fred had been absorbed with his thoughts and had hardly spoken to Lilly in the car, or in the house.

When she woke him up, at the appointed time, he jumped out of bed and got showered and changed his clothes as if it was desperate for him to get back to the hospital. He managed to eat a small portion of the meal Lilly had cooked, but he just used his fork with one hand and held his head in his other hand. Lilly saw Fred as a picture of fear and despair. He left in his own car and didn't try to contact anyone else. Lilly saw Bob and told him the state Fred was in.

'Lilly, I'm glad he isn't thinking about us, and is concentrating on Lucy. I hope we get some better news later today.'

Back at the hospital, Fred was pleased to see that Lucy was once again in the ward. She was laid flat in the bed, after the tests. She seemed dazed but she turned to Fred and recognised him. Fred clasped her free hand and pressed it.

'I'm glad to see you awake, Lucy. You must be feeling better.' She looked at him and slowly spoke.

'What happened to me, Fred? What am I doing here?'

'You're in Leeds General Infirmary. You were taken ill yesterday. The doctor sent you here. They're doing tests to find out what happened.'

'I don't remember much, but the pain in my head was very bad. I can't face it again.'

'Don't worry about what happened, you're getting better now. Just rest and build your strength up. Richard is coming to see you after he finishes at school this afternoon. We were both with you through yesterday afternoon.'

'I'm glad Richard is coming. I want to see him.'

'Well, you rest so that you are awake when he comes. Do you still have a bad headache?'

'It doesn't feel right, but not too bad.'

She closed her eyes. When Fred thought she was sleeping, he gently released her hand and went out to see the ward sister. He tapped on her door.

'Can I have a quick word with you, please?'

'Sure, you can. Take a chair, Mr Platt.'

'Do you know what happened to Lucy?'

'Yes, we have a diagnosis now. She had a subarachnoid haemorrhage. The sample of her spinal cord fluid confirms that it was a rupture of a blood vessel in the brain.'

'It sounds very serious,' replied Fred.

'It is very serious, Mr Platt, but we're treating her with drugs to reduce her blood pressure and stabilise her condition. We shall keep her under very close observation, but we hope she will slowly recover. It was as well that her doctor got her to the hospital as quickly as he did. We've asked the neurosurgical team to see her and it's likely that she will need an angiogram to identify the blood vessel involved.'

'What are the chances of her making a full recovery, Sister?'

'With this condition, the figures show that one-third die from the initial haemorrhage — Lucy has avoided that — one-third have a relapse, and one-third get better. So it is a battle for Lucy. You spend some time with her, Mr Platt, and keep her spirits up.'

'I'll do that, and later this afternoon our son Richard will come in when he finishes his lessons at school. I think she's keen to see him.'

Fred went back to Lucy and held her hand. He spoke to her from time to time and she answered him, speaking quite slowly. At least twice each hour a nurse came and took Lucy's blood pressure and temperature as well as the reaction of her eyes to light. At one time Lucy asked for a drink and Fred held a feeding cup so that she could take a few sips of water. Fred thought that Lucy was making progress. He hoped Richard drew the same conclusion.

Back at the garage Mavis and Bob were in the office,

planning operations going forward. They called David in to see them and Mavis addressed him across her desk.

'David, we're planning who will take on additional responsibilities, now that Lucy and Fred are out of circulation. We want to take advantage of your location on site now. You know the routine and we want you to take on responsibility for dispatching all the service buses and coaches, and receiving them when they return to the garage. And we want you to organise all the luggage handling. We hope, when you talk to the drivers, you'll pick up any issues that they raise.'

'That's fine by me,' replied David. He moved as though that was the end of the discussion, but Mavis intervened.

'Just a minute, David, let me explain the implications of this plan. We need to incorporate this change into your training programme. You will be appointed as 'Operations Dispatcher and Receiver on the Horsforth site' and we think it will be for a period of three months. All the staff will be informed of this and told that you are the contact for communications between the staff with Bob and myself. You will also have to put some time in with John Wall, assisting on the maintenance work. Bob will co-ordinate that with both of you.'

Bob joined in the discussion.

'The one thing that's concerning me, David, is the new frame cleaning system. Fred was involved in the design and manufacture of the system and he has concentrated on making it work. Are you and John familiar with the mechanics of the pressure cleaners?'

'We haven't spent much time on them, but John will be able to service them. We tidied up the one that Fred was working on yesterday. I'm sure we'll be able to keep them going.'

'We're giving you more responsibility, which is good for

your training programme, but you must keep up with your studies,' picked up Mavis. 'Bob and myself will keep our eyes on this site, and the movements of the fleet, on those days when you are at college.'

'I'll be able to do the early morning dispatching before I go to college, if that would help.'

'Yes, that will be a good help to us,' responded Mavis. 'We don't know how long it will be until Lucy and Fred are back with us.'

Richard finished his chemistry practical early and asked the chemistry master if he could leave to go to the hospital. He got an immediate agreement which indicated that Dr Poxon had briefed the rest of the school staff about his mother. He checked his watch and ran out of the school and just managed to catch the Maxwell bus into town. He arrived at the hospital at four o'clock, much earlier than Fred had expected. On the ward, Richard put his school satchel down and moved towards his mother.

'Look who's here, Lucy,' said Fred. 'Richard has come straight from school to see you.'

Lucy slowly turned her head and looked at Richard. He bent down and kissed her on the cheek.

'Oh, Richard, I am so pleased to see you,' she whispered. 'Let me hold your hand' Richard knelt at the side of the bed and clasped his mother's spare hand. Lucy looked across at Fred and she had a weak smile on her face.

'We are all together now, Fred.' Fred gasped at one possible implication of those words, but he pulled himself together and decided to look and talk positive.

'You're quite right, Lucy. We're all together and we are going to stay together until we have got you better and we can take you home. Don't you agree Richard?'

'Yes, I agree. You're making progress, Mum. You're so much better than you were yesterday. Everybody is asking about you. I've promised to ring Dr Poxon to report how you are when I get home tonight.'

They were disturbed then by the nurse coming in to take another set of readings, which she entered on the file.

'The readings are all slowly going in the right direction, Mrs Platt.'

Lucy smiled at the young nurse.

'I have got the two men in my life to help me now.' Lucy relaxed back onto her pillows and closed her eyes. She needed to rest after the excitement of the last half hour.

Fred and Richard stayed by Lucy's bed and quietly talked over the situation. Tomorrow was Saturday, and Fred asked what Richard had planned. He reported that he'd told the sports master that he didn't know if he'd be able to play for the first team in the cricket match with Wakefield Grammar School, in Wakefield. Fred said that he thought Richard should spend the morning at the hospital, but then play cricket in the afternoon. Later in the evening, when Lucy woke up, and was talking with them, Fred mentioned the idea to Lucy. 'Richard has a cricket match tomorrow, for the school first eleven in Wakefield. He's said he won't play as he wanted to be here, but I've told him to come here in the morning and then go and play at Wakefield in the afternoon. What do you think, Lucy?' Lucy turned to Richard and took his hand.

'Do as your Dad says, Richard,' she said with a smile. 'I'd like you to be here with me in the morning, but you should go and play. Then you can tell me how you got on when I see you later.'

'That's the spirit, Lucy,' said Fred. 'In a few weeks' time we will all be supporting him at a cricket match, when you get better.'

Fred and Richard left Lucy for the night and went home. They were pleased that she was improving, and they promised to be with her on the Saturday morning.

David had a meal with Lilly that evening. He showed her the two slips of paper he'd had to hand out to the teams on the service buses and the coaches that morning. One gave an update on Lucy, and the other described his role as Operations Dispatcher and Receiver on the Horsforth site.

'It's going to be late nights checking everybody in, and early mornings dispatching everybody out. I never realised that Fred was covering this as part of his job.'

'You'll be alright, David. It's a big help, living on the job.'

'Have you heard anything from the hospital?'

'Richard rang me and said that Lucy is improving. She's talking to them. They're both coming home to sleep tonight, and then going back to the hospital in the morning. Richard's going to play cricket in Wakefield tomorrow afternoon. I've made them some food. I think they might eat it this time, as they're more hopeful than they were last night.'

'I'll not see them. I'm going out now to see Joe North and the cleaning team, and check in the buses and coaches. We have a busy morning ahead, with six coaches taking tours with passengers. There are also four of our coaches, with two leased coaches, taking a trip to Skegness from Bradford. They'll leave early as they have to be in Bradford for a seven-thirty start. Mavis is coming in early, but Bob has some business tomorrow to attend to with his wife. So I am on trial.'

'You'll be alright. We have a big wedding that needs both taxis and the mini-coach, so I will be on trimming duty.'

Fred and Richard left before nine o'clock, and they saw the final loading of the two south coast tours. There was also a coach parked for the London tour which left at nine-thirty and a coach for a mini-tour which left at ten o'clock.

Fred comment to his son as they left the forecourt. 'I just can't pay any attention to the business now, Richard. All I can think about is Lucy.'

'You are quite right to do that, Dad. Everyone wants you to forget about Maxwell Motors and concentrate on Mum,' replied Richard. Indeed he wasn't sure if he'd be able to concentrate on cricket during the match. He'd told Dr Poxon that he would be playing to please his mother, when he'd reported to him last night that she was showing signs of recovery.

In fact, Richard had a good game. Leeds batted first and one or two of the early batsmen got low scores, so Richard got to bat. He stayed in to the end of the innings and scored twenty seven runs not out, from the total of 168. When he was called to bowl, he was also successful and took three wickets for eighteen runs to help Leeds win by 29 runs. It was a good result for Leeds, and Richard received congratulations from Dr Poxon and the sports master for his performance. His team colleagues were hesitant to speak to him, with his mother being very ill in hospital. From school he caught the bus into town and it was nearly eight o'clock when he got to his mother's ward.

Lucy was awake, and Fred was with her.

'Oh, I'm pleased to see you, Richard,' she said, holding out her hand for him to hold.

'How did the match go?' asked Fred.

Richard explained that they had won and he gave the results of his personal performance.

‘How about that, Lucy?’ said Fred. ‘Didn’t he do well?’ Lucy squeezed Richard’s hand.

‘Yes, he did very well. I’m proud of him.’

‘I am very proud of you, Mum.’ Richard gave her a kiss. ‘You are very brave and you’re getting better. I can see the difference each time I come to see you.’

‘I hope that I’m improving. I’m trying to get better.’

The next four days followed a pattern. Fred spent all day at the hospital, and Richard joined him in the evenings. Lucy had an angiogram on the Monday and a member of the neurosurgical team visited her each day. Fred was sure that she was improving. She was taking some solid food and her speech was clearer and her questions got more extensive. On the Tuesday she’d asked Fred who was looking after the house and he’d explained that Lilly and David had moved in. She approved of that and she was happy that Fred and Richard were being well looked after, as she concluded, with realism, ‘I think it might be a while before I’m well enough to go back home, Fred.’

‘Don’t worry, Lucy, about the time it takes. You had a bad turn. But you are getting better.’

On the Wednesday of that week it was the board meeting, and the atmosphere was sombre. Bob opened the meeting by giving apologies for Lucy and Fred. He then read out the latest position from the hospital — that Lucy was recovering, but there was a long road ahead for her to make a full recovery.

The first item on the agenda was a report on the modification of the organisation to take account of the absence of Fred and Lucy. The board appeared satisfied that the company could operate effectively in the short-term, and a few questions were asked about David Young. Both Mavis and Bob explained how he had performed excellently as an apprentice, and said that his knowledge of the organisation made him ideal to accept more responsibilities.

The rest of the agenda was straightforward, reporting that the results for the previous year had shown a record profit and it was agreed that the dividend should be seven percent. The London tours were settling down and doing well. Bob reported on the successful operation of the new garage extension and the cleaning and maintenance bays. Mike Best, when asked, gave approximate figures for the saving in costs by operating from the one site. He also reported on the use of the facilities by two other bus companies. The meeting concluded with a sandwich lunch, which Lilly had prepared and served in Lucy's office. The conversation over lunch was subdued and most members were pondering the uncertainty of the future.

Just after four o'clock on the Thursday morning, Fred was woken up by the telephone ringing. The call was from the hospital asking him to get over to the hospital as quickly as possible, as Lucy had suffered a relapse. He went into Richard's bedroom and woke him up.

'Come on, Richard, as quick as you can. They want us at the hospital. Something has happened.'

They grabbed their clothes and went to the car. They didn't think it necessary to tell Lilly where they were going, and why. On the quiet roads, Fred broke the speed limits to get to the hospital in the minimum time. When they got to Lucy's ward they were stopped from going to her bedside, which was surrounded by nurses and doctors. Even a member of the neurosurgical team was there. Clearly frantic activity was taking place trying to save Lucy.

After about fifteen minutes, the ward Sister and the doctor came to see them and asked them to sit down. The doctor explained that, despite the improvements and progress that Lucy had made, she had suffered another major haemorrhage and this time it had proved fatal. He said he was very sorry to tell them that Lucy had died. He knew what a tragedy it was for a woman like Lucy to be struck down in her prime, but this was frequently what happened with a subarachnoid haemorrhage. Fred put his head in his hands and his tears took the form of gasps and sighs. The Sister went over and put her arms around him. Richard went over to the doctor and shook his hand.

'Thank you for all that you've done to help my Mum. I think it was nearly an impossible task from the start, but everyone has tried to achieve the impossible.'

He went over to his Dad and took over from the ward Sister.

'Come on, Dad, try to be brave. We have a lot to sort out now.'

Before they left they spent a few minutes with Lucy, saying their goodbyes to her. Richard then found out from the ward Sister that Lucy's body would be taken down to the hospital morgue to be collected by the undertaker. The death certificate would be signed by the hospital and there would be no need for a post mortem. Richard took Fred's arm and led him down the corridors to the car park. Fred was blinded by the tears streaming down his face. When they got to the car, Richard led him to the driving seat.

'Pull yourself together now, because I want you to drive us home after we've had a few minutes to settle down.'

'Our world has collapsed, Richard. I can't contemplate life without Lucy. What shall we do?'

'We'll do what she would want us to do, Dad. We will carry on and build a new life without her. She will be watching over us and guiding us all the time. She has been a major factor in both our lives. We will always know what she would want us to do in any situation for years to come. Let's go home now, Dad.'

Fred pulled himself together, and slowly and reverently drove home. It was seven o'clock when they drove into the forecourt and they saw David having a word with one of the coach drivers. They parked and went into the house. Lilly was up and just starting to get the breakfast ready. She didn't dare ask the question.

'I'm going upstairs to have a wash,' said Fred. 'You tell Lilly what's happened, Richard.'

Richard took a deep breath and then faced Lilly. 'I'm sorry to have to tell you, Lilly, that Mum had another serious haemorrhage in the night and she passed away at a quarter past five this morning.'

Lilly immediately burst into tears and went over and clung to Richard.

'Oh, Richard, what a tragedy for you and your Dad to face. It will affect all of us. We were all so dependent on her.'

'Try not to be too upset, Lilly. We've all to be brave and sort out our lives without her. There is such a lot to do.'

Richard knew that he would have take on the role of passing on the bad news, as his father couldn't face doing that in his present state. He decided to go straight to the office to see Mavis when she arrived. She arrived within ten minutes and saw Richard sitting at the table. She pulled up short. 'Is it bad news, Richard?'

'The very worst, Mavis. Mum had another haemorrhage in the night and passed away at a quarter past five this morning.'

'Oh, Richard, I am so sorry for you.' She put down her bag and the papers she was carrying, and came round her desk and took Richard in her arms and hugged him tenderly. 'How is Fred?'

'Heartbroken is the only way I can describe him. I'll not be going to school, so I'll stay with him and sort things out. We'd better tell Bob. I need to pick his brains about funeral arrangements.'

'Just stay here and I'll get him to come round.'

Mavis called Bob on the phone and he said he would come round straightaway.

As soon as Bob came in and saw Richard, he guessed the news. 'Has it happened then?'

'Yes, she passed away after another haemorrhage at a quarter past five this morning," replied Richard.

Bob's thoughts focussed on relief at the outcome. He didn't say anything, but he'd considered that Lucy might recover but be seriously disabled, an outcome that he considered would have been unbearable for everybody. He had to do all in his power now to help Richard and Fred.

Richard stayed in the office talking with Mavis and Bob. He had a coffee, discussed the funeral arrangements, took advice from Bob on the undertaker to use and the church and its minister who would organise the funeral service. Mavis gave him a notebook and he wrote notes for reference. They also discussed a brief message to go out to the staff and Bob suggested that it might be advisable to publish a notice of Lucy's death in the local paper. Bob was sure many local dignitaries would want to attend the funeral, as they had a great respect for Lucy. He concluded the discussion with an instruction to Richard.

'Lucy was a wonderful person, Richard. I want you to arrange her funeral so that the respect we all felt for her is recognised and emphasised. Don't worry about the costs — that will all be covered by Maxwell Motors. Fred will be shattered, so you might have to play a major role in the funeral service. Your mother would want that.'

Richard went back into the house and Lilly told him that Fred hadn't come back downstairs and she hadn't disturbed him.

'I'll go and see him, Lilly. He's probably asleep, as he was exhausted when we drove back from the hospital. I'll probably have a nap, but I want to ring Dr Poxon at school first.'

David was again given the job of distributing the note about Lucy's death to all the staff. It was brief.

LUCY PLATT

It is with deep sadness that we have to report to all members of staff that Lucy passed away at five o'clock this morning in Leeds General Infirmary.

We will inform you of the funeral arrangements when they have been finalised.

As a mark of respect we would suggest that all staff might wish to wear a black arm band between now and the funeral.

Bob and Mavis

When the note was finished, and while it was being printed, Mavis went into a shop in Horsforth and bought three dozen black armbands.

David thought that his job of delivering the note to all the staff was a repeat of last week's exercise, however the reaction was very different.

'Another note from the office?' questioned one driver, with a smile. When he unfolded the note and read it his face turned white and he choked with shock.

‘Oh, God, what a tragedy. What’s going to happen to Maxwell Motors now?’

Several of the female staff in the bus station burst into tears and had to be comforted. David’s box of black armbands were taken up and worn by everybody.

Members of the public recognised that something drastic had happened and they asked about the black armbands. A number of them knew of Lucy and were also shocked to hear of her death.

At lunchtime, when the rest of the notes were issued along with the wage packets, there was no interest in the wage packets, but little groups of staff huddled together and discussed the news. Both David and Mike Best, who was there, realised that the staff were fearful for the future of the company. There was nothing that they could say to allay those fears.

Twenty-eight

Richard stood in front of the mirror in his bedroom, checking his appearance. His black suit, with a white shirt and a black tie seemed appropriate. He felt in his inside pocket to check that he had the notes he'd written to speak about his Mum during the service. It was to be a challenging day for him, but he knew that it would be even more so for his Dad.

During the past week Bob had helped Richard to arrange the funeral. Fred had stayed in the background and, for the past two days, had even spent some time in the maintenance bay with John Wall, while Richard, with Mavis and Bob, finalised all the arrangements. They knew it would be a major funeral, with people in the community attending as well as a good number of the employees of Maxwell Motors. The day for the funeral had been arranged on a Thursday in order to allow the maximum number of Maxwell staff to attend. A coach had been laid on from the Maxwell forecourt to take staff to the church and reception afterwards. The funeral was only seven days after Lucy had died, which meant that it was a tight schedule to finalise all the arrangements. Richard hoped that they'd not forgotten anything.

Lucy was to be carried into the church by four Maxwell drivers who were all the same height. There were to be no flowers at the funeral, but the coffin was to have just one wreath on it, which was in the form of a coach made of flowers in the Maxwell colours. It had been decided that one side of the church would be retained for Maxwell staff and close family and friends. To assist in this arrangement all these people had been given a green card to show when they entered the church. Elsie and David had been given the job of supervising the seating of the congregation.

The choice of music for the service had evolved as the week had progressed. Dr Poxon had agreed to give a short oration, about Lucy as a business woman, while Richard would speak about Lucy as a mother. Dr Poxon had reported that students were asking if they could be involved in the service, prompted after the success of the concert by the school pupils at the opening ceremony for the garage extension. So the night before the funeral, volunteers from the school choir and the orchestra assembled in the church to arrange the seating in the choir stalls and the position of the orchestra. The music mistress conducted them through the three hymns, accompanied by the organ. It had been decided to play the theme from Judas Maccabaeus, See the Conquering Hero Come, as Lucy was carried down the aisle after the service. The orchestra had the parts and there was a triumphant sound as the organ and the orchestra combined. The choir then suggested that they sang the words of the final verse and the chorus. The minister thought this was a good idea and he sought out the hymn books in the choir stalls and distributed them among the choir. The music mistress then organised a rehearsal.

'There are some beautiful notes for you tenors in this tune. I want to hear you revelling in it as you rise up above the sopranos,' she said.

They had a run through and it was a glorious sound. The minister was very impressed. 'It will make a wonderful finale to the service,' he concluded.

Richard went to his Dad's bedroom to see how he was getting on with his clothes. Fred was dressed and was putting on his black tie. 'I never dreamed I would be wearing a tie like this for Lucy's funeral so soon in our life. It's going to be difficult to keep myself under control today. I'll do my best not to break down, Richard.'

'You will not be on your own, Dad. I'll be sitting beside you in the pew and you will have Mavis on the other side. I will be at your side as we walk down the aisle behind the coffin. Mavis will be behind you and she will take your arm if you need her. Bob and his wife will be sitting in the pew directly behind us.'

'Thanks for all that you have done, Richard. I couldn't have managed without you.'

'All the information suggests that the church will be full. There will also be members of the grammar school and high school choir and orchestra supporting the singing. Mum will be getting a good send off.'

They went down onto the forecourt to await the funeral cortège, of a hearse and three large taxis. Only Pearl Featherstone was being left on site. The rest of the staff were gathered. Margaret came over and clasped Fred in her arms.

'Be brave, Fred,' she whispered to him. 'We are all supporting you today.'

Richard looked at his Dad and was pleased to see that he

was calm. The cortège drove onto the forecourt and the mourners climbed into the cars as planned. The funeral director, in his top hat, checked his watch and nodded to his drivers. He marched out into the road and led the way on foot, slowly up the route towards the church. There were some people standing on the footpaths to observe the funeral and the men took off their caps as it passed. After three hundred yards the funeral director slipped into the hearse and the cortège moved a little faster until it reached the road where the church stood. He then resumed his role marching in front of the cortège up to the church door. The minister was waiting, with the four coffin bearers, who were dressed in black and had polished faces and smart hair cuts.

When he got out of the taxi, prompted by Richard, Fred went over to the bearers and spoke to them.

'Thank you, lads, for carrying the coffin; Lucy would have wanted you to carry her.' It had the effect of upsetting two of the men, who realised the importance of their job.

On entering the church Richard looked around and saw that it was a full congregation, all standing and looking across at the procession. Richard took his Dad's arm and he felt him wobble slightly; Mavis moved forward and clasped Fred's other arm. When they were in their place, and the bearers were positioning the coffin on its stands, Richard glanced through the screen and saw the students in the choir stalls and the orchestra in place around the altar, all standing up and looking at the coffin. When the coffin was in place the funeral director and the bearers bowed to the coffin, the funeral director walked down the aisle and the bearers went to the side and took four chairs that had been positioned for them so that they could be a part of the service.

The minister looked around and addressed the

congregation. 'You have all come here today to show your respect for the life of Lucy Platt. From my discussions over the last week, with people who knew her well, I know she was a remarkable woman. It is very sad that she should have been so tragically taken in her prime. But her family and friends do not want this funeral to be a mournful occasion; they want us to celebrate her life and all that she has achieved. This service has been planned to be a positive and joyous occasion, made more so by the contribution of the schools' choir and orchestra, as from their contacts with Lucy they requested to be a part of this service.

Our first hymn is based on Psalm 23 and it will be sung to the tune Crimond. One verse is particularly pertinent to us all today:

Yea though I walk in death's dark vale,

Yet will I fear no ill;

For Thou art with me, and Thy rod

And staff me comfort still.

I would like the congregation to stay silent in that third verse, and listen to the choir.

From the side of the choir stalls, the school music mistress conducted the singing and brought out the harmonies of the tune. In the final verse of the hymn she asked for forte singing and powerful playing by the organ and orchestra. Richard felt that his mother would have been thrilled by the sound.

Richard had been given an order of service, and he was aware of the part being played by the minister in Bible readings and prayers, but his main concern was the oration by Dr Poxon and then, a little later in the service, his own reflections on his mother.

After prayers and a Bible reading, the minister announced the second hymn.

‘We will now sing a famous hymn with words by Isaac Watts. It will be sung to the tune *Deep Harmony*. Again, I would suggest that the congregation stay silent in the second verse and listens to the choir. The words in that verse are a call to peace and calm:

Sweet is the day of sacred rest,

No mortal cares disturb my breast;

Oh, may my heart in tune be found

Like David’s harp of solemn sound.

‘Lucy will today be passed over by us to the world beyond. The final verse is a great triumphant claim to what she will find:

Then shall I see, and hear, and know

All I desired and wished below;

And every power find sweet employ

In that eternal world of joy.’

In singing that hymn the school mistress did something she’d only rehearsed once: she had the choir sing the second verse unaccompanied. It was a surprise to many of the congregation to hear just the young voices of the choir, but all the singers were inspired, and they sang with confidence, and the harmonies were clearly heard. In the final verse everyone in the church raised their voices in acclamation.

It was then Dr Poxon’s turn and he took his place at the lectern. He paused before he spoke.

‘It is a challenge, in only a few minutes, to speak about Lucy Platt. There were so many facets to her. I have known her for over four years, and throughout that time she was always growing and changing. With her broader experience she developed into an excellent leader and manager. She is a brilliant example of a person who saw an opportunity to move into a different career. She worked as a shop assistant until she got married and started a family, then the opportunity arose for her to change the direction of her life. She went back to college and took a course in shorthand and typing, but she also did a correspondence course in business management, to broaden her options. When she passed these courses she didn't take the easy route to a regular job, but instead she joined an agency that provided part-time staff to cover temporary vacancies. She never failed to impress, whatever she was asked to do. In time, she was used to fill responsible posts in various companies around Leeds and her efforts were always widely acclaimed.'

'Lucy never applied for any job. The agency was asked by Bob Maxwell if they could suggest anyone to take over a role in Maxwell Motors. The manageress of the agency thought Lucy might be suitable, so she took her along to meet Bob Maxwell. Bob interviewed her and showed her around the company and during the course of that evening she made numerous suggestions of systems to apply so that its operations could be run more efficiently. Bob Maxwell was impressed by the breadth of Lucy's understanding of running a business. He offered her a job there and then, and she accepted it without even consulting her husband, Fred. Her title was 'Operation Controller and Office Manager,' which was open to a wide interpretation. Her title has never been changed, but her responsibilities have grown. She was told to expand the company, and she has certainly done that.'

'When she started, Lucy took a 'hands-on' approach: she obtained her driving licence so that she could drive the taxi; later she got her PSV licence so that she could drive a coach, which she did from time to time. We saw this on several occasions at the grammar school, when Lucy drove the coach taking our teams to sports fixtures around Yorkshire. It seemed strange to some of our students to be travelling in a coach driven by the mother of one of their fellow scholars, but she was a good driver and they came to enjoy the special service.'

'The expansion of Maxwell Motors under her guidance has been remarkable, and many of you here have witnessed it happen. She consistently applied one approach to any new business options. All new ideas were tried to see if they would work. If they did work, then they were expanded and exploited. She was also an expert at recruiting experienced staff who could fit in with the business objectives.'

'Lucy was a tough person when she had to be. I saw this on one occasion when a Maxwell coach came to the grammar school to take our sport teams to an away fixture. The coach engine developed a fault, just the day after it had been serviced by a maintenance company. Lucy brought a spare coach onto site and, after she had discussed the symptoms with the driver, she rang the manager of the maintenance company from my office. She required him to come on site and bring some engine oil with him. I only heard one side of the conversation, but I was fearful for the lashing that the maintenance manager would receive when he arrived!'

'Lucy became a shrewd businesswoman over the years. She managed the takeover of the Lidgett Bus Company, which was facing bankruptcy, in a matter of days. The green and cream Maxwell double-deckers on the Horsforth and Otley routes are used by thousands of people in Leeds to get around the city. The Maxwell coaches take tours around the country and their latest destination is London. The major change in the company in the last year has been the building and commissioning of the new garage extension, with state-of-the-art cleaning and maintenance facilities. This has allowed the concentration of all operations on the Horsforth site.'

'Lucy Platt was exceptional because she was an ordinary lady who had no illusions of greatness. However she worked hard and continued to grow her skills. She led by example. She required every member of her staff to also work hard and to grow their own skills. With her charm and personality they could never refuse her requests. She has left a legacy in the form of a company noted for its service to its passengers. For many in this church it has been a privilege to have met and worked with a wonderful person, Lucy Platt.'

Dr Poxon left the lectern and returned to his seat. He had touched a nerve for many in the congregation, and several were using handkerchiefs to wipe away tears. Richard looked at Fred and saw that his eyes were closed but he was calm and not overcome by grief. Richard was relieved.

The minister introduced readings from the Bible appropriate for a funeral service.

Richard's turn was next. He took the sheet out of his pocket to be ready to go to the lectern. He placed his double sheet of paper on the lectern and cleared his voice before gripping the sides of the lectern and looking around at the congregation. His voice was clear when he spoke and he hardly needed to consult his paper as he knew what he was going to say virtually off by heart. And he remembered to speak slowly.

'Lucy Platt was my Mum. She was always a first-class Mum. She provided me with a good home as a child, and I felt secure. When I started school she was always there to encourage me. Life was very good. It continued like that for a year or two. Then there was a big change. I remember the night when Mum announced that she was going back to school. It was a shock for me and Dad and we wondered how we were going to be affected. But she had it all worked out.

She might have been very busy with her studies, but she lavished her love and care on both of us. When she started working, and her hours extended, she organised for a neighbour to look after me in the morning before school, and in the evening until she came home and I never felt disadvantaged. It was the very opposite: I was getting love and care from all directions. My Mum supported me on the playing fields when I played rugby and cricket. She was a loud, and biased, supporter. It was embarrassing the first time she drove the coach and I had to own up to my team mates that she was my Mum. They considered that it was cool to have a Mum who could drive a coach.'

'My Mum always had a way of arranging things so that other people were helped and supported. I will just mention two cases. When John Bright retired from his job as a driver, Mum arranged that he should have a good send-off. He'd worked for Maxwell Motors from 1913, when he started as a lad looking after the horses. He gravitated to charabancs after the First World War and in the Second World War he served as a tank driver in the Western Desert and the Italian campaigns, being mentioned in dispatches on several occasions. He returned to Maxwell Motors and completed his career on the service buses. He was a gentleman respected by everyone. Mum organised an open-air buffet, on the forecourt, for John and his wife, attended by his fellow drivers and the press. John was presented with a cheque, but he also received a gold card which gave he and his wife free travel on any Maxwell bus or coach. His wife had a debilitating disease and this card allowed them to have trips to remember during the final period of her life.'

'When Sam Maxwell was terminally ill, Mum arranged for him to be in the office so that he could still see what was going on in the business. One day she took him in the mini-coach on a trip to Leeds Bradford airport, so that he could watch the planes. Near the end, she spent time with him in the afternoons, sitting with him in his bedroom. Mostly he was drugged and semi-conscious, but on the times when he opened his eyes she was there to talk to him.'

'My Mum was a very brave person. In the hospital, after her first haemorrhage, we saw her fighting with all her strength to get better. We were hopeful that she would succeed, but it was not to be. It has left me and Dad with the challenge of sorting out our lives without her. It's going to be tough, but she has prepared us for it. She has had such an influence over us both that, for many years to come, in the situations we meet in life we will think, 'She would want us to do it this way. She would want us to give that as an answer. She would want us to organise this to help a neighbour or a colleague.'

Richard paused before he spoke his final words, very quietly and very sincerely. 'Lucy Platt was my Mum. I will never forget her. I think she will be watching over me, and I will try never to let her down.'

There was a slight crack in Richard's voice as he spoke the last sentence. The eyes of the congregation were on him as he stepped down and returned to his seat, relieved. Fred reached over and patted him on his knee. From behind Bob Maxwell tapped him on his shoulder. When he turned around, Bob whispered, 'Well done, Richard.'

The minister moved into the final part of the funeral service, but first he referred to Richard's contribution. 'Well done, Richard; your Mum would be very proud of you. We now move to our final hymn. It is a hymn of triumph, acknowledging God's faithfulness and guidance, Great is Thy Faithfulness. At the end of this hymn will you please remain standing as we go to the Commendation.'

It was a rousing hymn and the congregation were relieved to have survived the orations about Lucy. The minister waited until there was complete silence as people put away their hymn books.

'Let us commend Lucy to God. Into your keeping, O merciful God, we commend your servant Lucy. Receive her into the arms of your mercy, into the joy of everlasting peace, and into the glorious company of the saints in heaven, through Christ our Lord. Amen. We will say together the Lord's Prayer.'

'The close family will now move to the burial in the graveyard adjacent to the church. They will shortly return to the church hall, and they hope that you will join them there for refreshments and a chance to talk together. After the closing prayer, the coffin will pass down the aisle to the glorious sound of the theme from Handel's oratorio Judas Maccabaeus, See the Conquering Hero Come. It is very appropriate for Lucy, I hope you will agree, when you hear the arrangement with the organ, choir and orchestra. The peace of God, which passes all understanding, keep your hearts and minds in the knowledge and love of God, and of his Son, Jesus Christ our Lord; and the blessing of God, the Father, the Son and the Holy Spirit, remain with you always. Amen.'

The organ and orchestra started playing as the bearers, supervised by the funeral director, took charge of the coffin. It took a couple of minutes before they were ready to move down the aisle. The music mistress looked over her shoulder and realised that the coffin would not have reached the church door when the music concluded, so she indicated to the choir that they should sing verse two and three of the hymn, assuming that the organist would realise what was happening. When the choir joined in with verse two there was a shiver through the congregation and they gazed cross at the coffin slowly moving down the church. It was a solemn and moving experience. There were many handkerchiefs deployed, by both men and women, to catch the tears. Richard and Mavis kept a firm hold on Fred. He had his head bowed as he didn't want to see the tears of the congregation.

Outside, the coffin was replaced in the hearse and the three cars were filled to go to the grave. It was a large cemetery and the grave was in the far corner. When they were gathered around the grave the bearers slowly lowered the coffin into place. The minister then spoke the words of Committal. 'Since the earthly life of Lucy has come to an end, we commit her body to be buried, earth to earth, ashes to ashes, dust to dust; in sure and certain hope of the resurrection to eternal life through our Lord Jesus Christ; to whom be glory for ever and ever. Amen.'

The people around the grave followed the tradition of throwing a handful of dirt onto the coffin. Fred hesitated and was the last to make his contribution. After he had cast his handful, he took a last look at the coffin. 'Goodbye, Lucy,' he said. Then he turned around to Richard and collapsed into his arms in a floods of tears.

The rest of the day was a hazy memory for Richard. He took his Dad into the reception and left him in the care of Mavis and Lilly. Fred elected to stay in a corner and not circulate among people. Several came to speak to him, but he didn't want to have a conversation with anyone. Richard went over to the choir and orchestra, who were grouped together, to thank them for their contribution to the service. They gathered round him and praised him for what he had said about his Mum. One or two of the girls gave him a hug and a kiss to support him in his grief. Others from the congregation also offered their condolences and praise for what he'd said about Lucy.

As soon as there was a move by some people to leave the reception, Richard arranged for his Dad to be taken back home with Mavis and Lilly. He stayed behind, along with Bob Maxwell, and said goodbye to the mourners and thanked them for attending. When he got back home he was exhausted, and relieved that it was over.

The general mood of the staff at Maxwell Motors was one of fear and apprehension. Little groups would discuss what would happen next. Would Bob Maxwell take the option to sell up? He had so relied upon Lucy to run the company, who could possibly replace her? Mavis was aware of the feelings, but she was reluctant to raise the matter with Bob. In the end, it was Bob who raised it with her three days after the funeral.

'Mavis, we have to arrange a meeting with the staff, to explain what is going to happen next. I have pondered about what to do and I will make my mind up in the next few days. Can you arrange a general meeting for the staff next Sunday morning, in some suitable place? We will have to make arrangements for as many as possible to attend and lay on transport. And I think we should arrange a special board meeting on Friday this week, so that we can discuss the future with the board.'

'I'll get onto both those matters straightaway, Bob and report back to you.' Mavis was as concerned as the rest of the staff about the future. She had simply carried on with the interim arrangements of her covering for Lucy when she was in hospital and it was the same with Fred, who'd returned to his old responsibilities, even though David was supervising dispatches and arrivals.

One thing that was under discussion was the role of Lilly.

Richard had opened a discussion with his Dad about their future domestic arrangements. 'We need someone to run the house, Dad. I don't see why we shouldn't have Lilly move in here on a permanent basis, if she will. I still intend to apply for a university course and if I'm away at university, I want to be sure that you are being looked after. I doubt if you could get anyone else as good as Lilly.'

'You could be right, Richard, but I don't want to rush into a decision. None of us knows what is going to happen to Maxwell Motors. Bob hasn't spoken with any of us as yet. He might decide to sell up and get out.'

When information about the board meeting and the general meeting with staff became public, everyone concluded that some decisions could be expected within the next few days.

But the next day a new factor appeared on the scene. Bob indicated that he would be accompanying two visitors around the site to see the facilities and how the operations were managed and he would like staff support to make it a good visit. Lilly was asked to provide a sandwich lunch in Mavis's office. News of this spread around the company and precipitated fears that Bob was definitely going to sell out to someone else. On Wednesday, the visit took place. Bob was accompanied by Fred, who demonstrated all the new facilities and in the office Margaret explained the way bookings were taken for trips and coach hire. Mike Best was called to Mavis's office to answer financial questions. Mavis was shocked by the detailed questions about turnover of the different businesses, but she noted that there was no discussion about the profit made by the company.

Mavis found it difficult to sleep that night, fearing that there might be no future for Maxwell Motors.

The Maxwell board met on the Friday morning. The

secretary of the board reported that there was only one item on the agenda, that being 'The Future of Maxwell Motors.' She then handed the meeting over to Bob Maxwell. He looked down at two sheets of paper on which he had made notes of what he had to say.

'We have all been through a traumatic, tragic experience, when we have lost a colleague, a friend and a key member of this company. The loss of Lucy has raised some fundamental questions about the future of Maxwell Motors. She was pivotal to the running of the compan and, to me, the overriding question has been, could we manage without her? And for me personally, did I want to continue to be involved in running the company? Could I face more responsibility at my age? I have sweated through these questions and reached some conclusions. Firstly, I do not want to have more responsibilities in the company. Secondly, I recognise that the company is in very good shape now, operating from the one site with the new facilities. Thirdly, every member of the staff has worked very hard to achieve the present performance levels. I believe that I can rely on them to carry on delivering the same high performances. It is my respect for the staff that has influenced my conclusions more than anything else. So I have drawn two final conclusions. Firstly, the company must continue, but be organised in a different way. Secondly, the financial structure of the company should be broadened. Let me deal with the organisation first. This must be spelt out clearly so that everyone knows where responsibility lies. These are the roles and titles I am proposing:

Bob Maxwell — Chairman. I will chair the board and be around, but I want to have limited operational involvement.

Mavis Freeman — Chief Executive.

Mike Best — Finance Director and Deputy Chief

Executive.

Fred Platt — Site and Engineering Manager.

Margaret Mason — Operational Controller and Office Manager.

Vacancy — Deputy Operational Controller and Office Manager.

Vacancy — Tour co-ordinator and tour designer.'

'I will be arranging for the required documentation and salary levels for all these posts to be issued to the postholders. You will note the two vacancies I listed. These posts will be advertised and suitable people interviewed. It is essential that the management of the company is strengthened as it goes forward. Mavis will be chief executive but she will not have her previous responsibilities as tour designer and tour co-ordinator. It is also essential that she has a deputy. It's fortunate that we have Mike Best on our staff now, so he will cover for Mavis as well as his financial responsibilities. We also need support for Margaret in the office. Over the years she has taken on more and more responsibilities to release Lucy for her general management role. That is why I have given her the new title, which was Lucy's, which we never bothered to alter.'

Bob paused and asked the board for any comments and questions. There were a few questions, but the main thrust of the board was to approve the proposals and support the continuation of the company.

'My second conclusion,' continued Bob, 'is the need to broaden the financial structure of the company. As some of you know, there are three hundred thousand shares in the company. I hold two hundred and fifty thousand and Lucy held fifty thousand. It will be necessary to transfer the fifty thousand into Fred's name, which will be handled by our solicitor. As a board, you agree the annual dividend on these shares. That has been seven percent for the last two years. In actual fact, the valuation of the company has increased, so that each share is worth around two pounds ten shillings, or in the new money, £2.50. Of course there is no trading in the shares, so we are not sure exactly what each share is worth. I feel that the total number of shares should be increased and I am proposing that an additional fifty thousand shares should be issued. I will tell you how this can be done, with your agreement.'

'I have been approached by a company, Sperry Transport, which is significant in the road haulage field. They have expressed an interest in being involved in Maxwell Motors. Their chairman, Mr Vincent Sperry, and his son, visited the site a few days ago and were impressed by what they saw and what they were told. They are prepared to invest £100,000 in the company for fifty thousand shares. My proposal to you is that we accept their offer, and that we provide a place on the board for the son, Mr Paul Sperry. Let me explain what the effect of this would be. They would be a shareholder, on the same basis as Fred Platt. Between Fred and myself we would control the company as the major shareholders. The £100,000 would give us ample spare money in the bank for any capital investment. We are in a fortunate position in that we have just about no debt at the present time, as we've financed the garage extension mainly from income. Could I have your questions and comments on this proposal?'

There was a discussion for a while, the main concern being what might happen in the future if Sperry Transport wanted to take over Maxwell Motors. Bob explained that to do that they would have to buy out the other shareholders. In his opinion they would only do that if they wanted to buy the company to run it as a profitable operation. That was very different from another bus or coach company buying Maxwell Motors so that they could close it down and take on the business with their own fleet. He emphasised that his aim for the reorganisation and the refinancing was to offer a future for the company with less involvement by himself.

The board were convinced that Bob was proposing a structure and a refinancing package that was the best possible way to run the company in the future. They agreed to the issue of fifty thousand shares to the Sperry Haulage Company, and the offer of a place on the board for Paul Sperry.

The general meeting with the staff took place in a relaxed atmosphere. Details of what had taken place at the board meeting had filtered out and most people concluded that Bob Maxwell had taken decisions that secured the future of the company. Some people thought that Mavis might struggle, initially, to be as effective as Lucy had been, but they were reassured that she would be getting someone else to take responsibility for monitoring and setting up new tours. They argued that she should know who to select for that role. They also thought it was a clever move to make Mike Best Mavis's deputy. He was considered to be a bright young fellow who would develop into a good business manager.

Bob spoke to the meeting and welcomed the forty-one people who were there. Each person was given a hand-out which listed the new organisation and the roles that people would play. He also took time to explain the financial restructuring. He concluded his remarks with a call to action.

'I decided not to sell up and leave Maxwell Motors to someone else, because of what you have all done to make this company what it is. I have also to tell you that I could not face pulling out and turning my back on all that Lucy had worked so hard to build up. So, my request to you all, is that you continue to work hard and support the new management team to keep Maxwell Motors the best bus and coach company in Yorkshire.'

There were a few questions, most of which were answered by Mavis and Mike Best. When it seemed to be nearing the end of questions George Clay asked to say a few words.

'I just want to say a few words on behalf of the staff, mainly to you, Bob. We are relieved at what we have heard today. When you recruited Lucy Platt, you made a brilliant appointment. We all admired her and agreed with what she was doing for Maxwell Motors. Like you, Bob, we all wondered how we could manage without her., but she left the company in a very sound condition. We all accept that the management team you have set up will be able to run the company well, and they will have our support. But most of all we thank you, Bob, for having faith in the staff. Most people in your position would have decided to sell up and take the money.'

George had got the mood just right. There were murmurs of approval for what he had said and there was a subdued, but sincere, round of applause. Maxwell Motors had a future.

Richard decided to go for an engineering degree. He applied for a place at northern universities in mechanical engineering, placing Manchester University as his first choice, followed by Sheffield, Newcastle and Leeds. His teachers at the grammar school considered that he should achieve good grades in Chemistry, Physics and Mathematics in the A-level exams, which would allow him to take an honours degree course at university. He wanted to gain some practical experience, so he met Mr Higson and discussed his plans. Mr Higson agreed to let him work in his company through the summer holidays in various jobs in his engineering firm. Fred was disappointed, as he wanted Richard to fill in at Maxwell Motors during the holiday period. Bob offered Fred his view of Richard's plans. 'The lad has made his choice for his career. Let him loose, Fred. Forget any ties he might have here to Maxwells. He must keep focussed on what he has to do to achieve his objective. He needs your help and guidance, but we all know that he takes after his mother as far as his hard work is concerned. He'll become a successful engineer.'

Richard's other objective was to finalise the domestic arrangements for Fred. 'We have to have a woman to look after us, Dad. Are you going to approach Lilly? We need to sort it out.'

'I think that's the best idea, to see if she will move in permanently. I'll want your help when I meet her.'

The next evening, when Lilly had finished with her housework and was preparing to go home, Fred came in from the garage. Richard arrived back from school at the same time. At the nod from his Dad, Richard took over.

'Can we have a word with you, Lilly?' Richard asked.

In her usual style, Lilly wondered what she had done wrong, but she took a chair in the kitchen.

'We have a proposition to put to you, Lilly,' said Fred. 'Go on, Richard, you explain it to her.'

Richard explained, quietly and slowly, that they would like her to move in permanently, as she had done when Lucy was in hospital. She would have her own private lounge, as they intended to create a small sitting room upstairs for her. There would be no charges at all for her living costs, and she would be paid a weekly wage for doing all the housework and any work for the company.

Lilly was embarrassed by the generosity of the offer. She asked for time to discuss the matter with David, but she thought the proposal was attractive to her.

That night Lilly discussed the proposition with her brother. He listened carefully and then made a comment which surprised her. 'It's a very good offer, Lilly. I'm sure you will be alright there. Fred will look after you. It will be a difficult time for him, getting over the loss of Lucy. I'm all for it. But I don't want us to give up our present house.'

'Really, David? I don't understand.'

'I want to take on the house. Now that we know that Maxwell Motors has a future, I'm sure that I'll finish my apprenticeship and I can settle down. There could well be a permanent appointment for me when I'm qualified. So I want to get married to Elsie, and we can live here.'

'That is a shock, David. I had never thought of you getting married, yet. Are you sure you're not too young?'

'Age doesn't come into it, Lilly. We're both in good jobs, so we can afford to get married. Having a suitable house available is too good to miss. We've been discussing options for us to get together for a while now. I'll talk to Elsie and I know she'll agree. You tell Fred that you accept his offer. I think me and Elsie will need a trip into Leeds to get an engagement ring.'

The following Saturday morning was a busy time for Maxwell Motors. Margaret was in the office handing out papers with passenger lists; Fred was there with David, accompanied by Brian Hunt and John Wall, with their luggage trolleys; Mavis was also hovering around. The two luxury coaches were the first to leave to go to Knaresborough and Harrogate. There were three coaches parked on the forecourt; two for south coast tours and one for the six-night London tour. Another coach was parked at the entrance to the old garage, ready to take a mini-tour to the north east later in the morning. Three other coaches departed at eight o'clock to take a trip to Scarborough from a club in Horsforth.

By mid-morning the hustle and bustle was over and, in the general office, there was a pause for the team to have coffee. Fred, Margaret, David, Elsie and Mavis looked at each other.

'All gone according to plan,' commented Margaret.

'Definitely,' said David. 'You can relax, Mavis. Maxwell Motors is back up to speed again.'

He squeezed Elsie's hand and they smiled at each other.